BEYOND DESIRE

THEA DEVINE

BEYOND DESIRE

BRAVA

KENSINGTON PUBLISHING CORP.

http://www.kensingtonbooks.com

BRAVA BOOKS are published by

Kensington Publishing Corp.
850 Third Avenue
New York, NY 10022

All Kensington titles, imprints and distributed lines are available at special quantity discounts for bulk purchases for sales promotion, premiums, fund-raising, educational or institutional use.

Special book excerpts or customized printings can also be created to fit specific needs. For details, write or phone the office of the Kensington Special Sales Manager: Kensington Publishing Corp., 850 Third Avenue, New York, NY, 10022. Attn. Special Sales Department. Phone: 1-800-221-2647.

Brava and the B logo Reg. U.S. Pat. & TM Off.

ISBN 0-7582-0550-3

First Zebra Paperback Printing: July 1993
First Kensington Trade Paperback Printing: October 2003
10 9 8 7 6 5 4 3 2 1

Printed in the United States of America

To Toni Benner, Kim and George Wong,
Alexandra and Maximillian, and Julie Morris
to commemorate a year of new beginnings

To Betina Krahn

To Carin Cohen Ritter, with all my gratitude

And to the men in my life, all of whom love to write:
Michael—for his cogent input and for letting me
borrow his books
Thomas—for sharing with me the exigencies of
being a writer
John—for sharing . . .

And, in memory of Mel Morris, best lawyer,
wonderful friend; kind and caring and treasured by
all who knew him: he will not be forgotten.

Prologue

London, England 1885

They called him a raider, and they called him ruthless. They called him a pirate and a predator, and they accused him of usurping their territory and undermining their achievements.

They called him a grave robber because his gift of *knowing* had pulled from the sands a thousand artifacts that no one would have discovered for another hundred years.

He had never sought his reputation, but he did not suffer fools gladly and had arrogantly stepped on a hundred toes and ruined a half-dozen careers and his exploits and his notoriety followed him like a curse until eventually the British Imperial Museum had no choice but to change his venue altogether.

They exiled him; they sent him deep into the deserts of Arabia with the dotty old Sir Peregrine deLisle to assist in his quest to find the fabled parchments of the Zoran which the Museum's authorities did not believe existed.

They banished him and gave him busywork—he who had unearthed the lost temple of Khalisz and the amphorae containing the ritual prayers of the mythical sect of the Setarah—and they thought that would quell the jealousies and deflect the political machinations of the Museum patrons who imagined their whims and decrees controlled the archaeologic sector.

But no one ruled him; he played that game for perhaps a year, and dove directly into the nearest bottle to try to drown his talent, his gift, his career and his defiance.

All he succeeded in doing in that time was taking giant steps closer to the hell that had consumed his father.

He had a craven thirst to drown that out as well. He saw it clearly: the drink was seductive, as silky and heated as a lover. But he could handle it, he could; he would not get dragged into the undertow. It was merely a matter of coming to accept his situation.

Nothing like his father—nothing.

Yet so much like his father that the day he hit bottom, with Sir Peregrine watching him like some benign old fossil, he understood fully and in his soul that a thousand miles, a thousand days and a thousand bottles could not divorce him from the drive within or from the gift that possessed him.

Hard lessons for a man as bold and brash as he, spawned in the potato fields of Ireland and as gritty and dark as the earth that had made him.

But he had always known things, and he had never been able to pinpoint the moment when he'd realized that something in his consciousness was working on some other level than everyone else's.

He called it the *knowing*, but it wasn't even that tangible: it was only a brief certain feeling of familiarity that registered in his mind as a sense, a presence, a comprehension, a direction—amorphous and sure all at the same time—acknowledgement that his mind was sensitive to things not perceptible in the ordinary course of events.

He resented it sometimes, that the *knowing* would shift his senses into places where he had no wish whatsoever to intrude. But there was no help for that either, and he had learned to accept his fleeting intuitions about other people's lives, which rarely lasted more than a moment in time—except . . .

. . . *Allegra . . . !!!*

And there it was again—that hellacious woman, Sir Peregrine's stiff-necked starched-up daughter—and he could not shut out his abject sense of her fear.

It was intense, pervasive, driven.

He pushed it away.

And he waited. He was so good at waiting . . . and then he felt something else, something insidious mixed in with the edgy fear that skirted his own powerful effort to negate her altogether; an ineffable sense of something hovering near—and then the impression . . . *dark and light . . . light and dark . . .* playing around in his mind, insistent, haunting, compelling . . . and muffling his sense of her panic like a blanket until he could feel it no longer.

Why?

Unnerving, as if some other consciousness were in control.

. . . *dark and light . . . light and dark . . .*

. . . *deliberate . . . ?*

—something, something . . .

He was patient, he waited. He knew all about waiting from the black hole of his childhood where the hours were counted waiting for his drunken lout of a father to pass into unconsciousness and for his mother's beaten body to heal.

Oh, he knew all about patience from his mother's firm resolve to keep the family intact and to impart to him the joy of living when all he saw day to day was his father's descent into the rage that compelled him to visit his madness and torment on them.

How much patience could a woman have, let alone a young boy, when there was nothing more to life than the living hell of a father's fury and a mother's determination to bury his deeds?

He remembered distinctly—and always—the sensation of feeling like a caged animal, and no other sensibility but the feral desire to kill.

And he remembered exactly the moment when he'd sensed the unbearable collapse of a consciousness pushed past its endurance, the day his mother saved him for the last time from his father's bile-driven wrath.

Had she planned it or had it been the solution born of the moment? He would never know.

But one day his father came home in an alcoholic rage and threw every last one of his books into the fireplace and came after him with a hot poker; and that was the day his mother could make no more excuses for a man with jealousy in his gut and murder in his heart.

Patience—he had scrambled up the ladder to his sleeping loft one step ahead of his enraged father with a drunken roar ringing in his ears: "I'll kill that rotten lazy gut-festering girl of a son you gave me . . ."

And then a mighty yank on the ladder, which almost toppled him backwards, and his mother's screams and then a heavy thunking sound at the bottom of the ladder . . .

Terror gripping him like nothing he had ever known before as smoke suddenly drifted upwards, blinding him.

His mother's power, seeking him: . . . *get out . . . get out . . .*

The flames leaping in an instant onto the brittle wood at the edge of the loft, singeing him—and him, watching in horrified fascination as the fire climbed up the far wall toward the ceiling . . .

. . . *jump* . . .

. . . *get out* . . .

The impressions coming thick, fast, frantic . . .

. . . *mother . . . !!!*

. . . *leave me* . . .

The bastard would die—

SHE would die . . .

. . . *no-o-o-o . . . !!*

The fire crackled overhead, threatening him, waiting to claim him and send him to the hell of his father's making.

He dove for the window and smashed the glass.

Dark down there—endless down there . . . freedom and redemption down there—or the devil and death . . .

He could still feel the moment of indecision, and the urgent commanding consciousness of her: . . . *leave me now—let me go* . . .

He was crying helplessly; he felt frantic, crazy . . . how could he leave her, how could he live with it . . . He climbed out the window a moment ahead of the crackling flames that whooshed across the floor in his path, and he hung dangling from the shard-laden sill that creaked and cracked under his weight.

. . . *oh God—motherrrr!!!!*

. . . *hurry* . . .

And the flames, booming onto the inner wall and around the

window frame, right down to the six inches of wood that were the only thing between him and the dead darkness below.

And he felt the flames and he felt *her* deep in the roaring furnace of the only home he had ever known: *thank God . . . thank God—let go . . . let go . . . let me go . . .*

And he let go.

And as he lay helpless and broken in the mud, and he heard the rending crack of the roof beams shifting, he felt the final nurturing sense of life that only she could give him: *. . . remember the joy . . . remember the joy . . .*

. . . remember me . . .

He had always known things, and he thought later as he understood that it was a gift of some power that it had begun with his awareness from her of all things.

"Never forget, Ryder my darling," she said as she watched him hunger for a world of knowledge beyond the potato field, "that in spite of the devil that consumes him, you came from the seed of your father, and your love of learning comes from the blessing of his joining with me. From that has come the good, from that has come another kind of thirst, and from that will come your joy."

And he still had it, that uncontainable, unslakable need to know everything, and that same obsessive patience that had compelled him into the field of his enchantment.

And the *knowing*, the thing that he had taken for granted in his childhood years with her, he had found it was both a curse and a blessing—like the memory of the two who had made him—and something he must live with for the rest of the days of his life.

. . . a blessing and a curse . . .

. . . light and dark . . . dark and light . . .

His father had been the darkness and his mother the light who had shed her eternal optimism all over her child even in the face of pure undiluted hopelessness.

. . . dark and light . . . light and dark . . .

The impression positively possessed him and made him think

of her and totally wiped away the urgency of the invasive Alexandra deLisle and her virginal terrors.

"Things must always get better," his mother would say, "There is always something wonderful just around the corner."

"A potato field has no corners," he would protest.

"A potato field is full of wonderful things, my darling. Look at the dirt; how did it come to be here? And how did God make it so that things could just grow in it? And how wonderful is it that the potato nourishes us all?"

"There are no potatoes."

"There will be potatoes, my darling, if not tomorrow then the day after or in the months to come. There is always tomorrow, there is always something beyond what we know now."

"How can you know that, Mama?"

"I know that, my sweet. There is always joy, even in the meanest moments."

"How can you stand to wait until it comes?"

"Because"—she would smile and hug him—"I am sure it will always be there."

Yet even her patience had run out in the end.

But her lessons had taken well. He had become a man of infinite patience, compelling knowledge and purposeful restlessness, and he often thought it was no accident that he had chosen to dig in the mists of time to discover the secrets of the past.

That was his nature: to want to know everything and to root around through eternity.

But he had never ever discovered the joy.

And so he had become a rebel and a nomad. He needed action and movement, and nothing more than a bed and desk wherever he settled for any amount of time.

And he had made money, lots of money; he had become jaded and willing to accept commissions from interested parties from Luristan to Tabriz, parties who had heard of his unorthodox methods and almost certain success, and that had allowed him to finally and formally resign from the Museum and its strictures and its rules.

But he had not abandoned Sir Peregrine or his concerns.

He had returned to London directly after Sir Peregrine's death, and now, two years later, he had come in pursuit of the greatest challenge of his life.

So it was only a matter of time until he would know why fate had chosen him to be the receptor of the consciousness of Alexandra deLisle. Soon enough he would discover what the cryptic impressions of dark and light would mean to him.

And as always, he was perfectly willing to wait.

Chapter 1

She could not get that man out of her mind.

Literally.

But she had almost come to terms with it, what with her father having seen a ghost before he died and her sister having mysteriously begun to walk in the night.

What was a sentient presence in her mind compared to that?

Sometimes she had had the disloyal thought that her father had totally invented the ghost, and sometimes, when she heard furtive footsteps in the hallway outside her bedroom, she thought nothing could be more real.

She sat bolt upright in bed as the footfalls descended the stairs in slow measured steps.

Damn and blast . . . She jumped up and out of bed, and she raced for the door, threw it open and dashed into the hallway.

It was black as a tomb as she made her way surefootedly towards the landing and slowly followed the sounds of footsteps down the stairs.

A moment later, she heard the click of the latch release and the soft closing of the door behind her sister's entrance to her father's study.

Alexandra moved down the stairs on silent cat-feet, her arm outstretched, her fingertips feeling the paneled wall in the short corridor just outside the study until they grazed the molded frame surrounding the door.

She listened for a moment, and as she expected, she heard her sister moving around beyond the door.

She turned the knob and eased her way in.

Allegra was at their father's desk, as always, rifling through his papers by the light of the full moon pouring through the expansive window which overlooked the desiccated rear garden.

Allegra was methodical, as she always was, and when her search of the desk yielded nothing, she dropped to her knees and began crawling on the floor, her fingers outstretched as if she were seeking some secret hiding place under the parquet, until she reached the far wall where she stood up and began a thorough search of the paneling.

"Allegra . . ." She always spoke, her sister never heard. Now she bypassed Alexandra as if she were not there and went directly to the fireplace which was on the wall backing the formal parlor.

Alexandra held her breath. She never knew just what to do about this inexplicable night walking. She had never tried to awaken Alexandra, and she had never told her. For two mystifying years, since their father's death, Allegra had continued this tormented search of their father's study, and Alexandra had yet to figure out why.

She knew there were secrets she had to protect, things she had sworn to do, and she could let neither her duty to her sister nor Allegra's aberrant behavior—or that obnoxious voice in her own mind—stand in her way.

Allegra approached the fireplace, always last in her search— and Alexandra fought an instinctive urge to pull her sister away from that wall and the fear that this time she would find the secret catch, the hidden stair.

Damn and blast! She could just see Allegra now, but she could hear, too well, her seeking fingers rattling over their father's beloved pewter pieces that cluttered the mantel shelf.

And then she heard the horrifying telltale scrape of something moving . . .

"*Allegra!* Allegra . . . !"

But Allegra did not hear her.

Instantly, blindly, she catapulted herself across the room at her sister.

She crashed into her heavily, felt herself falling, falling, her body cushioned by her sister's slimmer frame and then Allegra's head taking a nerve-shattering *thonk* as their bodies hit the floor.

Blast . . . blast . . . blast . . . Alexandra crawled off her sister's limp body in a panic.

"Allegra . . . *Allegra . . . !*" And she had never told her; it had been so much easier to pretend the thing didn't exist. Now . . . what if she were . . . ?

She shook Allegra, she smacked her cheeks lightly; but her sister did not respond.

Damn, damn, damn—she had come too close this time. There had to be changes . . . If only she would move . . .

She needed light, she needed water, a cover . . . She could not just leave Allegra on the floor . . . She needed to conceal the yawning blackness where the fireplace wall had been . . .

And she hated herself because she knew which of the two critically important things she would attend to first.

Allegra came around a heart-stopping half-hour later to find her sister sitting calmly beside her quilt-covered form, a table pulled nearby on which had been placed a kerosene lamp and a bowl of cold water from which Alexandra was patiently bathing Allegra's forehead.

"Where . . . what are you doing? That is horribly cold. What . . . where am I? What am I doing in the study . . . ? Alexandra . . ."

Alexandra drew a deep shaking breath. "My dear Allegra . . ." Her mind had been racing this half-hour, trying to decide how much she ought to tell. How easy it was to toss all her good intentions out the window in the face of Allegra's coherence and dissemble once again.

"I found you here," she said finally, as she squeezed the water out of the cloth and set it on edge of the bowl. "You must have fallen in the dark."

"In father's study?"

Alexandra shrugged. "It makes no sense to me either. I heard you going down the stairs."

. . . ah! too late; of course she would question that too . . .

"Never. I was in my bed."

"Yet you are here."

"I cannot credit this. And my head hurts abominably . . . I don't understand . . ."

Alexandra said nothing. What could she say when all this time she had chosen to say nothing about these nighttime sorties?

Allegra closed her eyes wearily. "This scares me."

"It is frightening," Alexandra conceded, and she did not have to pretend sincerity; she was frightened as well when she considered the possible explanations of her sister's ongoing night walking.

"But you were not too scared to follow."

That gave Alexandra pause; she could not allow Allegra to make her into a hero.

"I was too," she said leaping into the ensuing little silence and making sure to sound somewhat defensive. The lies . . . the lies . . . "I thought of thieves—and worse. I immediately went for a light and then onto the landing. I thought I could attack an intruder with the lamp. But that would have been a puny defense at best. Anyway, I saw you."

"And did you never think of father's ghost?"

"Never," Alexandra said resolutely. "It could only have been a thief . . . or my imagination."

Allegra made a move to sit upright and felt a faint dizziness. "Perhaps I am a figment of your imagination," she said gingerly.

"My dear girl," Alexandra protested instantly and, she thought, ineffectively. There would never be any cessation of guilt or anguish for her, and always Allegra knew it—viscerally, she knew it. And she used it.

"I am tired, Alixe, just plain tired. Tired of how we are living, tired of parsing out pennies from my inheritance when there is something we could dispose of that would bring us pots of money . . ."

Alexandra's expression turned stony. "Surely not *pots*," she said acidly.

"I do resent that you will not consider selling the bracelets when you know their existence could now validate all of father's work. Perhaps it is as simple as that; in my dreams I was trying to find them because I want to find a way out. And you want to wallow in false pride."

Always the bracelets—everything came back to them. "I will not dignify that with a comment. I care only that you could have been badly hurt, and I am grateful that I was awake and heard you in the hallway. Anyway, I am not as stiff-necked as you portray me. Come, do you feel steady enough to return upstairs?"

"I feel well enough to castigate you for not even considering taking advantage of the situation. Sir Arthur has very plainly indicated his interest in the bracelets."

"Very conveniently *after* father's death," Alexandra said stiffly, "and he assumes I know exactly where to lay my hands on them."

"Of course you do. You were always in father's confidence—how could you not?" Allegra could not keep the pain out of her voice. The hurts were still there; the wounds still bled.

"I won't discuss it tonight," Alexandra said, holding out her hands to her sister so that Allegra could balance herself against her strength.

"And when will you?" Allegra muttered, pulling herself into a standing position. "You never want to—oh . . . oh my—we never talk about it. Every time I broach it, you close up like a clam. So . . . Oh, that hurts. So when, Alixe? I mean, what if this happens again, what then? And what if I have been doing it for years and have never known it, what then? What if it turns out I need help, expensive medical help that must go on for years and years . . ."

"Stop it!" Alexandra commanded, pulling her sister into her arms. She felt chilled, flooded with the ominous sense that something terrible was going to come out of this one incident out of all those she had surrounded with silence. "Stop it," she crooned, her arms tightening around her sister's trembling, heaving body.

"I'm going to die in this place," Allegra moaned, burying her head on Alexandra's shoulder. "I am the princess and this is the dungeon and I am imprisoned here . . . How odd I never understood that before . . ."

"Shhhhh," Alexandra murmured, awkwardly smoothing back her sister's gold-shot chestnut hair that was so like her own. "Shhhh . . . it was a silly accident . . . shhhhh . . ."

She picked up the lamp and, slipping her arm around Allegra's waist to support her, guided her briskly from the room and out into the hallway.

It was paramount in her mind to keep her calm. "Shhhh . . ."

She turned and reached back to close the door. The room was

eerily dark, devoid in the blackness of any sign of habitation. *Dark . . . dark . . .*

The word reverberated in her mind for just an instant, almost as if someone had spoken.

Vibrations from Allegra, of course, in her mood of despair. What nonsense. She slammed the door shut emphatically and then quickly and efficiently got Allegra up the stairs to the comfort and sanity of her bedroom, away from the dark and from her morbid notions.

The ghost haunted her, and the bracelets. She held one of them gingerly in the palm of her hand the next morning, scrutinized it in the wavering light of the kerosene lamp on the table in the secret room below her father's study.

It was made of stone, and it measured two or three inches wide and seven inches around. One edge was ragged as though it had been snapped apart from its twin somehow. It slipped easily over her wrist, and it looked exactly like what it was: the primitive artifact of a primitive people. Her father claimed to have unearthed it in some unthinkably remote desert cave.

There were markings dancing around the ragged edges of both bracelets, untranslatable either individually or when the two halves were placed together. The artifacts appeared similar yet different, of the culture from which they came but foreign to it; and her father, who had become the custodian of them, had sworn to her that he would fathom the secret of them before he died.

For the two years after her mother's death, she had watched as he labored over their lettering and she had been his helper, his researcher, his confidante.

He had shut out everything and everyone in his quest, had abrogated all responsibility to his household and his youngest child. He was consumed by the bracelets, and all she could do was stand helplessly by and watch him fail.

Until the ghost.

The convenient, omniscient, *communicative* spirit who had come to him in a dream one night when he had fallen asleep at his desk, exhausted and enervated by his labors.

A spectre from the very past that haunted him, complete with the key to the markings, the missing pieces, the talisman of faith . . .

Even she did not know what was the truth and what was the dream. For a disturbing time, she had considered that her father might possibly be deranged.

"Oh, but here . . ." He had pointed excitedly. "Look—here. I was in this very room of the temple . . . The moment he explained it, I saw how obvious it was and that I should have seen it myself."

But nothing was obvious to her except the emptiness of the house which had been filled with the stone-hard bitterness of her long-suffering mother and the resentment of Allegra.

He never noticed either. Always self-centered and just a little vain, he had appropriated Alexandra for his own, as the son he had always wanted. It was immaterial that she was not the right sex: he prized her intelligence, he treated her as an equal.

Or, she thought now, as she twisted the bracelet in her finely tapered fingers, as a mirror; he had been talking to a reflection of himself all the time.

What was real?

Her fingers played over the time-eroded markings along the rough edge of the bracelet.

She had believed him—then—but no one else had. And she never knew what possessed him to present his hypothesis to Sir Arthur Hadenham, the head of the British Imperial Museum, complete with the ghost and the interpretation.

Her father had given his life to the Museum and his work. He had spent years in the field; his discoveries, his theories were respected and revered; his monographs of primitive civilizations were required reading at university; he was courted and lionized as only an intrepid explorer of the past could be. He lived for it; he fed on it.

Sir Arthur had been polite, condescending and a little removed. Perhaps it was time for Sir Peregrine to take a long deserved leave of absence. Perhaps he needed to conserve his energy now that he was older; perhaps he could use that time to make a thorough study of the bracelets, at which time the Museum would be happy to publish his findings. They would make him a consultant-at-large. He would lose nothing.

And neither would the Museum.

She had been sure Sir Arthur had made the offer in good faith, certain that he would never have to act upon it. It was clear that the bracelets were to be a closed issue, that they had never been considered of any import whatsoever.

So the find with which her father meant to cap his illustrious career became the impetus of his slide into oblivion.

It was then that he made the room beneath his study—in secret, as he did everything from that point on, and with her as his only witness.

But what could a daughter have done? He had always needed her more, had he not? If she had not brought his food, he would not have eaten. If she had not been there to listen, he would have talked to the bare walls of his underground room and she never would have known his secrets.

If she had not heeded him, she never would have known about the bracelets that felt so cool, so rough, so primitive in her seeking hands.

And if she had ever listened to her vindictive mother in the years before the woman's death, when her father was absent in the field, she would have buried everything with him when he died, two years after his wife.

Instead, she had buried his artifacts and his research in his room, as he had made her promise, where Allegra could not find them; and she had sworn to her sister that they were not among his effects when she had sorted through his papers and memorabilia in the hot claustrophobic days after his death.

All her father's friends came to the funeral, murmured their condolences and swore they would stand by Sir Peregrine's wife and two daughters. Then they departed, and their promises went with them.

All that remained of her father's legacy were the concrete items from his private collection that Sir Arthur, dripping sympathy, was perfectly willing to buy for the Museum.

Of course she had not by then catalogued everything, so it was a shock when Sir Arthur offhandedly asked about the bracelets.

"I know nothing of the bracelets," she told him, carefully phrasing her words and sending meaningful looks to Allegra who seemed about to open her mouth and say something quite the opposite.

"Well, it may be that you haven't come across them yet, my dear. Perhaps they will turn up."

"I found no bracelets," she repeated, casting a harsh glance in her sister's direction and then turning her grave green gaze back to Sir Arthur.

"Well . . ." Nothing discomposed him. "As I say, you may find them later on. Perhaps you might notify me?"

She said no more; and she had never sent word, but she should have expected that Sir Arthur would come around again with his sycophants in tow, pretending a friendship and a concern which he had not acted upon before either.

He wanted the bracelets, and for the first time since the tragedies of her parents' deaths, she wondered why—why now and not before, and why he had repudiated their legitimacy to begin with.

They were scruffy things, scrubbed to an ivory cleanliness by her meticulous father, each little line and swirl attended to with a fine wire brush to scrape out every vestige of dirt and sand. And they fit compactly in the palm of her hand as easily as around her wrists.

Sometimes, fancifully, she slipped one on each wrist, hoping that somehow she might be able to call up the mysterious ghost that had so possessed her father's last days.

And sometimes she cursed them because they were among the last few remaining things she had of her father and they had become objects of power, wielded by her sister, who craftily and unerringly played on Alexandria's guilt over her complicity.

She could not understand what it was about them that had fascinated her father and had compelled Sir Arthur to value them only after his death.

Nor did she understand how those insidious thoughts kept insinuating themselves into her mind, almost as if there were a voyeur spying on her and her deepest most private feelings, or why she first only became conscious of this after her father's funeral—and not before.

She felt she had no control, none; and she hated it. She wanted—and needed—to be able to touch everything so she would know its source and could contain it and understand it.

But she knew nothing and felt as if she were doing everything wrong and that the invasive presence in her mind knew it.

And maybe Allegra did too . . .

She stiffened at the sound of light footsteps overhead. Allegra, searching for her; she could hear her sister's voice faintly from above, and then, as Allegra got no response, her footsteps veered off in another direction.

Alexandra bit her lip and slipped off the stone bracelet.

She felt no urgency in seeking out her sister, and she took the time, as her father had made her promise, to replace the bracelets in the satin-cushioned carved-ivory casket in which he had kept them, and to put them back into the safe he had built behind one of the two beautiful tiled walls he had pieced together from fragments he had collected from the temples of Dudek on the plains of Alekkah where he had spent his final years.

Then she took the candlestick and carefully climbed up the narrow staircase which led to the door in the chimney breast.

Here was the one moment when Allegra could conceivably find her out: the door opened to her left so that there was one blind instant when someone could see her and she not see him.

She set the candlestick onto the ledge her father had built for just that purpose and slowly pushed the door open. Then, with one swift smooth step, she slipped sideways out of the door and shut it behind her.

A moment later, Allegra raced into the room.

"Oh, there you are. But I looked for you in here not five minutes ago."

"Well, I was out in the garden, taking stock as usual," Alexandra said briskly, hoping that Allegra would not notice there was no sign of damp or dirt on the hem of her morning dress, and that the French windows were not open. "I came to the usual conclusion that it is a lost cause, so that is that."

"Oh," Allegra said blankly, and then rushed on. "Well . . . let me tell you where I have been."

"I would like to hear," Alexandra said, perfectly amenable to any distraction which would steer the topic away from what she had been doing.

"Maybe not," Allegra said craftily.

"I am not an ogre," Alexandra said, but without heat. Allegra knew just how to manipulate her. She had taught her sister to do it, out of her own guilt. Allegra probably could not define it, but she was very good at getting what she wanted, and the midnight foray seemed not to have affected her at all.

"You are. You are monstrous sometimes in the weighty opinions you form without knowing anything or anyone at all," Allegra retorted. "Nevertheless, those who count themselves among our friends dismiss your prejudices as your merely being protective of me, and they seem to rather admire your ferocity."

Alexandra waved an exasperated hand. "Which brings you to?"

"Dzmura has come once again to Renwick House, and I saw him this morning."

Alexandra fought down her revulsion. "How nice."

"Exactly. He invites us to dinner tonight, Alixe, and I do so wish to go. He has always shown us the utmost courtesy and respect, and he has been a good friend to me."

Alexandra was not so sure about that. She turned away from her sister to stare out the unopened windows at the hopeless garden. Hopeless too to convince her sister that Dzmura was not an altruistic man and that his interest in Allegra had to stem from something other than her charm.

But she was hard put to know exactly what it was.

The man was hypnotic, as lean and sharp as a raven, with deep-set hooded eyes that missed nothing and a sensual mouth which spoke with the utmost deference to herself and to Allegra, his English exact and charmingly colloquial . . . and very suspicious somehow.

She had never liked him, but Allegra adored him, probably because he was so mysterious and broodingly handsome.

He had bought Renwick House some eight years before; she remembered it distinctly for it had been a time when her father was in the field and her mother was nursing grudges and having fainting spells so all her time was taken up with coddling the woman, treating her with possets and providing reluctant companionship.

So it had been Allegra with whom Dzmura had struck up what Alexandra considered a rather odd and ill-matched friendship.

Her sister, of course, hadn't seen it that way.

"He is so reserved, so proper. He has no children, you know. He is very considerate," she would say. "He teaches me things. He wants me to get on in the world in just the right way."

"And what way would that be?" Alexandra would ask, her tone of voice chilling, her body becoming still, as if frozen by a kind of latent fear.

"Oh, things about how to behave in company, and welcoming people to your house. He's very good at it; he's studied it, you know, because he is from a foreign country, and so he knows just how things operate. It's so much fun."

And Allegra had spent too much time with him whenever he was in residence. Alexandra had to believe Dzmura's motives were purely those of an interested neighbor and nothing more; she had her mother to contend with, and Allegra was lonely. Their father was always away, sending back cryptic letters like the one they had received about his newest protégé, Ryder Culhane:

The Museum sends me the young and impossibly self-destructive Mr. Ryder Culhane. He is angry and arrogant and quite full of himself. Still, he has talent and the requisite "eye," and so we go on to Alekkah in pursuit of the scrolls and whatever else might await us there. Do not look for me at Hidcote anytime soon.

"Anytime soon" had stretched into seven years and ended with the death of her mother, which had probably been the only thing that could prise her father from his fascination with hundreds of miles of sun-baked shifting sands.

Or maybe it was his fascination with Ryder Culhane: in her mind, she had always linked this unknown protégé with her father's prolonged absence which had placed on her the burden of her mother's consuming rage and ultimate death.

And because her own time had been of necessity taken up by

her mother's demands, Alexandra had blamed him as well for Allegra's having formed this unsuitable and highly questionable friendship with Dzmura.

She had never trusted the man, and whenever Allegra had been with him, she had felt alarm and great distress. She had nothing at all on which to base her active dislike of Dzmura—except that one thing, that one time . . . Her mother had been napping, quiet at last, and she had gone searching for Allegra in the most likely place, Renwick House, and when the manservant, Faoud, had not answered the door, she had gone around back to the garden to take a shortcut back to Hidcote.

. . . There—it had been there, although after many years, she tended to think it was something she had conjured up just because she felt so uneasy about the man—she saw them in the blinding sun glare of the summer afternoon, Dzmura, with his camera, and Allegra on a bench, draped in sheets which were expertly tucked and folded, her shoulders bare, her hair flowing down to *there* . . . one naked leg and foot peeking out coyly from beneath the draperies . . .

. . . Oh, it did not bear thinking about, nor did she do the melodramatic thing. She had been a coward then, after all, immersed in her own problems and those of her parents, and she had skulked away, and had never mentioned it, ever, to Allegra.

And somehow, she had convinced herself that it had been a delusion, just because she disliked the man so much; but afterward she never allowed Allegra to be alone with him again.

And she had had the sneaking feeling that Dzmura was well aware of all of this and that he was amused.

Since Allegra was not, how could she deny Allegra the pleasure of his invitation when they got out and about so rarely?

Allegra was a grown woman now. She had nothing to be afraid of, *nothing*.

"You are invited too, of course," Allegra's voice broke into her thoughts and she felt a frisson of fear: *why?*

She turned to face her sister, feeling a dread uncertainty about the motives of Dzmura.

"I am delighted to accept," she said calmly, noting without astonishment her sister's crestfallen expression. Allegra had expected an argument and a rabid refusal, and she had taken that power away from her.

At the very least, Alexandra thought, her sister had expected she might be alone with Dzmura at last, but she pushed that unwelcome thought to the back of her mind.

"Come, I will send Mrs. Podge's boy around with our acceptance. Do you know what you will wear?"

Allegra looked at her uncertainly.

"You are not immured in a dungeon," Alexandra said sharply, irked by the look. "And I am not a monster. Dzmura must set a tolerable table. I can put aside my feelings for one night to dine with him."

"But can you say it will be your pleasure?" Allegra asked sulkily.

"Not as much as yours, I am sure," Alexandra said, "but that is of no moment. You said you wished to go, and I am invited too and so we shall go."

Allegra bowed her head to hide her smile, and a thought wafted into Alexandra's mind: . . . *penance* . . .

She reacted violently: . . . *no* . . . *!* But in that same instant the thought was overlaid with the immediate feeling that of course she must appease Allegra after last night . . . it was necessary. It was only right.

Chapter 2

He had always disliked London and the dark wet fog that inevitably settled on his heated skin like a damp burnous.

London confined him; there was no room for a man to move, and he had no use for its amusements and diversions.

He kept a bare little room at a boarding house on Camberwell Road in south London, a convenience merely, because he never was in London often enough to warrant the expense.

Still, he was grateful for its austere familiarity when he had to spend time there. It was as close to home as any desert camp and a lot more luxurious.

He had been there a month, waiting with perfect patience for the moment he would confront his enemy.

He occupied his days with research, reading, walking, letting his senses open to the bombardment of impressions, waiting, waiting for the moment he knew would eventually come.

And at night he wrestled with the intrusive sentience of Alexandra deLisle.

He had seen her but once, just after her father's funeral, and she had blasted into his consciousness like an erupting volcano.

It was the most forceful, potent and powerful connection he had ever felt with another human being, and he had instantly wanted to run from it; he had felt an equally turbulent desire to combat it, to shut it out and shut her up.

... blasted hypocrite ... rot in hell ... devil ... charlatan ...

The impressions crashed into him, a tidal wave of fury engulfing him while her face remained impassive—all but her eyes, her glittery, sea green eyes spitting with enmity as she faced him across the threshold and said, "You are too late, Mr. Culhane. He's gone and been buried, and there is nothing for you here."

He said nothing and she made no move to close the door, her plain pale face reflecting none of her inner turmoil, her generous mouth refusing to speak all the hot resentment she felt.

He felt it too, shooting off in fiery little sparks like a roman candle, touching him everywhere with sizzling little fingers of grief.

He had not expected that she would not leave him. It almost didn't matter that she had no conscious choice about it; he was the receptor of her feelings and there was nothing he could do about it either.

He returned to Persia and found that he could not lose her in the deserts of Khuramafar or the valleys of the Zagros Mountains.

Nor in his sparse little room in a south London boarding house.

It was only a matter of waiting until he discovered the purpose and the reason.

So when he received the invitation, he was not unduly surprised; it was time and he was ready with this subtle provocation to confront his enemy.

They had known Dzmura, the wealthy international exporter of priceless antiquities, in Tirhan.

"I will not deal with the man," Sir Peregrine had said, "but you must—you must. Soon he will ask, and you will do what he wants, my boy, and let him try to lead you astray. But you must never let him know you are on to him. Then we will see what we will see."

He had found it not that difficult to pretend to succumb to the lure of the money Dzmura offered; his reputation, an open secret by then, had preceded him: he wanted money and he would suborn his precious gift to get it, a philosophy that sat very well with Dzmura.

Curiously, the money was the same whatever his opinion, and he was fascinated that Dzmura was always certain he would do it and vastly amused when he would not, and he never could define the difference between why he might do one and not the other.

"If I am caught, most excellent Culhane, it will be your reputation on the line."

"Exactly, so of course I must withdraw my services."

"My dear Culhane . . . we were only speaking in theory."

"The consequences are not theoretical, however, either to me or yourself."

"Nor is the money," Dzmura would murmur.

"Every man has his price."

"But you cannot paint yourself as an ethical man; you have diverged so widely from the work of the Museum, it seems all you wish to do is cast stones in the water and create disturbances."

"I have no use for the Museum; the Museum is hundreds of miles away. They have already claimed their credit and excavated what is left of my career."

Dzmura knew that very well and had made good use of it, particularly after Sir Peregrine was called back to England at the death of his wife.

But it didn't end there. Culhane received a note from Sir Peregrine seemingly minutes after the man's return home, delivered by hand, almost as if he did not trust the mails—or anyone else.

Damn the man! Not a half-mile down the road and cozy as scones with my family! How long has he been tormenting them—and me—thus? I will bring him down now, I swear it, and you must swear, if anything happens to me, that you will hunt him down and destroy him.

And then Sir Peregrine had died too . . .

And Sir Arthur had gotten to the estate long before Culhane returned to England, and he never would know what Sir Peregrine might have left for him.

But that was a consideration for another time.

Dzmura awaited him; the game was on: the cat might think he was stalking the mouse, but he believed the mouse was wilier.

He rode out to Lavering with only that one taunting clue as to why Dzmura had invited him there.

* * *

Lavering was not more than a half-hour outside of London, a place of expensive and expansive homes built by scions of the aristocracy and now given over to parvenus in trade who maintained them with all the ostentation their wealth could command. It was perhaps fitting that Dzmura counted himself among them. It was downright menacing that he had chosen to reside that close by Sir Peregrine.

Renwick House loomed before him in the dense damp twilight like some great hovering thing, its steep-pitched roofs looking like nothing so much as enveloping shrouds.

Not a light was visible on the well-marked track, but he had expected that as well; Dzmura liked effects that put him in control. He had come prepared with a small lantern and matches, and moments later, he was able to make out the front gate of Renwick House and to ease his hack through it and then dismount.

The scent of danger rippled into his senses, as amorphous as the flow of a stream.

. . . *dark and light* . . .

And the threat of something unknown, formless, unseen . . .

Instinctively he flattened himself against the side of the house, doused the light and listened.

There was no silence in the countryside. He heard the chirrup of birds, the riffle of the grasses, the faint lapping of water against rocks in a stream; the nickering of another horse came from somewhere in the distance.

And impatient footfalls and the strong invasive sense of *her.*

Of course, her. Of course Dzmura would make himself acquainted with Sir Peregrine's family.

She came careening around the far side of the house blindly and almost at a run, and he felt it again, that slithering cold sensation of warning.

She did not see him either; he reached out and grabbed her and pulled her tightly against him, his hand clamping over her mouth before she could let out a scream.

She thrashed about against him out of pure terror.

. . . *shhhh* . . .

The familiar . . .

... don't ...

She stopped clawing at him.

... you ...!

Him—resonating in her consciousness—*him* ... She sagged against him in capitulation. She could not begin to comprehend it.

He kept one arm around her and took his hand off her mouth.

"You are a madman," she whispered fiercely, jerking her body fruitlessly against his restraining arm.

"We'll go mad together," he whispered back. "Just hold that damned wasp's tongue of yours ..."

Hold her tongue? Hold her tongue? When he had held her very senses captive these two years?

"You are crazy. My sister is in there alone with that man, and I won't allow her to—"

"Shhhh ..."

He felt it again, that rippling sensation of danger, and then the presence of Dzmura, directly in his mind: *... it is safe ...*

And his first stunned thought: *... of course ...*

He relinquished his hold on Alexandra, and she almost keeled over.

"We will go in now."

"What?" He was deranged, he had to be. She would not walk one single step in his company.

"Come ..." He took her hand; she snatched it away. "You make nothing easy, do you?"

"Never," she shot back, "but of course you are very used to grabbing women in the dark and having them curtsy and say thank you very much."

Dear lord, she couldn't even see his face; she felt cornered, surrounded by the dark threatening shapes of foliage and trees—and the hovering feeling of disaster.

He felt a burgeoning desire to shake her. "And you never shut up—"

"—nor will I hesitate to scream—"

"—until you consider which is the lesser of the evils tonight, Alexandra—"

"—don't you dare ..." She felt like striking him, even if she could just barely see him in the dark; she was out of her mind with worry about Allegra and she couldn't see a foot in front of her, and all he wanted to do was trade clever words.

"Don't be stupid," he said brutally. "I have a light."

She hated him then, for having skulked in the darkness and waited to pounce on her. "Do you now?" she murmured as she heard the nick and scrape of a match.

The light flared, moved, flicked onto the wick inside the small lantern he held in his hand and immediately revealed his shadow-carved features.

She started visibly; in the dark and defined by shadows, he looked every bit as dangerous and crafty as Dzmura.

"Come," he said, holding out his hand.

She brushed by him and stalked down the path. What did he expect after he had all but attacked her?

He was right behind her as she approached the front door which faced well away from the road, almost as if Dzmura wanted to discourage the casual visitor.

He lifted the light to the heavy ornate knocker and raised it easily. It fell against the thick wood door with a gratifying crash.

A moment later, a turbaned manservant opened the door, and Alexandra stepped briskly into the vaulted foyer.

"Where is my sister?"

The servant did not answer; he took the lantern from Ryder's hand, motioned for them to remain where they were, and then withdrew, bowing obsequiously all the way down the hall.

. . . hate that man . . .

The thought no sooner tiptoed into her mind than she knew he had a presentiment of it, and she looked at him resentfully.

"No," he said easily, ignoring the gathering storm in her eyes, "I don't believe we've met formally."

"I know who you are," Alexandra said abrasively. "I just don't know what you are."

"But, my dear Alexandra, he is the most pragmatic Culhane," a voice interposed behind her, "and a trusted friend of your father."

Alexandra wheeling around to face him. "Where is my sister?"

Dzmura held up his hand. "You are ever so fearful for her always, Alexandra, and yet she has always felt safe in my house. Come . . ."

He gestured and turned, and Alexandra reluctantly followed him with Culhane but a step or two behind her.

"Put away your fears, Alexandra. Tonight we will merely be sharing a pleasant meal."

. . . not merely . . .

She could not suppress the rebellious thought. Something about this house frightened her, even awash with light and warmth as it was. There were still shadows, still things she could not grasp in a concrete way.

Dzmura was too pleasant—she mistrusted that. And the man behind her who could intuit her every feeling—he scared her; she could not hide from him.

But how could any man know her like that? It went beyond normalcy; it bordered the realm of the unquantifiable, of things she did not believe were possible.

Yet it was, and Dzmura was. And her sister's devotion to him was every bit as improbable and inexplicable as someone's being able to probe her thoughts.

Allegra came rushing at them from a doorway at the far end of the hall.

"Alexandra, Alexandra . . . what held you up? And who is this, Tebo? You never mentioned—"

"Did I not?" he murmured with a show of concern. "This is a business associate of mine—dare I say friend, most discriminating Culhane?—Miss Allegra deLisle, Mr. Ryder Culhane."

"Mr. Culhane," she said after a moment's hesitation, her questioning gaze on Dzmura and not on him.

"Miss deLisle." How like Alexandra she was, and how unlike. Her expression was fresh, open, guileless and trustful, her features a softened and somewhat blurred copy of Alexandra's, her body youthful and just past being gawky; and her hands went every which way as she talked, and impatiently pushed tendrils of thick tawny hair out of her bright green eyes.

They were not, Ryder thought critically, quite the same deep emerald as her sister's neither was her hair the same rich color,

nor did she have the same force of personality or the same tren-
chant timbre in her voice.

Only their features were similar, and side by side, did one not
know they were sisters, they might have been taken for twins.
Allegra's brow knit for a moment. "You were with father in
that horrible desert he liked so much better than us," she said accusingly.

"Now my dear . . ." Dzmura said conciliatingly, "the desert is
my home."

"Well, you never would have—"

"How does one know what one would have done had one a
family to consider, dear Allegra. Come, enough of this. I meant
this to be a happy occasion to celebrate my return to Lavering
and the renewing of my acquaintance with your sister and Mr.
Culhane."

Even Ryder looked askance at this, but Allegra bowed to his
silken solicitousness and never saw Alexandra's skeptical expression.

"Of course, it is ill mannered of me to bring personalities into
it."

"Very well then. Let me now invite you into my library, my
ever-curious Culhane. I am most anxious to see what you make
of it."

Culhane felt wary and suspicious but no one could have been
more charming than Dzmura as he played the excellent host. He
set a bountiful table, and he would not let one argumentative
word cross it.

He even managed to pull Alexandra out of her silence and into
the conversation, and he referred respectfully and with seeming
affection to several amusing incidents between himself and "the
most excellent Culhane," matters of anecdotal interest presented
with charming and self-deprecating humor.

Culhane felt he was watching a play and wondering just when
the author would reveal the theme, the menace and the twist.

Alexandra was not seduced either. Her taut body refused to
bend to Dzmura's charm. When his hooded eyes focused on her
now and again with dark speculation, she met his gaze defiantly,

almost as if she were ready to throw herself at him to put dista between him and Allegra, and she wanted him to know it.

"But you were telling me the most fascinating thing this afternoon," Allegra said guilelessly, breaking a pause in the conversation.

"We were talking of so many interesting things," Dzmura murmured, leaning into his dessert and bringing a forkful deliberately to his mouth.

Everything he did was deliberate, Alexandra realized apprehensively; he did not want to derail this topic of conversation, but he made it seem as if he did.

Oh God, when can I get Allegra out of here?

The words . . . *this afternoon* . . . resonated in the room.

Alexandra felt a frisson of foreboding. "Oh?" she said cautiously and carefully. "This . . . afternoon?"

Allegra leaped into the ringing silence. "Why yes. Tebo asked me to arrange the flowers for him and so while you were resting, I . . . well, anyway, we just got to talking and . . ."

. . . *losing her* . . .

It was an internal cry of pure terror that rooted itself right into Ryder's mind.

And then Dzmura, countering: . . . *groundless* . . .

But Alexandra was utterly unaware of the sentient duel between them; the message came to him, was meant for him. He looked at Dzmura, his face expressionless.

Allegra kept talking; no one was listening.

And then her words suddenly came into focus.

". . . about the thousands of artifacts that could be buried and never found. And that we haven't even scratched the surface of knowledge about the ancient religions, and there must be hundreds of ancient texts that could have survived somehow—"

"Like the prayer papers that Mr. Culhane so fortuitously discovered," Dzmura put in smoothly, seemingly seeking to stem the flow of her words.

Or maybe not, Ryder thought, holding his cup of tea to his lips but not sipping.

"Or those scrolls that my father was so sure he would find someday."

nura said.

talked about the intermeshing of known reli-
that might prove our ancestors worshipped
d the beliefs that have been imposed on us for

like a pupil who has performed her recitation
well.

"Did I? Did I say that?" Dzmura murmured. "Dear me."

"Things beyond that which we know," she prompted, hoping he would take up the discussion because something about the forbidden nature of it excited her.

"But we can only know what we know, is that not so, most practical Culhane?"

"But 'there are more things between heaven and earth . . .'" Ryder responded, the whole of his attention focused on Dzmura. But there was nothing. He could have imagined the impression of Dzmura's thoughts touching him. "How can we know?"

"That is your job," Dzmura said gently.

"But the thing that was so interesting," Allegra rushed in, ignoring them, "was the idea that religion really could also be the belief in evil and the darkness of man's soul, that in the struggle, evil wins instead of love and goodness. Imagine . . . a world of evil! Tebo says anything is possible. Is that true, Mr. Culhane, could it be?"

He shrugged. "Theoretically, based on concepts assimilated since a thousand years ago. Your father believed there was a written record of those beliefs, and certainly the discovery of such scrolls would be a monumental find and proof that such a sect of believers did exist."

"And you are the•very man to find them, most patient Culhane, for did you not conjure up the prayer papers of the Keturah out of myths and hieroglyphs and the power of your imagination?"

"You give me too much credit," Ryder murmured. "It was never my area of expertise."

"Yet you pursued it with Sir Peregrine. And were there not some similarities? Did not the Keturah worship the force of the ungodly?"

"So it could have been translated. It is equally apt to be interpreted as idolatrous gods, as I think you well know."

"Of course. I stand corrected. It is merely supposition for the sake of conversation. It was an exercise of Allegra's imagination and intellect to suggest to her a world served solely by the impetus of evil. The consequences are far reaching and unimaginable, and I see in Alexandra's expression that she is trying to even comprehend the improbable."

Oh, but she wasn't; evil sat within her grasp, taunting them all with the very theism he personified.

"My dear," he went on sympathetically, "even those of us with some passing knowledge of ancient religions cannot conceive of it. Every religious belief centers on a struggle between good and evil . . ."

. . . *dark and light* . . .

". . . and it cannot be otherwise that good vanquishes evil. Is that not so, most learned Culhane? Is that not an eternal truth?"

He felt Alexandra's distress as the matte-thick blanket of Dzmura's reasoning closed around him. He felt as suffocated as Alexandra, as walled in and taunted by Dzmura: . . . *test it* . . . *disprove it* . . . Yet his expression remained blandly benign.

And Allegra was blindly aware of nothing; it was as if she had been snapped off like a light and he and Dzmura were the only ones in the room.

. . . *dark and light . . . light and dark . . . who is the light and who is the dark, and who will win, most altruistic Culhane? He who must . . . who commands knowledge from beyond the mists of time . . . I await your challenge, Culhane . . . do not disappoint me . . .*

The moment passed: Dzmura smiled and waved a deprecating hand and murmured, "It is only a parlor game, most innocent Culhane, a conjuring trick, a magic act. But the power in the idea grabs hold and one cannot help but surrender to it. We—you and I—are not susceptible to suggestion; we deal solely in the concrete, the findable, the explainable. Have I not valued you for that, friend Culhane? I assure you I have.

"Ease your mind. It is mere prattle only, dinner table conversation, guaranteed to start arguments and foment strife. Ah, you relax now, Culhane. That is good. And further, as proof that I am only playing games, I offer you the hospitality of my home this night. It is beyond the time you can safely travel. No, do not protest, I insist.

"Now, Allegra, my dear, ring for Faoud. We will take up this topic some other time, over another enjoyable dinner."

Allegra reached for the embroidered bell pull which hung just to the left of Dzmura's shoulder in the ornate dining room.

. . . of course, you cannot win . . .

He perceived Dzmura's challenge simultaneously with the sonorous tolling of the bell, and then the impression of Alexandra's internal cry of distress: *. . . Allegra . . . !* as Allegra mechanically pushed herself away from the table and moved to stand by Dzmura's side.

Dzmura's face was expressionless, his steady hooded gaze as fathomless as the ocean.

"My darling Allegra," he murmured, and suddenly she smiled.

Alexandra's heart dropped as her sister came to life.

"Alixe . . . here is Faoud to see us home. Are you ready? Oh, Tebo, how can I thank you for such a lovely evening. You are so good to me."

"It is my pleasure," Dzmura said, rising also. "Alexandra, my dear. I hope this evening has changed your feelings about me a little."

The picture of them together that awful afternoon years before flashed into her mind. And then the unthinkable, the thing she had never ever allowed herself to consider: that it had not been the first time, and that it had gone on for years because she had just ignored it.

She felt sick, flooded with guilt and fear, and she had to hide it, from Allegra and from *him*.

"I do thank you for your hospitality," she said stiffly . . . *oh let me leave, let us leave . . .*

"And the ever-accommodating Culhane. I hope your visit has been a pleasure as well?"

"Most stimulating," Ryder said with a tart irony that was not lost on Dzmura. But he was looking at Alexandra, his mind awash with her pulsating need to get away from Dzmura; surely Dzmura could sense it too?

"I thought so," Dzmura said tranquilly. He turned to Allegra. "My dear . . ."

She grasped his arm, almost as if she could not stand without his support. "Oh, Tebo, maybe I come tomorrow?"

He ran a long finger down the side of her cheek. "With your sister's approval, anytime you wish when I am here."

"But you disappear sometimes like a cloud in the wind. Say you will be here tomorrow at least, and I will come early and we will talk some more."

. . . no-o-o-o . . . ! Alexandra, in anguish, as even Dzmura could see. He ignored it.

"I cannot refuse you," he said. He snapped his fingers. "Faoud."

His servant came forward on silent feet and motioned for them to follow.

At the threshold of the room, Allegra turned back to look at him just one more time standing so tall and elegant and aloof, the stuff of an impressionable girl's dreams. A participant in them for as long as she could remember.

Her body quickened at the thought of his attentiveness. He was the only person ever to take her so seriously—even when she was a child. And he asked for so little in return. Pleasing him and having him for her friend almost made up for the lack of everything else, including Alexandra's palpable dislike of him.

How could anyone dislike him?

"Allegra!"

Alixe again and always, pulling her against her will. She moved to join her sister reluctantly, her mind on the coming morning and what she might do to prove to Dzmura her pleasure at being able to have him all to herself again.

Chapter 3

She felt as if the ground had shifted under her and she had utterly lost her footing. It was the fog, the heavy, life-sapping fog that veiled everything in a distorted mist of illusion.

What was real? Or had she imagined everything?

She hardly heard Allegra's artless prattle.

"... have to admit, Alixe, he's not at all like you thought."

Oh, but he is, and worse ...

"... distinguished, mannered, elegant ... charming ..."

... dangerous ... manipulative ... sly ... cunning ...

"And you won't be mad if I visit tomorrow, will you?"

I will kill him ...

Or had she imagined everything? Ahead of them, Faoud with his lantern, wielded the light like a protective halo which would guard against the spirits of the night.

"... Doesn't Hidcote look positively dilapidated next to Renwick House?" Allegra moaned as the bulk of their house loomed before them. "Look at it ... ghosts live there, Alixe ..."

No, she thought bitterly, ghosts hide there: the shades of her malignant mother and her withdrawn and remote father. They infected the house, infecting the two of *them*—and in that single fog-bound moment, she understood that she reflected them and that she, like her father, had also failed her sister ... and her mother.

"Misses ..." Faoud respectfully held up the light so that Alexandra could reach for the bell pull to summon Mrs. Podge's boy to the door, and he waited patiently until it opened, before he withdrew.

Alexandra wheeled around abruptly as she stepped over the threshold, but the light was gone and he had disappeared like a wraith into the mist.

. . . Blasted fog . . . Ryder thought; it looked as if they were walking into a noxious cloud on their way to heaven or hell—even he couldn't tell.

The door closed behind them, sealing their fate as they proceeded into the night with the loyal Faoud, and Dzmura said, "So, most excellent Culhane, let us drink to a delightful evening."

He motioned Ryder to precede him into the parlor.

"We must drink first to the tenacity of Sir Peregrine who is no longer with us." He poured healthy portions of brandy from a cut-glass decanter into two snifters. "Come, Culhane, I am full of bonhomie tonight. No tricks, no hidden agendas. We are friends here tonight, as I offer you the hospitality of my home."

He handed one of the glasses to Ryder. "It amuses me to live in the fashion of the English. It is so opulent, so decadent to want and need such a house, so many rooms, so much furniture to accommodate one man who counts his wealth in land and tents and camels. The irony of it. To Sir Peregrine, most patient Culhane, who fully conceived of and who lived such a life not two miles down the road."

They lifted their snifters simultaneously, and Ryder let the first mouthful of brandy burn into his tongue and down his throat slowly and deliberately. This was his enemy whom he must not underestimate.

Dzmura was on his turf now, granted, but he walked it with the precision of a man who had learned how to traverse the most difficult terrain.

"And Sir Peregrine's daughters," Dzmura went on, holding his goblet up to the light so that it played on the deep gold in the rich liquid. "Yes, his lovely daughters. The backbone of that Alexandra—most admirable. And the sweet innocence of Allegra—ever desirable . . ." He lifted the goblet to his lips again and eyed Ryder over its rim like an eagle stalking its prey.

Ryder smiled grimly and lifted his goblet once again.

"Ah. And finally, to friend Culhane who searches so assiduously for the scrolls of the Zoran—to your success, my friend. May you find the ultimate victory . . ."

. . . if you can prevent me from stopping you . . .

Ryder smiled grimly into his glass. Here was the endgame— the tenuous warning, the delicate threat. Dzmura needed no other weapons but these.

"Ah, Faoud, back from safely escorting the ladies home. Faoud, the astute Culhane will occupy the Red Room." He turned to Ryder. "You will rest well there, Culhane; I promise, it will appeal to you."

It appealed to his sense of humor; it was a nightmare in red: walls in red moire silk, a thick carpet of red berber wool; red satin bedcoverings, red tapestry on the occasional chairs; matching red curtains; red accessories; a red dressing gown hanging in the armoire, precisely his size.

He paced the room alert as a cat. The challenge was on, issued subtly and artfully by a master of illusion who was well versed in conjuring up something out of nothing.

Dzmura . . . how elegant and logical.

How perfect that it was he who walked in the shadows and moved insidiously in the darkness. The chameleon who took on the coloration of his surroundings—

The wily consciousness that could infiltrate his at will—

Clever Dzmura to throw up a smokescreen in the persons of Sir Peregrine's own daughters who could have no knowledge of the things at stake between him and Dzmura.

But now the opposing pieces were finally engaged: Dzmura had outflanked him, but had not taken a pawn.

Nor had he been duped by Dzmura's opening maneuver.

Obviously it was only a matter of time before Dzmura attacked again.

. . . oh God . . . !!! oh God . . . !!!! Allegra !!! Allegra . . . !!!

The frenzy, the pulse-pounding fear in her consciousness awakened him and propelled him out of bed where he had settled finally, fully clothed, into a troubled and dream-wracked sleep.

. . . gone . . . gone . . . gone . . . oh my God, oh my God . . . gone . . . !!!

He felt as if he were running, here, there, everywhere, overset by pure panic and helplessness, enfolded by her deepening hysteria.

... she knew ... she knew ... oh dear God ... Allegra ... !!!

... A release, as if she had stopped in her tracks, gone numb with the sheer horror of it.

... find her—have to ... go ... must ... must ...

She was operating on pure terror-stricken panic now.

He felt her impetus to movement, unthinking, gut-level and frozen in a karmic litany: *... oh God, Allegra ... oh God, Allegra ...*

He eased himself out of the door of the Red Room into the pure opaque darkness of the hallway, and immediately scraped a match to flame.

The matte silence of the house felt as ominous as the fog. There was not a glimmer of light anywhere. The darkness was overpowering, intimidating.

He stood for a moment, his consciousness roaming, listening. He heard nothing, nothing. He felt space, yawning, empty, jet black space and an explosive urge to action.

Instantly he knew that Dzmura was of no moment now; he had dismantled the house sometime during the night and he had gone—a cosmic joke on him, after surrounding him with the trappings of a civilization to which he paid no court whatsoever.

He had just flung open the front door when he felt it—the distinct divisive pull towards the parlor.

He listened a moment, dissecting the feeling, deciding its truth, and then he moved towards the parlor and opened the door.

The room felt cavernous, cold, clammy. Empty.

But one object stood out incongruously: an album, placed precisely on the table that backed the stiff Chippendale sofa.

It was a luxurious thing, covered in fine tooled leather, a sentimental and burdensome thing with which a nomad like Dzmura would hardly encumber himself.

He touched it tentatively, seeking the sense of it, and then he opened it.

There was but one picture in it: Allegra as a child, stretched out on a garden bench, her youthful body draped in diaphanous silk, her expression sweet and coy at the same time, playing quite consciously to the camera's eye, and just beyond her, the shadow of her phantom cameraman, his mocking laughter echoing in the empty room.

It took him twenty long excruciating minutes to reach Hidcote, and he felt as if the fog itself were his enemy with its trailing fingers of mist reaching out to blind him, branches of trees whipping against his face in the damp wind, her exhausted chant a litany in his consciousness: . . . *oh my God, Allegra* . . . *oh my God, Allegra* . . .

A thick-waisted country woman opened the door to his incessant banging and shouting.

"Where is she?"

"Who be you?"

"Where is she?" he demanded again forcefully.

She pulled her wrapper tight around her throat. "You can't—" she started to protest, but he gave her no chance to stand her ground: he was in the house before she knew it and heading straight for the study.

"She ain't there," Mrs. Podge called after him.

"She'll find me then," he retorted and thrust open the door.

The room was lit and in monstrous disarray: papers were scattered everywhere, chairs tumbled over, desk drawers upside down on the floor, the carpet turned back in three places.

And there, by the fireplace, was a small panelled door swung outward. He moved towards it, ignoring everything else, and ducked his head as he entered its threshold and found the steep flight of stairs.

Here, the sense of Sir Peregrine was all pervasive. Below him, he saw a flickering light, candlelight, and he moved slowly and cautiously towards it.

He was instantly assaulted with impressions, and he determinedly closed them out as he stepped into the small square secret room in which Sir Peregrine had spent his last days.

He could not have imagined anything like it: a dungeon or an oasis, he didn't know which. It might have been ten or eleven feet square and two of the walls were a gorgeous mosaic of antique tiles. Just beyond the staircase were shelves on which were laid Sir Peregrine's tools, and in the center of the room was a plain scrubbed table around which were several chairs.

But the interesting thing was the tiled wall with the hidden compartment, its door swung open as if something had been taken and it was no longer necessary to keep its secrets.

... *hieroglyphs* ...

The impression was strong, almost overwhelming.

He reached his hand inside the vault. It was metal, like a safe, but its floor was carpeted with a length of velvet as if something precious had been stored there.

... *hieroglyphs* ...

The impression was insistent, overriding, but there was nothing in this odd, luridly decorated secret room that remotely resembled any kind of code or cipher.

He felt an urgency, suddenly, a dizzying whirl forward into time and then a lightning flash in his mind and the sense of something beyond what seemed obvious.

—the wall, the table—the opposite wall—

... *circles* ...

He saw them distinctly—round, thick, bone-white ... stone-hard—

And then he saw the pattern in the opposite wall of tile; it leaped out at him from the intricate maze of the mosaic, a perfect oblong, a twin to the door in the opposite wall, and embedded in the tilework, as clear as if Sir Peregrine had hand-written it, the code.

Hieroglyphs ... nothing Alexandra deLisle could ever have deciphered even if she had known what to look for: this had been left for him—*his* clue, *his* key. And not easy to translate in the dim light of the secret cellar.

He felt the press of time, as if every moment he was delayed would put Dzmura further and further away from him, and he was torn between the compelling urgency of finding him and the pull the impression exerted on him in this secret room.

Ten minutes passed like ten hours before he could decode Sir Peregrine's cryptogram, and then suddenly, without warning, the door to a second vault swung open, just as he heard footsteps pounding down the narrow secret stairs and then Alexandra's outraged voice: "*Get away from that wall!*"

But he did not move and he ignored the thready note of hysteria in her command.

"Don't be a fool, Alexandra," he said bluntly.

"No more a fool than if I trusted *you*," she retorted, her voice shaking with fury, fear and something else he could not define.

"We are wasting time. And I *will* see what is in the vault. Get over here . . ."

But she was there already, pressing the sharp tip of a weapon firmly into his ribs.

"Don't *move.*"

"We have no time for these games; Dzmura is gone and I would wager he has your sister—"

"*Noooo!*" She shoved the blade of the scimitar more firmly into his side in her anguish. "You bastard; and what do you know about it, having spent the night with that monster from hell?"

"I know I must see what is in the vault," he said impatiently, "and then I will know more."

"And why should I trust you?" she demanded.

"Because I found the vault," he said with almost irrefutable logic.

She sensed that she was almost ready to fall apart: it was too much—Allegra gone, the secret door ajar, her father's safe breached, the bracelets missing . . . and now Dzmura—she would *not* think about it—and a secret vault she had known nothing about, but which Culhane, having sneaked into her house, had found within the previous twenty minutes . . . !

"Move slowly," she said shakily, not willing to concede one single thing to him. It was her house, her father, his secrets . . . "Very slowly; I swear, I will kill you if you try something untoward."

He lifted one arm and felt the piercing tip of the weapon, the futility of her folly. He was convenient and there, and that was all Miss Alexandra deLisle needed.

He lifted out a plain wooden box, about eight inches square.

"Put it on the table," she directed.

The flickering light of the kerosene lamp enlarged it to twice its size. There was no lock.

"Open it," Alexandra said shakily.

He lifted the lid from its grooved slot and took out something wrapped in paper.

"I'll do it."

He swore silently, feeling time slipping and slipping away, and the mocking laughter of Dzmura deep in his mind.

"Oh my God, my God . . ."

She held it up to him, what was in her hands: two circlets of scrubbed stone, ragged at the edges, with cryptic markings encircling each, as large as bracelets, as old as time.

Chapter 4

They were the same, the same, and she had not hidden them elsewhere, and she couldn't think what it meant that there was a duplicate vault, a second set of priceless bracelets.

They fell from her seemingly boneless hands with a heavy thud onto the table. Instantly she reached for her weapon as he reached out to take one.

"Don't touch it!" Her voice was reedy, her emotions almost at the breaking point.

"Alexandra—" He wrestled with his impatience. Time . . . time . . . time . . ."I need to look at the bracelets, and then I am going after Dzmura."

"I'm going too," she said sharply, though she did not know where that bravado came from.

"I will find your sister, I promise. Don't waste time now, Alexandra; the more you talk, the farther away he gets."

"I am going too."

He held her gaze, a shadowed and stormy green in the dim light of the lamp, and he reached again for one of the bracelets.

She knocked his arm away with the scimitar, and they stared at each other, enemies almost to the death.

And then suddenly she dropped the sword, swooped up the bracelets and pulled them onto her wrists.

"Now you must take me with you."

. . . time . . . time . . . He jumped, barreling into her slender form and pushing her back hard against the tile wall.

"You . . . have no conception of what you are doing, what you

are saying; every minute . . ."—he felt her body straining against
his—". . . every second . . ."—she wrenched against him with the
almost superhuman strength born of her fear—". . . I delay . . ."—
her face flushed, her eyes hard and glittering with utter contempt
at his tactics—". . . he wins . . . he . . ."

His iron hands thrust her arms above her head. He was about
to force the bracelets from her wrists. ". . . God damn it . . ." His
body tightened with instant arousal as she writhed against the
thrust of his strength. "He . . ."

He couldn't force her; she balled her hands, and she arched
her body and twisted and shoved at him with the force of her anguish and fear.

He gazed down into her face; he had never seen a woman like
this, so utterly stubborn and intractable, so willing to pit her
power against his. He hadn't expected it; he didn't know quite
how to combat it.

He needed the bracelets.

A long heated moment passed and then he said slowly and in
a calm measured tone: "Dzmura will win if you do not let me examine the bracelets. He is answerable to no one: he will take your
sister and you will never see him again. Renwick House will fall
to dust—he will never return. I *must* see those bracelets."

Her world was turning upside down with those words: *he will
never return.*

. . . Allegra might never return . . .

Her heart constricted. If it were true, and if she even thought
there was a possibility of that, she had no choice but to hand over
the duplicate bracelets and leave Culhane to the pursuit.

But then what would she do? Sit home and wait?

Grow cold and barren with anguish and anticipation of an
event which would never occur? Was he crazy?

She had something he wanted, for whatever it was worth. And
perhaps he had answers for her—she had a hundred questions—
but she could not wander the cold fruitless rooms of Hidcote and
wait for that someday day when Allegra might return.

Her resolve seemed hard as stone.

"I will go with you, and we will talk about the bracelets."

"We waste time, Alexandra," he said, his tone dangerously close to anger and an underlying threat to wrest them away from her.

"*Now,* Culhane . . ."

She did not know where this iron strength was coming from; she only knew she needed to be able to *do* something, that on her wrists was the means to blackmail him and she was willing to do it, needed to do it, because her father had betrayed her and Allegra was in danger of her life.

She did not have time for his judgments or his protests; if anything, she felt more frenzied and helpless pitting her puny resources against his strength.

"Your presumption is appalling," he said grittily, losing patience fast. He forced her clenched hands more tightly against the wall. "I need the bracelets."

"And I have them," she bit out, "so you will take them by force or take me with you—no other way, Culhane."

He considered her rebellious expression. He did not know women like this; his women were always compliant, submissive in the way of the east. They never questioned; they always subordinated their desires to those of their men.

They would no more stand up to him than walk naked in the street. But this one was different, defiant. He needed to quell that insubordination—with scare tactics if necessary.

"Take you . . . take you . . . What use do I have for a virginal viper in the middle of the desert?"

Her body quivered with pent-up rage at his caustic dismissal of her. Dear God, she hated him—hated his smugness, his intrusion into her life, her mind, her pain.

She wrenched futilely against his hard and powerful grip, her body driving tightly against his taut frame; she had the instant impression that he was reining in his temper.

And then that he was leaning into her menacingly, intentionally trying to terrify her with the physical manifestation of his maleness.

"No use, Alexandra—do you hear me? You would slow me down, and I need to move fast. You don't have the stamina, you wouldn't survive a day in the desert. There is nothing you can do for me . . ."

She felt like kicking him, her need to take action settling into a massive determination to do whatever it took—anything.

"Nothing?" she interposed tartly. Oh Lord, was she really thinking of . . . She knew nothing about things like that—but it was so easy . . . She felt like a child putting her hand in a forbidden place, walking the dangerous edge just to challenge someone to slap her down.

"*Nothing?*" she repeated, thrusting her hips forward slightly so that her body nestled suggestively against his. "Truly nothing, Culhane?" And she understood finally, as the light changed in his eyes the headiness of the power of a woman.

She was like a child playing with fire, he thought, and he was angry because her slender body was potent enough to arouse him, even against his will. A stick she was, a slender stick with intelligent eyes, and she talked too much and knew too little, least of all about the importance of time and how he felt it slipping, slipping away . . .

And she saw her chance slipping, slipping away . . . and Allegra gone forever and herself alone at Hidcote, limping around its empty rooms getting older and older—forever.

She bit her lip. What did she know of the mysteries between a man and a woman? Did it matter? She had only to say the words, and they might be her magic carpet out of the prison of Hidcote.

Just say them . . .

"I will share your bed, Culhane."

He let go of her abruptly. "I don't need the bracelets that much."

She lowered her tingling arms slowly, grasping the bracelets so they would not fall off.

"I think you do," she said consideringly, and then she turned abruptly and erupted into a run, making for the small narrow staircase, and was out of sight before he could collect his wits.

By the time he got to the study, she was standing by the fireplace calm and composed, and the bracelets were nowhere in sight.

"Well, Culhane?"

Her voice was not even shaky, although she felt he held her life in his hands. He needed the bracelets, for what reason she could not guess since they were so obviously copies of the originals. But he needed them, and he wanted Dzmura, so she held the key and she had the power. Still, it took all of her guile and guts to push herself forward after offering the ultimate sacrifice.

They stood not ten feet from each other, and she could feel the power of his mind searching, searching; she shook her head, shaking him off.

And he thought, one last gambit; one last test. She was more formidable than he could have guessed, but someone as delicately nurtured as she could not withstand a litany of the reality of travelling with him.

"Do I understand you?" he said silkily. "You are offering me your body in exchange for the bracelets and coming with me?"

Was she? Was she? Was she crazy?

"Yes," she whispered without hesitation.

"And you understand what that means? That you are offering yourself to me fully, nakedly, in any way that it pleases me to take you. That you will submit to my desire whenever and wherever I dictate and that you will always hold yourself in readiness for me . . ."

He felt her fear—good—he wondered how much more he should heap on her plate before she gave in; she was damned stubborn, he saw it in her eyes as she comprehended exactly what he was demanding in exchange for her unwanted presence.

". . . and you will never refuse anything I ask of you, no matter what it is." Yes, he could see realization dawning in her eyes, the shadow of horror at this raw definition of his demands.

And he meant it all, she thought, her body beginning to shake as his heated, sensual words provoked a strange response in her. Words were powerful, and didn't she know it? Look at how her sister had been transported by words.

Nothing mattered now, nothing. Far from the sheltered walls of Hidcote, she would learn the secrets of women in the arms of a tyrant; she would give herself to him with the same brisk determination she did everything else in her life, and then she would have solved the great mystery in the life of a woman.

So be it. There would be no stain on her reputation that far from home; when she returned, it would be as if she were reborn, and that would be that.

"I accept your terms," she said, the calm hand of fate guiding her words.

... *I will do anything* ...

He read her obdurate resolve as clearly as if she had spoken aloud. There was no use arguing, not here, not now when the last moments that he could take action were still within his grasp.

He held out his hand. "The bracelets . . ."

"When we are on our way, Culhane—well on our way."

He read the flickering little moment of triumph in her too bright eyes, and he almost backed out. Almost.

But he believed in fate and the inevitability of destiny. There was a reason Alexandra deLisle was meant to come with him, and it had nothing to do with submitting to his needs.

Until he understood, he could handle her and he would use her; later he would lose her, and then she would see whose strength really won that day.

Chapter 5

They hurtled into the outskirts of London in the cold dense fog of an ominous dawn, with Culhane recklessly driving the aged and creaking deLisle carriage as if it were a racing curricle.

Alexandra hung on grimly as the carriage swung around a corner and went careening off down another road.

She had no idea where he was going; there was such a feeling of unreality about the whole thing that for one giddy moment, she thought she might wake up in her own bed and find it was all a bad dream.

But no, they were in the thick of the city now; dark gray-fogged shapes loomed outside the carriage window, amorphous and vaguely threatening.

. . . it is done . . .

The thought insinuated itself into her consciousness like the drifting fog.

It was done, and already she had come farther on sheer nerve-and mind-bending fear than she had in her whole life.

And what was she giving up in return? But this was the way of the world; she had been the one who had led the narrow closeted life. Because of it, Allegra had walked away—willingly or not—and she was forced to redefine her values and her life.

She saw in no uncertain terms what the future would have held for her: she would have stayed on at Hidcote forever, one of the two eccentric Misses deLisle, always skirting the edge of poverty, parsing out ha'pennies and living off the quarterly interest from Allegra's inheritance from their mother.

She would *become* her mother, grasping and emotional, resentful and repressed; and Allegra would be the one to leave and find adventure. But Allegra was always the bolder one, else how could she have appropriated Dzmura's friendship in such a calm and easy manner?

Was she not jealous of her sister? Had she always been? And bitter? Because tending to her mother and then her father—when he was home—had fallen on her shoulders?

Had she been angry all these years?

Because Allegra's sole function was to look pretty and let her family enjoy her company and her frilly little ways?

And because she, Alexandra, had always had to be the stronger of the two? The *man* of the family . . . ?

And was that why she had placed herself in this untenable situation—to prove she was a woman too?

No. That didn't bear thinking about either.

She wouldn't think about it. Somehow she would get out of it and that would be that; the important thing was to rescue Allegra.

The *most* important thing . . .

And why had she believed him anyway, she wondered, when she had been positive that Allegra had stolen the bracelets and was off on an odyssey to find Sir Arthur Hadenham at the Museum and offer to sell them to him?

In the dead of the night . . . sneaking behind her back . . . after all that talk . . . and with Dzmura hovering in the background . . . ?

And she—her bag packed once she had gotten over the paralyzing terror of Allegra's disappearance, because she had been so sure it was merely a matter of a quick trip into London and possibly finding Allegra along the way . . .

Bells—the sonorous tolling of the tower bells interrupted her thoughts: one . . . two . . . three . . . four . . . five . . . and then she was shocked back into her seat as the carriage drew to a shuddering halt.

A moment later, Culhane swung his tall frame from the driver's perch and she ducked her head outside the window to see exactly where he had taken her.

Dear Lord—Victoria Station . . .

She pulled back slightly as she saw Culhane move toward the

gaggle of urchins that habitually hung around outside the station, hoping to earn a penny assisting travellers with their luggage. She saw him speak to one of the boys, hand the lad a shilling, and then turn back to the carriage as the boy took off like a shot.

... Oh God, this really was real; she was really going with him ...

He thrust open the door. "Out, quickly."

"*Where* are we going?" she asked sharply, shrugging off his helping hand and climbing down.

"Wherever fate takes us," he said cryptically. "Do you believe in fate, Alexandra? Forces beyond anything we know that compel us to act in entirely antithetical ways?"

"I believe in what I can see," she answered stringently, "and what I see is a madman trying to force me out of a carriage on the nonsensical notion that things are *not* what they seem."

"Nor are they," he agreed calmly, "and *you* have chosen to cast your fate with mine, so come, Alexandra, we are wasting precious time."

His eyes were so compelling; they stared deeply into hers, reading things there, reassuring her with their depth and steadiness that he did not lie.

He was a hypnotist—he had to be—because suddenly she was walking through the bevelled glass doors of Victoria Station without a protest, not even caring what happened to her carriage or where they were going.

"You can renege," Ryder said softly, following her gaze as she stared at the awe-inspiring engineering of the archway that curved over the train tracks.

The noise was deafening; there were eight tracks, four of them occupied by the long sinuous snake of train cars in the process of being prepared for the next journey, their destinations as exotic to her as any overseas port: Bournemouth, Southampton, Torquay, Ilfracombe, Dover ...

On the other side of the building were offices and huge arched advertising boards and ticket windows and kiosks for baggage checks. Travellers were already queuing up or filling out baggage claims and then wandering off to take care of other business.

"I am coming with you," Alexandra said briskly. "That is our agreement."

"Very well then. We leave at eight," Ryder said coolly. "We may board at seven. Our carriage is the Pegasus on the Talisman line. We will be travelling to Dover and then on to Paris."

She really was crazy, she decided, not blinking an eye as he reeled off their destination; she was putting herself in sensual bondage to this man so she could go chasing off to exotic climes to find her sister who probably didn't want to be found in the first place.

. . . Paris, after all, with hardly any luggage, no papers, and all for the payment of a hundred hours in a car alone with a madman who was after a set of stone bracelets which were copies of originals that might also be fakes.

It made perfect sense.

And she was a fool.

She watched as he lifted his head, and his dark face, browned from years in the harsh sun, took on a wary expression. His dark expressive brows knotted for a moment, as if he were listening, listening. His mouth, so sensual against the map-sharp line of his straight nose, made a faint grimace, etching two deep lines on either side, which were fascinating to watch as he spoke.

"They have come this way."

His voice was like burnished walnut, deep, burly, with a faint unidentifiable inflection.

A formidable voice, powerful in its ability to persuade or intimidate . . .

And it said—what? *They have come this way . . .*

Allegra? Allegra had come this way? Allegra and . . . *who?*

He propelled her forward, using his body to press hers into motion as they heard a snapping noise behind them.

Instantly, he shoved her down into the milling crowd of waiting passengers.

She heard shouts, pounding footsteps, the crowd rushed forward and Ryder pulled her in the opposite direction as they raced towards the end of the platform and the shelter of the bulk of the train.

He hauled her back against the side of the car.

"Oh my God, what was that, what was that?"

He ignored her and pushed her up the nearby steps and into the vestibule of the car and over to the window opposite which overlooked the platform.

They saw the crowd surge forward like a great tidal wave to surround a man in flowing robes who went down in an undertow of public indignation.

A moment later, two men in uniform waded through the throng and pulled him up and into custody, and the crowd unwillingly dispersed; all the while Ryder watched with a slightly disapproving expression on his face.

"So be it," he murmured.

"What was it?" Alexandra demanded, turning towards him indignantly. "What shall *it* be? What is going on?"

She recoiled at the hard light in his eyes. "You have chosen, Alexandra, and now we have the consequences. Or did you think you had won the game by merely acceding to my conditions. Don't be naive. The man was merely a pawn, whose sole function was to distract and delay."

"Nonsense—he *shot* at us."

"And we are still alive, are we not? I won't even beg the point that things would be very different if you had stayed at Hidcote."

But there was something wrong with that assessment, she thought; she would have been alone at Hidcote, consumed with worry, with no protection, no guarantees. "I would be like a duck in water," she said trenchantly. "Could you be absolutely certain someone might not have attacked me there?"

There was a long pause as through the window over her shoulder, he watched the crowd disperse. He had never considered that Dzmura's web of evil might extend to Alexandra deLisle; after all, he knew she had been close to Sir Peregrine, and he could never ascertain what deLisle might have told her, what she might know.

"No, I couldn't," he said slowly, turning towards to the steps to signify the discussion was closed.

But she had a better sight line than he. A shadow moved forward, its long body shooting obtrusively into view, followed almost immediately by a man dressed in flowing robes and a turban, a man who seemed to know exactly where he was going and whom he was seeking; a man who looked exactly like the stranger the authorities had just apprehended.

She put out a futile hand to detain Culhane, but he was already one step down from the car.

She pulled back, expecting the worst.

But this man approached, his palms upwards, and bowed respectfully and greeted Culhane with the utmost familiarity.

"Culhane *caid.*"

"Khurt. I was hoping you would come."

"I have pledged to serve you."

"It is time."

"I have made the arrangements, *caid,* just as the boy said."

"For three."

"So I was made aware, *caid,* and I accompany you gladly."

He bowed again and a moment later disappeared into the increasing throng of passengers who were now starting to board their respective trains.

Culhane turned instinctively toward Alexandra who had remained uncharacteristically silent during this exchange.

She was hovering on the top step of the railroad car, her suspicious green gaze following Khurt's retreating form, her expression wary.

"There is time to change your mind," he said calmly.

She looked down at him, standing there so controlled and so sure of everything. So certain *they had come this way.*

But she would make sure he was not so certain of her. It was obvious she would have been in as much danger at Hidcote as travelling with him. So she would not back down no matter what happened.

Dzmura was everywhere: he felt it in his bones, he felt it in his mind, in the sweet-sour scent pungent in the air all around him.

It was the moldering stink of evil practiced by a man so amoral that there was but one recourse. Sir Peregrine had known it; he had tried to forestall it.

And to warn him that it was coming sooner than either of

them could ever have anticipated. Now he alone would have to take action.

So capricious fate had saddled him with this ungrateful stick of a woman who would hamper his every move; he supposed it was a saving grace that she did not scare easily, but he couldn't envision what he was going to do with her otherwise, his ridiculous bargain with her notwithstanding.

She sat stiffly on the flocked velvet bench opposite him, staring out the train window at the platform where the crowd had thinned and those remaining were only waiting for the departure of the morning Phoenix to bid a last good-bye to a loved one or friend.

But this was a woman with no loved ones, no friends, so utterly devoted to her father that she had left no room in her life for anything else, least of all a lonely and impressionable sister.

They had both been ripe for the schemes of Dzmura. How long had he plotted and planned only to see the outcome shape itself in an utterly unpredictable way?

Fate again, irascible, unforeseeable, undivinable and whimsical fate . . .

Fate had to be laughing.

The train lurched forward, throwing Alexandra off balance and she muttered something to herself as she propped herself up again and concentrated her attention on the still-crowded platform of Victoria Station slowly moving out of her view.

She felt mesmerized, outside of herself. The train gathered speed as the station receded into the distance. She felt the pull of the unknown and trepidation about what awaited her.

In her mind, she already perceived Hidcote as a prison and for a long glorious moment she thought she didn't even care if it moldered away into dust.

Culhane had obviously taken care of everything, he and the ubiquitous Khurt who now travelled in another compartment.

Khurt had even taken care of her carriage—yes, hired someone to drive it back to Hidcote—and he had procured the tickets and presented Culhane *caid* with a briefcase filled with money and necessities. Khurt had asked no questions and had properly withdrawn when Culhane had ascertained that all was in order.

And she—she need do nothing but prepare herself for the initial confrontation between them, the one in which he demanded she accede to the terms of their agreement and she refused to become his odalisque on a train headed for Dover.

And, in abeyance, she had the bracelets, the things with which she would entice him to take her with him wherever his journey led.

It would just be a matter of leading him on slowly, never giving in too soon—doing, in a manner of speaking, what she had done all along with Allegra in the matter of selling the bracelets.

She knew just how to play it out too; she had done it for years with her sister.

But he would not be so easy. He sat opposite her, seemingly relaxed, but something about the way he held his head spoke of supreme attentiveness.

Nothing escaped him; his changeable eyes noted everything and nothing, but nothing showed in his face. He was looking at her as if she were a specimen, his eyes a hard slate gray now, his expression impassive as always.

She took a deep breath and turned her attention to the scenery once again. There was no help for it: she didn't care if she was shot at or taken captive or Culhane took her on the compartment floor.

She had taken up his dare, and they both would have to deal with it.

Mid-morning a steward appeared, introduced himself and served tea, biscuits and a silver basket of fruit which he set on an ingenious little drop-leaf table that lifted up from under the window ledge.

Alexandra was ravenous—and as scared as she had ever been. Every time she thought about their would-be assassin, every time she tried to find a reason for Allegra's disappearance, she could not convince herself there was any logic behind anything that had happened.

For three hours she had stared out the window at the passing scenery without saying a word, and for three hours Ryder Culhane had not made one remark to interrupt the silence.

How self-contained could one man be?

And how would they get to Paris anyway?

Dear Lord, it was so unreal she could not conceive of it, yet she had taken her stand and here she was.

She directed her attention to pouring tea into the fragile cups provided.

. . . purpose to everything . . .

The thought shot into her mind, and she overfilled the cup so that hot tea sloshed over the side and scalded her hand.

She set the teapot down with a resolute thump. Obviously *she* had in some layer of consciousness clearly seen what she was *really* doing.

Here is what I am doing: I am travelling to Paris with a charlatan whom I allowed to convince me that my sister has been spirited away from London, and I agreed to become his strumpet in order to do it. Obviously I don't care if I am murdered in the process.

And that was the truth of it, plain and unvarnished, and the fact that he had convinced her so easily and she had acquiesced to his terms with no demur whatsoever made her as gullible as any victim in a penny-dreadful novel.

The notion so disturbed Alexandra, she could not pour her cup of tea. It was a testament to how persuasive he was: she had never asked a single question, and she had accepted everything he had told her in the heat of her terror.

An insidious little thought insinuated itself into her mind, and she aired it almost without thinking: or was she testing him?

"What if my sister has really gone to Sir Arthur?"

"She didn't," Ryder said flatly.

"How do you know that? How *can* you know that?" She began to shake with a kind of rage that he could be so sure, and she had no control whatsoever.

"I know," he said sharply, to offset the rising storm of her temper. But she knew that already; she wanted to understand the details, the things he couldn't explain and didn't comprehend himself. "It's an impression. It comes, and I trust it."

"God, I hate this—I hate you," she said vehemently.

"You made your choice," he returned coolly, seeking instantly to distract her from the disturbing awareness of his *knowing*. "In any event, it will not impede our impending union."

The heat of his knowing words enveloped her. There was no purpose to that cold-blooded assertion: he had done it to shock her, and she covered her fury by attempting to pour tea once again and ignoring the telling sting of the burn on her hand.

He would just love it if she handed over the bracelets and took the return train from Dover.

She lifted the tea to her lips, cupping its warmth hungrily in her hands, and eyeing him over the rim of the cup.

He had poured his own, as slowly and deliberately as he did everything else, and in the instant that he was not looking directly at her, she had the distinct feeling that his blatant declaration was meant solely to frighten her.

Then he looked up as if he had discerned her deduction, and she stared straight into eyes which had turned icy gray and she thought not.

He meant it: those were the terms on which she was with him, an exchange of her virtue for the vanity of redressing her sins.

She hated being closeted in such a small space with him. The air grew thick with the tension that emanated from her. She couldn't see her way beyond the next minute.

She hated the containment of their compartment and the explosiveness of all the things that hung in the air unsaid.

Her questions were palpable, so was her fear; she knew it. And there was no room to move, except as she wished to do expedient and private things in the little cubicle neatly fitted out right behind the bench where he sat.

She felt almost chained to the seat and muzzled by his preternatural knowledge of her. But the mistake was hers; there was no going back now.

She had no conception of time. They could have been travelling three hours or three days or through eternity; she couldn't tell.

It made her uneasy not to be able to hold onto the concrete, and nothing was more substantial than time. It measured her days; it was the bracket around which her life had revolved at Hidcote.

And now it had no determinable increments whatsoever; she

felt as if she were without an anchor. She had cut it loose herself out of her guilt and remorse.

And for what? She knew as little now as when they had started out, except that Dzmura was perfectly willing to kill them if they got in his way.

They travelled in silence; she couldn't think of one thing more she wanted to know that was not covered by the chilling realization that Dzmura would have no qualms about killing Allegra as well.

They stopped at Chapton and Lillingham so passengers could debark, and after Rittingbourne, their steward offered dinner either in the dining car or in the compartment, after which he would make up their beds.

She froze at his words, but Culhane ordered dinner in the compartment without even consulting her, and when the steward left, she rounded on him furiously.

"What did he mean 'beds'? Where are the beds? I'll tell you right now I'm not—"

He fought down his exasperation. "You're awfully particular for someone who wasn't even invited on this trip."

"And obviously you're not particular at all," she shot back angrily. "I will not—"

"Indeed you won't—not here at any rate. I like my comfort if you don't."

"I . . . you . . ."

"Exactly," he said bluntly. "Let me serve up some plain-speaking with your supper, Miss deLisle. You are a hindrance and an impediment, and you should rightfully pay for thrusting yourself into a situation you know nothing about. All you have to recommend you is the fact you are willfully concealing a clue your father meant solely for me, and since you have the audacity to act contrary to what he would have wished, you have nothing at all to say about anything—unless you have a change of heart and are willing to go back home."

Alexandra gritted her teeth. They weren't one bit further along in communicating than they had been at Hidcote.

"I am not going back, and we will not discuss the bracelets—yet."

"And when will we—after Dzmura has eliminated us all?" She made a strangled sound.

"Or did you not think it was that serious? You *are* naive, my dear Miss deLisle. You missed everything going on underneath your nose for ten years; why do you assume you have the power now?

"I will examine the bracelets, Alexandra; I hope I do not have to hurt you to do that."

"I will smash them to pieces if you try," she said grittily.

"And I will smash you—and leave you in the gutter beside them."

Dear God, what manner of man was this? What was he talking about? How could a simple question shift onto so many levels so quickly, uprooting her and all her preconceived notions in one swoop.

He left her with nothing; she understood nothing.

No, that wasn't true; she comprehended that he had threatened her, and that he didn't care a farthing for her: he only wanted the bedamned duplicate bracelets, and nothing would stop him.

Cold-blooded was not the word for him. He was a brigand pure and simple, aptly named, immoral as the devil, and steeped in sin.

Chapter 6

He hated the closeness of the compartment; the heat rose between them like steam, emanating from her determination to withstand him and his determination to get what he wanted and leave her at the first opportunity.

There was nothing honorable about it: there was too much at stake. And fate, as always, was standing side by side with circumstance waiting to interfere with his every plan.

He watched her sleep; she had been so determined to match his wakefulness, but in the end, she had put her head back against the pillow of the lower bunk and given in to her weariness.

He lay on the upper bunk, his arms behind his head, listening—hearing her, even in her vulnerable state, mentally consigning him to the devil.

Impressions bombarded him: solemn thoughts; romantic thoughts, the rhythmic clatter of wheels against track and the hypnotic sway of the car as the train ate up the miles like a hungry sinuous snake.

He watched her sleep; he had turned on his side and he had lit the wall sconce above his bunk, illuminating the car with just enough light so that one could climb into the bunk and plump the pillows.

Enough light to see the slender, shadowed and fully dressed form of Miss Alexandra deLisle reclining on the covers, persevering to the end in her resolve not to sleep in that bed.

He did not know what he was going to do about her.

In the dimly lit confines of the sleeping car, she looked angelic, vulnerable, even pretty with her sleep-softened features and that tangle of thick hair spread out around her head like a halo.

He could not imagine her naked, or moaning in pleasure. He could not imagine he was even thinking such things, but the burden of their bargain hung over him now like Damocles' sword.

If it came to that . . .

. . . he would lose her sooner than take her . . .

The problem was the damned bracelets . . . and if Sir Peregrine had meant them for him . . .

But why the secrecy . . . ? Why create an artifact and invent an elaborate story around it? And then why make a duplicate set and hide them away where no one but he could have found them?

Apparently she had found none of this specious, and she had protected the bracelets with the tenacity of a bulldog—at least from her sister.

None of it made any sense; Sir Peregrine had come home to bury his wife and then return to Alekkah . . .

. . . but he didn't . . .

. . . and he passed away not two years after his wife . . .

. . . with whom, by his own confession, he had had no great desire to stay and little or nothing in common . . .

Yet, he had stayed . . .

What had he told them then about the bracelets?

After he had sent the note, the warning—Dzmura down the road and cozy with his family—yes . . .

Sworn to bring him down; of course he couldn't return, not while Dzmura stayed in England . . .

And so he died.

Leaving a secret room and two sets of mysterious artifacts as his legacy . . .

And Miss Alexandra deLisle on *his* hands.

"*Do*-ver . . . ! Do-*verrr!* Thirty minutes to Dover station . . . Thirty minutes . . ."

The conductor tapped the compartment door window and was gone, singing out the arrival time to the next compartment and the next until his voice became nothing more than an elusive and otherworldly sound in the distance.

Alexandra stretched—and her eyes shot open. Daylight poured in through the window and Culhane was already up and about, his pull-down bunk stored, a cup of fragrant tea in his large hands.

He held it out to her and she took it without a word and sipped the steaming liquid. It went down hot, revivifying, nourishing; clearing her sleep-fogged throat and sending a jolt of energy to her fuzzy brain.

"Tell me about the bracelets," Ryder said, pouring her another cup from the cheery porcelain pot that was perched precariously at the edge of her bed on a tray. "And damn it, don't argue."

She rubbed her eyes with one hand and shook the sleep out of her head. "The bracelets . . . why?"

"We have twenty-five minutes, Alexandra; you won't reveal anything that will make them less useful to me if you tell me the circumstances of their origin."

She shook her head again, looking for the trick, and then she shrugged. "He had them with him when he returned from Alekkah. He said he had dug them up at Khuramafar."

"I see."

"What do you see? What could you possibly see?"

"You tell me, Miss Know-it-all deLisle. Your father returns from Alekkah with an artifact he claims to have retrieved from a dig at a place he hasn't been in ten years. He closets himself in a secret room, making a second set of these bracelets, and then hides them where nobody can find them. And one day, his daughter and the first set of bracelets suddenly disappear. You tell me. Give me the logical explanation that will cover those facts, Alexandra, and we will dispense with bargains and games."

She would not. It sounded demented, but she would never admit to him that she herself had wondered if her father were deranged.

"Take it one step further then, Culhane: my father claimed a ghost revealed the translation of the bracelets, the Museum spurned him and he died, and then Allegra began sleepwalking.

What logical explanation do you apply to those goings-on, tell me, and do you think it suspicious that you were the one to find the second set of bracelets? I think it is highly suspect, and I will guard them with my life."

"Yes, and well you might. I suggest you think twice before uttering such words lightly, because that is exactly what is on the line, Alexandra."

"And yours is not?" she demanded irritably.

"Let us say that I am more adept at protective coloration than is a hothouse English rose who knows nothing of the ways of the world."

"Well, I'll learn then, won't I?" she said waspishly as she set the cup aside.

"Or die in the attempt," he said coolly, and she looked into his slate-hard gaze and did not know if this was a threat or a promise, or who the greater enemy was: Dzmura or he.

Nevertheless, she had mapped out her own course and there was no turning back.

Khurt came for them long after the train shuddered into the station and most of the passengers had debarked.

"Culhane *caid,* it is time."

Culhane took her arm and pressed her out into the narrow corridor, and they slowly moved toward the exit with Khurt leading the way and stepping out onto the platform first.

"It is clear, *caid.*"

They descended into the bright brisk morning sun.

"The boat leaves at noon, *caid.*"

"Two hours," Ryder murmured, his hand still securely holding Alexandra's arm. "Two . . . We will attend to personal needs. We must obtain some clothing and whatever Miss deLisle feels is necessary to her comfort. Khurt . . ."

"It shall be done." He bowed and left them and Ryder steered her into the crowded station waiting room where the other passengers milled, trying to decide whether to walk or go shopping or find a restaurant open this early rather than purchase coffee and biscuits at the station concession.

How fortuitous that she had had the forethought to pack a bag on that seemingly long-ago night when Allegra disappeared. She had been able, before they vacated the car, to both change her shirtwaist and attend to personal hygiene, and she was feeling more comfortable just because they were among other people, which made Ryder Culhane and his veiled threats seem less ominous.

"We are being watched," Ryder said, his tone of voice matter-of-fact and not at all surprised or urgent.

"We . . . what?"

"Are being watched. Did you think it was over, Alexandra? The threat of Dzmura has only begun. But we are safe here; there are too many people. Khurt will take care of the rest."

Her heart sank. "The beginning? The beginning of what? Damn it, Culhane, I thought it had already begun."

"Damn it yourself, Alexandra; things would have been much easier if you had just given over the bracelets and not come with me."

"A lot easier if I had just stayed at Hidcote and killed myself with worry, you mean. And I still might never have seen Allegra again, while you would have carried off the only thing I shared with my father in his last days."

"And the thing you must share with me."

"And I will."

He looked at her sharply. "Believe it, Alexandra."

She did. She believed that he would abandon her the moment he got his hands on the bracelets, and she meant to keep them hidden as long as she could.

Everything after that was a blur; sometime later Khurt returned with two leather bags of some weight, one of which he gave to Culhane, the other he carried.

They got tea and biscuits at the station concession, but she lost her appetite as she scanned the passengers, trying to pick out the mysterious watcher in the crowd.

It was impossible; no one was dressed any differently, and everyone was engaged in some activity: conversation, reading a newspaper, looking through papers, drinking a cup of weak tea.

Two hours passed slowly, interminably.

At noon, they boarded a small narrow-gauge train which shot them across the viaduct and down to the harbor and the docks where they would board a tramp ferry to cross the Channel.

It was even colder there, and the water across the Channel looked as if it dropped from the horizon into oblivion, while behind them, the rocky cliffs rose like a fortified castle to protect them from harm.

"The watcher is still with us."

The ferry awaited them on the quay, and they moved with the crowd down the gangplank, onto the dock.

Khurt found the hiding place, convincing a newlywed couple to exchange their lesser seat in the hold for a more spacious place in the lounge where passengers were seated four across rather than around a crowded bench.

She remembered the moist air, the sense of waiting, the stillness, the calm face of Culhane as if he expected all of this; the tension inside herself, as if being in such close range with Culhane were not safe—he wasn't safe, she knew it; and she was frightened witless he would discover her secret and abandon her.

She remembered the heave and sway of the boat and the fact they could see nothing from their position. And the stolid expression of Khurt as he waited with them, all of them crowded into a space five feet square and furnished with a u-shaped bench and nothing else.

Once again, time receded into nothingness. It could have been hours or days and by Culhane's caution, they could not talk.

The trip took on the aspects of a nightmare; the lighting was dim, and they were separated from the others in the same pecuniary circumstances as the newlyweds: they could hear the deep murmur of voices in conversation, a word here and there, a laugh.

She felt isolated; she knew terror.

And she finally understood the power of Dzmura when, as they debarked in Calais, they heard the news that had swept the ship moments before: a young couple had been found dead in the lounge, and no one knew how it had happened.

* * *

At Calais, the continental train was waiting at the quay as the ferry docked, a sinuously curving line of beautiful green cars with the names set out in gold and red.

Here everything was a bustle of activity as passengers descended the gangplank amid the push and pull of porters removing luggage and various train managers attending to problems and compartment assignments.

"The watcher is with us," Ryder said as they waited their turn.

"How do you know?" Alexandra whispered.

"I know."

Again that certainty, that impalpable sense of urgency imparted by his sentient intuition. It was eerie and unquantifiable, and she didn't want to believe him.

But she believed evil surrounded them. Her sister was missing, her bracelets were gone; someone had shot at them and now two people were dead.

The investigation would not be exhaustive. There were too many passengers on board, and none of them had known the couple. This much the gendarmes had ascertained as they filed off the vessel and onto the dock.

Still, it caused a delay as everyone was methodically questioned and released to proceed to the Calais coach which would transport them to Paris.

It was a mystery which would never be solved, but someone among them had thought those newlyweds to be she and Culhane; they could have been the bodies in the morgue instead.

And so she believed him. Someone had been sent by Dzmura to trail them in their pursuit of Allegra, and they were in as much danger as her sister was. No one could be trusted—not Khurt, not even Culhane. She trusted him least of all.

He insisted that they be among the last to board, and they watched for fully an hour as everyone preceded them onto the train and began preparations for the journey.

"The watcher is aboard," Ryder said almost matter-of-factly as they moved forward finally to extend their papers and tickets to the train manager who then assigned them to an assistant who guided them on board.

They entered a compartment which consisted of two luxurious banquettes furnished with thick pillows, and an elegant Brussels carpet underfoot. The room was panelled in glowing walnut limned in gold leaf, the floor-to-ceiling panels hiding on one side a small closet, and on the other, behind the banquette, the cunningly fitted lavatory with its fold-away washstand and privy.

In this compartment, there was electricity: the assistant train manager proudly flipped the switch that illuminated the two sconces on either side of the curtained and windowed door and the little lamp at the window which perched on the swing-up leaf of the small table between the seats.

"There is food and drink available in the dining car. Dinner will be served by reservation from six o'clock onwards. Your steward will bring menus and take your reservations. Do call on me if there is any thing I can do for you." He handed his card to Ryder who thanked him gravely and watched him make his way down the narrow corridor to the next compartment.

Almost immediately their steward appeared, a bluff and rather gregarious younger man who was overly anxious to please. He reeled off the menu and the seating times, adjured them to dress and told them there would be a layover of several hours after dinner when they got to Paris.

They arranged an early seating and the steward, whose name was Cecil, withdrew.

Ryder pulled the thick woven satin privacy curtain over the window.

"Khurt will remain with us until Vienna, but he will take his meals in the stateroom so he can be on guard at all times."

"This is what we agreed, Culhane *caid.*"

Alexandra sank into the depths of the pillowed corner of the closet-wall banquette. Their pragmatic discussion scared her, as if it were an everyday thing to be pursued by a killer.

And then, she had the disturbing impression she was listening to a set piece between two con artists.

But how could that be? Her sister's disappearance was real. The gunshots, the mysterious deaths aboard the Calais ferry—

All a hoax to get her to give up the bracelets?

Inconceivable! Not even Culhane with his extraordinary sentience could have arranged to fake the murder of the newlywed couple . . . surely not?

For a pair of stone bracelets?

Just how important were the bracelets?

And how dispensable was she once they were in his possession?

Her thoughts were damped by the sudden huffing and chuffing of the engine, and the loud wail of the whistle that signified the commencement of their journey.

She felt the wheels grinding into the track and the sudden pull forward as the train moved slowly away from harbour and pier and began to incrementally build up speed until it was rocketing into the countryside among hills, farms and elegant houses.

The vista spread out before her through the largest of the five windows in the car which was centered over the drop-leaf table between the seats and was symmetrically framed by two smaller and narrower windows on either side.

But there was only so much scenery of interest after a half-hour of tense silence during which Culhane eased himself into the seat opposite her and Khurt perched uneasily beside him.

She began to wonder just how this journey was being funded and just where Khurt had come from on the heels of the shooting incident at Victoria Station.

Or was Culhane a conjurer too?

Oh, he had to be, and this was not the first time she had thought so.

She could see instantly by the expression in his eyes that he was aware of all the questions tumbling around in her mind; which would he pick to answer?

Or would he answer at all?

"I sent the boy for Khurt, as you must by now have realized," he said finally. "He has assisted me before, as far back as Khuramafar when your father and I spent six months at Killa Masir in a futile attempt to locate a clue to the parchments of Zoran. Your father found nothing else there, Alexandra, and he did not go back."

"Why would he lie?" she demanded defensively. "You would have reason to lie sooner than he."

"Or you," he retorted. "I could speculate, but you are not yet ready to listen to reason."

Oh but he was wrong about that. She was very willing to listen to anything that would explain where Allegra had gotten to and why he sought the bracelets.

"Try me," she said.

He sent her a skeptical look. "I think we will confine ourselves to the facts. Here they are: your father and I were digging on the plains of Alekkah when he received word that your mother had passed away. He made immediate arrangements to leave, just dropped everything and left.

"I gather that he began working on his underground room soon after your mother's interment; I don't know how soon after that he revealed the existence of the bracelets . . ." He looked inquiringly at Alexandra.

She shook her head. "It wasn't immediately. He was in shock over Mother's death. He hardly unpacked for a month—at least."

"And in the interim, of course, he discovered the viper nestling too close to the bosom of his family."

"He said nothing of this; we didn't know that Father even knew him."

"But after his discovery the bracelets appeared?"

"Yes. Sir Arthur had given him time off from the Museum, had told him to take as much time as he needed to get over Mother's death. Father said he had brought back some very interesting things with him, and Sir Arthur put him off. Another time, he said, when Father was feeling more the thing."

"And so there were the bracelets, and they were so precious he created a special hiding place for them?"

"Yes, and he spent hours cleaning them and picking over each of the symbols, trying to translate them."

"And came up with nothing."

"Not immediately. About six months later, he had the dream. He was working over the bracelets down in the secret room—about which my sister knew nothing, by the way—and he fell asleep and had a dream in which he swore an apparition appeared and took him back in time to the temple of Mastgard and revealed the secret of the translation to him. He took this to Sir Arthur and presented it, and he was laughed out of the Museum and asked to go on hiatus for his health. They didn't believe him, but the bracelets existed and he had them and I believed him."

"And now there are two sets of bracelets, Alexandra. So what do you believe now?"

What *did* she think? "My father found two sets of bracelets," she said firmly, even a little artlessly; but what else could she believe?

He shook his head. "I think not. I think your father *made* two sets of bracelets."

She threw her hands up as if to ward off his words. "No! Never! You said he made the second set, but now the first as well? You are lying. You! Why would he do that? Why?"

"Yes, why? I'll tell you why, Alexandra. Because he knew he would never return to Alekkah."

They dined on veal with mushrooms and Madeira sauce. It had been all she could do to make herself ready to go out publicly with Culhane when she was seething with rage at the implication that her beloved father had faked artifacts for his own reasons, his own gain.

He had suggested it before, but she had refused to consider exactly what he'd been implying.

This was on her mind as she reluctantly changed for dinner, taking with her the mysterious bag Khurt had procured for her, and finding within it as she unpacked in the lavatory not only toiletries but also a very tasteful assortment of clothing.

There were several shirtwaists, plain and lace lavished; there was a beautiful velvet jacket with a matching overskirt which tied around the waist and could be worn over her existing skirt or separately; there was a paisley shawl threaded in gold, as well as several belts, some hair ornaments, a nightgown and robe, a practical woollen travelling jacket which coordinated with her skirt, a pocketbook and a serviceable pair of boots . . . approximately her size.

The man was amazing. She could almost believe he knew her better than she knew herself.

She changed into the velvet suit and a fresh silk shirtwaist, and gratefully used the toiletries he had provided.

Culhane had changed as well from the severe dark suit he had been wearing now for two days to one of an elegant dove gray.

They looked quite the pair, she thought, as she caught a glimpse of them in one of the mirrors interspersed between the dining-room windows. Young and fresh and possibly newlywed, she thought in despair. As if they were off on the adventure of their lives.

They ate dinner in a simmering silence.

"It is necessary to appear in public," Ryder said. "We don't know if the watcher is aware that we know of his presence, or that we understand the death of that couple on the ferry was related to us."

"This is so unreal," she muttered, pushing a piece of sauce-soaked bread around in her plate. "How do you know, how do you *know*? Who among these passengers could be a murderer?"

"And who among them is prescient? Could you tell if you didn't know, Alexandra?"

The point was telling. "It's true," she muttered ungratefully. "Look at you. You look like a slightly overtired banker on his way to Paris on business."

"A *banker*, Alexandra?" he murmured, amused.

"Don't laugh at me," she growled, picking at her vegetable; she had to eat something. "I will not give in to the stupid idea that somehow you can sense things other people can't or that I am connected to you in any way whatsoever."

"*We* are not connected, Alexandra; we are *entangled*. And there is no help for that—it just is. I haven't fathomed why: I only know when—"

"After my father died," she interposed.

He nodded.

"And my father?"

"No, your father and I had no connection, only a complete and corporal understanding, Alexandra, which is why you must not impede me."

"Nonsense, I'm helping you. I have brought with me the bracelets and my knowledge of my sister . . ."

"You know nothing about your sister," he said irritatedly. "You have pretended for ten years that she is something she is not. Don't cross words with me about your sister."

"My dear Culhane, how marvelous. You know my family a thousand times better than I: you are now implying my sister is not the innocent I know her to be, and on top of that accusing my father of forgery. What next I wonder? You have yet to start on me."

"Then I would be pleased to begin, Miss deLisle: you are stuffy and priggish, spiteful and surly, and petty into the bargain. You are consumed with regrets, you are obsessive and dictatorial—in short, exactly what you seem."

She felt her whole body suffuse with a burning heat.

"And you sir are a humbug—a fake, an impostor, a hypocrite and a fraud—in short, a charlatan." She stood up abruptly. "You have won. I will relinquish the search to you, and I will return to London as soon as possible."

He grabbed her arm as she turned away and with very little pressure at all, he forced her back down into her chair.

"I appreciate the sentiment, Miss Alexandra, but it comes a little late, and so easily said when we're a hundred miles outside of Paris and a Channel's crossing away from England. Almost noble, too, except that you did not offer the ultimate sacrifice of turning the bracelets over to me."

"I'm sure you'll do perfectly fine on your own, Culhane."

"Yes, I will," he agreed coolly, and she felt like smacking him . . . *Obsessive, dictatorial* . . . she hated him, hated him . . .

He stood up and came around to draw her chair out for her. "Still we must observe the amenities."

"How civil is it to root around in someone's life uninvited?"

Alexandra muttered in an undertone. "You know nothing about manners, Mr. Culhane, nothing at all."

"I know enough to let you precede me out the door."

"Oh no . . . no. We need not stand on any kind of protocol here, Culhane. I would infinitely prefer *not* to have you at my back."

"Someday," he murmured, "I will make you take that *back,* but meantime I bow to your wishes, Miss deLisle. Don't back down now that you have backed out. It is merely a matter of getting back to our compartment and getting through the night."

Chapter 7

Her wariness heightened even more as she followed him down the crowded narrow corridors from car to car, squeezing past the next contingent of passengers on their way to dine.

There was an air of excitement among them. They spoke in pulsating murmurs, strangers who hadn't even known each other in London now comrades in adventure.

She felt as if they were going against the tide; *she* was the one courting danger; she was the one who had handed herself over to this scoundrel, the one who had a feeling of uncertainty about the consequences of her chosen course.

She almost resented the gaiety of the elegantly dressed crowd as they skirted her on their way from car to car. They didn't have to worry about sleeping arrangements or motives or implications or who was telling the truth and who lied. They didn't have a sister who might be in mortal danger, nor did they have to travel in the company of a man who unerringly knew what they were thinking.

She couldn't imagine what Culhane was thinking when he stopped so suddenly she almost fell into him.

The corridor was empty here, and dimly lit; all she could see over his shoulder was a row of closed and curtained doors, one of them the entrance to their compartment.

"Culhane . . ." she whispered furiously.

"The door is open." He spoke in an undertone. "Someone is—or was—in that compartment." He began to edge his way slowly down the hallway, and she followed uncertainly.

The door was ajar, and the lights were out; she experienced a tremor of apprehension when he moved to the doorway's side of the corridor and motioned for her to follow.

He waited another moment and then he thrust open the door with his foot and simultaneously switched on the lights.

"God damn it . . ."

She wedged in the doorway next to him, her heart pounding unmercifully.

Khurt lay on the floor amidst the remnants of his dinner, his head bathed in a pool of blood.

They arrived at the Gare de l'Est in Paris during the following hour, in late-night darkness when all was quiet and the city slept. The train took on several passengers and provisions, and they called for a doctor to see to Khurt's wound.

He was groggy but aware by that time, reclining on one of the banquettes, his head bandaged and rewrapped in his turban, his recollection of his attacker hazy at best.

"He came from behind, *caid*, or surely you would have known."

Ryder nodded.

"I called only for the steward to procure some dinner. Later, there was a knock at the door which I assumed to be the steward to pick up the tray. As I bent to retrieve it . . ."

Someone had come and cleaned up the food and the blood; still, there was a faint stain smirching the elegant carpet.

Alexandra stared at it from her corner of the opposite seat as Culhane paced the floor, stamping on it as if he could eradicate it with his anger.

"Dzmura leaves nothing to chance. He has warned us once again."

Alexandra bit her lip. "And what does such a warning mean?"

"Go back; don't interfere. The danger will escalate the closer we get to Tihran. The threat increases the longer you withhold the bracelets. But you know all this, Alexandra. But perhaps you require further proof of the wrath of Dzmura. It isn't enough that he has stolen away your sister and the original bracelets. It isn't enough that someone watches us and that two people have already been killed, that Khurt was attacked. You require something cataclysmic obviously. We must see what we can do to oblige."

She stopped listening; she just closed her eyes and shut out his harangue, but she could not shut out the truth of what he said. The incidents would continue. Innocent people would be trampled along the way. But she would hew to her course, never giving over the bracelets that Culhane wanted so avidly.

She wondered why. She wondered if she had even thought to ask him why in her stubborn need to use them to keep the upper hand and get what she wanted.

What was it about the bracelets that was so important to Culhane?

Yes, she would just ask him, but despite her intention to stay awake, she fell asleep just as she thought she was framing the question.

So there she was, he thought as he lay on his side in the upper berth, his head propped up in his left hand.

They were an hour out of Paris now after a two-hour layover; all was quiet. The steward had brought all kinds of apologetic treats to divert them from Khurt's accident, and the teapot and tray still sat on the narrow table by the seat where Miss Alexandra deLisle slept so soundly in her clothes, its swing-up leaf folded down to give him purchase to make up his own bed.

Khurt lay on the floor, as was his wont, protesting that he was comfortable enough, and that lying in a cushioned bed would only keep him awake on a night when he would treasure his sleep. He had taken some sedative; he slept as soundly as Alexandra.

The quiet was almost unnerving; Culhane probed the darkness seeking a clue to the watcher who lurked somewhere in the deep stillness of the night.

There was nothing, nothing, only the quiet even breathing of Alexandra, the heavier exhalation of Khurt, the clack of the wheels against the track, and the silence—the thick matte silence in which nothing moved, nothing spoke to him in the recesses of his thoughts.

Just below him, *she* slept with the conscience of a baby, and he didn't know if he admired or he hated her godalmighty stubbornness about the bracelets.

... *hair* ...

The impression formed in his mind coming from nowhere.

... *hair* ...

He mentally turned it over, chewing on it, nuzzling it trying to find the meaning behind it.

Somewhere outside his ruminations, he heard something—a faint scuffling sound in the corridor, there and gone in the space of a breath.

All of his attention focused on the corridor. Again, the sounds—the breathing, even, regular, heavy; the train wheels clacking even, regular, heavy; his heart pounding with the thrill of hunting a quarry ...

... the faint, faint sound once again, outside the door ... another long silence against which he heard the lightest screeching sound against the door window ...

... silence again ...

A waiting?

The same sound again, louder now, as if pressure were being applied—and then the dull thump of something banging against the door window ...

... the glass shattering ...

... his frantic whisper: "Khurt!" as he rolled off his bunk and onto Alexandra's supine body ...

... the door opening ... Alexandra struggling awake against the hot shocking weight of his body on hers ...

... a knife slicing through the air and embedding itself with an ominous thud in the wall above them ...

... Khurt diving for the sinister figure, catching his leg and tripping him up ... and then falling by the way as the intruder used his free leg to kick him in the head ...

... blood—the intruder scrambling away ...

And then in the dead, fraught silence of the aftermath: not a sound, not a breath; Ryder draped protectively over Alexandra's rigid and resistant body, and then the faint rustle of movement as Khurt dazedly pulled himself into a sitting position.

"Culhane, you snake," Alexandra hissed, giving him a convulsive shove. She was stunned when the pressure of his body eased and he jacked himself upright; she felt faintly bereft.

She maneuvered herself slowly into a sitting position.

Culhane knelt on the floor beside Khurt examining his head to the deprecating murmur, "It is nothing, *caid,* nothing . . ."

"It was a knife, god damn it." He reached up and flicked up the light switch to illuminate the compartment: the light reflected off of a quarter-round piece of glass lying on the floor; he picked it up and looked up at the door where a hole, exactly that shape, had been scribed in the glass and punched out.

He got up slowly, helped Khurt onto the edge of Alexandra's seat, and then pulled the knife out of the wall, leaving an ugly gouge in the panelling.

He held it in the palm of his hand, a dagger with a long blade and an ornately carved ivory handle.

Khurt fingered it. "It is lethal, *caid.* One cannot know what might be impregnated in the blade."

Culhane looked grim. "One can guess."

"The handle . . ." Alexandra said tentatively, and they looked at her. "The handle reminds me of something . . . The box where my father kept the original bracelets, it was made of ivory and I could swear the carvings looked just like that."

They reached Munich late the next morning at which time the window was repaired and Khurt once again subjected himself to the ministrations of the on-board doctor.

Alexandra sat looking out the window so she could avoid looking at Culhane. The remains of breakfast littered the small swing-out table between them; they were alone, the air heavy once again with the threat of danger and, for Alexandra, a deep feeling of unreality. This could not be happening to her because of a pair of stone bracelets.

The knife lay next to the coffeepot, an anomaly beside the china and the small silver bud vase that had come on the tray with breakfast.

Alexandra stifled an urge to speak because she was sure Culhane would just wade into her apprehensions, negate her fears and then go on and do whatever he wanted.

And that would not include her; Culhane could hardly stand the sight of her, all his threats notwithstanding, that was clear now. If he had had to carry through, she thought, he would have: that was his nature.

The thing that she had naively not understood was that a man could be aroused so easily: even in the dark and with the best instincts—to protect her from the intruder—his body, tightly crammed against hers, had betrayed him.

Enforcing his terms would have been easy for him; men did those kinds of things all the time.

What she had not anticipated was her own reaction, that the contact, body to body, would engender in her a most appalling hunger to experience it once again—and in the context of an equally appalling need she had never known she had.

How stunningly easy it was for him to arouse her, the virgin spinster with emotions held tightly reined, only to come unraveled at the first uninvited contact with a male body on the heels of his attempt to intimidate her so she would not accompany him.

She had to wonder, given her overpowering response in the midst of such grave danger, whether she had agreed to his terms solely because she would have no responsibility for what might happen or because she needed some righteous justification for what surely would happen.

But as always, she could read nothing in Culhane's expression: he remained as aloof as ever, his steady gray gaze focused on her and not saying one word; which utterly unnerved her.

He supposed he wanted to discomfit her; in her obdurate naivete, she had no idea what was at stake nor did she realize the degree to which she hampered him.

He was irritated that he had allowed himself to be held hostage to a pair of fake stone bracelets and a threat he had never intended to carry out.

She was the antithesis of the kind of woman he usually chose: virginal, abrasive, stubborn, talkative, plain-spoken, annoying, inflexible and unyielding.

A virago—with an unlikely body . . .

There were curves under that silky shirtwaist and velvet suit she had worn the previous evening and had now exchanged for her serviceable walking suit, her hair done up and out of her face.

He had been stunned at the heat of her and the power of the body thrusting beneath him in a futile attempt to throw him off; he had reacted, his mind skimming forward into a scenario that had nothing to do with the imminent danger or the adversarial entanglement between them.

He saw her naked beneath him, her wild hair in disarray, her hungry body seeking the domination of his, her volatile mouth begging for his kisses, her eager hands pressing him deep deep deep into her hot wet core . . . he saw . . . he yielded for one lost moment to the fantastical idea of it before the hiss of the knife returned him to reality.

And now there she sat, much as she slept, her left profile toward him, her right hand propped up under her chin, her expression pensive and determined.

She would not give up the bracelets. He felt the powerful insistence of it; the artifacts were her insurance, and she would use them however she could to make him do what she wanted.

He felt a virulent urge to just shake her.

. . . hair . . .

The impression streaked into his thoughts from nowhere, persistent, pressing—

. . . hair . . .

—something he was missing . . .

. . . or something he had noted already—

. . . her hair—bound up and away from her face—he had marked that, and how thick it was, untamable, always secured one way or another off of her face as if it were too much trouble to deal with altogether . . .

So thick a man could lose his hands in it, tracing the springy waves and curls, burying himself in the sweet enveloping scent of it . . .

He wondered . . . he envisioned it, inviting and moist between her legs, opening to him, only to him, naked and submissive, demanding the heat of his ramrod possession, yielding to her need to reveal everything to him . . . to *him*—

... hair ...

... so much hair ...

The thought of it pulsed right through him; he wanted it, he wanted to touch it and feel it—to slide it between his fingers, to pull out the pins and combs so it would shimmer down to her shoulders and over her taut naked breasts ... and the bracelets would fall ... right into his hands—

He thought it and he reacted instantly, levering himself over the small fold-up table, to reach with both hands for the loosely pinned fall of her hair—

And he felt it, he felt it—she fought him—she smacked his hands away, she scratched him, she kicked at him as he reached and pulled at the tendrils of hair and something fell out and rolled across the carpet.

She shimmied out from under him and dove onto the floor.

He came flying after her, pinning her where she lay, facedown on the carpet, her hands clasped around the object over her head, her body pushing and pumping, trying to throw him off.

Which meant she could not protect the other bracelet.

He braced himself on one arm and felt the thick strands of her tumbling hair.

Instantly she reared back and rounded on him with her right arm, catching him off balance so that his right arm folded under him and he collapsed onto her again.

"Culhane ..." Her tone was dangerous, feral. She hated herself for giving her secret away; more, she hated him for taking advantage of it.

She felt his body slide several inches up hers, so that his hands touched hers, his lips were just at her ear, and the forceful thrust of his manhood just nestled between her buttocks.

And she was torn between two powerful sensations: she wanted to defeat him and she wanted to yield ...

She felt his hand in her hair again, and she shook her head violently—a mistake because that loosened the pins with which she had fastened the second bracelet at the base of her head, and it fell with a dispiriting thump and rolled six inches toward the door.

They grabbed for it simultaneously, and miracle of miracles, she got it first. His large hot hand closed over hers the moment her fingers secured it.

He had immobilized her in every way now, and so who had won? She had the bracelets and he had *her*, with her one arm spread-eagled out toward the door, the other over her head clutching the bracelet as if her life depended on it.

She was bombarded with sensations: her overwhelming fear which kept both of her hands knotted around the bracelets; the heat and hardness of his body pushing into hers almost involuntarily; the faint pulse of his breath beside her ear; the sway of the train as it rounded a curve, her body heaving with it to press more tightly against his loins; her hungry and unexpected yearning for contact; the flick of something moist against her ear, shocking in the intensity of the feelings it aroused in her . . .

They were at a stalemate, and she must be the one to surrender.

She thought her heart would pound right through her clothes; she thought he could hear it, it was beating so loudly. Her sense of time dissipated and she felt she never wanted to move again.

Her body was melting; she imagined her clothes sloughing off like a second skin until there was nothing between them but her naked yearning.

There was no sound but the heavy beating of her heart. In the rising excitement that gripped her, she heard the ragged and heady draw of his breath by her ear, and she sensed his tightly leashed arousal.

He didn't move, but there was that one purely male part of him that kept elongating incrementally against the cushion of her buttocks, that kept pushing and rooting with involuntary little shifts of his hips to drive himself so tightly against her that she would feel his power despite her clothes, and because of her desire.

He didn't want that—he could have sworn he didn't want that. He didn't want her, he didn't; but as he lay sprawled on her, inhaling her scent, envisioning his fantasy, feeling his unruly male tension escalate to a fever pitch along with his fulminating anger, he experienced the keen edgy drive to strip her shimmying body and her rebellious nature and master her and leave her begging for more.

"The time has come," he murmured in her ear, "the bargain must be met."

"Never," she hissed, her body bucking up against his to meet the thrusting stiffness taut against the layers of skirt that covered her buttocks. Immediately she felt the heavy weight of him pressing downwards on her buttocks, forcing her down and down until she was almost flat against the floor except for that teasing little curve of her rear wriggling against him.

She could have lain that way forever; how could she have known she would love the heat of his huge body enveloping her, the tight fit of his ramrod length against her?

She should have been afraid, should have been screaming for her life.

Nothing could have prepared her for this, not the size of him or the feeling of him all over her; nor her elemental response to him, as if her body had ached for some tactile acknowledgement of her desirability and she had not known it—and then the instant he touched her, she had craved it with such intensity that there was nothing left but to surrender to his wanton heat and her blood-pounding arousal.

She felt a tentative sense of power: that her movements could provoke the thick lush atmosphere of the forbidden and the desired.

The time had come; she had been waiting, but never had she thought she would be a willing participant.

It was like floodgates opening—a waterfall of sensation that could not be held back and which might drown her if she could not maintain control.

How clever men were, with this most potent weapon that could reduce a woman to a swoon of opulent yearning; it was irresistible—the tension, the heat, the lusting for the forbidden, knowing that there were no boundaries beyond forever.

"You feel me," he murmured in her ear.

"Yes," she whispered; she could not deny it when she cradled him in the sensual curve of her bottom, where he rocked against her in writhing little thrusts.

"You want me."

How could she say she wanted him when she knew nothing about what *wanting* meant. But these opulent feelings—yes, these she wanted.

"I will not renege on our bargain."

"You want me."

"*Never*. I will"—she gasped as he took her earlobe in his teeth and pulled gently—"fulfill the terms of our bargain."

Oh God, he was just pulling and sucking at her ear—she couldn't get away from it; she bucked and wriggled against him, shifting her body one way and then another like a horse that yearned to be broken.

Her hips were strong; she caught him unaware as he was invading the delicate shell of her ear, and she lifted him and rolled him off of her.

He grabbed her around her middle before she could leverage herself away from him and, with heart-stopping strength, pushed her onto her back and straddled her.

"Now, Alexandra—"

She licked her lips. "A bargain is . . ."

He watched the war of her emotions, her naive prudery against her burgeoning passion.

Nervy virgin . . . "You remember our bargain."

She hesitated a moment; did she remember it? Or was she merely seduced by the raw power of all those hot sensual unimaginable feelings? Or was the prim virgin undone the first time a man evinced a need for her body?

Did it matter?

"You will never refuse anything I ask of you," he whispered seductively, "*no matter what it is*. Do you remember?" He watched her face and the growing sensual excitement in her eyes. "I remember, Alexandra. I remember. And I want you now. Tell me what *you* want."

Her lips flexed, aching for the honey of his kiss, dry with the knowledge something explosive was about to happen.

"I don't know," she whispered, some sane part of her, the cool virginal part of her still reluctant, still resistant, knowing the ways of men—*hating* the ways of men—ravenously curious about the ways of men, and women.

He bent close to her so that his lips were almost touching hers. "You want my kisses . . ."

Yes, yes . . . She closed her eyes as her excitement tore at her nerves; the waiting was unbearable . . . but she hated the words, she hated them. Still, what did it matter in this war between them; the end would justify her submission, it was merely a matter of time.

She licked her lips again and felt the hot wet flick of his tongue against hers, then the thick crush of his mouth over it and the invasive feeling of his tongue rooting against hers, delving deeper and deeper into the virgin recesses of her mouth.

This was the honey-hot kiss she had yearned for; she couldn't get enough of it, that thick slick wetness of tongue against tongue exploring and foraging mouth to mouth; it was unimaginable, she never could have dreamed it in a hundred years, and she wrapped her arms around him to pull him deeper into her mouth.

The sensation trickled and twined its way down to her very core and resolved into a sharp darting feeling at the apex of her femininity.

He eased himself away from her just as she arched up into his kiss once more. "Now, Alexandra . . ."

"Tell me," she whispered, her body tight and taut with explosive feelings, her lustful words heightening every sensation. "Show me, show me what to do . . ."

He settled his mouth back on hers again and moved off of her so that he could slide her skirt upwards.

Somewhere in that deep lush kiss, he reached up and locked the door, then resumed his slow leisurely exploration of her hungry mouth until she thought she would expire of the sheer pleasure of kissing him. He knew it; he eased away once again, hovering near to her swollen lips so he could drop hot little kisses on her mouth as he commanded her. "You know what to do," he growled. "You were born knowing what to do . . ."

"I know nothing," she whispered, shuddering with excitement.

"You know everything . . . you know you want me. And you know I want you, in the most elemental way possible. Alexandra, it is time to enter the bargain, but you must tell me . . . tell me, Alexandra. Tell me you want my touch, my body, my pleasure—tell me . . ."

She caught her breath as she wavered on the precipice; such seductive words, such a seductive mouth. All the secrets of the forbidden life of women to be laid out before her at her command.

. . . his touch, his body, his pleasure . . .

. . . and he desired her touch, her body, her pleasure . . .

She almost swooned at the thought of it.

"Tell me, Alexandra."

She heard his volatile whisper and felt the breath-catching throb of his desire.

In the dark, in the dark all things were possible, even an unholy bargain between a virgin and a charlatan transmogrified into this swooning cloud of passion and need.

She couldn't bear not to know, not to feel.

"Show me, teach me," she breathed, and she felt him grab hold of her undergarment and gently strip it away from her flushed skin.

Heated, urgent, her body swelled with wet wanton desire, undulating with the sheer ripe sensation of being open and naked for him.

He settled one last long kiss on her hungry mouth—and then he moved, downwards and downwards, and downwards again until he buried his face in the luxuriant bush of hair between her legs.

He inhaled her perfume, and she arched herself against him, holding onto the bracelets as if they were bonds, as hard and abrasive as he who bent in obeisance before the power she commanded.

He was nuzzling her, exploring her; she reeled with the sensation of his probing her most intimate self, the self she did not know, the self she had known forever.

How was it possible to know and not know this devastating feminine pleasure, to be so familiar with it that she knew when to bear down into its seductive coiling ecstasy; to be so willing to submit to its lush wet carnality a sensibility that had held itself firmly and frighteningly in check?

Was it him—or was it her—in the throes of this insane amoral freedom where she knew no one was watching and no one would ever tell?

She didn't know, she didn't know; she felt herself thrashing wildly as she pushed against the suckling, waves of voluptuous sensation eddying through her, unexpected, unforeseen, rippling over her like the tide, pulling her with the force and thrust of a nature of which she had no control.

And then—a voice intruding into the atmosphere of luxuriant carnality, and a heavy banging at the door: Khurt's voice, rimmed with anxiety:

"*Caid! Caid!* Are you there? Are you there?"

The mood of insensate sensuality dissipated instantly: she felt stupid, gullible, used. She wriggled away from him, using her hands to lever her out of his way, and he jacked himself onto his knees, muttering imprecations. and scooping up her undergarments.

She stared at him resentfully as he called out: "Everything is fine, Khurt," and he motioned her to the lavatory.

She felt like the veriest strumpet as she scrambled to her feet, still clutching the bracelets, grabbed her underthings and crept into the privy.

She heard him unlock the door, saying: "A precaution only while you were gone . . ."

A heavy lie, that, even to her listening ears, was as heavy as the bracelets weighing down her hands.

She looked at herself in the little mirror above the washbasin. She looked absolutely no different; nothing had changed except that now she had been initiated into the realm of the forbidden and there was a knowing light in her eyes that had never been there before.

The man was unscrupulous and oh so seductive; she ought to have known it. She *had* been naive.

She wondered to what lengths he would go to possess the bracelets.

She wondered to what lengths she would go to withhold them.

She slipped them on her wrists, one and then the other, and covered them with the sleeves of her jacket.

Dispassionately, she examined her undergarments, now in

shreds, and balled them up into a piece of refuse which she crammed into the wastebasket.

What lengths? she wondered, as she smoothed down her skirt and bundled back her hair into some semblance of order.

It struck her suddenly that with her capitulation she had gained some power; and it might even be possible to sometimes command the game.

Why not? Who would censure her here or even know of her licentious behavior?

She shook off the erotic thought. Why would she ever want to abandon her reason like that again? Women who acted against reason invariably got hurt.

She turned away from the mirror, satisfied with her appearance, and immediately her naked lower torso was caressed by the silky petticoats beneath her skirt.

She felt it keenly, that sense of erotic bareness, and that telling little itch between her legs reminding her of the shimmering pleasures to come.

She resisted it, resented it. But every movement she made as she set herself to rights only reminded her of the voluptuousness of yielding her nakedness to the carnal desire of another.

She felt the swelling of her body, its memory having nothing to do with reason or vengefulness. She was acutely aware of her distended lips and the memory of the force of his kisses.

The astounding thing was, as her body recreated the sensations, she instantly wanted more—without rhyme or reason or logical need; she wanted more and more and more.

She touched her lips in wonderment, closing them around her forefinger as if that succulence could assuage the sudden stiffening of her body as it arched into awareness.

She caught a glimpse of herself in the mirror as she turned to open the lavatory door.

She saw it in her eyes and in the insolent smile on her face. Her sensual side understood it even if she didn't want to.

If he wanted the bracelets, he could just come and get them.

She couldn't wait.

Chapter 8

She wondered how much Khurt comprehended. He was, if anything, even more stoical than Culhane, and his expression, she was delighted to observe as she sank into the seat opposite him as the train left Stuttgart, was positively carved in stone.

Culhane's burning gray gaze immediately flashed to her face—her hair; she saw it. And to her mouth, so obviously exposed to his rough kisses, which had to be noticeable, even to Khurt.

She felt a telling heat wash over her face, but she did not back down from his hot, knowing eyes.

The moment she licked her dry, swollen lips, the tension rose like a blast of steam.

She understood it too: she had said the things he commanded, and had opened herself to his carnal kisses. He could not forget any more than she.

He was waiting to see whether she would recoil from the utter shamelessness of it, or whether she was so brazen she would beg for more.

She would not beg. Never would she beg: she would entice him and provoke him until he could stand it no longer, and then he would become the supplicant, not she.

The thought was utterly beguiling, and the perfect way to turn the tables on him: he had not expected his own response; he surely could not have predicted hers.

She wished Khurt were not there, but that was an entirely selfish thought; she wanted to play with her new power, regardless of the danger or the consequences.

And the danger was real—the next attack might take out all of them. Dzmura was relentless, but she had known that.

"I must see the bracelets," Culhane said, and there was no inflection by which anyone could have guessed what had passed between them.

"You must tell me about the bracelets," she countered, playing for time. "You have said enough about my father, certainly; surely I deserve some explanations."

The stone gray glint of his eyes told her just what he thought she deserved. "Your father was *not* a saint; the first set of bracelets are not a brilliant archaeologic find: your father concocted them—and that ludicrous story—just as he made the second set and hid them away for *me* to find."

She felt her hackles rising. "Why? Why would he do such a thing, Culhane?"

He hesitated a moment as if he were trying to decide how to frame his answer. "Because he was the only one who knew where to find Dzmura. He just didn't expect to find him on his own doorstep. He made it all up to lure Dzmura out in the open."

"And then he died," she said caustically.

"And then he died."

He wasted away, sick over the Museum's rejection of the bracelets' provenance, she thought combatively. What more could it have been? The bracelets were real; Culhane's version was the fairy tale, and she would have found the duplicate set eventually, she was certain of it.

"You would never have found the duplicate set of bracelets," he interposed irritatedly, following the stormy trend of her thoughts by the increasingly rebellious look in her eyes. "And the story would have ended like this: your sister would have been abducted, the bracelets would have been destroyed, you never would have seen her again, and you would have rotted the rest of your days in that mausoleum."

"Oh, but surely you would have come to the door selling secrets and answers, Culhane."

"And I might have bedded you too, to get what I wanted. It is my bad luck you turned out to be a termagant, but there is still time to come to terms. I merely need to see the bracelets, Miss deLisle."

"But if I allowed you to see them, Mr. Culhane, you might leave me to rot in some other antiquated mausoleum, since my purpose will have been served. I would have fulfilled both requirements of the bargain, would I not? What use would you have for me then?"

"None whatsoever," he said bluntly, but the expression in his eyes said otherwise.

She bit back her fury at his cavalier dismissal of her, and she saw he was instantly aware of her anger the moment it overwhelmed her senses.

Damn him and damn him . . . I am as easy for him to read as a book, she thought, and she resented being so open to him.

She felt suddenly powerless against so all-enveloping a consciousness. He was right; her father was a fraud—she surreptitiously felt the bracelets, her fingers rubbing the incisions as if they could tell her what Culhane would not.

She pulled out every bit of perversity within her to summon up a disdainful smile and a dismissive shrug.

"Well, so you see, Culhane . . . it is for that very reason a woman never gives away all her secrets."

And, she thought venomously, this is perfect venue with which to make him pay and pay.

. . . and then he died . . .

The words skirted around the edge of his consciousness, teasing him, and then skeining out into nothingness.

He yanked back the thought. Alexandra deLisle thought her father had just wasted away out of disappointment and disillusionment, while he understood that Sir Peregrine had been racing against time.

And how skillful he had been, playing his eldest daughter like a fish on a line, making her part of the process and consummately acting the part of a man drowning in bitterness.

Could he ever have envisioned that his foolhardiness would lead to *this?*

The worst part of it was his daughter's insolent naivete, a stick of a woman turned into the serpent in his very own Eden.

Well, that would be easy enough to combat; but her stubbornness was something else again. He had expected gratitude at the very least, both for his taking her on and for saving her life; but she had no conception of the forces at work.

She believed what she could see, she had said, and the bracelets were something she could both see and hold onto with all her might. He would probably have to break her wrists to remove them, because he had given in to one or the other irresponsible impulses just because she was Sir Peregrine's daughter. And just because he had thought he might have some use for her somewhere along the way.

Fate . . . There was no other reason, no other explanation.

But now he did not have the luxury of time.

He would end the thing in Vienna, reclaim the bracelets and leave her there.

The doctor sent a note that he wished Khurt to return to the infirmary and perhaps spend the night.

"There is too much danger, *caid,* I could not leave you unattended."

"Nonsense; if something further happened to you I would remain unattended: forever. We must take every precaution, on both our parts. I will insist that security check the compartment several times during the night in addition to their normal precautions."

Khurt bowed. "It shall be as you wish, *caid.*"

They escorted him to the infirmary on their way to dinner, and saw him settled in the doctor's capable hands.

Then Culhane sought out their steward, Cecil, and arranged for security to make several passes through their sleeping car.

And finally, they sat down to the second seating at dinner.

This night, she wore the silk shirtwaist with the velvet skirt and the shawl, which she fastened around her shoulders with a glittery little jet pin that had been among the effects in the suitcase Khurt had provided.

She thought how odd it was that in the midst of the turmoil that surrounded them, she and Culhane could calmly sit down to dinner and wade their way through each course without speaking a word except to whomever occupied the adjoining chairs.

And she clamped down on the unnerving thought that when they returned to the compartment they would be utterly alone.

But that was meaningful only to her. If she did not have the bracelets she would be of no use to him whatsoever. Had he not told her that barely two hours before?

She squared her shoulders, wondering if he meant to come after her and force her to relinquish them this night.

She felt a shiver of—what? apprehension . . . excitement?—course through her body. The possibilities took on a life of their own; it required no thought, just memory, and it was as if her nerve endings functioned independently of her mind.

And perhaps that was all to the good; she had no experience at all at playing the strumpet, but she wanted to, and that was both strange and perfectly sensible to her.

Men were vulnerable in that regard; even Culhane was susceptible, and if she did not allow his careless hurtful words to affect her, she would prove he was not immune once again.

She felt streams of pleasure just ruminating on that delicious notion, and she understood how seductive the dance between men and women could be, how enticing and destructive.

But if it were not Culhane? Sanity insinuated itself into her thoughts. What then? What then?

Was it him? She shook that thought away: she couldn't want him, she wanted the power and the gratification to be had in the pursuit of forbidden pleasures—the control.

Her body stiffened with remembrance and arousal. She marveled at how simple it all was, how natural. One taste of carnality and her body craved it again; morality entered into it not at all.

It felt both liberating and sinful, as if she had become dissolute somehow because she had submitted to her baser instincts and come away the victor.

And yet she was the same, wanting only another bite of the

fruit of temptation, willing to take the first step and make the first move in order to subjugate Culhane to her burgeoning need for him.

She played it out over and over in her mind during dinner since she did not want to converse with him and only had to nod in answer to their table companions, who seemed intent on doing most of the talking.

Waiting only intensified her hunger; the dinner was long and leisurely with at least five courses and dessert, and she was sure her hand was shaking with excitement by the time coffee and tea were served and she reached for the sugar.

He noticed nothing, or he pretended not to. Perhaps he sensed her tension as she stirred the sugar into her coffee and gave the appearance of taking part in the desultory conversation, and perhaps he was viscerally aware of every scenario she had plotted throughout the long two-hour dinner.

He said not a word to her as they bid their dinner companions good night a half-hour later. Nothing, as they passed through the corridors of the three cars previous to theirs. Nothing, as he unlocked the door to their compartment and let her precede him inside.

She hesitated a moment as she stepped over the threshold. The darkness was shadowed by the diffused light from the corridor, and he stood limned against it, the phantom lover she never could have imagined—formed, featureless, perfect—intoxicated with her, coming after her as he shut the door to enclose them in a tight hot little world of tense anticipation.

She knew better than to throw mundanities into the air; she felt him grasp her arm and draw her back toward him and against the door where he leaned into her, breathing in her fragrance, her scent, her hunger.

"You have waited all night for this," he murmured, lifting her face to his in the palpitating darkness and crushing her mouth under his.

She made a contemptuous sound that might have been a protest, but she did not fight that hot wet invasion of her mouth that sought only to dominate her, subdue her, arouse her.

Her body arched into his, awakened from its trancelike state of imagination into the lush realm of his forceful penetration of her tender mouth.

She couldn't get enough of it; she wanted it. She could barely hang onto the little voice of sanity in her mind which insistently reminded her that if she succumbed, she would give him the upper hand.

But those kisses! Long, slow, disastrously delicious kisses wreaking havoc with her common sense; that gorgeous knowing tongue delving and darting into everywhere, her body streaming with pent-up excitement that was almost unbearable.

He was so smart; he knew everything. He knew women, he knew *her* in no time at all . . .

In spite of the fact he had no use for her *whatsoever.*

Except for this—except for *this* . . .

And how like a man, how unutterably overbearingly like a *man.*

It was as if she had been doused with cold water; all the heat dissipated instantly, and she wrenched away from him so violently, he took a step back. She switched on the lights, and they stood facing each other, panting, in the stunning brightness.

She wanted to cut him up into little pieces and stamp on them. "You have it all wrong, Culhane," she said finally when she had some control over her hostility. "*You* were the one yearning all night for that. And I know it was worth the wait."

The tension between them ballooned outward as she stalked past him to the lavatory and slammed the door behind her.

And it hadn't even been hard to do. He might be fuming, but he would come running, she was sure of it as she touched her throbbing lips and peered at herself once again in the mirror.

She had come close, so close to just melting in his arms—and if she had done that, where would she be now but at his mercy?

No, it was meant to be the other way around, she thought, as she unfastened the pin and removed the shawl.

Already her pulsating body urged her on; there wasn't a pause between memory of his kisses and the desire to yield everything to him, and only him.

She was beguiled by the wonder of it as she untied the black velvet skirt and unbuttoned her shirtwaist and let them slip to the floor.

She had prepared well for this eventuality. All night long her naked limbs had been caressed by the supple lining of the velvet skirt; all night long her gartered black silk stockings had hugged her thighs, a sensuous contrast of which only she was aware, that of being simultaneously dressed and undressed.

She wore nothing else underneath but the black sateen corset that was trimmed with lace and silk and used elastic instead of steels to shape.

She thought it shaped her very well, pushing her breasts upward so that they seemed to want to spill out from the confining cups and curving over her hips to an inviting downward point.

And what if Culhane walked in the door this very moment?

Her body seized with that heady uncontrollable feeling of pleasure, and she raised her arms to lift her hair off her neck.

Her body arched forward, almost as if she were offering herself.

Yes, that was just right: she would offer and let him take ...

... let him come ...

She wanted to envelop his mind with the sense of her; she wanted to will him into that little room with all the power of her femininity. She wanted ...

... *let him come* ...

She concentrated her desire directly at him, until the waiting, the excitement pulsed to an unbearable pitch.

And then—

"Damn it, aren't you done yet?"

He pounded on the door once, just once, and it opened almost as if he had breached it by pure strength and fury.

And she was there, molded by the low light and the minuscule space, her back to him, bent over retrieving something, her shawl, her enticing bottom naked and brazenly shimmying in her effort to grab onto the material, the bracelets circling her wrists like slave bracelets.

And then she realized he was there and sent him an insolent look over her shoulder, braced her hands on her thighs and just waited as if she knew he could not resist the temptation of her nakedness.

As if she were waiting to feel the hot clasp of his hand against her cushiony bottom; as if she were inviting him to slide his hand into that sweet crease between her buttocks.

She knew he would not refuse such a blatant invitation. She looked away as he moved towards her, so that she could experience the sheer shock of pleasure at feeling his hand cup her buttocks and slide all over them, caressing their rounded contours; and then the agonizing wait for him to work his hand between her legs to that tingling pleasure point.

Oh, and then something different, something incredibly powerful and voluptuous, his fingers pushing inwards and inwards, so gorgeously unexpected and erotic that she arched herself and thrust against them.

How many fingers? Two, three—yes—more, more . . . She felt him grasp her hair and pull her head back to meet his kiss.

"Who wants . . . who wants?" he whispered fiercely against her lips before covering them with thick wild biting kisses that sent her bucking against him, and he knew it was not only she who wanted.

He wanted, he needed, he felt the mesmerizing glimmer of something beyond his pure male possession of her, and it was good, it was good.

He held her nakedness in his hand and her tongue in his mouth and she undulated frantically against the inescapable push of his fingers in that secret wet place between her legs, and he wanted to drive that pleasure deep within her forever.

Something was coming; she didn't want it to end. The push was inexorable, his kisses utterly devouring; her body pumped against him urgently, insatiably, spreading against him to give him the greatest purchase to deepen this erotic carnal caress.

She wanted him deeper and deeper, and harder against that shimmering pleasure point; she loved the feel of him *there*, thick and unrelenting and she wanted to escape whatever it was that was coming.

She couldn't bear it, she couldn't . . . one more step, higher and higher, one more . . . she thrust against him wildly, seeking the far pleasure that was an instant beyond her grasp, an instant . . . building, building, shimmering with promise, breaking suddenly and without warning, she wasn't expecting it—and there it was, peaking and breaking, and she stepped off the peak and fell into a luminous, shattering, bone-melting ecstasy.

He never broke the kiss.

Still, as the final shimmering sensations rippled away, she felt herself bearing down, seeking more and still more, almost as if her body would not relinquish the pleasure.

She wanted *him* there forever, always; her body writhed against his in memory of the sense of his claiming her there. She hated him leaving her there, removing himself ever so slowly so he could cup her buttocks and lift her tightly against the iron length of his manhood.

It bulged against the vee between her thighs, pulsating, prodding, as demanding as his kiss.

She wriggled against it, seeking his elusive hand; she enticed his kisses in mute supplication, winding herself around him so as to give him purchase to take her again.

She lost herself in his hot devouring kisses, in a haze of luxuriant yearning; she felt him working at his clothing, working at her, his hands feeling her legs, the erotic crease between her buttocks.

She felt him shifting her, lifting her so that she suddenly straddled one of his naked hairy thighs, her legs spread, the lush excitement in her focused against his heated skin.

His hands took her everywhere, sliding over her shoulders, her arms, brushing the cups of her corset seeking the hard thrust of her taut nipples beneath the stiff cloth.

He waited a long sensuous moment for her to deny him; she didn't, and he stripped away the impeding cloth to close his large hands over the pure nakedness of her large rounded breasts.

She arched herself into the swirling heat of his caress as he took the weight of her firm breasts into his hands and moved his thumbs across her pebble-hard nipples.

She almost swooned; the sensation was like a thick spiralling dart right to her feminine core.

She leaned into the rock-hard thickness of his thigh, pressing, rubbing, riding him as he explored the contour of each tight taut nipple.

The rigid naked flesh of his manhood nudged her thigh, and she lifted her leg to enfold it against her.

She felt liquid, expansive, explosive; her body simmered with sensations radiating from his expert fondling of her nipples.

He knew, he knew *her;* he knew just when to touch, just when to squeeze—oh, and especially when to just hold them between his fingers, so lightly that she had to thrust herself just that much more boldly against him to feel it.

She never wanted it to end. It was like she was riding an opulent cloud of molten sensation and there was nothing but this gorgeous little world of sumptuous feelings and the hard heat of his nakedness supporting the frenzied drive of hers.

She could not get enough; his sultry kisses only heightened her ravenous urge for culmination. Her hunger was fathomless, hectic. She strained against him, undulating her body in a dance of yearning, wild and sleek, tormenting in her abandon.

Her body vibrated with erotic tension; and in that one tumultuous moment when she was at the crest of all that explosive feeling, he took her thrusting nipples between his fingers and he gently squeezed.

She swelled, suspended, and then it spilled, crackling like lightning all over her body, incandescent, glittering, a long silver slide of sensation up and down, white-hot, sizzling, blinding . . . exquisite and so all-enveloping that his thrust of flesh against flesh and his long low groan of repletion was lost in the hot aftermath of her ecstasy.

She felt the sticky wetness against her inner thigh coupled with the soft moist kisses he lavished all over her mouth as he gently eased away from her.

She wound herself around him, and he lifted her and carried her into the compartment and lay her down on the seat and then stood back to look at her.

She looked like a goddess, with her hair in wanton disarray, her lips swollen and eyes knowing, the disputed stone bracelets cuffing her wrists, long black stockings encasing her shapely legs and her corset in shreds at her narrow waist.

She looked like the embodiment of ripe femininity, and his manhood stiffened with his powerful desire to possess her.

She felt the living heat of his desire and her body stretched in mute invitation as she curved her legs one over the other to entice him by obscuring her seductive sex from his hot gray gaze.

... *yes* ...

She thought it, she felt it, her body surged with it, shimmering with lush moist need for it.

His nakedness aroused her when she had never known anything about a man's body or his prowess; there was a symmetry to him; in how his broad shoulders tapered to his narrow waist, how the power of his legs and thighs was complemented by the jutting root of maleness that was the essence of all he was.

She remembered the feel of it pumping against the soft flesh of her inner thigh; her body took the memory of his expert hands fondling her and played it back in her mind and made it so real it seemed she could feel it all over again.

She felt the lust of wanting instantly, and the something more that they had not even begun to explore that had to do with the ramrod length of him probing the hot wet pulsating core of her.

She wanted him there. His towering sex was meant for *there*; she wanted the feel of his voluptuous thrust into her wanton heat. She wanted to contain the hard thick granite length of him in all its primitive glory.

And she wanted the elemental force of all that lusty power focused solely in her.

... *yes* ...

She parted her legs and undulated her hips in brazen invitation.

... *yes* ...

He came to her slowly as if he wanted to stretch out every last voluptuous moment before he mounted her.

He knelt on the edge of the seat to give her full view of his stone-hard manhood, and she reached out and slid her bracelet cuffed hand down the hard long length of him and marveled at the rigidity, the size of him and at the fact that her satin sheath could enfold every last lusty inch of him.

She shuddered with excitement as she fondled the iron-hard length of him, waiting, waiting for the ultimate moment when she would feel that thick, ridged tip slide between her legs and press forcefully against her velvet fold.

And suddenly he was there, thick and hard and penetrating and jutting into her with one hard primitive thrust that tore into her with a twisting unexpected pain.

And he was there, there, *there,* kneeling between her legs, his body canted slightly, and his thick rooting manhood quiescent within her, and all she wanted to do was get away, get away.

This was possession, this impossible cradling of this tormentingly filling maleness; this was inescapable, this was pain—and she had not known, how could she have known that all the lush provocative wanton feelings would lead to *this* . . . ?

She bucked against him, trying to escape the invasiveness of him, the pure immense virile power of him; dear God, how did women survive it?

But she knew: all the fondling play beforehand lulled them into a haze of submission so that men could overtake them and trap them by wielding this carnal staff of power.

Never again, never again—everything else but *this;* anything else but this full potent possession that barely left her room to breathe, room to move.

She shifted her hips upward again, against the heavy weight of him, the huge fullness that nestled deep within her and she felt something, she felt something.

Her body twinged with it, the pain receded, and she reached for it again with a jouncing undulation of her hips against his intrusive hard heat.

She watched, her green eyes glittery with sensual awareness, as he lowered his head to her breast and took one taut hard nipple into his mouth and tugged on it.

A stream of molten silver slid down her veins to her ripe velvet core, and she levered herself upwards to meet it.

 . . . *yes* . . . *this* . . .

... this was different; his ramrod length was so deep within her that she gyrated against the hairy root of him, and it aroused her.

The pain dissipated to be replaced by a shimmering building excitement as she accepted this primitive fusing of their bodies.

His thick hard volatile manhood was the center around which her body rotated, and she did not know whether he possessed her or it was the other way around.

It didn't matter; he had thrust the whole of his imperious maleness so deep within her that she could feel it still elongating as she wriggled against him, seeking that something that made her breathless with excitement.

She wanted him hard and potent only for her; she was greedy for his throbbing lengthening sex now.

She understood the powerful depths of a woman's carnal appetite.

She heard the rhythmic pounding of her heart in concert with her body's tensile and subtle thrusting against him.

But he was so quiescent within her; and the pounding grew more forceful and she suddenly realized that it was outside herself, that someone was at the door knocking and calling to them.

He mouthed *you,* and she felt her body's urgency deflate and reluctantly called out: "Yes?"

"Cecil, ma'am, come to make up the beds."

"Oh . . ." She didn't know what to do; she didn't want to give up this beguiling world of lusty sensuality, but she had no choice: he slowly slowly removed himself from the seductive heat of her sex, and withdrew into the lavatory.

She couldn't believe it; in the space of thirty seconds, the explosive sensuality between them utterly evaporated.

She lifted herself up on her elbows, frantically seeking something with which to cover herself, calling out, "Just a moment, Cecil."

Damn and damn . . . She grabbed her bag and rummaged for the robe that Khurt had so thoughtfully provided, threw it hastily around her flushed and unsatiated body.

There . . . She pulled open the door and Cecil entered, his arms full of fresh linen.

"It will take but a moment, ma'am," he murmured, averting his gaze from her very seductive body which was fully outlined by the drape of her silky robe.

"Only a minute . . ."

Her breasts were taut-tipped tempting mounds clearly visible through the thin material. He could just see the tips of her black boots beneath the hem. He didn't want to see anything else. Not anything.

He raced through the bed-making as if someone were timing him, pulling down the berth and climbing up on her seat to spread out the sheets and tuck in the covers, and then stepping down to reverse the banquette seat to the mattress and making that up quickly with the precision of a military commander.

"All done now ma'am."

"Thank you, Cecil."

She closed the door carefully behind him, locked it and made sure the shades were firmly fastened on the door window.

Her heartbeat accelerated as the clack of the train wheels underscored the silence. She took a deep breath, inhaling the drift of fresh air that Cecil had brought into the compartment with him.

She wondered at the ease with which the air of steamy enchantment had utterly vanished. Her corset itched her tender skin now, a symbol of his hectic passion, and she only wanted to remove it and forget the whole thing.

She untied the robe and unhooked what was left of the corset and tossed it on the floor near the little closet.

And she looked down at herself, at her full upward tilting breasts with the enticingly engorged nipples; she cupped them, feeling the heft of them, wondering what he felt when he touched them, knowing what she felt when he sucked her perfectly peaked pointed nipples.

Again, the memory lived in her loins; her body reacted with the same streaming wetness to just the thought of it, and she hurriedly whipped her robe tightly around her.

But her straining nipples pushed tightly against the thin material; she could see them perfectly outlined and it was as if they were naked and inviting a man's touch.

She felt the power of her naked nipples. If he walked out the door right then, she knew the sight of her stiff pointed nipples thrusting against the flimsy silken robe would instantly arouse him to granite rigidity.

Her body twinged: she wanted to see it. She wanted him to walk out the lavatory door naked, his potent maleness in repose, and she wanted to see him elongate to a ramrod hardness at the sight of her.

There was power—to incite a man to carnal arousal with the promise of your body. She loved the heady thought of it; she wanted to do it.

Her body spurted with excitement at the thought of it.

She was naked beneath the robe but for her long black stockings and the little kid boots. She liked the contrast between the whiteness of her body and the dark stockings.

She liked the sheerness of the robe as it hugged her every curve, and the way it left nothing to the imagination.

All she needed to do was tie it more tightly around her to emphasize her thrusting breasts, her lusciously stiff pointed nipples, her flaring undulating hips . . .

She knocked lightly on the lavatory door. "The steward is gone." And then she threw herself onto her newly made-up bed and waited for him to come to her.

He slipped out the door all naked, his lusty manhood quiescent, to find her reclining on her bed, her right arm supporting her, the sensual curve of her body outlined clearly against the fragile silk robe, which was pulled so tautly around her that the lush hard nipple of her left breast was delineated as clearly as if she were naked.

He reacted, and his virile sex lengthened.

She shifted her body slightly, wriggling the curve of her buttocks against the back cushion as if she were trying to make herself more comfortable, and it spurted again, elongating just that little much more.

"Good night, Culhane," she murmured, turning her body over so that she was on her stomach and her hiked up robe revealed the pillowy curve of her naked buttocks and the long lush line of her stockinged legs.

She watched through hooded eyes as his manhood stiffened still more.

She ground her hips suggestively into the blankets so that her naked bottom shimmied with provocation.

And she watched as his ferociously virile sex elongated into its full thick ramrod hardness before her very eyes.

She loved it; she wanted to make him crazy with wanting her, with the new-born power of her body.

She was heady with it.

She yawned, and then turned onto her back, angling her legs so that the robe fell away and she was naked from the waist down and fully revealed to him.

His powerful maleness rammed out still farther, jutting upward and outward, stiff as a bone as she watched, her body creamy with excitement at provoking him into this forceful vigorous erection.

She lifted herself on her elbows and parted her legs.

"I'm not tired anymore," she whispered.

"Perhaps *I* am," he answered in kind.

"Perhaps I can arouse you," she murmured suggestively, and she could have sworn that his erection lengthened yet again.

"A stimulating thought; what could you do?"

"Something to make your pulse quicken?"

"A taste of that might be very, very tempting."

"With what can I entice *you?*" she whispered coyly, and to her eyes he got bigger still.

"The lure of your nakedness sucks me in."

Her body reacted this time, at the thought of his mouth tugging at the taut peaks of her nipples. She felt a starburst of glittery expectation.

She coiled herself upward slowly to her knees, deliberately arching her body toward him so that her pointed nipples were clearly defined. "A voluptuous thought," she murmured, and he flexed outward again.

"Arousing," he agreed huskily.

She looked down at her protruding nipples and then back up at him. "Inciting," she whispered as she slowly untied the knot around her waist and let it fall to the bed.

Immediately the edges of the robe parted and his inflexible sex moved again.

She lifted her shoulders and shrugged out of the robe.

It slid down her body into a pool around her thighs and she rested her cuffed hands on her knees.

She looked like nothing so much as his thrall. The thought sent his senses spiralling and brought his manhood to lusty new lengths as he gazed his fill of her luscious nakedness.

"I see I have managed to excite your interest," she murmured in that faintly suggestive tone of voice.

He would have sworn he couldn't get any harder. He wanted to cover that fresh mouth with kisses. He wanted to . . . but of course she was goading him.

She was loving this little scenario that was arousing him beyond endurance; she adored watching his naked sex jutting into thick hard explosive life.

She wanted to show off her body and tempt him with the nakedness of her breasts and those succulent pointed nipples.

And he could be enticed; her voracious virginal acceptance of his fondling and feeling of her naked body was intensely seductive.

Her explosive need to arouse his naked manhood to its full thick engorged glory, to provoke it and watch that happen, totally enslaved him.

And her insatiable appetite for their sensual coupling, her ravenous response to his greedy kisses almost seduced him beyond endurance.

But that was the way with virginal temptresses: they embraced the forbidden and behaved as if they had invented fleshly pleasure.

And perhaps she had. Or perhaps only the two of them together could create that towering insensate ecstasy.

And now she waited, her body fully naked and urgent with churning desire, her hungry gaze fixed on his jutting member, and it spurted upright yet again.

Together . . .

She licked her lips as if she were imagining the hard feel of it against the softness of them, and he loved the passiveness of her waiting, and her cuffed wrists, her wild hair and insolent look as she silently enjoyed his arrogant perusal of her nakedness.

His manhood jolted to life once again, and he wanted to enslave her with her hungry desire for their coupling.

Together—

He brushed away the thought and came to her slowly, presented himself to her, hard and hot, throbbing and ready for her carnal kiss.

That look was in her eyes, insolent, unyielding. "It is very hard to tempt you," she whispered, leaning forward and closing her lips around the very tip of him.

His hand shot out and entwined itself in her hair to pull her head backwards to force her hungry gaze up at him, and he climbed onto the bed and straddled her legs so that the full long length of him nestled tightly between her breasts.

"And yet I'm so easily satisfied," he murmured, and crushed her waiting willing mouth under his.

She groaned as his wanton tongue invaded her mouth, taking her, forcing her . . . Her arms slid around his narrow waist to press his huge hard sex more tightly between her breasts. Her fingers found the rounded softness of his buttocks and crept teasingly toward the erotic crease between.

He moaned as she boldly touched him there and wrenched his mouth away from hers. "Your kisses sate me."

She caught her breath. "I want more than my kisses to satisfy you."

He growled savagely under his breath at her shameless offer and took her mouth again with that same forceful thrilling invasiveness.

He made it a hot wet little world of their own; he dominated her, he goaded her, he aroused her until she was soft and compliant in his arms.

He kept his hand entwined in her hair, pulling her backwards so that he could delve deeply into the heated recesses of her mouth and she could hide nothing from him.

He made her quiver with yearning for his seeking torrid kisses. He made her hunger for them, demand them; he made her melt for them.

She could only hold tightly onto the naked cushion of his buttocks and *feel*.

Her body turned liquid, nectarean; her nipples expanded and pulsated with naked yearning. Her lips swelled under his forceful kisses, and she offered them up for more and more as he tugged at her thick mop of hair to force her to open her mouth to him more fully.

The hot tight little world of their wet lush kisses closed in around them.

She quivered with her wanton carnal need; his body shuddered with the relentless force of his determination to enslave her with his hot potent kisses and then with the unyielding power of his towering manhood.

He heard the fierce moan in the back of her throat, and he eased his lips barely an inch from hers. "Your nipples tempt me."

. . . *yes* . . .

His lips roamed downward from hers, pressing against her neck, her jaw and as he moved himself away from her breasts, her shoulder, the curve of her breast . . . until he licked the turgid tip of her breast and closed his mouth around it.

The sensation almost sent her spiralling out of control. His virile manhood nudged the underside of that breast as he tugged on the hard pointed nipple.

She reached for him, grasping him tightly, and moving against him as her body took control.

Somehow he moved her legs out from under her, and laid her against the back of the seat, still sucking and pulling at the pure pleasure point of her nipple, until she felt she would explode.

He felt that twinge of give in her and he relinquished her breast, knelt down between her legs and pulled her body towards him until her feet rested on the opposite banquette and his lusty manhood was nudging the velvet fold of her sultry sex.

She braced herself for the voluptuous slide of him within her. He hovered above her, watching her face, holding her eyes as he probed her intimate heat delicately, tentatively, erotically until that one final tormenting thrust and then he drove into her and positioned himself just where he could see every nuance of passion play over her face.

He held her arms immobile as he rocked forcefully against her and watched her.

She felt every potent inch of him possessing her, felt her power in the hard hot restraint of his hands. She had him in bondage to her, and she reveled in her spewing desire for him.

Her volatile need for him escalated as if her body knew no bounds.

She undulated against him, enticing him with her sinuous movements, begging him to take her.

He plunged savagely into the hot honey of her torrid sex, her churning hips inciting him, inviting him, meeting his every gyration and rotating against it in an ecstasy of excitement.

Who was tempted and who was enslaved? He couldn't tell; he was lost in the pistonlike pumping of his body, lost in the creamy resonance of her desire, bonded to her shimmering writhing form.

He was molten, he was satin; she bore down on him, parting her legs to their fullest so that he could connect with that tingling pleasure point and make it explode.

And the moment she yearned for it, she felt volcanic with it. Her body tensed against his galvanic thrusts, her hips rocketed against him urgently, possessively.

She felt the glimmering of it suddenly, and then the full unbridled eruption of it cascading between her legs and sizzling all over her body in great shocking seismic waves.

It was a maelstrom of sensation, an avalanche, a storm; she rode it out, she rode it, her body clamoring, insatiable, drawing him into the keen relentless spasm of his own drowning release in concert with hers.

And then, still cradled within her, he levered himself onto the bed with her, and they fell asleep together, their bodies entwined.

Chapter 9

He woke up when the train stopped in Munich. Everything was silent except for the faint shuddery huff of the engine as it was continually stoked. The soft lights of the compartment still burned, and he was still nestled beguilingly between her legs.

He disentangled himself with some difficulty and slipped out of the bed and then rooted around for his suitcase. He found it in the closet, which made sense, and delved into its jumbled contents, searching for his watch.

Two o'clock. Damn—only two o'clock.

Or perhaps that was good. He felt wide awake, while she remained deeply asleep, her body seemingly boneless under the cover, her chest rising and falling with intensive regularity, her head propped against a pillow under which her cuffed wrists were lightly crossed.

He hadn't thought he would find opportunity in the dead of night on the Orient Express after an explosive sensual exchange, but there it was staring him right in the face.

He retrieved his pants and shirt from the lavatory and settled himself on the seat opposite her. Taking care not to hit his head on the berth above, he reached forward and lifted one of her hands, let it drop back onto the bed.

She didn't stir.

He took her hand again and held it for a while.

She didn't move.

He slowly began working the bracelet off her wrist, and almost instantly, she balled her hand defensively in her sleep and wrenched it away from him.

He cursed and reached for her other hand, but she snatched it away almost as if she were awake and aware.

"Culhane..." Her voice was sleep fogged and angry. "I knew you'd do this."

"You don't know the half of what I'll do," he muttered, climbing onto the bunk and straddling her prone body, his hands still holding hers immobile.

"Culhane..."

"You're dangerous, Alexandra. I need the bracelets, and you just won't cooperate."

"I have *cooperated*," she hissed through gritted teeth, now jolted fully awake. "What are you doing? Damn you, *what are you doing?*"

But she knew: he was ignoring her bucking body and binding her wrists with a length of sheet. The instant he tied the knot, she jerked up her arms and sliced them downwards towards his head.

He caught the blow on his chest, and she felt his fulminating fury as he held her hands against his chest and slowly and ruthlessly pried open her fingers, then roughly removed the bracelets from her wrists.

"I hate you."

"Go back to sleep, Alexandra. Your anger won't profit you."

"I *won't*. I'll—"

"Turn over and go back to sleep, or I'll tie you to the bed as well."

She made a tense movement to get up in defiance of his orders. The iron clamp of his hands stopped her. "Alexandra..."

She hated it that he now had the power. She felt impotent, stupid for not having divined that he would try something like this.

"All right. Get off of me. I won't try anything."

He didn't trust her; he waited a moment, and then another, as he became increasingly aware of her quiescent naked body beneath him.

In an instant he wanted her, and he hated the irony of it. *Use her and lose her . . .*

It wasn't going to work that way now—but he didn't want to think that.

He wanted her quiet and asleep.

He climbed off her slowly, just waiting for her to make some move. But she lay there rigid, wrapped defiantly in that shroud of a sheet, waiting and waiting, determined to wait him out.

He eased into the opposite seat, the ragged edges of the bracelets biting into the palm of his large hand.

She jerked her body sideways so that her mouth was positioned to take a bite out of his hand.

"If you try it," he said, his voice dangerously low, "I will see to it that you don't awaken until we reach Bucharest. *If* then."

He meant it. She was absolutely sure he would have no compunction about keeping his word.

She levered herself backwards until she touched the cushion of the berth, and she lay her head down on the pillow reluctantly.

A brittle silence enfolded them: she was determined not to fall asleep.

And he waited, with all the patience he was capable of calling up. He was prepared to wait for the rest of the night and into the morning because of the tension in her shrouded body and the anger in the air.

But he had the bracelets—and he had all the time in the world to wait.

And finally, she slept.

He held the bracelets up to the dim light of his berth.

And there they were, ugly and unprepossessing . . .

. . . a duplicate set of bracelets that were copies of fake artifacts Sir Peregrine had tried to pass as originals by concocting a story about a ghost giving him the key to the translation . . .

. . . and which Dzmura now possessed . . .

And by now Dzmura knew what he had just discovered: the lines did not match and something was missing.

He clamped down immediately on the first thought that jumped into his mind. He didn't have to deduce anything until they reached Alekkah. It was far more important to have the bracelets.

—And to make some kind of record of them . . .

Quietly he reached for his briefcase and removed a stiff board about the size of a sheet of paper and the thickness of a book cover. He placed the bracelets on this, balancing it on his knees while he dug for a pencil and a sheet of tissue paper.

He wrapped one bracelet in the paper and painstakingly made a rubbing of the markings on it, and then those of its twin.

These he sandwiched between two blank sheets of writing paper, clipped them all to the writing board and returned that to his briefcase.

He took the bracelets, several sheets of tissue paper and his suitcase into the lavatory. There, he wrapped the bracelets in the tissue and then removed everything from the suitcase to access a small pocket which was ingeniously hidden on its bottom.

It was designed particularly for the concealment of small items and artifacts that were to be spirited from the country of origin without official sanction, and it was especially constructed for the transport of fragile things, this rigidity giving the suitcase its balance and shape.

He tucked the bracelets within padded and steel-framed confines, repacked the suitcase and returned it to the closet.

He was asleep by the time the train churned its way slowly out of Munich station.

Alexandra awakened to darkness with a long sensual catstretch of her naked body, the scent of sex still in air that was pungent with possibilities.

Her mouth felt ripe still from his kisses, her body buoyant with the memory of that transcending pleasure, which was instantly superseded by shock, for her hands were unbound and it was morning, he was asleep and the bracelets were nowhere around.

Instantly she wanted to jump on him, attack him, kill him.

She hated herself for succumbing to sleep.

She propped herself up on her elbows and strove for a semblance of calm. The first thing she had to do was get dressed; she needed light, and thank the fates he hadn't torn off her robe. She got up, whipped it around her body, tied the sash tightly and then sat down on the bed to think.

She had to think.

She didn't want to think.

Who had the power now?

And who had really had it all along?

Did she want to admit he could have forced her to turn over the bracelets at any time?

Indeed . . . what had he *forced* her to do at all?

But how could she have known she would love sensual play so much?

Damn and blast . . . She felt the surging terror of losing control. Every possible scenario raced through her head, not the least of which was that he had no reason now to keep her with him.

He could abandon her tomorrow—and he had nothing to lose.

How stupid she had been; all that heated carnal coupling with a man who thought she was obsessive and dictatorial . . .

What had she been thinking? That she had *him* in the palm of her hand?

Here was the truth: he had used her to get what he wanted, and that had not been her naked body.

Damn, damn, damn and blast . . . A gush of pure humiliation washed over her; games, she had thought they were playing games. Instead he had been playing for real, and he had gotten what he wanted all the way around.

Her cheeks burned, remembering . . .

That part was simple: she just wouldn't think about it. But his possession of the bracelets was something else again.

She felt cheated every which way. More than that, the bracelets belonged to her and she wanted them back.

"They are safer with me," Ryder said lazily from his berth above her almost as if he could sense her determination.

"But *I'm* not safer without them," she said tightly, speaking into the darkness, which she hated, "and you stole them and I want them back."

"You are not invulnerable, Alexandra."

"Nor are you," she put in viciously.

"Nor am I," he agreed edgily, "but they are more secure with *me*. There is nothing more to discuss."

And what about me? she wanted to ask, but that would have been humbling herself a lot more than she had already.

Besides which, he could not have figured out what the incisions on the bracelets meant—not yet. It wasn't inconceivable that she might find them.

"Ever a man," she threw out maliciously, "*nothing more to discuss*—because he has decreed it. I should say there is a lot more to discuss; perhaps the security on the train should be notified that something has been stolen. Perhaps I should run through the corridor screaming, 'thief, thief.' Perhaps I should . . ."

She heard a rustling sound and then he was right beside her before she could even react.

"Shut your mouth," he growled menacingly and clamped a hand over her parted lips.

"Mmrph," she retorted heatedly, ramming an elbow into his ribs.

He relinquished her mouth instantly and grabbed her by the sash of her robe. "You little bitch—that hurt."

"I surely hope so," she said fervently, swinging her body away from him violently. "You bastard . . . you . . . you lecher!"

He pulled back and she came crashing back against his hard body.

"Excuse me, Miss Alexandra deLisle, I *don't* recall that anyone forced you to do anything you didn't want to do."

She ripped away at her sash, frantically untying the knot before she responded. "How did I know I wanted to do it before I did it?" she demanded, pulling against his iron grasp once again, once, twice and then the knot came undone and she hurried across the compartment, feeling her way in the awful darkness.

"You damn well know now," he muttered, balling up the sash to toss it aside. And then he thought not.

"With a debaucher and a thief for a teacher," she spat out, backing up against the door.

"And a tease and a tart just aching to be tutored," he said brutally, moving towards her slowly, slowly.

She felt his anger palpably in the darkness. Oh, the darkness was not her friend, not now. She thought of a hundred things she would rather do than confront him in the darkness with his wrath and her bile.

All she had to do was turn on the light.

She edged her hand upwards, the palm of her hand flat against the wall.

His large hand slammed against it, effectively immobilizing her. "No lights, Alexandra; you maneuver so beautifully in the dark."

She felt a wave of heat suffuse her; he was so close to her, and she felt so vulnerable with her robe wide open and only the darkness between their conflict and their desire.

"And you are so expert at manipulation," she said with some bitterness. "You know all the right moves, Culhane, all the tender places."

"Don't I?" he murmured. "Don't you?"

He was so close.

"I am so tender, if you touch me I will dissolve," she whispered as she felt the heat of his body and the touch of his breath.

"If I touch you I will solidify."

The image of the thick jutting flesh of his manhood flashed right into her mind; she could almost feel it.

The heat between them rose like steam.

In the dark, the dark where things like possessions are of no moment when one is about to be possessed carnally, voluptuously, explosively.

Her traitorous body would always betray her now; it possessed a memory of its own which ran on a separate track from her common sense. It divined desire, it embraced the erotic and the forbidden.

Her insidious body wanted all the delights that awaited her in the dark; her nipples stiffened, her ripe femininity was wet with yearning. Her mouth recreated his demanding kisses, her body the feel of his hands in her most intimate and secret places.

Her body would never forget those things now; she could not live without them. Her father's legacy was nothing compared to the wanton need he aroused in her.

Still, she could not give in to her profligate yearning . . . yet, not yet.

He was that close to her, and her heart began pounding wildly in her chest. Her body arched towards his as if she were offering him her breasts, but he could not see them in the dark.

He still held her hand; he felt her subtle movements, and in his mind's eye he could picture every naked inch of her and wanted her again.

It was insane, but he felt wild with the need to possess her. He needed her mouth, he needed her hard pointed nipples, he needed her hot willing woman's flesh—he needed *her*.

She wanted him to take her; he sensed it, he felt it: she needed not to give in to her desire—she wanted to submit to his passion.

He tightened his hold on her hand and moved a step closer.

She caught her breath as he aligned his hips against hers and she felt the distinct massive bulge of his towering sex.

"Don't say anything." His words were a breath against her lips.

"I don't—" she began heatedly.

"You do," he contradicted coolly, reaching out to grasp her other hand to pin it against the wall. "You do." He moved both of her hands up above her head and grasped them both in one of his. "You want."

"No—"

"You need." His free hand traced a line down her face to her neck and then her chest, and finally the cleft between her taut breasts. He rested his fingers there between the soft mounds erotically separated by the lifting of her arms, and then he stroked gently that delicious space between the heavy curves of her breasts, where he could feel their contours and imagine her tight nipples peaking against the thin silk of her robe.

"You demand." His hand moved downward, caressing her midriff and the slight swell of her belly, and downwards again to the thick thatch of feminine hair at the crowning point between her legs; it rested there.

"You crave."

She made a little sound at the back of her throat as his fingers grazed her provocative fold.

"You yearn." His fingers stroked her there, lightly, caressingly, maddeningly; and she wriggled against them inviting them to explore.

"You can't wait," he growled as he gave in to the wanton wriggle of her hips and filled her with his hard probing fingers.

She parted her legs and thrust her hips downwards to ease his way. And then he was there, and she moaned at the sheer erotic sensation of it.

"You love this."

She groaned.

"You want more."

She couldn't speak; her body turned liquid as he played with her, all in the dark, just as she had imagined an hour or so before.

"I want to give you more, Alexandra, but I have a problem."

"What, what?" she breathed, grinding her hips downward to elicit every voluptuous feeling.

"You'll never fall asleep, and you will be searching my belongings before daybreak."

"I—oh . . . no—ohhh . . ."

"Yes, yes, Alexandra; I know you, I know how you think. I will give you completion, but you must give me compliance."

Her mind, her heart, her sex were all concentrated in his carnal probing of her most intimate womanhood; she hardly heard him—or maybe she heard him and she didn't care what he required of her. It didn't matter as long as he did not stop provoking the luscious creamy feelings that shimmered inside her.

"Come to my bed then," he commanded.

"I don't want to move."

"We'll move together."

He lowered her hands, still holding them, and with his fingers still inserted between her legs, he stepped carefully backwards and guided her toward his berth.

"Now, Alexandra, slip off your robe." He released her hands, and she shrugged the robe off of her shoulders.

"I want you up in my berth."

"How . . . why?" she whispered, concentrating all on the light feel of his fingers still between her legs.

"It's hard and tight up there, and I want you as close to me as possible. I'll help you up."

"I don't want to move," she protested again.

He withdrew his hand. "Now you do."

"I hate you."

"I want you." He ran his hands from her waist to her buttocks and caught her up and lifted her so she sat just at the edge of the berth.

"I want your hands."

"Why?"

"This is the compliance part."

"I already did the compliance part," she said stringently.

"I would not have called it complying," he murmured, his voice just faintly amused.

"I believe it's called resistance."

"And will you resist me now?"

Could she resist him when she knew it had been her choice to play those forbidden games in the dark?

She extended her hands towards him and felt him wrapping something around them, something slithery and light, with the tensile strength to immobilize her.

She heard the soft slide of his removing his clothing and felt the heft of his weight as he swung up beside her, his hands directing her where he wanted her—flat on her stomach with her arms over her head.

Dark, dark, it was so dark, so close up in this berth; she couldn't see, she couldn't act, she could only feel and inhale his scent, it gave her the strangest sensation of power.

He was now at her mercy; if she denied him her passion, he had nothing, absolutely nothing.

She even mulled it over for a while in her mind as his hands slowly began their bold erotic exploration of her body, starting at her shoulders and moving downwards to caress the sensitive curves of her breasts, downwards more to the small of her back and to just where it flared into her hips and the pillow of her buttocks.

He rested there to let her feel the heat and size of his hands, and then he began the more intimate carnal probing of her body, two hands this time, seeking, spreading, stroking, feeling, sliding finally to the pulsating core of her.

Here she could not deny him; here was where she wanted him, all of him, every towering inch of him. She shook off his knowledgeable hands, rolled her body this way and that as if she wanted to turn on her back, and he finally stopped her by sliding his arm under her belly, lifting her, and driving his ramrod sex home.

And this was different too; he was above her and behind her with the sensual shimmy of her buttocks in his hands as he lunged into her in short thick pistonlike strokes.

He did not cover her; she could not touch him. All she could feel was the rampant drive of his hot hard sex and his large hot hands on her buttocks registering her every undulation as she met his thrusts.

She had been waiting for this, yearning for this, wanting him to take her like this so she could fire her anger into the burning desire to be naked in his arms.

She had never felt so naked and so aware of him. His whole focus was on her eternal femininity. Her whole body was centered on the power and virility of him at that one intimate point of smoldering carnality.

She loved this different reverse coupling and the fact she could only feel the explosive male essence of him pounding into her, rock hard, lusty with possessing her, primitive as the ancients whose lives he explored.

It took but a moment over and above this thought for the glimmering sense of something coming. Just a moment for the break of rapturous sensation to start building into something more turbulent, more fierce.

This one, oh this one—her body gyrated wildly pulling the sensations from his titanic thrusts—this one and this one . . . her body pumped against him, wringing it out, wrenching it out as the cumulative feelings coalesced in that one churning center of her being; she couldn't stop the tumultuous rotation of her hips— on and on and on and on until the exquisitely shimmering sum- mit of feeling erupted like a volcano and spewed her away in a sumptuous paroxysm of sensation.

She couldn't get away from it; it was an avalanche, burying her under a torrent of fathomless pleasure.

Her body heaved with it; she shook with it, trying to buck him off, and he kept coming on and on until she was ready to scream with the relentlessness of it.

She couldn't bear it, she couldn't . . . It was more and more than anything she had experienced so far; it was uncontainable, roiling around inside her long after he had stopped his furious thrusting. Long after he had rolled her on her side, still nestled in her, so that they lay back to front and he idly caressed her stiffly peaking nipples and the wetness of her feminine hair.

Long long after, with her hands still immobilized, and her body still the receptacle for his volatile manhood, she felt the power of his carnal domination and the keening pleasure of her surrender even while he had still not given her his.

It would come, it would come. She felt the urgency of his fingers as they played with her naked nipples; her own body stiffened once again with suffused excitement as her nipples bulged and he began seeking the pleasure point between her legs.

She felt him move as she wriggled against him, seeking the pressure of his fingers again.

She was insatiable. All that galvanic pleasure still was not enough.

How could it be enough with his fingers sliding all over her velvet heat and arousing her all over again? Stroking her turgid nipples, fingering them, squeezing them into hot hard arousal . . . She could not get enough of it, and he knew it.

He had all the time in the world. All the time his ferocious manhood would give him in its ravenous urgency to rush to completion.

But he couldn't; he wouldn't. Her body was too fascinating, too tempting, too ready to explode once again under his expert handling of her.

Her nipples were hard points of passion, just made for his caresses. Her voracious femininity had awakened only for him. He held her tightly, so she could not move against his rock-hard total possession of her.

He wanted to stay that way all night, just fondling her nakedness and thrust deep inside her.

But his lusty manhood ached for relief. And he heard the soft moans of her rising excitement as he experienced a ferocious urge to drive her to still another white-hot culmination.

He meant to start slowly, but he couldn't. The feel of her nakedness cupped against him, the thrusting power of his potent manhood, her writhing reaction to his caressing her taut nipples, all drove his body to frantic excitement and he began again the short quick forceful thrusts that had launched her into that smoldering culmination.

But instead, almost instantly, it was he who felt the oncoming surge of pleasure; and he couldn't stop it. It coiled and twisted around him, all over him, convulsed him and catapulted him into a racking wrenching release that drained his mind, his soul, his energy, his hands.

They rested, one on her breast, the other between her legs; he felt her give, and heard her poignant moan of pleasure, and then he slept.

And he awoke to the thumping pummelling of her fists against his chest and daylight filtering in through the pulled window shades.

"Damn you, Culhane, damn you."

Sometime during the night they had separated and he had turned his back to her. He rolled onto his right side and levered himself up on his elbow to look at her.

"A different story this morning, Alexandra? Are you never consistent—or is it that I've effectively circumvented your lust for hiding things from *me?*"

"*Nothing* is hidden from you, you beast," she muttered angrily. "Now untie me."

"Oh, I think not. I love having you at my mercy."

"Well, you've already had me and I'm not feeling particularly merciful, Culhane. So just untie me."

His cool gray gaze flickered over her enticing nakedness. Not a stick. Nor stiff-necked. And that alluring combination of her obdurate nature and her wanton willingness almost galvanized his desire all over again.

He jacked himself upright abruptly. There was no time to give in to the tempting thought of her tantalizing sex.

None. He swung his legs over the side of the berth and eased himself down lightly.

"Time for more mundane matters, Alexandra. Come."

"Well no, Culhane, I believe I will just lie here like your everyday strumpet and await your pleasure, since my hands seem to be tied."

His manhood stiffened instantly.

"And yet nothing between us is binding."

"The very thought makes me feel so secure, Culhane. Of course, I'm getting nowhere. And your restraint, by the way, was admirable."

He gritted his teeth; he had never met a woman of so many words. He wondered if she ever shut up other than when she was moaning with pleasure beneath him.

"Trust me or truss me, Culhane," she added maliciously. "Of course, my teeth are very strong—I wonder if I . . ."

He picked up his clothes and headed for the lavatory. He had to ignore her: breakfast was due imminently—and Khurt. It wouldn't do for Khurt or the steward to find them coupling on the floor.

He slammed the lavatory door emphatically behind him.

Alexandra leaned over the side of the berth, and then slowly rolled off it and down onto her bed.

God, she must be a sight: her hair all wild, her wrinkled black stockings down around her ankles, and the blasted sash of her robe wound just tightly enough around her wrists so that she could not work the knot free with her teeth.

Still, that little inconvenience would not prevent her from searching the compartment from top to bottom if that were necessary to find where he had hidden the bracelets.

Even with her hands tied, she could open the closet door, and if she leaned in far enough, she could run her hands all over the walls, search pockets and shelves—and suitcases.

His was there, alongside hers, and she opened it with no little difficulty. The hard part came next: using both hands as one, just digging in and lifting out each item of clothing and tossing it over her shoulder until the thing was empty, then canting her body to her knees so that her weight was on her legs, and leaning into the suitcase to feel around inside.

She was so quiet.

She was too quiet, he thought from the confines of the tiny

lavatory; he heard no noise whatsoever and that was very suspicious.

He threw on his shirt and eased open the lavatory door.

And there she was, rooting around on the closet floor, on her hands and knees, her tempting buttocks wriggling alluringly.

His lusty manhood shot right out from under his shirt and he padded across the room and knelt behind her.

She felt him there. Then his hand slid familiarly between her buttocks, and her whole body twinged with immediate arousal.

"Damn you, Culhane."

"Tell me to stop, you vixen."

His hand reached farther, stroking her moist feminine fold, and she wriggled backwards against him.

"You are a bastard."

"And you just can't stop, you wanton; you love flaunting your body and my express wishes. It's almost as if you were waiting for me to find you here. I would guess you were. And that you didn't find what you were looking for—but I did."

"And what was that, oh wise Culhane?"

"A naked and willing woman lying on my closet floor. Just what I need to begin my morning."

"How do you know she's willing?"

"I can sense it; I hear her breath catching as I caress her. I see her body stiffening with excitement because she knows I'm that close and she knows the feel of me deep and hard inside her. I see her swollen lips still ripe for kisses. I feel her wetness just at my touch. Her body arches to give me the ease to take her. She's very wet for me, she's so willing for me—you are, Alexandra, aren't you?"

"No," she moaned, curving herself into his hands and almost begging for his touch.

"You want me."

"No."

"Right now."

"No."

"I'm feeling you, Alexandra; you're begging me."

"*Never.*"

Both hands now in an orgy of caresses. "You're so hot for me, Alexandra."

"No," she whispered.

He lifted her so that her buttocks were canted upwards to give him better purchase to push at her with his granite manhood. He heard the groan deep in her throat.

"Your body just opens for me, Alexandra."

"It doesn't," she breathed and waited with tremulous excitement.

He pushed again and little corkscrews of glistening pleasure spiralled all over her body.

"You love that; you want that."

"*No.*"

He pushed again and her body spasmed.

"And now, Alexandra . . . ?"

". . . I can't—"

"You will."

She felt it, felt it intensely. It was as if his ramrod sex were the center of the world and she wanted it fixed in her. But him—only *him.* "Yes, now, yes . . ."

He drove into her in five ferocious pumping thrusts and she bore down and instantly the spangling pleasure exploded within her, all golden this time, molten, slithering through her womanly core and radiating out all over her body.

That, and then his wild plunge into the whorling ecstasy of her culmination, drove him to the eruption of his final drenching release, and he collapsed on her bone-weary and lethargic body.

There were things you did in the dark, in the sensual coupling and the privacy between a man and a woman, that if you thought about them, you could never look a man in the face again.

Alexandra sat in her usual place by the window, watching the passing scenery and toying with a biscuit which lay on her plate on the small fold-out table.

Her body felt languorous, cleansed of all tension and fight, buoyant with awareness and repletion.

They were due in Vienna in two hours, and she didn't want to move. Culhane was off somewhere and Khurt was due to rejoin them at any moment.

Everything had reverted to normalcy: the remnants of breakfast on the fold-out table, the cold cups of tea and coffee sitting next to the fat little silver pots, the crumpled napkins.

The seats were now turned back and stripped of their linens and covers, the upper berth tucked away and the laundry taken. The two suitcases were lined up neatly in the closet.

And herself, neatly dressed, looking the picture of a sedate young matron—except that she suddenly didn't have much to wear. Her corset and one of the two undergarments she had packed were in unwearable condition. Her silky blouse was crumpled, as were the black stockings which hung, wringing wet now, over the towel rack in the lavatory, and she had only one change of blouse besides to wear with her travelling suit.

And he had not returned the sash to her rumpled silk robe which now lay neatly folded in her suitcase.

The one next to his.

She was sure he had hidden the bracelets in his bag. She had searched it thoroughly again that morning after she had painstakingly gone over every conceivable inch of the sleeping car for a possible hiding place.

Suddenly restless at sitting alone in the compartment, she got up and went to the door and looked out into the corridor.

It was bustling with passengers racing for the last seating at breakfast, who, by the snippets of conversation she heard, were full of high good humor at the prospect of a short layover in Vienna.

She closed the door carefully behind her and joined the fray just to remove herself from the constricting atmosphere of the compartment.

But it was equally claustrophobic in the corridors. She slipped by knots of passengers engaged in conversation and finally stopped at the end of a long line waiting to get into the dining car. She decided to wait there a bit with the idea of ordering some more tea.

However the line did not seem to be moving, and as she stepped out of it and craned her head to see if there were some delay at the front of the queue, she caught a glimpse through the window of the second sleeping compartment in that corridor.

She saw a man and a woman in heated conversation, gesticulating, and she saw the man look up suddenly as if he had suddenly become aware that someone could see into the compartment.

Then the shade came furling down violently, and he wasn't there anymore.

And she wondered if she had imagined what she had seen.

The man was Khurt.

She felt a moment's uncertainty, but then it seemed perfectly clear.

The man was *not* Khurt—her imagination was running wild—because Khurt was with the doctor and was due to join them before the train arrived in Vienna.

The line moved, slowly, slowly, and she wondered if she could just waylay any steward, ask for the tea and then go back to the compartment and wait for Khurt.

A passing car manager told her they had suspended service to the cars until after Vienna, but she was welcome to stay in the line for the dining car.

She decided against that and had just left the line when she felt a hand grasp her arm.

"What the hell are you doing wandering around?"

It was Culhane emerging from the dining car, his briefcase under his arm. Instantly her hackles rose. "I finished searching the compartment, and there wasn't much else to do," she said acidly as he practically bore her through the connecting corridors towards their sleeping car.

"I don't doubt you did, Alexandra. In fact, I was sure you would."

"While you probably stuffed it all in your briefcase when I wasn't looking."

"Take a look," he said, proffering the case.

She looked at him, startled, and then opened the leather case and rummaged around inside.

"Nothing," she said in disgust, handing it back to him. "So the only other possibility has to be that you tied everything up while I was . . . dressing . . . and dangled it out the window."

He smiled a trifle grimly at her mordant humor; it wasn't a half-bad idea. "You will just have to check that out when we get there."

They made their way easily through the succeeding two cars and into the hazy air of the one next to theirs.

His arm shot out to bar her way just as the connecting door burst open and the car manager charged into the sleeping car, shouting, "Fire! *Fire!* Move . . . *move!*"

Ryder moved; he shoved Alexandra aside, pushed past the car manager, thrust open the connecting door between the cars—and walked into a wall of billowing smoke and the blazing remains of their sleeping car.

. . . Culhane . . . !!!

She thought she screamed it; she buried her face in her hands as she felt the blast of heat beyond her and he disappeared into smoke.

. . . Culhane . . . !!!

He would die, he would die—she couldn't let him die! She made a move to go after him, but the car manager held her back.

"He can't go through, ma'am. He has to come back or die."

"But what's happening? What are you doing?" she screamed as she fought him ferociously. *"Culhane! Let me go, let me go!"*

"Ma'am, we cleared out all the cars surrounding it, and we've got men working from the opposite end of it, where it's less dangerous. Ma'am, your husband won't be foolish, I promise you."

"But there could be someone else in there," she said agitatedly. "What if—"

"Don't ma'am . . ."

"Damn it! *Culhane,*" she cried frantically. "God, I can't bear this—it's so hot!"

"You'd best go back to the dining car, ma'am. Your husband will come soon. He'll probably come through any second now. You hear me, ma'am? Don't go another step farther."

"The whole train could catch—"

"No, ma'am, no. We're not twenty minutes outside of Northwest Station. It will be fine, ma'am, I promise you, if you'll just get back to the dining room with the other folks."

She wrenched out of his grasp and dashed to the door; then her heart plummeted. The heat was brutal, and the smoke clogged her throat and made her cough violently.

Culhane was nowhere to be seen.

Chapter 10

She was in the dining car, waiting uneasily with the other passengers when the train finally pulled into Northwest Station where a battalion of pump trucks and fire fighters were already waiting.

And Culhane had not reappeared.

The minute the train stopped, the conductors and car managers began the evacuation. Everything was to be left on board; passengers were to get to safety immediately; the cars would be safeguarded and no one was to worry about his possessions.

They filed out of the end car reluctantly and crowded around the station office to view the blazing car.

It was horrible. Alexandra pushed to the forefront of the spectators by the line of pumps spewing water.

But she saw nothing save the sputtering flames and the charred outer skin of the railway car, she heard nothing but the frightened murmurs of the crowd behind her.

Dear lord, where was Culhane?

And what would she do if he—if Khurt . . .

Oh no, there was no profit in thinking that she might be stranded in Vienna with no clothes, no money, no papers . . .

She concentrated on the rush of fire fighters boarding the train to water down the sizzling embers.

It was a mess, the whole outer shell of the car blackened and peeling, the window shades burned away, and what little she could see of the interior as black and charred as the outside.

. . . oh God—Culhane . . .

They were still hosing down the car when the conductor

mounted a dais and, with a horn, issued instructions to the milling passengers.

"There will be a minimum three-hour delay. We will be disconnecting the damaged car and the two cars on either side. The passengers in Triton, Jupiter, Juno and Athena have leave now to go aboard and pack. The company has made arrangements that anyone who wishes may spend the intervening time at the Hotel Leidesdorf on the Adalstrasse. Carriages have been arranged. You have only to notify your steward or car manager and you will be returned to the station in good time. I thank you."

The crowd dispersed, and she tentatively moved forward with those who were boarding the train.

She bit her lip and stepped into the vestibule of the boarding car. No one challenged her, no one detained her.

She moved through the connecting cars slowly, carefully, cursing Culhane, damning him for leaving her to cope with the fear that she might never leave Vienna.

And then she hesitated, consumed by agonizing misgivings about approaching the burned-out skeleton of the compartment they had shared, fear of what she might find there.

She eased her way through the passengers who were tentatively entering their own sleeping cars. The smell of smoke was thick and overwhelming; she almost gagged on it as she got closer and closer to the connecting door to their car.

She made her way cautiously, watching for conductors or anyone who looked official and who might stop her.

She absolutely refused to think that she might find Culhane in some kind of trouble—or dead.

She slipped through the first door, and slowly opened the second and walked into the scent of scorched wood and cloth, the smell of something still burning; the compartment was a smoldering charred mess in which nothing was distinguishable.

Culhane stood in the center of it, his suit and skin all sooty and singed, his briefcase tied ingeniously around his waist with the sash of her wrapper and his attention focused on what had been his berth.

She wasn't even glad to see him and he knew it; he swiveled towards her just as she stepped over the threshold.

"Don't say anything; I'm a bastard and a rotten son of a bitch for leaving you. I got that. We have to get out of here in one minute: the railroad officials are coming to examine the car, and we don't want to be in it."

She gathered her jumbled wits. "But . . . Khurt . . . ?"

He looked down at her. "They took someone out of here," he said grimly. "But this was meant for us—for real."

She backed away. "No . . ."

"Five incidents now, Alexandra, and two murders. There is no question. And Khurt"—his expression darkened and he seemed to be listening for a moment—"*someone* died in here."

"Could *he* . . . ?" She couldn't finish the question.

"Anything is possible."

"I saw him talking to someone earlier, when we thought he was still with the doctor."

He jumped on it. "Where?"

"In one of the cars, farther towards the dining room. A woman. And then suddenly he just wasn't there, and I thought I had imagined it."

"Nothing is *un*imaginable. *Nothing*," he reiterated. "Come, we can't do anything more here. This way now—they are coming through the head cars behind us."

"How do you know?" she demanded as she allowed him to push her out the opposite connecting door from the one she had entered.

"I just do," he said, and for once she didn't doubt him.

They slipped quickly through the adjoining cars and came out onto the station platform from the rear of the train.

"They will want to talk with us as well—but not now. Not until they find the frayed wiring by the upper berth light—as they were meant to. Then we will talk. Come . . ."

He grasped her arm and pulled her away from the station house. "I can't go in there like this; there has to be a place where I can clean up."

"The Hotel Leidesdorf," she said. "They've made arrangements there for the passengers."

He thought about it a moment. "That will have to do. It will just—the watcher is still with us, Alexandra. Hurry. To the nearest cab, and we'll figure out the rest after we get there."

It was a most impressive place, the Hotel Leidesdorf, rising five majestic rococo storeys above its arched and cavernous entryway, which was designed to make lesser mortals fear breaching this elegant domain.

To assure that none did, uniformed footmen attended the front door, their job to screen prospective guests and to keep out any who sought merely to spend an hour or two warming themselves by the massive lobby fireplace as opposed to registering for the lavish and exceedingly expensive rooms.

These guardians of the "gate" had been instructed to look out for the passengers of the Paris to Constantinople Orient Express and to direct them to the west suite of rooms, where they might tidy up and order room service for which the railroad would absorb the expense to ease the burden of the unexpected layover.

All of this the footmen explained to the passengers who straggled into the hotel in various stages of irritation. By early afternoon, they were fairly certain everyone had arrived who was coming, and the management bent its attention to assuring that everyone was fed and made comfortable in the lounge where the guests could amuse themselves at cards or billiards, reading or conversation by a roaring fire.

"The last thing we need is conviviality," Ryder muttered as he surveyed the room on his return from a hasty washup and brush-off which cleaned him up but did nothing to disguise the condition of his singed and rumpled suit.

"What *do* we need?" Alexandra asked cattily, having spent the intervening minutes taking care of her own appearance and now looking no less the worse for wear than he.

He looked down at her. She had scrubbed her hands and face, but there were still telltale smudges of soot in the places she hadn't thought to wash. And her hair was in bad need of combing; all she had done was fasten it back with some pins the matron in the lavatory had lent her. She had brushed the cinders from her skirt and her blouse as best she could, but her clothing had evidently suffered in the fire.

They looked nothing like the elegant passengers who lolled in the lounge waiting for a few boring hours to pass.

"We need everything," Ryder said decisively, "And most particularly we need not to be here. We must get out of here *now*, Alexandra."

She looked at him for one irresolute moment, and then he grabbed her hand and they ran.

The Cafe Landtmann was frequented, as everyone knew, by students and intellectuals, and so they did not look sorely out of place.

They sat at a table at the rear, sipping *kaffee*, and saying little because Alexandra had no doubt he already knew exactly what she was thinking.

Even though her thoughts were a jumble: Khurt might or might not be dead, the fire was yet another attack on them and everything was gone—*everything . . .*

. . . everything . . . ?

But he had his briefcase and their papers—that he had had the forethought to take with him. It lay on the table between them, cinder dusted and slightly the worse for wear, flat with papers and nothing else that she could tell.

She felt that she was going mad. Did she really care about the damned bracelets now, though she had fought a losing battle to blackmail him with them?

She thought not. She wondered how he was going to pay for the little food they had ordered in spite of the fact that neither of them felt like eating.

And she was especially curious as to whether he had any explanations for her now that would make more sense than his accusing her father of being a liar and a counterfeiter.

"Don't worry about money," he said crisply, sensing her immediate concern. "Everything is taken care of. I have a standing arrangement with certain banks throughout Europe since I have always needed to travel on short notice; so there is no problem there. We will find some clothes—soon—and we will keep moving until we can return to the station."

And then? And then? Even he didn't know. *Use her and lose her.* He had gotten what he needed; he could just leave her to Dzmura's mercy now. And Dzmura would make very good use of that unbridled voluptuous sensuality of hers.

It made perfect sense to do it—she would be the decoy, to distract and divert Dzmura whose tentacles reached everywhere. Except how could he do it . . . *now?*

She sensed some indecision in him, and it scared her.

Instantly, she envisioned him abandoning her to the zealots who argued heatedly in one isolated corner of the cafe.

"Why?" she asked tentatively, and then with more heat, "*Why?*"

"Dzmura is everywhere—I told you. You can trust no one."

"Not even you?" she murmured before she could contain the thought.

"Not even me," he said soberly, ignoring her caustic tone. "Least of all me. I have what I want, do I not, Alexandra?"

"But I don't," she snapped. "All this travelling and these violent threats, and there is no sign of Dzmura or my sister, and you won't tell me what it means. So how do I know?"

"*You* have no business being here; you should have stayed at Hidcote and trusted me to return your sister. But you wouldn't and now things have changed drastically and it is time to rethink the consequences."

"Tell me what there is to rethink: we are no closer to finding my sister; we have been subject to three attacks on the train alone and now Khurt—or someone else—is dead and I am still utterly dependent on you, only now you already have the one thing of value I had to barter."

He sent her a lazy look of amusement across his table. "Oh, I think not, Alexandra."

"Nonsense. That was all fantasy and imagination from someone's underground memoirs."

His smile deepened. "Isn't it too bad that it's all in my head? A woman could barter away a man's soul with such carnal sensuality. We made a bargain . . . you do remember?"

"What are you saying? Nothing has changed."

"The terms remain the same, Alexandra, except that my expectations are higher and so, I think, are yours. And no, nothing has changed except that I now possess the bracelets and I am willing to fulfill the terms of the bargain in spite of that."

She gritted her teeth. "But, my dear Culhane, this is a bargain in which *you* cannot lose."

"Nor you," he retorted, "but you would never admit it." He toyed with his sugar spoon for a moment, again hung on a moment of indecision. "Or"—he made up his mind—"I can make arrangements for you to return to England in the same luxury to which I have accustomed you; you can then remain at Hidcote until I track down Dzmura and your sister. So make your choice now, Alexandra, but let it be the honest one."

How sure of her was he? Even he didn't know. Or why he made the offer or whether he even really wanted her to go.

But he was very certain of what her decision would be—of what he wanted her decision to be.

And she was certain she didn't want to go home; she didn't need to think about it more than thirty seconds.

"I want to find my sister," she said tightly, refusing to give him the satisfaction of claiming victory over her. He had really done nothing of the sort; it had been merely expediency. In the dark, it was almost as if it hadn't occurred.

He nodded. He had expected nothing less, no admission that her decision was compounded of guilt and passion. It didn't matter: fate had handed her to him and he could never deny fate. Whatever he felt had nothing to do with it.

And now he had to make her understand while explaining as little as possible.

"This is the endgame, Alexandra: Dzmura is a man of vast interests and enormous power in his own country. He has a network of comissants and diplomats who carry out his orders. The watcher who has been following us is an agent of Dzmura, but we do not know whether it was an unknown or whether Khurt betrayed us. And so we must move with the utmost care: every action will predicate a counteraction. Dzmura enjoys a good chess game, and I will warn you now that he does not like to lose."

She shook her head wearily. "I don't understand any of this. Why take Allegra? And the bracelets—are they gone? Did they burn? Why the bracelets?"

"I went back to the burning car to retrieve the bracelets: I have them. They are charred to the point where nothing can be deciphered on them; they are useless as they are now—until we have the time and the safety to try to salvage them."

"They meant to destroy them," she whispered.

"I don't know. It could be that—or us." He took her hands. *"Why?"*

"I only have theories, Alexandra. Your father was renowned for his search for the parchments of Zoran, and he believed that in Alekkah he had come across something very powerful but unverifiable. And then your mother died and he returned home to find Dzmura in residence right next door when he expected him to be in Alekkah. I think that is when he produced the bracelets and on them *he* chiseled the code that was meant to lead me to what he had found.

"And because he did not trust Dzmura, he made a second set of bracelets and he hid them where he knew only I could find them . . ."

"And then he died," Alexandra said mordantly.

"And then he died."

"Because of the bracelets? What is so important about the bracelets?"

"Two things: one, whatever your father discovered, Dzmura does *not* want it to be found; and two, they are not bracelets."

". . . not?" she said faintly.

"*It* is a votive candleholder, actually a set, which your father broke into thirds. And there's a missing piece."

. . . oh dear lord—she saw it all instantly. Since they did not have the missing piece, they were courting danger with every move they made; their enemy would be watching, waiting for the moment they found the key to its hiding place . . .

Or did she believe him? *Did she?* He had said trust no one, and his tale was as farfetched as any ghost story her father had concocted.

Her father . . . He had purposefully shunted his family aside to pursue some secret, the clue to which he had incised onto a pair of stone bracelets in order to communicate with . . . *Culhane?* . . . *Really?*

. . . And she was going to continue on a journey with this madman? Oh, she had had it right the first time: a pirate and a madman and not necessarily in that order.

Suddenly she felt uncertain—distrustful and unsure. It was a fairy tale, utter nonsense, grown men pillaging continents in a race to possess—what?

Who could believe it?

And *he* could have staged the accidents, hired someone to attack Khurt and set that fire. If Dzmura could have agents, couldn't he? And could they not commit murder in the name of some reprehensible higher purpose?

He had said it: anything was possible, and that did not only apply to Dzmura.

But none of this mitigated the fact that Dzmura had abducted her sister and that Culhane was now her only resource. She did not need to make a decision; she had understood all along she had only one choice.

The matter of clothing was crucial. They would be making no more stops until Bucharest, with only a brief layover in Budapest: seventy-two hours of limitless travel, alone, together, with not even the tempering presence of Khurt.

She had chosen.

Or he had.

"It is impossible to buy ready-made; this is a city of royalty, society and loyalty to one's dressmaker. We need some newspapers."

"We will find clothing in a newspaper?" she said skeptically.

"We will find fire sales, which is as good as, if you don't mind a little fire damage, and I daresay *we* won't," he injected at her dismayed look, "It's the fastest and least expensive way to get hold of something to wear—when you're desperate and don't have time. We don't have any time, Alexandra. Waiter!"

He paid the bill, pulled her out of the cafe with alarming speed and hurried her up the street to Alserstrasse, where he paused for a moment as if reading a map in his mind and then turned left and walked until they reached the Gurtel, where, at an intersection, they found a kiosk which sold a bewildering array of newspapers and periodicals.

He chose two, a daily newspaper and a weekly, paid for them and hailed a cab.

She felt as if she'd been lifted up by a whirlwind; he knew everything: where to go, what to do, and he even had enough command of the language to make his needs known.

He told the cab driver to wait several moments, that he would pay extra fare, and then handed her one of the papers while he rifled through the first.

She looked uncomprehendingly at the gothic lettering— *Schwarz Gelb*—on the masthead.

"Ah . . ."

And he read the language too; she was properly impressed.

"Driver . . ." He dictated an address and the cab lurched forward. "Let me see the other." He handed her his newspaper, *Abendpost,* and made quick work of scanning the *Schwarz Gelb.* "Nothing here, but this is a weekly."

"And what does it say, in the first advertisement?" she asked curiously, still feeling reluctant to obtain clothing in this way.

"Words to the effect that a certain well-situated couple have been devastated by an unfortunate fire in their residence and seek to dispose of some water damaged property, including furniture and clothing, in order to raise some money to tide them over in this troubled time. I believe. So . . ." he looked out the window. "We are here."

Here was an elegant house on the Ringstrasse not far from the Cafe Landtmann, and it was not obvious from the facade that the inside was a smoky ruination.

Culhane rang the doorbell and a maid answered, and a moment later the lady of the house appeared; then he spoke rapidly, and with great conviction, Alexandra thought, wishing she could understand the words, and soon the woman invited them inside the house.

Everything she and her husband wished to sell was laid out in the double parlor with the curled and blackened wallpaper. Overhead, the frescoed ceiling bore evidence of water stain and the center panel of paintings was charred.

There was no furniture and the strong smell of smoke prevailed. Along the fireplace wall were racks of clothes and all around were small oddments of furniture: little tables, porcelains, paintings with scorched and gilded frames; a great Axminster carpet with an edge burnt off and spots of water stain; some jewelry of no intrinsic value; some statuary which had been broken in the course of saving the house.

It had been a backed-up flue, and the cost of reparation was so great, the woman and her husband had no choice but to divest themselves of as many of their belongings as possible in order to start over.

The woman was a little heavier and shorter than Alexandra, but her clothes were of the finest tailoring, though it was quite obvious that she had reserved what remained of her most fashionable *tailleurs* for herself.

Still, among the discarded items, Alexandra found several well-made jackets of jersey—the previous year's styles perhaps, but she didn't care—and matching skirts; a plain morning suit of wool cashmere; a severely cut dress of blue serge with black velvet trim; and a dress of amber satin with puffy lace-trimmed sleeves.

These she set aside, along with three blouses made of silk and linen, with decorative pleats and tucks and lace edging and the fashionable gigot sleeve, and a green silk wrapper with sawtooth lace trim, all clothing of finer quality and greater expense than she had ever owned in her life.

The amber dress did not fit, and she was absurdly disappointed, especially after having felt enormous hesitancy about buying some other woman's clothes for her own wear.

The rest of the garments could be tucked, tied, pinned and tacked invisibly to fit her more slender body and she was satisfied with that. She had no need of amber silk . . . still, it was such a beautiful gown. You could hardly see the minuscule holes where embers had caught and been brushed away. Nor were they detectable on the plainer darker clothes. And the odd water spot could be disguised.

She watched him lay their choices before the woman, including a wool cashmere suit and a suit with a cutaway jacket for himself, and negotiate the price.

They settled amicably after five minutes of haggling.

"And the price includes a suitcase; Madame knows our story and is properly sympathetic," Ryder said, behind the disappearing back of the woman. "They have more clothes and baggage than they know what to do with. Madame is just tired of last year's wardrobe, I think, and she might well have set the fire to force her husband to buy her new attire."

Madame returned in moments with a well-worn leather suitcase which she set on a table and then carefully packed the things they had bought in with an expertise of a veteran traveler.

Ryder thanked her with all the formal obsequies which were repugnant to him and expected by her: "I lay myself at the gracious lady's feet in thanks for her generosity in our reciprocal need and with gratitude that we were able to mutually assist each other."

"I convey to you and your lady a hand kiss for the occasion of your fortuitous purchase of the newspaper with the advertisement that led you to my door and our fruitful negotiation," she replied in kind as she bid them good-bye.

"And so," Ryder said, hailing a cab and mindful of the time, "a fire sale and we can present a respectable face to the world in fashionable clothing acquired for very little money."

He climbed into the carriage after her. "Driver—the Northwest Station." The cab lurched forward before he had time to settle himself.

Alexandra turned her head to look wistfully at the house on the Ringstrasse.

"Alexandra? I take it you have overcome your aversion to used clothes? I wonder how you will feel when we arrive in Tirhan. Trust me, amber dresses with lace-encrusted sleeves would be utterly useless there."

She shook her head irritatedly; she ought not to have even thought about that dress again.

She hated the way he could penetrate her inmost thoughts. She wasn't even allowed any puny little regrets.

And they had so much longer to travel; the wonder was anyone had any enthusiasm after all the time that had to be spent on trains and waiting.

Seventy-two hours to Bucharest—if the rolling stock had been replaced, and if the railroad officials had no questions that might detain them still further.

They came to the station just as the last of a group of passengers were boarding and hurriedly took their place in line.

"Ah, Mr. Culhane," the car manager greeted him. "A word with you." He motioned for an assistant to take his place and led Ryder and Alexandra to a more private place on the platform. "Now then"—he consulted his passenger list which was clipped to a hand-held board—"you have been reassigned to the car named *Triton*. Your former compartment has been gone over thoroughly by the police and we have deemed the fire accidental, due to a bad electrical connection. We think the poor soul who was caught in the fire had turned on the light and the thing just exploded into flames. I take it that person was your travelling companion?"

Ryder nodded.

"We have been asked to hold up the journey just a while longer while you make positive identification and arrange the disposition of the body."

"Madame will attend me."

"She need not," the car manager protested. "I will call the steward to show her to the car, and he will make her comfortable; in any event, we will not be long."

"Nevertheless, I'm sure Madame wishes to come with me," Ryder persisted, and the car manager, giving up, motioned to another lackey to find a conveyance.

Madame didn't wish anything of the sort, Alexandra thought resentfully as they waited; she could have been snuggled up on that nice large comfortable seat with a cup of tea and something substantial to eat.

. . . *safer* . . .

Her heart dropped; of course, how easy it was to forget that there was someone after them and that she did not have the wherewithal to protect herself.

If his story was true, and his suppositions sound . . .

She could never be alone again.

And neither could he.

Chapter 11

She slept, wrapped in the luxurious silk peignoir of an elegant Viennese lady of means who had had some bad luck, and she hadn't found it as difficult as she had thought to don another woman's attire.

Or had she become another woman altogether by wearing things that were not her own? Someone utterly unlike the suppressed virginal *her* who could have become just like her mother?

She let that interesting thought block out everything else, including the horror of entering police headquarters and knowing that Culhane was going to face the corpse of someone who had died violently and identify it as Khurt.

And he did so, quietly, calmly; and then they returned to the station. The sky had not fallen and everything was fine.

Except . . . someone else had died, the bracelets were blackened beyond use, Dzmura still had her sister and the mysterious watcher was still after them.

She did not want to think about that, not at all.

But she was; her mind, in its semiconscious state, conjured up a dream, and she was back on the Ringstrasse, alone, climbing the steps of the stately fire-damaged townhouse, dressed in an outfit she had purchased from the lady of that house.

But the person who opened the door was Allegra, bidding her to enter and come into the parlor, saying her husband was due home at any minute.

And in the parlor, laid out in proper and expensive coffins were her father and Khurt. And when she turned to Allegra for some kind of explanation, her sister had disappeared.

There was nothing else in the parlor but the two coffins and she could not get out of the room; locked in with the earthly remains of the two men, she was frantic with fear.

And then she heard Allegra, exclaiming joyously through the locked door, *Oh Alixe! My beloved husband is here. I've kept you here just so you could meet him.*

She heard a key in the lock and backed away just as Allegra flung open the door. *Darling Alixe, aren't you happy for me? See who's here . . .*

She moved aside so that the person behind her could enter—Dzmura, his hands outstretched and on them the cursed bracelets for which he had killed and had abducted her sister.

Dear Alexandra—I've just come from Khuramufar, and I know everything . . .

And then Allegra glided into the room, wearing the amber dress, her arms outstretched supplicatingly, her wrists encircled by the second set of bracelets all charred and blackened.

She heard herself screaming, You *don't know everything, you don't . . . you don't . . .*

And then a voice inside her mind thundered, *Run!*

And she turned, and she ran, but there wasn't anyplace to run and she crashed through the windows and felt herself falling . . . falling . . .

And Allegra above her laughing wildly, clapping her hands, full of ecstasy and crowing, *It's over, it's over . . .*

She jolted awake, shocked and disoriented, her heart pounding with fear, her mind not comprehending that it was morning and Culhane sat folded into the seat opposite her, watching her almost as if he knew what she had dreamed.

It took her a moment to come to terms with the fact that she was not in the house on Ringstrasse.

She struggled to maneuver herself upright, and he made no move to help her.

He was waiting; she saw it in the hard set of his gaze and in the firm way he poured tea from the tray beside him on the seat, handing it to her without a word.

Revivifying tea, to warm her vitals and warm up her vocal

cords. She sipped warily because the dream was still with her and eerily real even as they sped away from Vienna.

"Tell me what you dreamed."

And there he was, ever sensitive and instinctively knowing before she did what was going on.

"I was back at the Ringstrasse," she began hesitantly, "at the house; I was wearing one of Madame's outfits—a skirt, jacket and the blouse with the high tight collar. And Allegra opened the door . . ."

She almost couldn't bear recounting it. The words hung in the taut air of the compartment as if they had a life of their own: as if the dream were real and the conclusions to be drawn were absolute.

"She said, 'It's over . . . it's over . . .' So clearly. As I fell I heard it. And laughter—hers, Dzmura's—I don't know . . ."

"And he said . . . ?"

" '*I have just come from Khuramafar and I know everything.*' " She shuddered as she repeated the words.

"And the house—tell me again?"

"Exactly as it was when we were there, except for the items the woman wanted to sell. The fire damage, the fireplace, the door in the same place—everything. And the coffins."

She shivered again.

"How did you know who was in them?"

She thought about it for a moment. The dream-Allegra had not opened the coffins, yet she had known.

"I just knew," she said slowly. "There was no question, but it was frightening."

"And the locked door—you couldn't get out?"

"I tried and I tried . . . and she called Dzmura, her husband . . . "

"Yes," Ryder said, and it didn't seem to shock him the way it had stunned her. "It makes sense."

"Are you crazy? Dzmura and my sister make sense?"

"There are a litany of symbols in your dream, you know."

"No, I don't," she hissed, distracted by his complete acceptance of the logistics of the dream, "but it obviously goes without saying that *you* do."

"Listen: the coffins, an old building, falling, a suit with a high-

collared blouse, the bracelets—closed doors, locks, the fire damage, even the corpses you couldn't see, and your attempt to run
away—these components all have symbolic interpretations, all
negative, and all connoting failure and mistrust and unhappiness.
Even the corpses you couldn't see—they signify the end of something of great consequence to the dreamer. And the bracelets . . .
It is no accident that Allegra characterized Dzmura as her husband; bracelets symbolize matrimony . . ."

". . . No . . . !"

He didn't say anything more.

". . . How do you know? *How?*"

He didn't answer, almost as if it were a question that she need
not have asked and the answer was, he knew, that that was how
it had to be.

She leaned back against her pillow, exhausted and frustrated . . .
the end of something of great consequence to the dreamer . . .

. . . The end of everything as she had known it . . . as she
stewed in her guilt for not having prevented Dzmura from ab-
ducting her sister. *That* was what all the symbols meant, short
and simple. She would never forgive herself, and this was obviously going to haunt her dreams.

But to take that guilt within the context of her dream to the
point of Dzmura and her sister being married—that she did not
understand at all because it was utterly inconceivable.

"And he said"—Ryder interrupted her thoughts—"he had
just come from Khuramafar." He mused on that for a moment.
"He had just come from Khuramafar . . . and he knew everything . . ."

She shook herself out of her feeling of malaise. "And I said he
didn't. What could be meaningful about that?"

He didn't answer for a long moment and then he said, "That
is what you told me your father said—"

"That he had just come from—but he hadn't; he said he had
found the bracelets at . . ."

"Exactly," Ryder interrupted briskly. "The thing at the bottom of why you dreamed it that way. But the implication was
that he had just come from there, wasn't it? You didn't assume
that he had been at Alekkah all that time before he returned

home, nor was he notified of your mother's death at Khuramafar, was he?"

She thought back, her brow knotted. "No, we sent the telegram to Alekkah."

"Yet he said he had found the bracelets at Khuramafar; and they looked just like the usual artifact?"

"Yes."

"You could have assumed—you don't know how far away that is from Alekkah, but it is several days' journey—he responded to the telegram immediately?"

"I think so. And then we received one, giving details of his travel arrangements."

"... And all that took some time," Ryder went on, almost as if he were talking to himself, outlining the story, trying to fit the puzzling pieces into her foreboding dream. "But still, more immediate than if he had had to traverse the distance between Khuramafar and Alekkah and *then* respond to the telegram, the question remains: *why* did he tell you he found the bracelets *he* counterfeited at Khuramafar?"

He looked at her expectantly, and she shook herself again because she had not been totally listening. "Why he . . . *what* . . . ? Why he told me?" She gathered her wits, trying to follow his deductive course when she had not heard a word he said. "I never questioned why he told me. I believed him, Culhane. Why should I not?"

"Indeed; but the fact remains, he disrupted his life and yours—and Allegra's—and even mine in the pursuit of Dzmura. So, if he is forced to return home and has been crippled in the chase and knows there is nothing more—especially because his quarry has cornered him on his very own turf—and he produces an artifact he claims to have found at a place you now know he has not been in ten years . . . why would he do that?"

She couldn't see where he was going with that reasoning. "He wished Sir Arthur to believe that he had been engaged in legitimate Museum work there," she said testily. "Nor would he have been the first in the field to pretend he had gone someplace he hadn't."

He ignored her argumentative tone. "I hadn't considered that conclusion, actually; interesting because the focus is also on why it was important enough that you dreamed it. It made some impression on you, even if you didn't know it. So it seems likely that your father wanted to leave me a further message—and that can only be that there really is something to be found in Khuramafar."

In light of all that, she wasn't in the least surprised when she automatically chose the twin of the garb she had worn in the dream and the high-collared blouse to go with it.

She hated having no underclothing and only the thin black stockings, but the style of the blouse was such that it draped over her breasts and waistline in the new fashion and disguised what might otherwise have been obvious. The previous day, she had requested some pins as well as some personal items from the steward; these he had provided so that now she could twist the waistband of the skirt and fasten it more tightly around her waist. The jacket covered everything else up very nicely, and when she viewed herself in the mirror, she thought she looked rather stylish though somewhat harried.

She did not like Culhane's conclusions. After all, what could Dzmura be hiding—besides Allegra? He exported antiquities; they had always known that. He was slick and dangerous, but she had always understood that, if Allegra had not.

He had been her father's enemy? There had been absolutely *no* hint of that. And he had never come round in the years before her father's death. Allegra had not mentioned him, and Renwick House had looked abandoned.

None of this made any sense. If she could just comprehend why Allegra had gone with him . . .

—no . . . That was wrong; she had meant why he had *taken* Allegra—

. . . or had she? Was it even remotely possible that Allegra had gone with him . . . *willingly?*

The thought was like a dash of cold water in her face.

Allegra adored him.

Dear lord—Allegra *worshipped* him . . .

How prophetic could a dream be?

She sank onto the edge of her seat and saw him watching her, a peculiar light in his eyes, and she rounded on him accusingly.

"You thought of that."

"First thing," he agreed coolly. "Why did *you* think Dzmura invited us all to dinner?"

She felt as if someone had punched her in the stomach. She knew exactly why. To show *her* how important he was to Allegra.

"Yes," he said, reading her horrified expression accurately. "And more than that, to show all of us how much power he could wield. He waved his wand and we came, and then he played games with us. He was looking for the bracelets, you know. He could not break into your house himself, so he engineered the next best thing."

Her eyes widened. *"Allegra?"*

"He is a master of many arts. It isn't inconceivable that he hypnotized her somehow."

Her body felt cold . . . the ritual searches and the periodic nature of her sister's obsessiveness, the way she never saw her, the way she never knew . . .

She bit her lip. Culhane had surmised and he had not told her; she hated him for that—and she hoped he intuitively raised that thought right out of her mind too.

"I don't understand why he wants the bracelets," she said finally, his voice hoarse with anguish and frustration.

"I don't know for sure; I'm guessing. But since we have only just deduced that your father made them, I think it's safe to assume Dzmura has always known. In point of fact, your father made a great fuss about them, as you've told me, and created an impossible story around them. Why would he? For what reason? Look at the chain of events: Sir Peregrine is home and not in Alekkah, nor is he intending to return anytime soon because, as he discovers, Dzmura is flaunting the fact that he lives right down the road from him.

"Your father begins working on the bracelets; Dzmura withdraws, watching to see what your father will do. And suddenly there are these bracelets and the story concocted about them that sweeps the archaeologic community which then brands Sir Peregrine a senile old fool.

"Sir Peregrine waits for Dzmura to move. Probably Dzmura is seeing Allegra without anyone knowing about it. By your own admission, you were busy with your mother and then with helping your father with the bracelets. Probably you were never very aware of what Allegra was doing.

"And so he has time, Alexandra—all the time in the world to track down his enemies and wreak revenge. Always, he can afford to wait.

"And very soon, your father dies and Allegra begins seeking the bracelets, because Dzmura knows it is only a matter of time before I return to England and he will have to match wits with me.

"He knows that I have been on his trail, and that I *will* be able to decipher the bracelets. I am more of a danger to him than Sir Peregrine ever was because I can come after him. And I will. And this is what he fears:

"That I will be the only one in the world who knows exactly where to find him."

She didn't ask why; Dzmura's power was all pervasive. She almost didn't need to know. But she never expected his next words.

"I think he killed your mother in order to pull Sir Peregrine off the track and get him away from Alekkah."

She shook her head violently. "No . . ."

"He was there."

Yes, he had been, he had been; she remembered the day, the moment between him and Allegra she never wanted to think about again. Her mother had been so sick. And she had been so busy. And Dzmura had been there . . .

. . . been there, been there . . . The words reverberated in her mind like an echo. Who had been there? She and Allegra and no one else except Dzmura, and who knew what power he had had over Allegra even then?

But she knew, she knew; she had just pushed it out of her consciousness and had refused to use that knowledge to make any other inferences.

"I don't want to know any more," she whispered.

His face was impassive. "The danger remains. I possess the bracelets and now the knowledge that there is a missing piece. Dzmura wants them, make no mistake about it, Alexandra. We are not even one step ahead of him, nor do we even have an inkling as to whether your sister even wants to be rescued."

"Nonsense," she snapped. "Of course she does. And you know where to find her. So that is what we'll do. And if you won't—I will, and I won't count the cost."

"Damn it, you haven't had to," he retorted, jacking himself upright and pacing furiously around the small compartment. "This is not some serialized adventure in the Strand for God's sake. Nor is it some medium in which you can work off your tedious guilt about how things should have been. Things happened the way they happened. Fate and circumstance can't be planned. The intrusion of a Dzmura could never be reckoned by provincial innocents living in a goddamned nunnery outside of London. Dzmura could not have foreseen your father's clever plan. Nor could you have foretold his retaliation. And that is the end of this bloody nonsense."

But it wasn't. It had always been cause and effect: if her father had not stayed in Alekkah because of *him*, he might be alive today. The lure of working with Culhane had drawn him when he might have finally made his peace through being at home; everything that ensued was purely because Culhane had gone to Alekkah, and not because her father had stayed.

They made the early seating for dinner; she felt so overwrought by all the revelations she could barely taste what was on her plate.

And Culhane was disinclined to talk; rather he had the air of a man constantly at attention, as if he were soaking in every nuance given off by everyone around him.

"This trip is debilitating," she muttered as he unlocked the door to their compartment on their return. "It's endless."

"It takes roughly two weeks to travel from London to Tirhan," Culhane said mildly. "You just never thought to ask."

She threw herself into her seat and stared out at the darkness. "And so now we lock ourselves into this room tight as a drum and wait for some unseen watcher to attack."

"He is out there," he said, settling himself opposite her. "It is only a matter of time."

She bit her lip. "If you mean to scare me, you don't."

But he knew better; her mobile face reflected her uncertainty and her wariness. The whole story defied belief, from her father's concocting clues to their chasing after her sister who might or might not have been a willing dupe of the omniscient and powerful Dzmura.

And Culhane's theory that Dzmura had had some complicity in her mother's death didn't even bear thinking about.

It was even harder to credit given the sane atmosphere of the dining car, where couples and families and strangers dined together companionably in a world where there was no Dzmura, only the faint thrilling rush of courting danger by venturing into exotic climes.

Sanity sounded very seductive.

"Can we order some tea?" she asked finally, seeking some way to grasp onto order and normalcy.

. . . Tea. *There is nothing saner than tea,* he thought. In spite of the fact that they had drunk gallons of it already that day. Tea was the great leveler. It brought calm, quiet, contentment, warmth.

And it was something to do.

He rang for the steward and fairly soon the man returned with the usual tray and porcelain pot, the scent of it permeating the room and dissipating the tension.

Until Ryder locked the door and carefully drew the shades.

She had poured by then and sat in her corner, swirling the liquid around in her cup before she took the first scalding sip.

Tea—so normal, so mundane, so *hot* . . .

He cupped his own and inhaled it.

The heat and scent of it permeated his head and cleared his mind. He understood completely the attraction of ceremonies grounded in the ritual of drinking tea.

It required both caution and abandonment of the senses. It demanded that you move into it slowly and savor the moment. And it rewarded you with warmth and delicacy of taste and refreshment.

And after you were done, it could parse out your future.

He looked at his cup thoughtfully and then transferred it to his left hand and rotated the cup left to right several times to disperse the tea leaves.

She watched him curiously as he went through this little rite and then looked faintly annoyed as he stared down into his cup.

He set it aside. "Let me read yours. Take it in your left hand . . ."

She nodded and followed his movements exactly and then handed over the cup.

"Ummm," he murmured, holding it in his left hand and gazing into it. "So . . . this is how the predictions work: it graduates downwards, with the rim, or the part closest to you, indicative of present time; the sides mandate the future; the bottom anytime beyond that.

"The handle as I hold it represents you, so that whatever I read closest to the handle will transpire soon.

"And immediately, I see a long journey . . ."

"That is hardly a prediction," she said dryly.

". . . a number . . . two, two—the number of days until you complete this aspect of the journey. But still, misfortune seems to hamper you; there is waiting danger—"

"You are making this up," she interrupted exasperatedly.

"I wish I were, damn it! Still, the danger is diminished somewhat because you have someone who will protect you, and there is an initial—Z—and things will not be easy for you. There is a man who is interested in all things relevant to you. But you mustn't make hasty decisions because very much further on in the future, you will find happiness."

"How nicely steeped in reality that little parlor game is, Culhane. At least this time you left me some hope."

He handed her back the cup without comment and then wiped out his cup and poured another for himself.

"It is what it is," he said finally.

But she found this frustratingly fatalistic. "You believe that?"

"I believe in fate—I told you that. And I don't fight it."

"I *do.*"

"Still, the great wheel moved and here we are and nothing you could have done would have changed it."

She hated his saying it because that made her feel even more at the mercy of the unknown. Or maybe it was just because of Dzmura; if there hadn't been a Dzmura there would be no need to debate the hand of fate.

That thought was interrupted by a brisk rapping at the door. "Bed change," the steward sang out. She rose to unlock the door to admit him, and he entered with his armload of fresh linen; but he wasn't Cecil and he had a gun.

"*Don't move.*"

Alexandra froze. Culhane stood poised, alert; not at all intimidated, not even surprised, she thought.

The steward tossed the linen onto Alexandra's seat and pushed the door closed behind him with the heel of his shoe.

He held out his hand. "The bracelets, please."

Everyone knows about the bracelets, Alexandra thought wildly.

"They were lost in the fire," Ryder said calmly.

"Oh, I think not, Mr. Culhane. I feel certain you still have them. You, Miss deLisle—search him."

She looked at him and he nodded imperceptibly. She moved over to him and began tentatively running her hands down his arms and down the jacket that was one of his purchases the previous day.

There was nothing in his pockets, nothing concealed in his shirt, nothing behind his back under the jacket, nothing in his pants pockets.

Through inscrutable gray eyes, he watched her slowly pat every inch of his upper body, and she couldn't tell for one moment what he was thinking or what he intended to do.

"Go on, Miss deLisle—his lower torso too. Don't be afraid. There's nothing there to be afraid of. Every place you can think of, Miss deLisle and I mean that."

His tone was so snide, so nasty, she just knew he would have no compunction about firing the gun if she refused to cooperate.

She knelt down in front of Culhane and began feeling his legs slowly, the right one first, her gaze at a level with his most private parts, her face stinging with anger and embarrassment that he had to be subjected to this.

"Stay down."

Culhane, *sotto voce,* barely discernible through her quaking fear.

"Don't take your time about it, Miss deLisle; I'm perfectly willing to tear this place apart—after I blow you apart."

Her hands started shaking.

"There's nothing, nothing."

Boom! He fired once into the ceiling. "Would you like to rephrase that, Miss deLisle?"

She swallowed hard. "He doesn't have the bracelets."

Boom! He fired into the floor just to the left of where she knelt.

"Perhaps you can try again, Miss deLisle. He may have secreted them with the crown jewels, if you comprehend my meaning."

She bit her lip and hesitantly slid her trembling hand between his legs and into the soft center of his manhood.

Boom! He shot into the soft, back pillow of the left-side seat. "Don't enjoy it too much, Miss deLisle, because I'm aiming right there, next."

She sucked in her breath and looked up at Culhane. His face was impassive, his hard gray gaze fixed on their tormentor.

"The bracelets are not there," she said finally, removing her hand from the solid warmth of him.

"Don't move."

Culhane let out a barely discernible breath in the mounting tension.

"Miss deLisle . . ."

She didn't move.

"Miss deLisle"—in his voice was pure impatience and hair-trigger anger.

—*"roll over—now!"*

She heard Culhane, ducked and rolled onto her left side towards the lavatory door, and he dove over her prostrate body and into the rising arm of the intruder, the shot blasting into the ceiling as Culhane crashed into him and they fell to the floor.

Boom! Another blast, this time into the panelling, as Alexandra scrambled to her feet looking for something with which she could immobilize the assassin.

They rolled around on the floor, Culhane's fingers like an iron manacle around the maniac's gun hand, and she jumped out of the way, one of her feet coming down hard on the assassin's arm.

He stopped thrashing for one moment, and she jammed the heel of her boot into him again. And again. And then with super-human effort, he thrust himself against Culhane's body and pitched him onto his back. Culhane retaliated instantly by ramming him sideways and throwing him onto the floor again and they wrestled furiously for control of the gun.

And then she couldn't see it—she thought it was between them, or that Culhane had pushed his arm downwards so that if he fired, the bullet would carve a hole into the outer wall of the sleeping car.

She thought, she thought . . . They grunted with fury now, pulling, pushing, tugging, kicking. The assassin was deft, dirty—he was biting and spitting and scissoring his legs in an attempt to squeeze something between the bony part of his knees.

Culhane restrained him through sheer will, his hand bending and twisting the man's gun hand until it seemed like only the devil could make him relinquish his grasp on it.

And then he lifted the man's hand and rammed it against the floor. And again. And again.

The hand went limp, but the fingers still maintained their death grip on the trigger.

And she couldn't do anything; there wasn't one thing, not one object, she could use to defend herself and help Culhane.

And then the man's limp hand tightened and jerked upwards as he used it to lever his body forward which took Culhane by surprise.

The assassin's hand came up between them, and Culhane wrenched himself away, just as the gun went off and the bullet blasted into their assassin's chest.

And she saw it. She saw the blood spurt from the wound, the man's hand relinquish the weapon as, almost instantly, the life and the force of his hate flowed from his body.

Culhane inched backwards and kicked the gun away from the now limp hand towards Alexandra.

She picked it up and tossed it onto the seat, staring in horrified fascination at the body.

"We have to get him out of here," Culhane said, and she looked at him blankly.

"The son of a bitch tried to kill us. There will be no nice burials for him. Open the window."

"Are you crazy," she said.

"You think I'm going to recite prayers for this maniac? Open the damned window!"

She climbed onto the seat and crawled to the window, released the locks and turned to look at him.

He got to his feet and awkwardly lifted the body over his shoulder like a sack of potatoes.

"Watch out. Don't look."

She didn't think she could, and she wondered who was more cold-blooded. Then the thought came that if Culhane were not, they might not be alive . . .

She heard him slam the window closed emphatically, then the slick clicks of the locks as he set them back in place.

She turned slowly to look at him.

His face was drawn, his eyes stone cold.

"*Requiescat in pace,*" he said tightly. "And may the bastard's soul rot in hell. Now let's get some sleep."

Chapter 12

He slept, soundly, exhaustedly, bonelessly, for such a large man.

But she couldn't sleep; she was frightened of dreams, and of the reality that they could add another attempt, another death and a frightening theory about her mother to the litany of events surrounding their pursuit of her sister.

And it was even scarier to think that all Culhane's party tricks and his speculations might have a grain of truth in them and she would be better off returning to London and leaving the chase to him.

It was so tempting to think about going home.

But she didn't want to go.

She wanted to find Allegra and *then* go home, and she couldn't do it without him.

It had been very clear all along that he could do it very easily without her.

She stiffened with fear. The only irrefutable thing that aligned her with him was the fact that Allegra was with Dzmura.

Everything else about the situation could be readily interpreted two ways, including the events of this night.

. . . What if the whole thing were a ruse to scare her off? What if the assassin wasn't dead, and it was all a carefully thought-out and eerily acted plot to frighten her away?

What if the dream had no symbolic consequence whatsoever and he had just made it all up?

And the tea leaves, for God's sake . . .

What if the lady of means in the house on the Ringstrasse had hypnotized *her* somehow so that she would have that horrible dream?

Anything is possible . . .

He had said it—why? To throw her off the track? To make him seem both candid and beyond such tricks? And now he had the bracelets.

How stupid had she been? To offer herself to her enemy and then just fall asleep?

He was a seductive monster . . . as sincere as life and as treacherous. The only vestige of power she had now was her passion.

Her passion was sure to betray her.

She turned restlessly and punched down the mound of pillows on which she reclined. She was still dressed. She had known she would not be able to sleep, had felt fretful and apprehensive, and she knew why.

She was trying to remember every last thing that had happened between the time she had received her father's letter about Culhane and his death.

Everything compressed into a jumble and she suddenly was in a maze, running, running. She was naked, and it seemed to her that her hair was so long it covered her nudity but did not impede her progress. She was afraid and sensed that she was being followed; she wanted desperately to know who pursued her.

She burst out of the maze and into the woods and searched frantically for someplace to hide, running here and there until she came upon the hulking trunk of a huge dead tree.

The thick bark scraped her skin as she inched her way around it, and not a moment too soon. Her nemesis was on her heels, and she could see, she could see . . . it was her father—but it wasn't. It was his face, but his body was that of a dwarf; and he was panting from exhaustion as he stopped to survey the line of trees that bordered the woods.

Alexandra. . . Alexandra. . .

She heard him calling, calling . . . but it wasn't his voice; it was her mother's, eerie and plaintive, echoing through the woods . . . *Alexandra, come to me, come to me . . .*

She stood frozen in place behind the tree.

It wasn't her father, it wasn't her mother. She wasn't in the woods—and yet she was, and it looked like Vienna and it seemed she had always known it.

Alixe...Alixe...

She knew that voice, but she wasn't going to budge; what if it wasn't her sister? And worse, what if it was?

She peered around the crusty trunk of the tree.

The dwarf was still hovering by the border of the woods, but this time, he bore the face of Dzmura.

Alixe...Alixe...

He was calling her, but it was the voice of Allegra reverberating through the dense trees; and she cowered against the old dead tree, sinking down to its roots and huddling there until she suddenly realized she was actually sitting on something.

She reached beneath her bottom and pulled out a pair of boots, kidskin tie boots, her boots, and she felt so relieved to have something of her own, she put them on just to warm her cold feet.

But there was still the matter of the dwarf with the changeable faces and damning voices.

She had to get away from him, she had to; she felt the fear creeping up again because he was coming her way and she had to move ... When he came parallel to the tree, she darted behind him and ran for her life.

But the verdant walls of the maze had turned to stone and she couldn't get away, and again she had that febrile sense of being followed.

And the voices, interchangeable: her mother, her sister ... echoing in her mind.

She clapped her hands over her ears and kept on running; and suddenly there was a window in the wall—escape, welcome, wonderful escape. She ran to it, threw it open and something leaped onto her cold naked body and knocked her down.

An animal, vicious and purposeful, seeking its prey. Its yawning jaws were inches away from her head, and she closed her eyes, surrendering to death—but nothing happened.

When she opened them again, the wolf-face had turned into Culhane—and she screamed ...

... and screamed, wildly, crazily, physically pushing his weight off her body . . . kicking, wild as an animal herself. He was coming after her, his arms like a vise around her to contain her roiling body . . .

Alexandra!

The wolf knew her name.

Alexandra!

The wolf was the dwarf, and they were trying to get her . . .

"Alexandra!"

She was being shaken violently and awoke with a start to formidable darkness and the sense of a presence weighting her down, and she wasn't sure that she wasn't still in the throes of her dream.

"Culhane?" she whispered uncertainly.

"I'm here," he said roughly.

"You can move now."

"I think not; you went a little crazy."

"I'm awake now," she assured him, but she still wasn't sure. She pushed at him, and he felt whole and hot and real, but he didn't move; there was no give in him at all, which was exactly what he was like for real, she decided, so she must be awake.

"You were screaming."

"Yes." She closed her eyes, and she could see it—could hear them, her mother and Allegra—and she hadn't the slightest doubt the dream arose out of her guilt and her feeling of complicity; she did not need Culhane to interpret it for her. "I remember screaming. There was a window—and a wolf that I thought was going to kill me. And then he turned into you."

"And you still kept screaming."

"I probably did," she agreed tartly, very aware now of his weight pressing down on her body which, in one way was comforting and protective, and in another, as dangerous as the threat of any wild animal. "I really am all right now, Culhane, do you suppose—"

"No, I don't."

She drew in her breath with a faint hiss. The darkness enveloped them, and she could not get the sense of that dream out of her head.

Maybe he knew it.

His touch was soft and soothing. She felt no sense of urgency in him, only the solidity of his weight and his presence—the reality of him enclosing her and making her feel safe.

What kind of sorcerer was he?

In an instant, all the sensation of the dream had evaporated; she felt weightless, tranquil, somnolent.

There were no barriers here; there was just the darkness, and him, and a little world of their own, and that was enough.

She thought she slept.

The darkness enfolded her, and his arms; he was close, so close he seemed to slip into her consciousness almost as if he had always been there. She could not remember a time he had not been part of her in the deep rocking darkness of that night.

It took nothing at all for him to bare her skin to the melting feel of his. The touch of him nourished her, pacified her, heated her.

It was enough to lie in his tight embrace and feel the darkness beat against her naked skin like the palpable desire that hovered just out of reach.

She wanted nothing of passion this night. She wanted the warmth and merging of naked skin against naked skin. She could feel the texture of him, so different from her, and all encompassed in the world of darkness he had created between them.

His arms, his legs entwined with hers, his head pillowed softly just near hers, his lips a breath away from her ear.

She inhaled in concert with him, taking his life force into her own and examining the rhythm of it with an elemental curiosity.

She moved her hand against his bare hair-roughened chest to feel the pounding of his heart.

His breath quickened and excited her own.

Movement against her leg and the ineffable sign of his overt arousal rubbed gently against her skin.

Soft . . . he was so soft, unfurling for her slowly and patiently, resting the lengthening of him against the long line of her; there was so much time in the dark, there was no rush in the dark.

Nothing moved in the dark. There was only the soft soughing of their breathing and the fluttering urgency of her burgeoning need for him.

Slowly, slowly—the darkness hugged her, and she felt the push and the prod of him tight against her leg. She had only to move it to welcome him home.

Softly, softly, she felt the sweet pressure of his kisses in the dark, and gently so gently she moved so he could fulfill that soft promise.

He slipped into the moist haven of her. She turned to join with him, and side to side they rocked together in the soft ancient rhythm of mating.

So gentle it was, so beguiling, this soft lush merging; skin to skin, mouth to mouth, self to self, all by feel, all in the dark.

Time spun outward, endless, immeasurable, luxurious, all their own.

Her body felt luminous, skeined with gold, all hot and elusive and threading through her veins. It was subtle, tantalizing, supple in the way it spiralled just out of reach and smote her with little darts of pleasure that penetrated her vitals.

She was like satin, all slick and sumptuous, suspended for one lustrous moment in that glittering space between the crackling break of sensation and the culmination.

And then she moved and it poured through her like molten gold, sliding radiantly all over her body and eddying away into soft tendrils of pleasure that went on and on and on . . . and he came, erupting convulsively, pumping his seed deep into her shimmering alluring sex.

And time stopped.

And they slept.

When she awakened, she couldn't remember how she came to be naked in her bed and in his arms.

She had a vague recollection of a soft glistening sense of pleasure, but surely that had been a dream . . .

Or maybe not.

The scent of their sex permeated the compartment; her clothes were on the floor, his beside them, and his legs were wound around her body as if he meant to keep her where she was.

She felt a clamoring panic and an instant desire to escape him.

"Oh, I think not," he whispered lazily in her ear.

"You don't think," she snapped, wrenching against the forearm that held her, an iron bar across her midriff.

"May I say neither do you?" he said acidly. "But you don't need to *think* to obey the terms of a bargain."

"Thank you, but we've done that already," she muttered, struggling against him.

"But I prefer you wide awake and willing."

"And I prefer you far away and disinclined."

"You win," he said, dropping his arm abruptly.

She wrenched away from him and swung her legs over the berth. "I like winning, Culhane."

"I know you do," he said as he heard her groping awkwardly across the dark room towards the lavatory door; the light switched on suddenly, and then the door closed behind her shadowy naked form.

When she emerged, five minutes later, she could just see him across the room, lying back comfortably, his hands behind his head, waiting . . . and watching.

Something in the taut set of his body as he lay there struck an answering chord in her, and she understood suddenly the nature of the power of a woman.

His sole focus was on her; he couldn't see her clearly, he could only imagine the whole of her naked body that he had touched so intimately in the dark.

But she could see him, the full sprawling length of him, the blurred features of his face, and she could imagine the touch, the feel, the scent of him in the dark.

And her body twinged with the memory as surely as his did, instantly, blindly, yearning for the replication of it.

It was a wonder, her body; just the shadow of it could command the stiffening respect of his. Their memories were simultaneous and powerful, linked through their flesh, not through their minds.

He had only to see her, the outline of her limned against the low light behind her, and his desire initiated the demand.

Her body and no one else's, and his was hers to command.

The feeling was heady, potent.

She compelled his desire through the memory of her naked and willing in his arms. He wanted the recreation of the naked essence of her surrendering in the dark.

She did not need to ask what to do. He was all there for her, rigid and perfect and waiting, and all she had to do was take him and make the memory.

Wordlessly, she climbed onto the berth and straddled his hips so that his rampant manhood was aligned against her buttocks and he could see her finally and fully in the wedge of light that sliced into the room.

She felt the power of her nakedness as his hands began the slow slide from her thighs up to her midriff and still upward towards the heavy swell of her breasts.

She canted herself forward for him and braced her hands on his shoulders as he cupped her breasts and thumbed the taut thrust of her nipples.

She felt a spangling rush of pleasure, and then the imperious nudge of his manhood.

Slowly, she sought the firm ridged tip of him, and in the throes of the lush pleasure of his fondling her nipples, she settled herself slowly and delicately downwards and downwards until she covered the whole ramrod length of him.

The sense of containing him was stunning, the awareness of control utterly extravagant and it was all she could do to stay still and savor it when she wanted to ride him until he was insensate with pleasure.

She writhed against the towering length of him as he caressed her straining nipples, teasing, jolting, circular little movements that increased in intensity as he fingered and squeezed her pebble-hard tips into a glittery spasm of pleasure.

Her hips rocketed against his in response, her body undulating feverishly against the sensation he created in her naked nipples.

He squeezed them gently, gently, her body silently screaming with urgency; and she ground her hips downwards against him, as she bounced, wriggled, gyrated against the hot hard power of him, enticing him, tantalizing him, surrendering to the sensual power of his expert hands, demanding that he yield to her potent erotic sex.

And in that one perfect moment, she lifted herself and ferociously plunged her body downward just as he reared his hips back and drove his pumping manhood upward explosively, and they collided in a frenzied and shattering carnal culmination.

She rode it, rode it out, pumping every last drop of his spuming release from him until she was sure there was nothing more, nothing ever again, not in her, not in him, and that the perfect memory of it would be enough to bind them forever.

And then slowly, she sank to his chest, and truly fell asleep.

They reached Bucharest the following night, and in the morning, they packed before breakfast and the final short run to the seaport town of Varna where they would take the ferry across the Black Sea to Istanbul.

She stared out the window as their train edged ever closer to the sea.

Somewhere in the far distance, Dzmura awaited them. And with him, the final clue to the puzzle of Allegra.

Yet nothing that she saw looked exotic or unusual. Here was a countryside as fresh and verdant as any in England. There were thatched houses and grazing animals, and she had one unsettling moment of thinking that the train had indeed turned roundabout and she was in England and the whole thing was a gigantic hoax.

But then, far away in the distance, she could see the light litmus blue of the horizon, and a sense of disaster crashed down on her.

The steward knocked on their door, singing out, "Varna Station in one half-hour, Varna Station in one half-hour . . ."

"*He* is none the worse for wear," Alexandra murmured. "Obviously a man very used to the eccentricities of his passengers, even if they want to lock him in the pantry."

"Are you all set? Take the shawl. The voyage will be cold and rough; you'll want to be as warm as possible. We'll be at sea about eighteen hours."

She looked shocked, but there was, as with everything, nothing she could do about it: Varna was the gateway to the east by the easiest and most direct route.

She dug out the shawl and wrapped up the bar of soap and the pins and baking soda the steward had given her and placed these in the suitcase. Culhane added the few items the steward had acquired for him, and the spare ill-fitting suit purchased in Vienna, and they were packed.

A waiter came and removed the breakfast tray. Another came to strip the linen and reverse the berths back into seats.

Twenty minutes later, the train pulled into the small station at Varna, where, down rolling streets that sloped down to the sea, they could see the docks and the rusted and creaking ship that would ferry them to Istanbul.

Alexandra fought her feelings of misgiving as they cautiously made their way out of the compartment and into the corridors to debark.

The air already was fresh and clear and cold and she drew the shawl more tightly around her shoulders as Culhane preceded her out of the vestibule of the Midas car and onto the platform of the station.

It was like a big farewell party, with the passengers crowding around to exchange addresses and good wishes.

There were carriages waiting here to take them down to the docks, and slowly, passenger by passenger, the crowd thinned out until only she and Culhane were left—which was as he had planned it.

So they were the last to arrive, the last to go aboard and the last to be assigned a stateroom; no one but the officer in charge had knowledge of their whereabouts.

And as night darkened over the sea, they were the last to fall asleep, each keeping a silent vigil, certain the other had given in to the lulling rolling of the ship and the thought of the long night and the reckoning ahead.

Chapter 13

Her first impression of Istanbul was bright white glaring light. She had never seen such intensive sunlight in her whole life. Her clothes and her skin absorbed it; she almost melted in it.

It was a city in which old and new clashed, domes and minarets intermingled with more modern European buildings, and those were interspersed with towering palms and orange groves and the gates and walls surrounding the city.

Beyond, the sun reflected off the Bosphorus onto the white-wash of the native houses. Narrow alleyways crisscrossed the city like throbbing veins, leading ultimately to the bazaar with its tented vendors and extravagant merchandise.

It was a panoply of color and movement and seismic heat; Alexandra began to feel faint.

Ryder sensed it. "Look, the hotel is just there, courtesy of the Orient Express. Not everyone wants to go native—immediately."

"But you would, were I not with you?"

He shrugged. "I have friends certainly, but your presence will raise more questions of etiquette than we want to deal with right now. You need a room, a bath, some clothes for this heat—and a hat. Don't argue, Alexandra; I'm not going to abandon you."

But she wasn't so sure. He was on home ground now and needed her less than ever, and that special sense of power that always embraced her in the dark moments of their passion inevitably dissipated in the light of day.

It just wasn't enough to coerce him to take on the burden of her inexperience; she could see it clearly. It was one thing to be chasing after Dzmura through the streets of Europe, quite another to pursue him past the mystical gateway to the desert.

But did she not know that outside the ornately carved doors was the teeming sunbaked city, she would have thought she was in one of the more gracious European hotels.

Even though the decor had a faintly Eastern cast, with the extravagantly tiled floors and inlaid furniture in the lobby and the rugs scattered everywhere, there was a quiet sense that things were done here just the way they ought to be.

And she needed that bath, she needed a real bed. The sea journey had been rough and rolling at best, the accommodations minimal.

Nor had she known whether she was a good sailor. She did now, with one horrible bout of nausea as her baptism, then her willful stubbornness taking over and refusing to allow it to happen again.

The room at the Summer Palace Hotel seemed as big as a house after sharing the close confines of a sleeping car for almost a week, and it contained a separate room for bathing as well as a smaller privy.

This was luxury, and an unstated elegance. The decor could have been said to be spartan, except that it reflected the opulence of the East; the bed, centered in the room, was covered with silks of glowing colors and a pile of satin pillows. Intricately designed rugs covered the glowing parquet floors, and the ceilings were high, the windows arched. Sunlight filtered through painted wooden lattices. The cabinets for clothes were built into the walls, their latticework doors painted to match the room. Two small dressers of hand-rubbed walnut stood beside the bed and against one wall. Alongside the windows were a small round table and two chairs.

There were no electric lights here; on the dressers and on the table were oil lamps and on the walls brass sconces for candles.

"A seductive room," Ryder observed in a hushed voice. "Just take off your clothes and sink into sensuality."

"Even here," she murmured, gliding over to the window to peer through the latticework onto the sun-shimmered blue of the Bosphorus.

"Especially here. The scent of the forbidden permeates the air and the hedonistic gluttony of the pashas dominates lives. It's all around you, Alexandra. You can touch it, feel it, take it anytime you want."

"Every man wants a harem," she said tartly, trying to interject a feeling of reality into the suffocating perfume of their rising desire.

"Or one woman who can be his harem—all things, all the time."

"And how can that be when it is true that all these women do is bathe and adorn themselves—and sit around naked awaiting the whim of their master?"

But even as she said it, she could envision herself so, adored and adorned, reclining seductively on that very bed, naked but for jewels and veils artfully concealing and revealing.

There would be slaves to do her bidding and the finest of everything for her delectation. She would spend her days solely thinking about and readying herself for him, devising new ways to expand the horizon of their pleasure.

All her body need do was mine the memories of their past encounters and willingly submit to the opulent pleasures of surrendering to him, solely at his want and whim.

She would be Scheherazade, seeking new ways to rewrite the carnal story of their lives.

But when the time came that he tired of her, she would have to yield to a younger, fresher, firmer body and that she could not stand.

And could he read the sensual scenes being played out so graphically in her mind?

"I would love to have you naked and waiting and willing to submit to my every desire," he murmured seductively. "The women are taken young, and they know no other life. But you would come to it freely, as a prisoner of your passion and your voluptuous desire to join only with me."

To be his odalisque, to be naked and ready only for him . . . she sighed at the luxurious thought of it. But one could not give him such control so easily.

"And what does your harem slave receive in return? Surely the same fidelity, the same availability, the same naked readiness to be taken at my want and whim?"

"You would think the same rules applied, would you not, that if a woman submitted herself in all her nakedness to the passion of the one who desired her, that he would offer the same willing capitulation to her needs and her passion? But here it is not so; here the man rules supreme and the woman must yield her nakedness whenever he wishes to take her."

How powerful were his words and fantasies; he spun them like silk all around her, trapping her in her rising desire so easily she could almost have begged him for the privilege of becoming a slave to his desires.

The luxurious bed and its tactile covering beckoned to her. She wanted to feel the silk beneath her skin, she wanted to sink into the lush creamy satin pillows, naked, and await him there.

She felt so hot suddenly, so damp with succulent yearning. Her clothes were an impediment to all those lush forbidden desires that, were she ready and waiting at his bidding, she would be experiencing even now.

And he watched her and he wanted her; she could see the enticing throbbing bulge of him and her memory supplied the knowledge of the rest.

"So," she murmured dreamily, "she spends the day suspended in an erotic dream, preparing herself, and hoping that the memory of her naked surrender is so carnally gratifying to him that he can't survive without her yielding her voluptuous nakedness to him again and again. Imagine *him* a slave to her erotic femininity. Imagine if she denied him the sight of her nakedness when she is his to take as he pleases."

"But that would never happen."

"Anything can happen," she whispered. "You said so yourself."

"And if I wished to take you?"

"I would submit at your command."

"Then I command it: lie on the bed."

She sent him an insolent look, hesitating for a moment as if she might refuse, and then she climbed onto the pillows and reclined there like the most compliant of slaves.

"Lift up your skirt."

She twisted her body slightly and, with that same haughty look, pulled at her skirt, slowly raising it higher and higher over her stockinged and gartered legs, upwards still to reveal her bare thighs and the curve of her buttocks, and higher still until the hem brushed the thick thatch of feminine hair between her legs, and then she paused provocatively, a breathless excitement skeining through her body.

"Lift up your skirt."

He repeated it calmly but with an edge to his tone that set her tingling nerve endings keenly on edge.

Now she willed him to demand to see her nakedness. Now she wanted him to yield.

She waited, savoring the hot arousal of revealing herself to him on her terms.

He knelt at the edge of the bed and waited.

She licked her lips and slid one hand downwards over the sumptuous curve of her buttocks.

He removed his clothes, slowly and deliberately, as she watched, releasing the power of his jutting manhood to the flame kindling in her greedy gaze.

She lifted the skirt a fraction more so that now he could see the shadow of the lush curling hair that crowned her femininity. And she waited, savoring the fact that he had given her his unrestrained nakedness in response to her challenge.

He came closer to her. "A man does not wait on the provocation of the woman who is the slave to his desire. This defiance would bring harsh measures to assure his woman's compliance— he would never accept such flaunting of his wishes. If he demanded his woman lift up her skirt, she would pull it up instantly and without coyness and show him that tempting nakedness he wished to see. Now lift up your skirt, Alexandra, and let me see."

She felt the greatest pull to resist him and the greatest desire to submit: which was the stronger when excitement ran rampant through her veins?

But she knew the answer: she raised up her skirt for him because *she* wanted it and not because he wielded the power.

And he knew it; he lifted it right out of her mind and waited for her to give in.

Slowly, slowly she bared herself to him, and slowly slowly he made his way towards her until he could just reach the inviting softness of her thighs.

And then, slowly again, so slowly, he parted her legs and lifted them around the hard jut of his hips so that his lusty manhood was poised directly at her feminine fold.

Then with one forceful thrust, he took her; she was his, willing and ready and waiting for that drive of virile domination.

She understood it completely; a woman could submit to that rampant power and sumptuous pleasure, could want it always and endlessly for her own.

He was the center, the rock around which her feminine source revolved; in that explosive moment, he was the world.

He held her hips and watched her face; he could feel every nuance of her movement as she met each subtle thrust of his masterful sex.

This was different, this was new; her hips were canted upward so that she felt each firm stroke to the fullest.

This was his power, this was his strength; and all she could do was surrender to its breathtaking potency.

She could not prolong it, the pure erotic feel of him pumping tightly and tautly against her escalated her excitement.

He owned her; he could possess her forever. He felt a pure crystalline moment of joy as her fathomless pleasure built and built as he drove deep within her carnal core.

And suddenly it came, pure and crystalline, cascading through her like a waterfall, a gush of sensation, a wash of erotic pleasure so stunning that she felt she might dissolve.

And he was so deep within her, feeling the rush of her shuddering body; he moved; he twitched his hips to press his rigid manhood home—and he ejaculated in a spewing culmination that took five minutes to subside.

He held her eyes, he held her body as the volatile sensations rippled away into memory. His memory was hers; she felt it, she understood it and she knew she was in his thrall.

* * *

Sometime later he left her, and arranged for her bath. Shortly after that, a parade of hotel stewards came marching through the door bearing pitchers of hot water, followed by a maid bearing a tray with soaps, towels, perfumes and oils.

She shed her clothes languorously and slipped into the steaming marble tub. The water felt rich against her body and was redolent of scent.

She floated, her body weightless; water lapped against her nakedness as she languidly washed herself, sensing its movement in her very pores, her every sense heightened and radiantly aware.

At these moments when she was alone her femininity unfurled and the carnal memory of the hour past became a prelude to what could come later.

Her erotic need could never be sated. He had made this voluptuous little world, and he could now wall her up within it. She felt wanton, willing to surrender her nakedness all over again.

Her body was sumptuous with yearning; the lush backdrop of the pillowed bed beckoned to her and she climbed onto it, still naked, her body glistening with the bath oil, and stretched herself out on the satin pillows.

The thick material felt creamy against her skin. The lustrous colors glowed against her sinuous nakedness.

She sensed her own power, her abandonment to the lure of the senses. She had never felt so feminine or so potent; a hundred men might have killed to possess her just as she lay, but she was enslaved by the desire for only one.

She was drifting into a dreamy sleep when she heard the door open.

She knew it was Culhane by the way her body stiffened with contained excitement. And she knew what he saw, her glistening naked body in supplication to him.

She heard him setting something on the floor, and then came the interminable waiting, the essence of her thralldom to him, the waiting while he paced the room and feasted on her nakedness from every angle.

His eyes touched her and she writhed with excitement as he savored the nature of her wanton capitulation.

She stretched her body like a cat, shimmying with overt invitation, but he made no move to come to her. He stood across the room, indulging himself in the pleasure of her nakedness.

She felt that impatience to bend him to her will, but slowly the attentuated thrill of the waiting added a pungent excitement to her yearning.

Time dissipated in concert with her growing hunger for him.

And then, suddenly, a drift of delicate silk was enveloping her loins and she sensed the weight of him kneeling on the bed beside her.

And his mouth dragging slowly and hotly over the silken caress of the fabric at the curve of her buttocks. He kissed her there through the silken web of her desire, and he kissed her there; at the flare of her hips into the soft pillow of her buttocks, and he kissed her there, at the dark round mark on her hip, and there, on the silken promise of her burgeoning nipples. And there, through the veil of silk on her luscious lips. And there, through the silken shroud of her femininity.

Just *there* . . . and she rolled over gently and into his arms, there, and invited his kisses, there.

And he took her, there, and she ground her throbbing sex against the scorching heat of his silken tongue, there, until there was nothing but her writhing nakedness and the silken spasms of her total surrender.

And later, while she slept, the sensuous silk draped over her shoulders and back, he undressed himself and mounted her, pressing himself inside her and covering her with the languid weight of his body, while she was all unaware.

She awoke to the heat of his nakedness possessing her, fully and deeply and she arched her buttocks firmly against his hard male root.

There was no movement between them and only the space of a breath between his lips and her ear; she could hear him and the rising excitement pounding in his chest.

And she could feel him in the most elemental and primitive

way possible. He nestled against her, shimmying to press himself deeper within her.

She pretended to ignore him and tried to go back to sleep.

He pressed against her more firmly.

She turned her head away.

"And what if she . . . ?" he murmured in her ear. "And I told you, she cannot." He thrust against her again, and again she ignored him.

He grasped her hair and tugged on it to pull her closer to his mouth. "You were born to be an odalisque, and naked in my arms. That is your nature and why you waited willingly for me. And now it is my wont to take you as you sleep, and your only choice is to submit."

And as he whispered into her ear, he began swiveling his hips against her in a hard tight rhythm that she could not escape.

He drove into her like a piston, in short thick explosive thrusts; he wanted her surrender, and he felt in the volatile heat of his forceful possession of her the resonating response that he sought.

And suddenly, she was open for him, in motion for him, urging him on with the lure of her churning body until he could withstand no more and he catapulted involuntarily into a galvanic and drenching release in total abject surrender to her.

In the morning, Alexandra wrapped the translucent drape of silk around her spangling body, went into the bath and slipped into the water which still remained from the day before. It lapped against her skin, cool and rich, soaking into her pores and alleviating the intensifying heat.

She wrapped the silken shroud around her hips, knowing it hid nothing; she had packed all her forbidden secrets in the dark.

Or perhaps not. Culhane lay awake, watching her progress into the room, his naked body sprawled across the sumptuous satin pillows, waiting, waiting, his male root thrusting out of its thick nest of hair like a separate part of him, waiting, waiting for her.

The room was shadowed and heavy with the scent of their

shared sensual memory. Time stopped, fragmented by their rising desire.

Her body grew taut with it as she moved her hips provocatively; had she planned for this, counted on this when she had stepped out of her bath and into the realm of his erotic world?

Did one never experience enough of the forbidden fruit of desire, or was it she alone who could not find satiety?

In the filtered light of the morning, in the aftermath of his tumultuous possession of her, she knew her sole yearning need was to provoke him past all endurance until there was nothing but his driving passion to possess her and only her.

And she loved the way he looked at her; she wanted him to look at her just that way, as if he knew her and he could never know her and there were infinitely more secrets to be explored and revealed and her nakedness enticed him on to a journey of erotic discovery.

Her body was perfect; she had never felt it more than when she stood naked before him, and watched the slate gray of his eyes slide over her like a touch.

Her nipples tightened into two taut peaks, her hips writhed as if she could feel him there, her body stretched, remembering the pleasure, inviting it all over again.

And he was aware of each subtle enticing movement.

Her body shimmered with awareness. Her emerald eyes glittered with the deep wanton knowledge of carnal memory.

She waited only to obey, and he waited to command only to draw out the unbearable erotic excitement between them.

His body got harder and harder as she squirmed with the waiting, and he could feel her explosive tension and his own.

"Strip away your concealing silks," he ordered finally; then he watched with great pleasure as she twisted her body so she could untie the knot which rested on the erotic little mole on her hip and the silken material slid to the floor to pool around her bare feet.

"And now naked odalisque, come to my bed and I will tell you how you may pleasure me."

She came to him without protest, her body tense with need, and she knelt on the edge of the bed.

"Lie down," he ordered, and she gracefully rolled onto her back and waited with heart-stopping excitement as the heat of his body and the erotic scent of him radiated out to her in waves.

He made her a bed of rich satin pillows, positioning them just under her hips so that her body canted upwards, and so that her legs were wide apart, straddling a saddle of satin, revealing everything to him in that way.

She licked her lips as he made no move to mount her; his eyes possessed her and she involuntarily ground her hips against the lush softness of the pillows, seeking some tactile hard heat and finding nothing but a soft empty promise and her spiralling carnal need.

"You will not move."

"Take me then."

"My odalisque has not yet learned," he murmured, prowling around the bed like a sleek panther. "I make the demands."

"Someday," she ground out in the throes of her voluptuous yearning, "I will have my own harem—ten men who will do my every bidding. I will have them every which where, Culhane; there will not be a part me that will go untouched when I command. Think of it, just think of it—the pleasure of it ..." She groaned at the thought of it, at the pure vision of it: all that powerful masculinity naked in her hands.

The thought of it made him even more rigid: he could see it—that glittering green gaze smoldering with insolent surety that she had only to snap her fingers and each of the ten naked muscular thralls would be slavering to do her every bidding.

"But now the pleasure of it is mine," he growled, "and your nakedness is mine, and no one else will ever touch you while I possess you."

Ah, the eyes, the eyes, turning haughty with a defiance that no harem slave would dare reveal. Only she, most wanton of them all, waiting only to submit to his desire, understanding fully her carnal nature—and his.

She lay there amidst the opulent satin pillows, her body stretching and undulating, wild and wet with longing for the joining with him.

He knelt beside her and laid his hand on her tender inner thigh just below her arching womanhood, and she moaned at his hot pleasurable touch.

He moved, positioning himself just where she could see his thrusting naked maleness, and he moved his hand slowly so that it covered the whole of her feminine mound and rested there so she could feel the power of him encompassing all of her.

Then he shifted so that he was crouching over her, balanced on his knees slightly above her shoulders, his granite manhood cradled between her breasts, his hand still cupping the moist yearning center of her.

And then suddenly his fingers slid within her and she grasped his legs tightly as an intense wave of pleasure rolled over her.

This—this, she had been waiting for this—the pure naked feeling of thrust and hardness and movement within her; it didn't matter how or what, it was the essence of him possessing her, and she bore down on the penetrating thickness of him, raked her fingers across his naked flesh in ecstatic submission to his will.

His mouth scraped across her belly, downwards and downwards, until his tongue nestled at her pulsating point of pleasure just at the moment she wanted it there.

She felt the rocking of his body against hers as the rigid flesh of him caressed the soft rich flesh of her in concert with her movements, her pleasure.

This was what it meant to be in thrall to her carnal instincts—this voluptuous willingness to open herself to anything, to do anything, to experience everything nakedly and fully and utterly at his hands.

His hands enslaved her, his tongue tormented her with its sensual surety of just where she needed to feel its wet hot caress.

Her body met him, compliant, rich, hot, wet, submissive to the knowledge of the voluptuous pleasure to come.

She felt his mouth all over her, simultaneously with his thrusting fingers and the forceful drive of his towering manhood against her soft flesh.

She was naked and full of pleasure for him, only him, just as he wanted, his naked odalisque at his command, where she wanted to be—forever.

Her body tightened and her hips gyrated upwards violently at the sudden jolt of pleasure the thought gave her.

. . . naked forever in this rolling, roiling, crashing flood of sensation that spumed through her blood like a violent waterfall breaking over the hard wet edge of rocks and slick slippery mud . . . primitive, elemental . . . wet, wet, wet . . .

. . . wet on her body, wet between her legs, hot wet vestiges of pleasure as he succumbed to the convulsing heat of her, jamming himself against her soft lush flesh, taking her wholly into his mouth at the moment he spewed his hot wet pleasure onto her body . . .

And it was done; he lay heavily on her body, his face buried between her legs, his senses fully aware of her abandoned surrender to him, of the sticky residue of his desire between them.

He felt her curious hands exploring him, and he inhaled the perfume of her sex, a perfect moment in the aftermath, as seductive as anything he had ever experienced.

They lay still this way together, listening to the sounds of morning permeating the silence: the street sounds below their window, the wail of a horn, a loud cry from a caravan passing through the bazaar, the shuffle of footsteps in the corridor beyond the door, the light flick of a door being opened—a shadow—he did not know if they were asleep or aware . . . a dream invading their erotic world and bringing them back to reality—

He jolted awake suddenly into silence and fingers of sunlight streaming through the latticework shutters.

She was asleep, her arms over her head, her nakedness provocative even in repose.

Slowly and carefully he eased himself off her to the scent of something different in the room.

He saw it by the door then: a small folding table on which someone had placed a brass tray with a fat porcelain teapot and two cups. And the scent pervading the room was chocolate, rich, sensual and hot.

It woke her. She propped herself up on her elbows as she watched him take up the pot, pour a thimbleful of its contents into a cup and take a tentative sip.

And then he became aware of her and jutted into life at the very moment he might have fallen down dead.

The sour taste was there, just under the perfume of the chocolate; Dzmura knew they were here and there was no time, no time.

She saw a different kind of tension envelop his body, and she scrambled to her knees.

"We have to get out of here—fast," he said tensely. "We have to leave almost everything. Get that bag—there are some underthings in there. Take those and this tunic, the boots. You have to cover yourself completely. Don't argue—just do it."

But doing it meant donning the body-shrouding tunic and veil of the streets and a pair of thick leather boots, well used and broken in to be sure, but not the stuff of her erotic dreams.

But all that had dissipated at his barking command.

In five minutes, they both were dressed, he in a long woollen cloak and desert headdress that made him look as exotic and foreign as any man she had noticed in the streets, and she in the voluminous tunic which covered her entire body, the matching veil which revealed only her eyes.

Everything else, except his everlasting briefcase which he had tied around his waist once again, lay in disarray on the floor.

"We will need to obtain a new wardrobe in Tirhan anyway," he said practically as he rubbed some henna from a little clay pot into his face. "I wish your eyes were not so green. Keep them down as much as possible. They must not suspect we are not what we seem."

She had so much trouble shifting her mind into the realms of danger. And it was so easy for him.

It was over, the sultry capitulation of the morning and the night before; it had become just another fantasy realized and he could heartlessly expunge the memory.

But she could not, so where did that leave her? There was nothing there: he was galvanized into action and she had reverted back to being a nuisance. In the light of day, a killer still pursued them and nothing was black and white; and everything was gray.

He threw some money onto the bed, pulled out the gun and then eased open the door.

"The way is clear," he whispered. "Keep your head down, Alexandra; the women here are veiled and submissive, and you will do exactly what I tell you. Are you ready?"

"Yes," she breathed, her assent barely carrying beyond the muffling material of her veil.

She felt her heart pounding furiously as he stepped into the corridor; and then she couldn't see him, and a horrible wave of panic washed over her.

Rashly, brashly, she followed him into the hall.

Chapter 14

Anyone could have been the enemy.

She could see only the hem of his *aba* and nothing else—she could have been following the wrong person for all she knew.

And the heat, the heat was abysmal, a testament to his wisdom in having her discard all her clothing. Under the enveloping folds of the *feradge,* she still felt as if her body would melt in the heat.

The air was close and still, dust occasionally swirling up and around her on little bursts of energy from the movement of the crowd, and rent with the sounds of conversation and haggling.

They were walking the bazaar, the most auspicious place to lose oneself in the whole of Istanbul.

They looked no different from a hundred others pacing back and forth among the stalls, examining some merchandise here, bargaining for some food there, arguing the provenance of a piece of antiquary stoneware across the way.

They moved in a leisurely way, which belied their need for haste; now and again, Culhane would pick up something and inquire as to a price, and then carry on a heated harangue with the stall owner, asking the nature of the ancestry of one who would demand such an outrageous sum for such an inferior item, and eventually he would put the item down and they would move on.

The slow pace of their progress grated on Alexandra's nerves, even though it was obvious he knew what he was doing. They had melted into the crowd, become a part of its color and noise; and anyone having spotted them and followed them from the hotel would not have set them apart from dozens of other people milling around the bazaar.

The worst of it was, he had told her nothing; there had been no time for explanations, only spur-of-the-moment flight to the busiest part of the city where, at some point, they could slip through the crowd and make their way—where?

She was wringing wet from tension when they finally skirted the outer edges of the bazaar and cautiously followed a crowd of natives down yet another circuitous route through winding streets and back alleys which finally let out onto a main highway and a railway station around which there was bustling activity.

It was as he had expected. "There is a train," he murmured. "It will take us to Tabriz, and that is enough for now."

"But how do you know?"

"I know. Come, I will make the arrangements. But nothing is certain. Danger is all around us."

She could feel it, she was sure she could, as she followed him into the station house and settled herself on a bench as inconspicuously as possible amidst the crowd of travellers already milling around and waiting for the train.

Head down, veiled and submissive . . .

She was the very picture of a woman of the harem in city dress, but there was nothing submissive about the combative line of her body as she bent her gaze and avoided his altogether.

"The train leaves within the hour," he murmured, suddenly standing beside her.

She nodded her head slightly to indicate she had heard him.

But they could not carry on a conversation; their language might be remarked upon: a spy might be lurking about in spite of the fact that Culhane sensed nothing untoward about the passengers who waited.

But anything was possible, he had said so. Now in addition to everything else he had killed a man, he possessed the weapon of a murderer and she had allowed those hands that had killed to seduce and possess her.

Anything was possible, and everything was probable in the company of a man who could conjugate dreams and read tea leaves and intuit her thoughts in the blink of an eye.

For the briefest disloyal moment, she wondered if her sister was safer with Dzmura than she might be with Culhane.

It was the most rickety-rackety train imaginable. They sat among a raft of passengers who looked exactly like them and they did not talk, and for two days Alexandra stewed in a kind of simmering fear that nothing was what it seemed and everything was upside down and the other way around. She almost believed that if she went home to Hidcote at this very moment, she would find Allegra there safe and sound and worried sick about *her*.

While she would have been changed irreparably because she had believed the improbable stories of a madman and had gone with him to Persia by bargaining away the last thing of value she had left.

And it did no good to reflect on her gullibility and stupidity when he had the money, the power, the secrets—all—in his insanely seductive hands.

Two days, two long interminable days during which they had no conversation and he had treated her exactly as if she had been his woman, in the custom of the country. She could barely contain her irritation and she knew he knew it.

They arrived in Tabriz the morning of the second day and debarked into a sea of excited bystanders who had come to see the arrival of the train. Alexandra was pushed and prodded along by both the crowd and Culhane who had hold of her sleeve and was forcing her the way he wished her to go.

She wasn't sure she wanted to comply. Tabriz was the mirror of Istanbul, heat and dust and golden minarets reflecting the sun. But there was less of a sense of urgency here, at least in those around her, and only Culhane who hurried her along seemed to be a man with little time to lose.

They came eventually to the bazaar and here, as before, he slowed his pace, poking through one stall and another, making comments and issuing insults and leading her through a series of streets devoted to various crafts—leatherworking here; the coppersmiths, their tools resonating like drums as they beat the metal into submission, there; the grain merchants behind them, quietly measuring out the lifeblood of the city in their brass scales—until they entered the area where merchandise was sold.

Here the stalls were larger to accommodate all manner of goods from exquisite carpets to foreign armaments and every last seller leaped out of his stall at the sight of a prospective buyer and begged him to "Buy here, buy here; that man there will cheat you, but I will give you the fairest price . . ."

Once again, she sensed that restrained urgency in him; his seeking, his bargaining seemed serious; the words spewed from his mouth, and a moment later, he handed over the money. At the end of a half-hour, he had an odd assortment of things tied onto the back of a young and somewhat recalcitrant mule.

He had bought two ill-fitting sheepskin coats, several woollen blankets, a brazier and a sack of coals, four goatskin flasks, a bag of dates, a keg of water, a cork helmet, and a box of dried meat.

She was so tired she stopped keeping track, and when he led her to what passed for an inn, she was grateful for the respite in spite of the crudeness of the place, the pallets that passed for beds and the awful stench emanating from the street.

He left her there for a half-hour more, and when he returned, the thing was done and there was no use protesting about it: he had seen to everything. They would be travelling by mule, with a caravan that was leaving for Tirhan early the next morning.

The road to Tirhan wound through the mountains, but Alexandra had not expected the bone-chilling cold or the snow or the landscape that changed from barren to breathtaking in the blink of an eye.

Nor had she foreseen that she would still have to play the role of the subordinate woman, swathed in the abominable tunic and veil and wrapped in blankets and the sheepskin coat as the caravan made its way through rain and wind, mud and snow, over the rise of the next low mountain and the next, with nothing for company but her own thoughts and her waning interest in the events around her.

Culhane was nowhere to be seen; but then, he could not be observed in casual conversation with her if they were what they seemed. He would only share her meagre blanket at night surrounded by the body heat of the animals, the light of the coals and the low murmurs of men pitching their tents.

There was something infinitely more uncivilized about this than anything else; she was no more to them than an animal herself, a necessary burden at best, just as she had characterized her usefulness to Culhane.

She had days and days in which to think as the caravan paced slowly through the rise and fall of the mountains and sloped down the long winding trails to the barren plains.

They passed other caravans, and little villages in the middle of nowhere, set along an improbable sward of green; they passed a frontier fort, and they plodded through endless arid plains and then up into the hills and mountains again, following the track of those who had gone before.

They saw purple sunrises and glowing orange sunsets and sometimes a vista so beautiful it took her breath away.

And time crept by as they fought the elements. They were often buried in snow and camped along the outskirts of one small village after another in order to wait out the weather.

In all of this, she could do little but some of the cooking for herself and Culhane. Even at this she was inept with the brazier, while he had the skill.

She imagined the others joking about her and wondering what it was that kept Culhane so steadfastly by her side.

In the end, she had no one to rely on but herself for company and she inevitably retraced the unbelievable events that had led to this moment on a muddy dirt road in a torrent of rain, riding a mule in a caravan trekking its way to Tirhan.

They came to the gates of the city in the pouring rain moments before the portals were to be shut, and they made their way through gratefully, exhausted, drowning in rain and mud.

But within the walls it was not much better; the streets were a sea of mud, and while kerosene lamps lit the doors of shops and houses, there was no way to determine where they might find a room for the night.

Alexandra sat stiffly on her mule, waiting for the moment

when Culhane would give her a clue as to how they were to proceed. She watched him exchange obsequies with the men of the
caravan and settle some money upon them, which they waved
away at first and then accepted gracefully.

She watched him move finally towards her wretched little
mule, take it and the pack mule by the reins and begin to lead
them through the muck of the city streets.

She didn't even have the strength to ask where they were
going. She didn't care, as long as there was somewhere she could
lay her weary head.

A mile down the road he turned into still another gate, but beyond this point she could see a house with lights streaming from
every window, and she could see movement, carriages bustling
down the long driveway with Culhane trudging behind them,
two tired mules in hand but no break in his stride.

As they got closer, she could see people, she could hear laughter, and it was like a dream, a party in a place of civilized people
where there would be warmth and beds and a hot bath in the
morning.

It really had to be a dream—a nice one from which Culhane
could not nitpick dark elements, making it into something nasty.

And Allegra would be there, her hair done up, dressed in a
lovely white dress, virginal as she ought to be because she had
never met Dzmura and he had not abducted her, and everything
was just as it ought to be.

They drew up to a side door of the house; Culhane stepped up
onto the porch and knocked, and immediately a swarm of servants poured out of the door.

She was home, Alexandra thought blindly as she felt their
hands lifting her off the mule, and she hadn't gone to Wonderland.

And then she fainted.

He had taken her to the British Legation to Sir Barclay Gore,
who was ever welcoming of his countrymen and who saw nothing untoward in Ryder's arrival in the middle of the night with a
bedraggled native woman in tow.

Alexandra had come around by the time they had whisked her

up into one of the guest bedrooms and peeled off her mud-caked coat and tunic and veil.

By then, a phalanx of servants were preparing a bath and several maids were rummaging through the wardrobe of Lady Gore to provide her with something *proper* to wear.

They had lifted her into the bath, into the warm soaking water that permeated her pores until she felt she was almost drowning in it.

And then a sweet young maid washed her hair; another dried her off, and a third powdered her all over and then helped her into the silky peignoir provided by the generous Lady Gore.

And after that, tray after tray of wonderful food arrived, the likes of which she had forgotten existed in the ten long arduous days since they had left Tabriz.

When Alexandra had finished eating, the servants plumped up her pillows and covered her with a thick duvet and placed a glass of warm milk at her elbow. They lit a fire in the fireplace and lowered the wick on the kerosene lamps so that all she could see were the shadows of the dancing flames and they waited while she drank the milk and willed herself not to think.

But that part was easy in the face of such luxury and civility. She would never leave it again—never.

Allegra had to be close, she had to; where else in this godforsaken country could Dzmura have taken her?

Alexandra would find her soon and take her back to civility, and then this whole nightmare would be a thing of the past.

It was such a comforting thought—wholly unreal and she knew it, but it was, after her stoic endurance of the trip from Tabriz, just the cloudlike fantasy on which to fall asleep.

The Legation house was like an oasis in the desert; here everything was of the finest, imported from Britain in extravagant abundance, whether it was food, clothing or furniture. Lady Gore believed in comfort and in providing for her fellow countrymen in the gracious style to which they were accustomed.

Still, there was some concession to native arts: the floors were tiled and covered with gorgeous Kerman carpets, and low tables with beautiful inlaid designs were scattered about. There were wonderful overstuffed chairs and the windows here were not covered by the everlasting latticework, however, and the delightful library provided a vista overlooking an interior quadrangle of gardens. In this room Sir Barclay worked at a massive mahogany desk, his back to the view.

And there were servants everywhere. They woke Alexandra gently with a tray of fragrant tea; they brought her dresses from which to choose so that she might join Lady Gore and the other guests at breakfast; they sent someone to help her bathe and do her hair.

All this luxury after the deprivations of the caravan—it hardly seemed possible that Sir Barclay could maintain his usual lifestyle in the midst of a country that lacked such amenities.

Alexandra arose and allowed the maids and servants to do with her whatever they were accustomed to doing for Lady Gore, so it was a full hour before she appeared in the dining room where a leisurely breakfast *en buffet* was in progress.

She had not dreamed it: there had been an elegant party the night before, and since some of the guests had come from as far away as Kum, many had stayed over and were now seated informally around the dining-room table, partaking of tea, coffee, toast, biscuits, milk, dates and all manner of fruits, potted fowl and assorted dried meats.

"Ah," Lady Gore said, rising up to greet Alexandra as a maid led her into the room. "My dear, who would have thought there was a lovely well-bred English girl under all that mud and all those veils? Do help yourself. After all that time in caravan, I don't wonder that you would be ravenous for civilized food."

But Alexandra's stomach rebelled as she faced the array of breakfast offerings, and she wound up taking another cup of tea and some toast and joining Lady Gore at the table where a seat had been saved for her.

Lady Gore fired off the introductions with the ease of a rifleman: here were Lord and Lady Ruskington, the Hadringhams, the Honorable and Lady Langhorne, the very available Lord Frederick Alderson, employee of the Imperial Bank whose tour of duty would shortly be coming to an end; and Colonel and Mrs. Rosedale of the Indo-European Telegraph.

Alexandra learned to her surprise that there was a rather large population of Europeans, comprised not only of the diplomatic corps but also of missionaries, civil servants, the military and investors who had brought their capitalistic mercantilism to the bazaars of the east, and that Lord Barclay Gore was the nexus around which this complex society revolved.

Periodically he entertained these Britons, always he was aware of plots and schemes through his network of spies and informants and he held the reins in Tirhan with a certain grace and a bluff bonhomie which made him very likable, even to the veriest stranger such as Alexandra.

But Gore had known Culhane forever, it seemed; Lady Gore was quick to point this out and the fact that Alexandra was Sir Peregrine's daughter did not hurt matters at all.

"We were so sad to hear of your father's death," Lady Gore said sympathetically. "He spent many hours here with us, educating us on the lore and antiquities of the country. Did you not know?"

She hadn't; it struck her again that there was much about her father she had not known. She had thought of him over the long ten-day journey from Tabriz, wondering whether he had made the same trip in the same primitive way, and what it was about Persia and its mysteries that attracted him so.

And now here were Sir Barclay and Lady Gore, fast friends of her father, a man she had never really known.

She felt disoriented: she might have been at a neighboring house in Lavering instead of in the middle of a Persian desert and she might have known these people forever. Her father had had a life which had not included his family—or her—until he had decided he needed her.

And for what? To be the keeper of secrets that only Ryder Culhane was meant to know?

She wondered bitterly whether her father had intended her to be one of those secrets.

But Hidcote was a lifetime away now, erased by the urgency of finding Allegra, wiped away by death and murder, expunged by her symbolic dreams and governed by her explosive and unforeseeable passion.

"I didn't know," she said after a long pause. "Father talked very little about his work in Persia—until he came home for the last time."

"Oh, but it was so very interesting; he would spend months out at Alekkah and then come back to civilization, as it were, here in Tirhan and bring with him the most interesting artifacts and stories. In fact, he stopped here on his way back to England when your mother died and left several fascinating pieces with us," Lady Gore said. "I really believe he meant to retrieve them when he returned, but he never said so. Perhaps you'd like to see them?"

"Certainly," Alexandra responded, but this was the last thing she wanted to do at the moment, and she didn't understand why. Lady Gore had preserved a piece of her father's life for her, out of kindness or the possibility of monetary gain if the artifacts proved valuable, she did not know.

What she did know, as she followed Lady Gore into an anteroom to the library which was crowded with display shelves, was that she resented the years her father had not spent with her and the fact that these people might well have known him better than she.

Everyone crowded around as Lady Gore lifted a highly decorated water jug off one of the shelves. "Well, there was this delightful piece from the remains of the home of some ancient Shah ... Look at how well the colors have been preserved; of course it was well known that your father was searching for the parchments of the Zoran, and he was absolutely sure they would turn up in some container like this even though they are reputed to be only legendary. You do know the story? A Zoroastrian high priest named Kartir corrupted the master's teachings and practiced the worship of evil. Branching off with his followers he led a sect which is said to exist to this day. It does sound like something out of a penny-dreadful novel, but after Khartoum and those murdering zealots ... well, anything is possible ..."

She moved to another shelf. "And here—in this velvet case—is an ancient amulet from the arm of some powerful harem beauty. The beading and goldwork have almost been obliterated by time, but it is common knowledge that the black arts were—and still are—practiced behind harem walls. Sir Peregrine believed that this amulet represented a follower of the Zoran and that this very mutilated and incised lettering was a Kartesian prayer invoking evil spirits.

"And finally," she moved to another cabinet, "there is this very odd pair of cylinders which have incised symbols around each end . . ."

Alexandra's breath caught in her throat and she reached out to take one of the cylinders Lady Gore held up.

"They look like bracelets," Lady Gore was saying as Alexandra turned the one she held over in her hands, not even hearing the rest of Lady Gore's recitation.

. . . *Bracelets . . . How could my father have known that Culhane would eventually wind up at the British Legation? He had planted the whole thing: the idea of the bracelets. He had done it all before he left Tirhan because the danger was imminent even then; Dzmura had been a threat of some kind for which he had to make provisions. But why? WHY?*

The whole thing was like a spiderweb, fragile and carefully constructed to trap its prey—but who was the spider and who was the fly?

She balanced the cylinder in her hands, recognizing immediately that the markings around the edges were extensions of those on the pair she had once possessed and would complete the motif, translating it into something meaningful.

But did Culhane know? How could he? Her father had planned this all out of his knowledge of her, of Culhane and of the proclivities of Dzmura almost as if he had known he would never make it back to Persia . . .

She closed her eyes as the enormity of that thought hit her, and her hands tightened around the cool stone cylinder as if it were some kind of lifeline.

. . . *He had planned it all . . .*

And in her hands was the answer to everything. She had only to find Culhane, they could clean the bracelets just enough to translate the key and then they would know everything—*everything.*

She suddenly sensed him in the room behind her and opened her eyes and looked up.

He was there, and she saw by his expression he had known; of course he had known, how could he not? And she was mortified by her stupidity.

Lady Gore replaced the one cylinder on the shelf and indicated that Alexandra should do the same with the other when she had finished examining it and then rejoin the company in the dining room.

The stifling little anteroom was empty in a moment, and Alexandra and Culhane faced each other across a recriminating silence.

"I wasn't sure I would find them here," he said finally.

"Of course not. You bring all of your indigent colleague's daughters here after you test their mettle over the mountains. How much don't I know, Culhane? How much have you kept secret?"

"There *is* one thing you don't know," he said consideringly. "The bracelets are gone, and I don't know whether they were taken in Istanbul or here—"

"*What!*" She wheeled on him. "Are you crazy? Stolen? By whom? When?"

His expression remained impassive, and she couldn't even tell whether or not it mattered. They were so close, so close, but to what she did not know.

He shook his head. "I don't know. I assume someone lifted them here because I assure you they were in my possession the entire time we travelled."

But did she believe that? That he had just laid them where someone could walk out the door with them? That Dzmura could insinuate his people wherever and whenever he wanted and no one would be the wiser?

Anything was possible . . .

Instinctively she reached for the second cylinder even as she felt a crashing sense of futility.

"Then someone didn't know about these cylinders," she said tensely.

"Someone might—now. Do you have pockets in that dress? No? Wait—the tiebacks." He extracted a small knife from his pocket and cut away the tieback from one of the curtains at the only window in the anteroom, and then he took the cylinders from her, threaded the fabric through them, looped it and tied them together.

"Lift up your skirt now—quickly—and fasten them to the steels. That's it, lower down so the flare of the hem covers it. All right. That is all we can do for now. We have to get back to the dining room before anyone remarks we've been too long gone."

He guided her quickly through the library and back down the hallway to the dining room. By then the Ruskingtons had excused themselves, as had the Hadringhams and the Langhornes. Only Colonel and Mrs. Rosedale and Frederick Alderson remained to keep Lady Gore company.

"Finish your breakfast, my dear," Lady Gore invited her, and then, addressing Ryder, "and help yourself to something, Ryder dear; everything has been refreshed and is nice and hot. Freddie has to leave in moments and wanted only to pay his respects to Miss deLisle."

Alexandra eased herself into her seat beside Lady Gore, and Ryder took a place opposite her.

A servant appeared and poured the tea and offered biscuits and fruit. The conversation ebbed and flowed around the previous night's party, nothing more sinister than who had flirted with whom and when the weather would finally turn.

It was all very redolent of another time and place, as if life went on no matter what happened.

Alexandra listened politely, sipping her tea, eating whatever food they placed before her, perfectly aware that under this veneer of civilized behavior, someone was a traitor and that now her life was in danger too.

Chapter 15

She had walked ever so carefully up the stairs after breakfast, aware of the stone cylinders bumping against her shins despite her efforts to take tiny swaying steps.

"A good little rest after breakfast," Lady Gore advised her, "is the best antidote to that beastly journey from Tabriz. It took me weeks to recover. Go on then. I'll send one of the maids to call you for dinner."

She wondered if someone was watching her, wondered how likely it was that Dzmura had had the forethought to plant someone in Lord Barclay Gore's household for the express purpose of stealing a pair of stone bracelets that he didn't know would turn up there.

The thought stopped her cold just as she reached for the doorknob, and a wave of cold dread washed over her.

She let herself into her room and shut the door emphatically behind her. There was a lock, but she turned the key so fast she wrenched her wrist, then stood with her back pressed tightly against the door as she tried to rub away the pain and all the questions that begged to be asked now that the emotion of the moment was stripped away.

Finally she walked over to the bed and sank into its feather softness and lifted her dress to untie the cylinders.

So there they were, a pair of puzzles meant to fit between a pair of cylinders hidden in a house thousands of miles away.

It was unbelievable. She felt the web tightening around her. It was all so unbelievable.

Dzmura was everywhere, Culhane had said it, but Culhane had been the one from whom the bracelets had been stolen.

And her father had left the key to the puzzle hiding in plain sight at the legation: *Why?*

What would the cylinders reveal once they were pieced together, and why was it so important that Dzmura would abduct her sister, steal the original bracelets and then kill to prevent anyone from finding the rest?

Who knew the answer better than Culhane? And who did not have the bracelets anymore after all of his subterfuge to obtain them?

It didn't make sense. Nothing made sense, and these two ragged cylinders sitting on the counterpane made the least sense of all.

Her father ought to have buried them somewhere instead of leaving them where his enemies could find them.

Why would he have done that?

And who among the guests of the Gores could have known they were coming and planned to attend the party the previous night for the express purpose of stealing a pair of primitive artifacts?

What would happen when Lady Gore discovered the cylinders missing?

She could hardly remember how the whole thing began: the sleepwalking, the sense of Culhane reaching into her mind; the bracelets hidden in a secret room; the ghost and the last months her father had spent in that secret room; that awful dinner with Dzmura and the undercurrents . . .

. . . Oh God, yes—and Allegra's disappearance that night, her own shameless bargain with Culhane . . . It seemed a lifetime ago . . .

. . . and then the pursuit and the attacks, the deaths, the fire, the gunman . . .

. . . all this in aid of finding Allegra and pursuing Dzmura to what end she had yet to discover—

Except that her father had lied about everything . . .

. . . in order to preserve and present Culhane with the clues to finding Dzmura . . .

Only consider it, she thought, eyeing the cylinders: duplicate bracelets, duplicate clues, duplicate puzzle pieces. All to evade the all-pervasive net of Dzmura, who was everywhere.

And here was the inevitable conclusion: her father had found him somewhere, and it was important enough for him to fake an artifact to leave a message for Culhane.

—and it was urgent enough that Dzmura did not want it to be found, and he used Allegra to prevent it—

—underestimating her father who had already prepared the duplicate set of bracelets, knowing full well that Culhane, were he to come and find them, would understand instantly that a piece was missing—

—and having prepared for that contingency by leaving the missing piece in a place where it very likely might go unnoticed forever . . . or be found in a hurry if Culhane understood the clues and took up the pursuit . . .

How devious her father had been, and how torturous was his plan; when had he devised it? Before or after he had received news of her mother's death? On the trip from Alekkah to Tirhan so that he would have the cylinders ready to dispose of along with the other artifacts he would ask his dear friends to keep for him?

And wasn't it fortuitous that they knew nothing about the antiquities of the land in which they represented their homeland?

They probably never showed that room to anyone; they probably kept all those little gifts out of kindness and laughed behind their hands at the primitive antiquities they would eventually bury in the rubble of the Legation House when they left.

Her father had known that.

Her father had been tracking Dzmura for years . . .

Culhane had said that, she was almost sure he had said that, and her father was his mentor. He had a stake in it that had nothing to do with finding her sister.

She wished she could remember everything he had said—her brain was fogged up with despair and fear and her wary uncertainty.

He could have lied about the bracelets being stolen.

But to what purpose?

He did not need her to accomplish his purpose; he never had.

She picked up one of the cylinders and ran her fingers around the incised edge. A votive container that her father had somehow cracked into three pieces after chiselling a message into it.

He had then pretended it was an artifact he had unearthed at some place called Khuramafar—

—where Culhane said he had not been for ten years or more . . .

Yes, that she remembered. They were going to Khuramafar because her father had lied and that was meaningful.

What else might her father have said that would have significance to Culhane—and was that why he had not balked at taking her with him?

The net tightened again—she felt it: all the facts, all the surmises woven around her, her father's last little lie.

She picked up the second cylinder and examined it. But she found only what she might have expected: that it was identical to the first in the way the bracelets were identical to each other, and that the incised markings on it meant no more to her than they did on the other bracelets.

They had chased across continents to find them, and here they were, in her hands, as mysterious to her as the bracelets she had believed to be her father's labor of love.

Why could he not have told her?

Oh, but he had been treading on such thin ground to begin with by seriously presenting the fiction of the ghost—how could he have told her?

He knew he was going to die.

NO!!

No!! She could not bear to think—But he had known Dzmura was right next door for those two years—he had to have known it—Culhane did . . .

. . . and Culhane had said that Dzmura had drawn him away from Alekkah with the death of her mother . . .

Plots within plots, all so horribly unbelievable she thought she might lose her mind.

Once again, she had that jarring feeling of unreality which came from sitting in a quintessentially English bedroom with the deserts of Persia stretching out right beneath her window.

Which was the reality? Was she here or was she there?

And if she left the room and walked to her father's study and into the secret room, would she find the bracelets exactly where she had left them a month ago?

She bit her lip and pushed one of the cylinders over her wrist; it slipped on as easily as if it were meant to be there.

And the other . . . then she stared at her hands because, except for the ragged edges, she could have been looking at yet another duplicate set of the bracelets that had been stolen.

She had reached no conclusions by the time she was called to dinner. The maid provided a dress of moss green jersey with a pleated collar and hem and figured black velvet accents. She said it was a year behind the fashions, which didn't much matter in the desert.

Nor did the fit matter either, but the maid must have taken a nip and a tuck here and there because Alexandra looked very well in it as she surveyed herself in the mirror inside the massive armoire which was one of the furnishings in her room.

It only remained for her to conceal the cylinders, and since the skirt and the figured velvet undersleeves were too narrow to hide anything, she asked the maid to procure her some hairpins. She then pinned them up into her hair just as she had before.

When she finally made her way downstairs, she found Lady Gore in a high-collared dress with diagonal striping and lace and button trim which did nothing to diminish her size moving among still more assorted guests whom she had presumably invited to the dinner, supposedly informal in deference to her guests' travel fatigue.

Alexandra smiled brightly at Colonel Rosedale who had not yet left, and searched for Culhane who was not, as she instantly discovered, present.

Lady Gore drew her into the company with a compliment as to how well the dress suited her and a comment about her father whom everyone had known, and the conversation went on of its own volition from there.

"And will Mr. Culhane be joining us for dinner?" Alexandra asked with some audacity later when he had not appeared and she was beginning to feel greatly annoyed that he had left her to face this all alone.

"Oh . . . My dear, Ryder never stays to dinner at the legation, ever. He always makes his own arrangements when he is in Tirhan. You understand, my dear. Men have their needs when they are as footloose as he is. You may be sure he will be well taken care of."

She didn't like the sound of that one bit, and her frustration at her own constraints overrode her doubt and anxiety.

The worst thing was, she had walked into it with her eyes wide open. He had told her exactly what to expect, how things were here, but she supposed she had thought in some secret part of her that she would be the one who could dare to be different.

Instead she had had no choice but to play the role, and now he was assuming she would just buckle down and continue the charade.

Veiled and submissive . . . She was to put blinders on her eyes and not see what was going on in front of them, and if she had any inkling, she was to bow and kowtow and lower her eyes and agree that whatever he did was perfectly fine with her.

Never!

She must show him then that rules applied to men as well as women, and if he could enjoy himself in the company of other women, to whatever extent, she, too, could find enjoyment.

And it was really quite simple, when one understood how to go about it. He had taught her much in this ensuing month. She could now read all the hungers in a man's eyes, and she knew to a certainty how to deflect and how to invite. She saw herself becoming another person once again in the guise of a guest in a house a thousand miles away from everything she had ever known.

So simple really.

Just reach for the forbidden and it will find you . . .

An artful look here, an arched eyebrow there, a delicate reference with a double meaning—she could not have been more charming or more desired in the male guests' eyes.

She tempered her walk to draw their gaze, she lowered her eyes becomingly when a sly innuendo passed her lips, she drank with them the nectar of the senses and felt heady with power and control.

So easy to do when one knew how.

And she knew that Lady Gore had remarked upon it, quite simply because she was the youngest most attractive woman in the room and all the male guests' eyes were riveted on her.

She had the sense to restrain herself at dinner, but that did not quell the interest in her, and she subtly encouraged it right under Lady Gore's eyes.

Why not? She cared little what Lady Gore and her friends might think. Her gratitude for their hospitality was waning every minute that Culhane remained absent from the Legation House.

What if he left her there forever?

No . . . no, that was the wine thinking and not her practical self. But she felt so far from commonsensical that *anything was possible* . . .

And besides, Culhane was not there to see it, so it was a hollow victory at best. By the time the evening drew to a close, she was very willing to retreat to her bedroom and nurse her grievances in private.

Instead, she fell asleep.

And she woke up abruptly to the awareness of someone's hands fumbling with her dress in the dark.

She screamed and wrenched herself away from the groping hands, rolled her body as hard as she could to the other side of the bed.

She heard the door burst open underneath the high note of her scream, and then the sound of flesh beating on flesh and grunts and groans.

And suddenly there was a light at the door and Lady Gore appeared in her nightdress, holding a kerosene lamp high and surveying the scene from the lofty height of righteousness.

Colonel Rosedale lay facedown on the floor, his corpulent body straddled by a seething Culhane who sent her a searing look where she lay, huddled against the edge of the bed.

"Well," Lady Gore said haughtily, "I think that's quite enough of that. We will say no more about it except that it should be a lesson to those who play with fire in a country where every sensibility is a tinderbox. Good *night!*"

She turned on her heel, and the room was curtained in darkness once again.

Another hand reached in and set a lamp on a nearby table and withdrew. Then Colonel Rosedale climbed heavily to his feet, his face beet red with humiliation.

"Be careful where you abuse male provenance, my dear Miss deLisle. In some places, screams are accounted mere moans of pleasure and are ignored in that polite society."

He stamped out of the room, slamming the door behind him, and Ryder turned the key in the lock, then stood watching her as she slowly climbed back into bed.

She made a picture sitting there defiantly against the pillows, her collar torn away and the figured velvet inset in her bodice ripped from its hooks.

Her hair was in disarray as she ran nerveless fingers through its strands, seeking the cylinders she realized must have fallen to the floor in her escape from Colonel Rosedale's fumbling fingers. Finally she pushed some straggling wisps away from her face and gave up the search altogether.

The silence stretched out, tense as elastic, and he said nothing as she poked and prodded her hair and her dress in order to avoid meeting his gaze.

"So," he murmured, and she looked up at him, startled. "So . . . the naked odalisque was intent on proving her power tonight . . ."

"Did I not?" she asked silkily, determined to attack him before he could devour her. "Did not a man become so impassioned of me that he literally broke down the door and tried to take me? What he did not understand was, I had not chosen him, but if I had wanted him, he would have groveled at my feet."

"And instead he groveled at mine."

"It is the thing a man must learn: that a woman has the right of possession too."

"Yet, from what I hear you enticed them all. I wonder who next will try to break down your door."

"Why those among them who would make me moan with

pleasure—and those who would like to try," she answered artlessly.

"But there is only one man who is your master; you can serve no other. He would kill you otherwise."

"Why may he savor all the possibilities and his chosen one not have the same privilege? Many men with expert hands and beautiful bodies must come to his court. They could pleasure her just with voluptuous words. Would she not love to walk among them in all her glorious nakedness and know that they all ached to possess her? And would she not desire to choose just one and savor the experience with him as her master does with his hundreds of slaves? I think she would—I know she would."

"But this master has entered a carnal bargain with just one willing slave, and she will not flaunt her nakedness anywhere else but in his bed."

"I wasn't naked."

"You might just as well have been; they were all envisioning it. That dress hides nothing of the curve of your hips and the sway of your buttocks. And was it you who tucked the material tighter around your breasts? You were so innocent that a man was overcome by lust and broke into your room tonight with the intention of stripping away your clothes and possessing your nakedness. And all because you deliberately used the power of your body to entice him. In this world, that means only one thing."

"I see," she murmured. "And you use the power of your maleness to shop for fresh flesh in spite of our bargain. That is forgivable in the land where such dominance reigns supreme. You may feast on all the nakedness you desire, while I must solely await the moment to do your bidding. This is no bargain. If I continue waiting, I am truly a slave. I would rather find my pleasure elsewhere, Culhane, than try to anticipate the moment when you will desire me."

"The anticipation is part of the pleasure."

"Anticipate me then, Culhane, walking down the hallway naked and seeking firm youthful flesh to mate with mine."

She made a move then, in fury and frustration, and he grabbed her arm and pulled her back to him.

"You *are* mine, you know," he growled, feeling something totally beyond the coursing pulse of possessiveness and pushing it firmly away.

He thrust her back on the bed, where she promptly rolled over, propelled herself to her knees and began ripping off her dress.

"I am my own," she retorted grittily, tossing sections of the dress behind her, to the side of her and over her head until she was covered in nothing more than her stockings, pantalettes and corset.

"You are *mine*, according to our bargain, and if you cannot or will not continue to accede to its terms, I swear I will leave you here and you may make whatever bargains you like with any of those milksops you were chasing after tonight."

That stopped her. She paused in her furious disrobing.

"I accept those terms," she said insolently, and continued unhooking her corset with feigned intensity.

He was close to blowing now; she heard him huff with impatience as her nerveless fingers pulled at the corset hooks and her body arched towards him as if to belie her audacious words.

"Do you now? Do you? And which of those milksops will crown you his love slave and spend himself more than once a month between your legs? Who among them knows how to pleasure your nakedness? The fat frog who could not even strip off your clothes with any subtlety? The lizard with the slimey hands who could not keep them off of you? Did you think Lady Gore did not notice? Or that I would not hear? You want the cold and clammy, the tepid and the dead. Oh yes, by all means, strip off your underclothes and go walking among them; see what pleasure you derive from being their receptacle."

"But am I not that to you?" she murmured.

"You belong to me by the terms of our bargain. You have no right to anything more," he said tightly. But he knew why he felt like throttling her, and it had nothing to do with bargains or fate or anything else he had veiled it with in order to negate his own need for her.

"So it is the same, and you, just as they, will go seeking firmer flesh no matter who lies in your arms. That is the way, is it not? And it will always be so."

She paused as she reached the last hook of her corset, and then slowly she unfastened it and let it fall at her knees.

And there were her nipples, hot and taut and begging for his caresses, and she could not negate their need.

Slowly, she hooked her fingers into the elastic around her pantalettes and began sliding them down her thighs, and as she reached her knees, she sat down on the bed and pulled them off her legs and tossed them over her shoulder.

All that remained now were her stockings. She bent her one leg to balance her body as she began removing the silky hose, and then reversed her position so that the bare leg supported her weight as she slid the second stocking slowly and provocatively down her leg and threw it at him.

He caught it, stretched it out so that he could slide the soft silk across his face and inhale her scent, and she waited and watched him and hid nothing from him.

And then slowly, with that same provoking insolence, she swung her long legs off the bed and made a move towards the door.

He grabbed her from behind, thrusting his iron bar of an arm around her waist and hauling her nakedness roughly against his body.

"You . . . are . . . mine," he rasped into her ear: how else could he tell her, as he fought her wildcat body and her flailing arms and finally and futilely threw her down on the bed and pinned her with his weight.

". . . Now . . . now . . ." Her body writhed beneath him as he wrestled with her hands and arms and finally jammed them over her head; immediately she quietened and watched warily as he groped for her discarded stocking and then began tying it around her captive hands.

". . . Now . . ." The stocking was soft, soft, but stretched, it had a tensile strength and he wound it around her wrists with merciless speed. ". . . Now . . ." as if that could contain her volatile body, as if now she would understand.

He eased himself off her naked form and pulled her up to stand rebelliously before him.

". . . Now . . ." The bed was covered with a nice flat canopy of Bruges lace draped over a rounded stretcher just within reach.

He lifted her arms and took the ends of the stocking and tied them around the stretcher so that she was poised, arms upraised just at the foot of the bed between the two posts.

"And now," he whispered, "now we will see who can pleasure the naked odalisque better than her master . . ."

He knelt behind her so she could not see him, and he began his wicked exploration of her body with his mouth, his tongue, his hands, knowing as he must that her every sense was heightened to a screaming tension by this perverse bondage.

She felt him behind her, probing every part of her thoroughly and intentionally and she backed into his caresses, writhing against him, inviting still more.

Her body arched voluptuously with each delicious foray of his hands and tongue, every sensation expanded by the immobilizing of her hands.

She did not want him to stop. Whatever he was doing, she wanted him to keep doing it forever; her body shimmied for him, her legs parted for him, she moaned for him in her pleasure, she willingly gave her nakedness to him if only he would never stop.

He rested his hand there, splayed and probing just where she wanted to feel him, and with the other he slowly made the journey from the writhing curve of her buttocks to the lush rounds of her breasts, winding himself around her so that he was sitting on the bed facing her with his legs on either side of her thighs.

Slowly he took one taut pointed nipple into his mouth and then the other; back and forth he went between them, pressing her closer and closer against his massive erection as he sucked and pulled on the hard peaks of her breasts until all she could do was moan and push herself against his avid mouth to demand more and more of his ravenous sucking.

The sensations intensified, fed by the sense of the weight of her breasts beneath her uplifted arms; her head fell back in sheer abandonment. She felt him moving, pushing, thrusting the granite length of him between her legs so that she straddled the hot throbbing essence of him.

She bore down on him, his hot hand guiding her as he began a turbulent suckling of one lush nipple, drawing it tightly into his mouth and shaping it with his tongue.

And then . . . and then . . . She bucked against the ramrod length of him, pumping her body against the turgid heat of him as he pushed her and pulled her with his hands and his mouth, and she abandoned herself to the hot hard pleasure-suck of her nipple and his wicked, knowing hands and the power of his nakedness between her legs.

And it didn't stop; it centered in her lower belly and radiated upwards and upwards to the very tip of her nipple and then it exploded downwards and downwards into a long hard gush of sensation that rippled over her body like a storm.

She cried out then, and he removed his mouth and pressed her still closer to the heat of his body and his rampaging sex.

He drew himself up against her, slanted his mouth over hers for a long and ravishing kiss. He felt her body give against him as he took her mouth as greedily as he had taken her nipple.

She writhed against him, helpless to push him away, at the mercy of probing fingers which inched her body tighter and tighter against his and the hard heat of his male root.

He wanted her to feel it, to know its primitive force and its potency, to beg for his ramrod strength to possess her; he wanted to drive his jutting male power deep into her feminine core so that she would know forever who had mastered her nakedness and to whom she owed her joy.

It was in his kiss, that ravaging, ravishing kiss, as they stood bonded together body to body, so close that there was not a breath between them, his knowing hands feeling and pushing and pressing her hips more tightly against his.

"And now," he breathed against her swollen lips as he broke the kiss for a moment, "which bargain will you keep? Who will you wait for, naked and willing, whenever he desires you?"

She leaned into his mouth, rubbing her breasts against his chest. "Convince me once more," she whispered, seeking his mouth. "I can't seem—"

He crushed her lips against his ferociously. Her body twisted against his, seeking his nakedness, begging for his expert caresses.

"This is the bargain," he murmured, moving his lips a tantalizing lick away from hers. "You are mine and I want you naked always—in my presence and when you wait for me; I want to know that I can take you where I want you and when I want you. That is the nature of an odalisque, and that has been the bargain, whether you choose to acknowledge it or not, with no other threats and no coy little displays of power."

"Yes," she whispered, angling her face upwards again for his kiss. "Please . . . now . . ."

He fit his mouth against hers again, slowly and deliberately this time at the very moment he probed her velvet fold and purposefully thrust himself within.

He heard her groan at the back of her throat, welcoming him there, and he pushed himself deep within her in concert with his hot possession of her mouth.

She was ready for him then, wet with anticipation, and he could hardly restrain himself against the seductive sway of her hips.

Her intensity was enthralling, her capacity for pleasure was utterly ravishing and her willingness to play totally beguiling.

He had never reckoned on that, or that he would fall in thrall to her passionate nature. He could not get enough of her, and sometimes he thought his need was an enchantment unleashed by his nemesis, sometimes he thought it his greatest joy.

He knew only he could never let her go. That was as much as he would acknowledge, even in his deepest longings.

But all he needed to know at that moment was that the bargain was met once again. She was his, and that mesmerizing notion catapulted him with one forceful driving thrust into a shattering culmination.

In the land of his enemy, where he had come of age, he could take nothing for granted.

Deep in the night, he awakened suddenly with the pressing sense that he must examine the cylinders more closely.

But for that, everything else was in readiness, and he had only to tell Alexandra the outline of his plans.

The enemy was everywhere; the bracelets were gone—gone and perhaps negligible. He had been too lax in the home of Sir Peregrine's friends, and here, where he thought he would find sanctuary, he had found treachery instead.

The enemy was wily and fast. He had discarded his briefcase for a pouch he could conceal on his body, and it lay now on a chair across the room with his clothing.

There was no light in the room: he had snuffed the candle when he had released her and carried her to the bed to bring her once again to shuddering completion.

But he needed no light: his senses guided him, and he slipped off the bed and groped around on the floor, finally locating them under the bed where they had rolled, just beyond the dust ruffle.

Stealthily, then, by the light of the nub of the candle he carried to the small desk on the opposite side of the room, he removed two folded sheets of tissue paper and his pencil from the pouch, and he began the delicate task of making a rubbing of the markings on the cylinders.

He knew it at once as the incised hieroglyphs became clear, and he understood his feeling of urgency.

The cylinders were fakes. They were in mortal danger if they did not leave the Legation House immediately.

Chapter 16

It was too easy in the night to prowl around the Legation House.

Before they departed, sneaking away like thieves, he had returned the cylinders to the anteroom and retrieved her tunic and veil, then locked her bedroom door behind them.

In the kitchen, they foraged for nonperishable food and water which he bundled into a linen tablecloth about to be laundered.

Afterwards they hid in the stable, surrounded by its fecund smells and a torrid sense of menace, until first light of dawn, when he saddled a horse and they cautiously crept away from the house, skirted the main gate, sought a break in the wall and made their escape.

He had planned it all. Waiting for them near the bazaar was a wagon and a mule team outfitted with everything they needed for the three-day journey to Khuramafar.

The air had warmed; the weather might be turning, the *charavadar* told them, and the roads would be clear all the way to Killa Masir.

He paid the muleteer the rest of his money and waved him away. There was no buying silence: the word would be passed soon enough that the *kafir* and his woman had bought supplies and headed south.

The enemy would know, but at least by then they might have a lead of several hours.

He tied the horse to the wagon and settled Alexandra into the wagon bed.

It was done.

By the time the sun showed the mid-morning hour, they were four hours past the gates of Tirhan.

And now, where before it was unremittingly cold, it was stiflingly hot.

She had had to wear the tunic and veil, and he was dressed in the local way so that they would present the appearance of a couple journeying from Tirhan to some new settling place.

Nothing about them was unusual, judging by the travellers, the caravans and the one burial procession, they passed.

But once again, conversation was limited as he drove the mules over the rutted roads, now dried from the previous winter storms, across the flat and endless plain toward the mountains on the distant horizon.

Slowly, slowly they veered southwest, following the road, and as daylight shaded into darkness, they came upon a small grouping of mud houses, a village in the midst of nothingness, but when they stopped to explore, they discovered the hovels were crumbling to ruins and the village had been abandoned.

Nevertheless, it was a stopping place for the night, and he found among the ruins a little reservoir of water, brackish and distasteful, but when boiled in a tin on the brazier sufficient to moisten their food so they could save what liquid he had in the supplies for another time.

After a meager meal of cheese and dried fruit, they moved the coals into one of the mud huts where there was space for spreading out their blankets, and where, from the road, neither their wagon nor their accommodations could be seen.

It was close in the hut, and it reeked of the ripe scents of those who had abandoned it long ago and of the dried mud beneath their feet.

He lay back on his blanket and watched her moving edgily around the hut, still dressed in the shapeless tunic.

The air between them thickened appreciably as she understood what he was waiting for.

"Surely not here?"

"Why not here? That was the bargain. Here it is warm and

close, and we are well fed and contained for the night. What is different about here?"

Her body twinged with the memory of the naked voluptuous pleasures of the night before, his ravaging kisses, her breathless submission to his demands.

... *always naked in his presence* ... Last night she had yearned for it, begged for it, surrendered to it. She had given herself to it, and now she must perform her part of the bargain, even here, as she had agreed in the throes of her ungovernable passion.

And he waited, and in the waiting, her excitement expanded; her willful body demanded the pleasure, fired her urgency to obey his commands.

She lifted the formless tunic over her head and tossed it to one side. The dress was an easy matter with buttons down the front and a clean slide to her feet as she shrugged out of the sleeves. She kicked off her boots and shimmied out of the pantalettes, and in her stockinged legs and her tantalizing corset, she presented herself to him, kneeling by his side, her legs parted to invite his caress.

"This is not our agreement," he said with a harsh huskiness in his tone.

"Strip me naked," she whispered, leaning her covered breasts into him.

"If I comply, you can never hide your breasts from me again."

"Do it," she begged, her body swelling with excitement. She watched with voluptuous impatience as he inserted his fingers between the corset's cups and tore it away from her body.

"And now the stockings to complete the bargain. This is what we agreed: naked and willing, wherever and whenever ..."

"Kiss me."

"The odalisque does not make demands."

"Who will know?"

"You will know that the bargain is not met. Take off those stockings, and then ..."

"Strip them off for me," she begged, watching his face, pushing the boundaries deliberately and out of the fulminating excitement of the moment.

She felt his one hand grasp her buttocks firmly and then push her so that she fell backwards with her legs tucked under her.

"The stockings, odalisque, and then you will have fulfilled your part of the bargain."

She smiled grimly and lifted one leg to brace it against his body, well aware that the slight stretch of her leg revealed everything to him.

"Help me," she pouted, deliberately leaning back to emphasize the lean line of her body and her leg.

She moved her stockinged foot downward, seeking the bulge between his legs and rubbing it with the flat of her foot. "Help me undress," she begged him, as she felt the ramrod length of him elongate under her sensual massaging.

She dug her toes against his towering erection. "Take off my stocking for me," she whispered entreatingly as she continued to slide her foot all over his surging manhood.

"You are like iron under my foot. So powerful. So forceful. Let me feel you naked. Let me see you. I want you naked for me, ready for me the way I am wet and ready for you. Strip my stocking and let me feel you . . ."

He couldn't resist that, he couldn't . . . her whole body was moist with longing; she was desperate to feel his hands on her, to make him capitulate to her.

"The odalisque does not make demands."

She would break him, she swore it. The air between them was thick with voluptuous need; her body streamed with the wet hot yearning he aroused in her.

"When you are naked for me, odalisque, then . . ."

A world of meaning hung in that word: all the fecund pleasures of her times with him were contained in that one little word: . . . *then* . . .

. . . Then his wicked hands would probe and pleasure her most secret places . . .

. . . Then the naked force of his manhood would possess her in hot driving pleasure . . .

. . . Then she would want only to surrender to him always and remain his naked odalisque forever—

. . . Then . . .

Slowly, unwillingly, she bent forward and eased off the offending stocking until her bare foot rested against the inflexible bulge of his manhood.

"The other one . . ."

She shifted her body slowly and placed her other foot next to the bare one on the thick jut of his sex, then worked off the other offending stocking with equal resentment while he reclined there like the pasha he was and watched her every movement.

"And now . . ." he murmured as she tossed the stocking over her head. "And now . . ." His eyes grazed her two naked feet pushed up against his granite manhood. "Now you have met the bargain, and you will never defy me again."

She looked at him sulkily. "Sometimes a woman wants to play."

"Odalisques do not play."

"Boring," she muttered, withdrawing her feet and tucking her legs under her again.

"Have you been bored, odalisque? Or has it been that the thought and sight and scent of you has aroused me past endurance and you have reaped the rewards? Have we not bypassed the inconsequentials, the coyness, the games; and have we not been able to pleasure each other beyond your wildest imaginings? Bored, odalisque? I think not."

"But the odalisque can never say no."

"And she lives always in anticipation of the next coupling, which, in a harem of one, is more often than any odalisque has a right to expect or demand. So, wherever we are, you will expect and anticipate that I will want you for my pleasure, and you will not deny me with coy games and prudish modesty the sight and the feel of your nakedness at my command."

"But you may refuse *me* the sight and the feel of your nakedness?"

"So that your excitement and need grows with the memory of it and with renewed anticipation of the pleasures to come. When an odalisque is confined in this way, naked and steeped in all the luxury and pleasures of the senses, she can only bend her thoughts to recollecting the pleasures of submission, which heightens her craving for the next carnal coupling. Her master will either continue to take her to his bed or choose another slave; she then will center all her energy on making herself desirable to him once more."

"How tidy for him."

"An odalisque lives for pleasure."

"And does not the pasha who controls her? Only he has the choice. It is monstrous."

"But still, the thought of it resonates in you; you love the freedom of your nakedness and the pleasure of your body, you want to be naked for me, you want to be my odalisque. You love the carnal excitement of our coupling. And why? Because you have bargained to surrender your nakedness to me. And you want it, you crave it, now. You can't wait for it. If you could spend your life in my harem, you would come willingly, begging each night to couple with me. You would never put on clothes again if you knew you could be naked and mine as long I desire it. You were born to be naked, born to fit with me. You want me now, but you swear you won't beg again. You will just tempt me with your insolence, and that look . . . that look—"

"The only one looking is you," she spat out. "No, I won't beg again; I told you I wanted to see you naked, I told you I was wet and ready for you. Now you can beg—and don't tell me an odalisque cannot command her master's desire. Why should you play tormenting games with me when I willingly stripped myself naked for you?"

"Not so willingly . . ."

"And why? Because I wanted to feel your hands undressing me; because I wanted to feel the iron power of you naked at my feet. Instead, I must beg for the privilege of your pleasure. Oh no, not me. I can sit naked before you and not succumb to my erotic need. And I will. Tonight your naked odalisque does not wish to explore the pleasures of the senses."

"Tonight," he growled, "my naked odalisque will beg me to possess her. Tonight"—he raised himself to a sitting position and began removing his clothes—"tonight . . ." Within moments he had stripped off all his clothing and had resumed a reclining position on the blanket. "I will let you look your fill, and we will see what we will see . . ."

Her body was permeated with erotic heat. In the light from the brazier, his naked form was all planes and angles and musculature and narrow pumping hips from which the jut of his towering manhood thrust from its nest of wiry hair as if it were reaching for her.

Presenting himself to her, taunting her with his naked power, certain that she was not proof against the memory of forbidden pleasure, he lay there, supreme and supine, in all his primitive maleness, waiting and waiting; silent, secret, watching, wanting, rigid with passion, explosive with need.

And she sat there, haughty and disdainful, her body taut with hunger, waiting and waiting; silent, scornful, watching and wanting, consumed with the carnal power of her nakedness.

The air grew thick with erotic tension. Neither spoke. Neither moved. Her body grew hot with longing. She could not take her eyes off him.

Her body flexed with the memory of him. She stiffened her spine, and her nipples tautened to pebble-hard points to entice him.

Her body was ripe for him, her mouth honeyed with yearning for his kisses, the nectar of ecstasy lush between her legs.

It would take but a word, a sign—and only from him; but she would never give in, never.

They sat through the night in apposition to each other, each obdurate, strained, utterly purposeful in their determination not to be the one who would yield . . .

He woke her the next morning at dawn, having already lit the brazier, watered the mules, prepared some fruit and cheese for their breakfast and boiled up a tin of tea.

She was cold now with the memory of his withholding, and it was as if the pleasures of the dark became forbidden by light of day.

She scrambled into her dress and tunic and took the cup of tea he offered without a word.

Only after she had eaten and they had packed away their meager stash of food and she had donned the veil and sat primly in the wagon bed once more, only then did she say, "I hate this, I hate it."

"It is necessary. There is still another day's travel to Khuramafar, and the horse cannot bear the burden of both of us and our saddlebags for such an extended time. Tomorrow morning, we can abandon the wagon, and that will give them something to puzzle over. Perhaps we will gain an additional hour."

"It takes so *long*. How can you be sure of anything now?"

"We are following the clues your father left me. I thought that was clear to you."

"Nothing is clear, and as time goes on, everything gets murkier and I am more and more certain we will never find my sister."

"You've had no more dreams since we debarked at Istanbul. We are clear that your father meant for us to travel to Khuramafar. And we know that enemies pursue us, that they are not above counterfeiting, or infiltrating the homes of friends or murder. What is not clear?"

"Why? Why, why, why? Why Dzmura, why my sister, why the counterfeiting and the duplications and the lies and the pursuit? Why *you?*"

He snapped the reins and the mules moved forward, but he did not answer her question immediately.

They traversed a mile and more before he spoke, and even as he explained it, she did not comprehend.

"Your father spent his archaeologic life searching for the scrolls of the Zoran, which are the prayer papers of an ancient sect of *daevas*—worshippers of evil, followers of Kartir, who was a Zoroastrian priest. It was long believed that the religion had died out, although there are vestiges of it still in India; but here, Islam took root over Christianity. Still, it was thought that one small stubborn group hung on and went underground, where the vices of evil were practiced and perfected, and that the latter-day priest of this sect lives in the guise of Dzmura.

"It is thought that it was he who fomented the disaster at Khartoum, that the *mahdis* were a war-mongering splinter group of zealots determined to spread the doctrine of Kartir throughout the world.

"But all religion is a battleground between good and evil. Dzmura operates in hiding, arming his minions for the next great armageddon; and no one can prove it.

"Your father meant to find him. He stumbled one day on an altar of the Amesha Spentas, who are the immortals of the Zoroastrian religion. But the dedication included an eighth, a *daeva*, and symbols and icons which were of a more recent vintage, and in a place where it had been long supposed Zoroastrianism had died out.

"As he searched more and more at Killa Masir and Alekkah, he found even more subtle clues that the sect existed to this day, and as he got closer to linking Dzmura to the priesthood of the sect, he moved closer to signing his own death warrant.

"I was aware of all this; your father was my mentor, my father, my equal. I revered him. And I felt Dzmura's power spreading all through Persia and beyond. We agreed he had to be stopped, but we did not know how.

"Your father determined he would keep on searching for the scrolls of the Zoran as a cover for his search for Dzmura's followers.

"I quit the Museum and began undertaking various unsavory commissions, chiefly to root out Dzmura, whose business dealings had always been questionable at best. We were sure he would come to me eventually, and he did. He was a dealer of antiquities who had no qualms about counterfeiting or stealing, and he always needed a provenance which he knew could be provided for a price.

"I was on a commission for him when your father received word from Lavering of your mother's death, and it was my very bad luck to be stuck in the snows of the Zagros Mountains on my way to Alekkah when he left.

"There was only a note—he had no time for anything more until he was on his way with various artifacts, one supposes, that he wished to take with him.

"Perhaps it was then his ghost appeared and gave him the idea of breaking up the votive candle holder after he inscribed the map of Dzmura's whereabouts on it. But that is the whole of it: the so-called bracelets are a map to Dzmura's stronghold, and the missing piece was not at the Legation House.

"Without a doubt your father made the duplicate set of bracelets because he felt certain that Dzmura had forces at his command that could ferret out anything; I don't think he dreamed that Dzmura's secret weapon was his own daughter.

"I believe she had been programmed for many years. And I think your father playacted the disillusioned archaeologist with great panache. He probably felt if his story, weird as it was, could smoke out Dzmura, who then was in England, it would be worth the loss of his reputation.

"I think he knew the danger; I think he was even aware that Dzmura might have had a hand in the death of your mother, to force him to abandon his quest. And Dzmura more than likely was involved in your father's death somehow. He probably felt, after the proper amount of time, he could dispatch your sister to find the bracelets, never realizing that they were not in the house proper.

"By then I had entered the picture. And thus the dinner and the challenge and the reason we are pursuing Dzmura all over the Hamadan Mountains.

"He is dangerous, he is armed, he has psychic capabilities and he is determined to persevere. He must be stopped. I will do it, and that is the why, Alexandra, you are with me. I will need you to successfully remove your sister from Dzmura's gilded cage, which is the last and only thing I can do for your father."

It was noon by then, and they seemed to be no more nearer the mountains than before.

"They are following us," he said suddenly.

"How can you know that?" she asked fretfully.

"I know it. You know I know it. Dzmura will stop at nothing to keep his secrets. But his agents do not possess his powers. We must be wary, and fast. There is a place ahead, a village, where we may be able to get another horse. We will leave the wagon there."

Now she felt fear: the mules plodded along as if they were not being trailed and no one could kill them. She, however, was aware of her mortality and of the danger of Dzmura.

The story was finally woven into whole cloth. Now it made

sense. Later she would come to terms about whether the quest to find Dzmura should have taken precedence over her father's duty to his family.

Later she would deal with Dzmura's culpability in her parents' deaths.

Later she would cope with all that had happened since Allegra had disappeared.

But for now her world encompassed only the sunbaked road, the distant mountains and the palpitating danger which made her the more determined to survive.

Chapter 17

The village was situated in the shadow of the Hamadan Mountains adjacent to a small lake. Here there was some semblance of prosperousness: the lake fed an orchard and a sward of green where horses and various animals grazed. The men of the village were artisans, workers of leather, makers of saddles. And the women were hidden out of sight.

The village was accustomed to the advent of strangers because of its situation along the road to Hamadan. The men were traders, always with a surfeit of food and animal flesh to exchange for something more valuable.

They were not impressed with the offerings of the *kafir* and his woman, who cowered behind him with proper deference.

A wagon had its uses, certainly; they saw little of these things along the route to the mountains. Mules were the transportation of choice, but the two pulling the wagon looked as if they were about to drop.

From behind the cover of her veil, Alexandra listened to Culhane adroitly arguing. She understood nothing except the urgency of proceeding as soon as possible, and she knew that these stubborn people could hold them up long enough for their enemies to find them.

Culhane climbed up into the wagon and threw out everything they had accumulated: the brazier, the bag of coals, a pair of boots, the sheepskin jackets, several blankets, the tablecloth with the food wrapped up in it—and it was this the village men leaped upon of all the articles heaped at their feet.

Here was something to be prized: finely woven cloth, the likes of which they were not familiar with.

They argued furiously for a half-hour before concluding the bargain, and when they were done, Culhane had in hand two reasonably vigorous-looking horses, two jackets, the blankets and a basket of food for their journey. He had also acquired the good will of the villagers and an invitation to take a meal with them.

"But what did you tell them?"

"I told them the mules would fatten up, that they could use the wagon to haul their crops, and that my woman was not part of the bargain. The chieftain was most disappointed, but he has directed that you attend his wife while we break bread in his house."

She wasn't prepared for this. She had naively thought they might conclude their business and be on their way.

There was nothing in Culhane's expression to indicate that this delay discomfitted him in any way, and following the custom, he never even looked at her as the chieftain led him away.

One of the men motioned for her to follow him to a house, at which he knocked lightly on the door.

It opened a crack, her escort withdrew and Alexandra hesitantly pushed her way into the dwelling.

The room that she entered astonished her; from the outside she could never have imagined the opulence of it. It was almost as if the chieftain had imported the luxury of a palace into this mud hut in his village, into the house of his particular woman.

The walls were tiled in dazzling colors, and the floors were strewn with carpets. On the benches along the walls were piles and piles of luxurious pillows, and on a brass table nearby was a steaming pot, an assortment of cups and tidbits to eat.

The woman who came forward to meet her was dressed as extravagantly as any queen. She wore a transparent gold-embroidered gauze chemise over which was a skirt of figured silk and a vest embellished with jewels of various colors set off by swirling gold thread. Her cap of velvet matched the vest, and a wimple of snowy crepe was appended to it and fastened under her chin.

She wore jewelry the likes of which Alexandra had never seen, her arms covered by bracelets adorned with shimmering jewels, a golden collar around her throat. There were jewels in her plaited hair and miniature flasks, suspended by golden chains from her waist, exuded a flowery scent.

She lifted her hand gracefully and motioned to Alexandra, beckoning her to sit, to partake of tea and fruit; and Alexandra reluctantly joined her on the banquette.

She spoke, but Alexandra shook her head to indicate she could not understand.

Then she called out and another woman appeared, less expensively dressed, her body rounder and fuller and somewhat more squat than that of the beauty who waited expectantly for her to speak.

The woman said a few words and Alexandra recognized the language as French, of which she knew some phrases and some words, and with this meager vocabulary, she managed to have some conversation with her hostesses.

They were young. The one was the mother of the chieftain's children, the other, who was bedecked with jewels and silks, was his wife.

They had migrated there some years before, and her husband headed a tribe of nomads who, by virtue of the location, could now settle in one place and prosper.

Their sole duty and joy was to serve their husband and provide him with sons.

They offered her some dates and apricots and replenished her tea and did not ask her much about herself because she had such a limited vocabulary.

She felt time slipping away. There were no windows in this diminutive seraglio, no sense of hours, days, weeks; no comprehension that anything existed beyond the walls where they willingly immured themselves.

They knew nothing else, and she knew so much more which they could never comprehend.

She felt overwhelmingly distressed for their lot even as she understood they embraced it fully and joyfully.

It seemed she had spent a lifetime with them before the soft rapping on the door summoned her to be reunited with Culhane.

She pulled the veil back over her eyes and bid the two ladies adieu; but just as she was about to depart, the woman who spoke French called her back.

A gift, she explained, from the *femme,* and she thrust something into Alexandra's hands.

There was no time to examine it or do anything but hurriedly express her gratitude even as she had one foot out the door.

It closed behind her, emphatic, final, like the sealing of a tomb, immuring its secrets forever.

Culhane awaited her astride the one horse.

"Of course you can ride?" he murmured.

"I can *not,*" she said acidly, "but that shouldn't matter."

"I would think not. But you can't straddle it. There's a step on the other side. Hoist yourself up—they won't help you, and I must not since you should not even be doing this—and hook your leg around the pommel. We'll fix things after we are out of sight of the village."

She found the step, and somehow, awkwardly, managed to lever herself up into the saddle—a frightening proposition being so far off the ground and on such extremely precarious seating.

"Just hang on," he advised, and turned back to the chieftain to exchange compliments and farewells.

"*Now!*" he whooped, and immediately propelled his mount into a gallop.

Hers responded with a jolting rocketing motion that almost landed her at the chieftain's feet. She grabbed for whatever leather she could grasp, and hung on for dear life as her horse beat its way after him, down the track and finally, mercifully, away from the village.

They made a camp at the base of the mountains in the freezing cold of the night, and they huddled together near the horses, fully dressed in the sheepskin jackets and wound around with the blankets to keep out the cold.

It was the worst night of them all, bitter and unsheltered and fraught with the possibility that they could be attacked at any time in the open air.

Morning could not come fast enough for her. She was sure she could never sleep, but somehow the time passed and she was not aware of it until light broke behind her eyelids.

"Khuramafar is just over the mountains, a half-day's trip by horseback at the most. But we have to keep at it, with no stops. Are you up to it?"

She thought longingly of tea, but they had nothing with which to build a fire, and only some cold water which had partially frozen in the goatskin flask.

"I need something to eat, and then if you could tie me onto the saddle somehow, I'll be fine," she said gamely, but she wasn't sure she could hold on for another step let alone the miles they would have to course up a mountain and down again.

There was a chunk of table bread in the basket and some cheese and fruit. They washed these down with the freezing water.

"She gave me something, the chieftain's woman."

"Did you look to see what it was?"

"Not yet." She produced a square of blue handkerchief, which she had tucked into her sleeve, and carefully untied it. Inside the folded-over square was a chain made up of alternating gold-and blue-enamelled links.

She held it up: it was quite long, surely it would dangle as far down as her thighs, and it was quite lovely.

"You know of course that color has great significance in the harem: blue is the color of hope, usually in the form of something romantic. The chieftain's woman prays for you."

She sent him a skeptical look, then wound the chain around her neck and tucked it beneath the tunic. She tied the handkerchief around her wrist.

As she shaded her eyes and looked up towards the mountains she took a deep breath.

"It is time to go," he said, gathering up the basket and the blankets. "Try to keep as warm as possible: tie the veil around your neck and your hair, and wrap one of the blankets around your legs as well."

"How close are they now?" she whispered, feeling danger in the icy edge of the air.

He stood very still for a long moment. "They cannot have yet reached the village. They are hours away by my calculation and probably still sleeping now. Come—it is time to go."

He helped her mount, this time astride, and seated her in such a way that he could spread out the blanket to use the ends to tie her legs tightly to the stirrup straps and around her waist to secure her to the pommel.

And then they began the swift ascent through the scrub at the base of the mountain trail.

She thought she would die of hunger, thirst and the pummeling her body was taking as the horses picked their way swiftly through the brush and up the endless mountain trails leading almost vertically upwards and upwards as if the ancient gods had made a path right to heaven.

There was no stopping-off point, no village, no plant life, no plateau—only the bare face of the mountain and the stinging winds as they reached an altitude thousands of feet above where they had begun.

They shared the remaining water and some fruit, without dismounting, and then plunged onwards; she was sure they would be riding that mountain forever.

But within an hour, they reached a levelling-off point from which they could see the valley.

And there, spread below them, was a skein of houses stretching from the base of the mountain to cluster around a fort and continue up the side of an adjacent mountain; here was vegetation and a glint of water in the valley all the way off into the sunset.

"Khuramafar," Culhane said, shading his eyes against the sun. "Dwelling place of the ancient tribe of the Astilbe and site of the Palace of Bazzi which is still in the process of being unearthed. There is much that has been discovered here and still much to be found."

And they reached it by sundown, galloping into the shallow bowl of the valley in a race with the shadows and halting at the edge of the village.

"We can find accommodations here," Culhane said after a long, seeking pause. "We will dismount and walk the rest of the way."

He untied the blanket around her, and she gratefully and some-what shakily slid to her feet.

"I don't think I can walk . . ."

He took the reins of both horses and motioned for her to cover her face and to walk several paces behind him, and slowly and resentfully she followed him into the town.

The "accommodations" were nothing like what she had imag-ined: merely a room in a *caravanserai*, one of several, into which as many itinerant travellers as possible were crowded for as long as they could pay.

The room was windowless, the walls thick dried mud, the floor was spread with dhurries so that there was some warmth underfoot. Built all around the perimeter of the walls were sleep-ing platforms, and heat rose from a firehole in the center of the room which was also used for cooking.

There were four others in the room with them and only one platform allotted to them both, a problem Culhane solved by spreading their blankets on the floor alongside it and sleeping there, while she had the pleasure of the straw mattress covered with the none too clean dhurries and one of their saddles for a pillow.

But she was so weary of travelling, she didn't much care and fell asleep the moment she lay down.

In the morning she awakened from a dreamless sleep all wrapped around in her tunic, veil and blankets with the necklace gift tight around her neck almost choking her.

For an instant, she thought everything else had been the dream, but there was nothing more real than the scents and smells of the *caravanserai* early in the morning, with the brightly burning *tandur* in the center of the room and the babble of the travellers who shared the room.

And then she smelled honey, and she opened her eyes to find Culhane seated cross-legged just by the head of the pallette, dip-ping a piece of flat bread into a bowl of honey.

She grabbed it out of his hand, and then she realized she had to disentangle herself from her clothing and the covers, and she sheepishly handed it back.

There was no water, no way to wash, no food provided except what Culhane could scavenge: the bread and the honey, and the water they had brought with them which they then used to wash their hands and faces.

By then it was mid-morning and there was no way to conduct a conversation in the dormitory room of the *caravanserai* and Alexandra wondered exactly what Culhane had in mind to do now that they were at Khuramafar.

They saddled the horses, but they walked through the village, with its bazaars and its mud houses and mosques side by sides and palaces of the well-to-do set on stepped back terraces up the mountains.

The village was vibrant with noise and commerce; they passed the rug-makers, and the tin-smiths, and the bakery where a company of peasant women were mixing together the flour, water and leavening for the flat bread they baked every morning and sold at the bazaar.

They heard the faint wail of a pipe summoning the faithful to prayers at noon, and as they walked farther away from the village, they came upon a garden of apricot orchards, almond and date trees, where palm, chicory, garlic, grapevines and a host of other vegetation not in season grew, alongside a small field of wheat and barley.

Above this they saw a cemetery, its white crypts ghostly and forbidding in the bright white sun of the morning.

They were heading farther and farther from the village, towards the fortress and the terraced hills.

"Now we ride," Culhane said, and he came around to help her mount and then swung up on his horse. "Across that ridge and down in the second valley, we will come to the Palace of Bazzi. Your father was working there many years ago. There are excavated rooms and places of silence where we can talk."

He led the way, and once again, she hung on fearfully as her horse picked its way surefootedly over obscure terrain. But this wasn't nearly as scary as crossing the Hamadans or the trip from Tabriz. It took less than a half-hour before they were cantering down into a valley which looked like little more than rock formations and plateaus to the untutored eye.

The sun was at its zenith as they dismounted and tied up the horses, so he spread a dhurrie and laid out a meal of blanket bread, sweetmeats and milk.

And the milk was cold and clear and fresh, not strained or mixed with anything else. She drank it gratefully, thirstily, before she even tasted the bread.

"My father worked here," she murmured, when she had satisfied her hunger and could take more appropriate note of their surroundings. "It looks like nothing."

"You have to go down into what they call a *serdab,* a kind of underground room which is accessible at both sides—through what looks like a tunnel cut into the rock. There is just enough room to walk upright, and the whole is laid with marble and supported by thick carved arches, and when you emerge, you are in the courtyard of the palace. It was your father who found the *serdab* and oversaw the initial excavation."

She nodded. "Yes, I remember; he did write about it. And then he was called back to Alekkah and it was a great disappointment to him."

They were silent for a time. To her, the setting was strange, the chiseled rock and the high sun and the obliterating sense of timelessness as if nothing ever intruded on this place.

"The Museum withheld funds and the site was abandoned; no one comes here, and there are already myths about why the *kafirs* chose to discontinue the excavation."

The matte silence settled around them once again. In her imagination she could envision the energy of the dig, the native workers, the shouts, the chants, the bustling sense of adventure as each foot of the *serdab* was uncovered inch by painstaking inch.

Her father had lived for the adventure, despite the tedious nature of the work. He had loved the moments of infinitesimal discovery, the triumph of deduction and the unearthing of that which had been buried for centuries.

He ought not to have married her mother, she thought mordantly; he should never have had daughters. He ought to have been alone so he could have devoted his whole life to wandering and excavating and never have had the yoke of duty binding his ambition. He could have finished the palace. He could have walked in the paths of ancient tribes and found insight into the ages.

She felt a tearing sadness at his having been so constricted; what had he really been like? She had never known. There had never been a hint of any of this, ever, in his letters or his demeanor when he had returned home.

There had only been that single-minded devotion to work which had so enraged her mother, and which, latterly, she had always suspected, her mother had used to make herself mortally ill.

But even that was not so, if she could believe Culhane. All those months of caring for her and shunting away the needs of Allegra . . . and all of it had been a part of some great villainous game of cat and mouse that her father had known must surely culminate in his death.

She did not sense his presence in Khuramafar. He had not been to this place in ten years, yet he'd told her that here he had excavated a pair of bracelets which had turned out not to be bracelets.

He could have left no other message here.

The weight of centuries pushed down on her shoulders.

"We have made this journey for nothing," she said into the still silence.

"There is a reason your father told you what he did."

"Then *you* must discover it with that bloody intuition of yours."

"It doesn't work that way, Alexandra. There is a reason fate compelled me to bring you here. This is the last thing I can do for your father, and I feel strongly that he meant us to come to Khuramafar, that he left something for us here, something that is relevant to the bracelets."

"As opposed to the cylinders we left at the Legation House. How could you decide unequivocally they were fakes?"

"It was too easy a clue. A word about your father and suddenly Lady Gore produces the very item we need to complete the puzzle? I think not. Dzmura is everywhere. I think your father deliberately left counterfeit cylinders—Lady Gore surely could not have told the difference—and was canny enough to leave more subtle clues."

"You think he just left clues in some kind of trail?"

"Yes. And I think they lead in this direction for a purpose."

"Perhaps he really did come here—for a day or two—well before—"

He sensed the thought she was about to voice: "—well before he got word about your mother. Because he was getting too close, and Dzmura knew he had come here. That might be why Dzmura had to deflect him in some critical way . . ."

"So he wouldn't actually have lied . . ."

"Only by omission." He levered himself upright suddenly. "We need to explore the ruins." He moved towards the horses and then stopped. "I'll put the horses out of sight. Take the saddlebags and the blankets. If we have to stay here, we have provisions for a night, and a lamp. Quick . . ."

She didn't know what he sensed or why it was suddenly so urgent they proceed, but while he concealed the horses, she quickly dragged the saddles and then the bags to the mouth of the tunnel.

When he returned, she placed everything inside the underground room while he kept watch. Then he ducked in and joined her.

There was no time to admire the architecture. She had a distinct impression of coolness and of a cluster of slender columns spaced proportionately across the room. The floor and walls were marble; their footsteps echoed as they quickly pulled their belongings through the room and, a hundred feet distant, out into a courtyard.

The sun poured through here and onto a mosaic of brick and tile work, in the center of which was an ornate stonework fountain. Surrounding this was one side of the excavated palace—a series of arched, carved stone entryways which led to various rooms off the courtyard.

It was like walking into another world, into the vast stillness of the ages where nothing had changed and everything was immune to the ravages of time.

A half-dozen rooms had been uncovered, four of them leading directly off the courtyard.

The tilework was intricate and covered the walls and floors, each room in a different design and different colors. In three of the rooms some tiles were cracked or missing. But in the fourth, it was as if the princess of the palace could walk through the door in the next minute.

This was not a large room: there was an arched entryway. Two arched windows looked down on the valley, and several niches and shelves were built into the walls to hold her precious belongings. A stone bench, as long and wide as a bed, with an inlaid design of gold and copper, stood against one wall. There was a fire pit in the center of the room, recessed into the floor and surrounded by a ledge where the princess could rest her feet for warmth.

They brought their gear into this room and spread out the blankets and Alexandra began to remove the shrouding tunic.

"Don't do that yet. You need that protection from the sun. We are going to search this place, top to bottom, beginning with the outside courtyard."

And they did. He did not know what they were looking for, but he was certain they had to find something.

The late afternoon sun bore down on them as they went over the courtyard inch by inch on their hands and knees until shadows edged across the tiled floor.

"There's nothing there," Ryder said finally, grimly. "I was hoping . . ."

"Another set of cylinders . . . ?"

"They undoubtedly exist, but they are most likely hidden somewhere in Tirhan."

"But why? Maybe he had done the thing long before he had gone back through Tirhan. Maybe even before my mother's death. Just because he knew he might not have communication with you."

"Perhaps," he said noncommittally, "or perhaps"—a new thought struck him—"perhaps he returned to England by way of Baghdad in order to come here."

"Which means the real cylinders could be secreted here and he left the counterfeits at the Legation House to throw Dzmura off the track."

"Maybe . . . maybe—"

"He could have started for Tabriz and gone south. Why was it you assumed he travelled the same route we did?"

"Indeed . . ." he murmured. "Yes, Baghdad makes sense, and then through Damascus to Istanbul—very possible . . ." He looked up at the sky. "There is no point to continuing out here. I must think about this. We will stay the night in the princess' chamber. Go make yourself ready."

The change of subject was so abrupt, she could only stare at him. *"What?"*

"Nothing has changed, whether we are at the Legation House or in the Bazzi Palace. Go make yourself ready and do not waste my time or the night."

She stamped into the princess' chamber and furiously shucked the tunic and veil and the beautiful necklace. He was vile, utterly vile—and single-minded in his pursuit of gratification. Nothing interfered with it, nothing.

He had meant to teach her a lesson the other night, but she would never capitulate unless she wanted to, though he had not been chastened by her defiance.

She had already learned the lesson of the harem: the pasha had the power and the women had none. They were ornaments and toys to exist at his pleasure and his whim.

Her own passion-fogged gratification was irrelevant. It was. It *was.*

But her treacherous body told her otherwise. She was shuddering with suppressed excitement as she furiously paced the room.

. . . Go make yourself ready . . .

The lord and his command—she wanted to throw it back in his face. And she simultaneously wanted to strip off her clothing and make herself ready for him.

"Are you naked, odalisque?"

Her breath caught. "I—"

He strode into the room. "You keep no bargains, do you? You toy with my temper, and you waste your passion. All this time I might have had the pleasure of your body, yet you waste our time. All day long you have been covered up, away from my sight. For two days I have ached for you. And still my odalisque refutes the bargain and denies me."

Her heart pounded wildly. "Let me see. Let me see how hard you want me."

"I think not, odalisque. You should have been naked in anticipation of my need."

Her gaze drifted downward, between his legs; in her mind's eye she envisioned him as he had reclined in the scurrilous mud hut, explosively waiting for her to obey his commands. As he was waiting for her now, throbbing with unrequited passion, aroused to a towering lust for her by the mere thought of her naked body.

This was the power of an odalisque, unbearably arousing in its potency.

"You hardly gave me time."

"It takes no time to rip away civilization for the pleasures of the flesh," he rasped, "and too much time to find ways to defy me." He came closer and closer and she began backing away. "I will strip you, the way you begged me to do the other night."

He grabbed her hair and pulled her unmercifully towards him until he could grasp the collar of her dress. "This is my strength, odalisque, to make you obey," he declared and he pulled at the garment brutally, tore it down the front with one sharp yank.

She wore very little under it: the chemise and pantalettes and the black stockings, and he pitilessly ripped them off of her body and threw them out the door.

"Now, odalisque," he growled, still holding her hair, "now you are ready for me the way I am ready for you."

"Let me see how ready," she whispered, thrilled to her core that he wanted her so desperately.

"Oh no, no, odalisque—that you did not earn."

"But then I would remember how much even the thought of possessing me aroused you," she whispered coaxingly, as he tugged still tighter on her hair. "Let me feel you."

He caught her hands as she reached out to cup his massive erection. "You will feel how hard I am, odalisque. Tonight." He lowered his mouth to hers. "Tonight we will not waste my passion." He crushed her lips and delved for her tongue.

She sagged against him as the wet heat of his mouth invaded hers. Her body writhed as her spiralling need escalated with the flick of his tongue. She opened her mouth to him and begged for his hot thick kisses.

He lifted his mouth from hers for a torturous moment. "Naked and willing, odalisque, begging for my passion . . ." He covered her mouth again and pulled her head backwards so that he could delve more fully into the heated depth of it.

"Now . . . take my saddle to the center of the room and kneel over it." He plunged into her willing mouth once again, hard and quick and thick, and then he let her go and watched her move to obey his command, then getting on her knees and leaning her body into the curve of the saddle seat.

She looked just as he had envisioned her all day, with her upper torso resting on the floor and the seat of the saddle lifting her buttocks deliciously to invite his caresses.

He wanted her instantly, volcanically; he tore off his clothes and clamped his hands onto the lush curves of her buttocks.

She almost swooned at his harsh touch; the waiting, the waiting—had he not said the anticipation only heightened the desire? Her imagination went spinning into memory, the feel of him, the first ramrod push of possession; the full, tight feminine hug of his rampant manhood contained fully and deeply within her . . . the waiting, oh the waiting . . .

She felt his hands positioning her, lifting her to give him full purchase in this thrilling reverse way. She loved it that she could not see him, that she could only imagine the towering thrust of him until the very moment she felt it and that his sole possession of her would be by the very male essence of him.

She arched her body to entice him to her, shimmying her hips, begging him to take her.

. . . the waiting . . .

It was as if he knew her impatience, as if he wanted to prolong the excitement of his joining with her, as if he wanted her to submit to her erotic nature and her need for him—and only him.

He heard her heavy breathing, her panting, her begging moans as he grasped her buttocks and waited a long long moment to watch her writhe with anticipation of his first possessive thrust.

Her body was tense with longing, shuddering with voluptuous excitement.

And he waited; he waited with the thick ridged tip of his manhood poised for the very moment he would drive into her wanton sex, his hands flexing with tension, his body taut with wanting her.

His . . .

. . . his . . .

She pushed herself demandingly against his hands.

. . . his—he pushed himself against the lush wet cleft of her womanhood . . .

. . . naked—he thrust into her with all the power of his body—

—odalisque—he drove into her like a piston, hot and hard, and long and strong and primitive as a rock—

He took her—

He gave to her—

And the moment she felt his powerful possession of her, there was the shattering starburst of pleasure exploding all over her body like fireworks, hot and soaring, petering out into a glowing sizzle until there was no more sensation but the furious pumping of his body against hers, driving and driving and driving into a volcanic explosion of sensation that wrung him to the core.

And then . . . the silence of repletion.

Sometime later, he carried her to the stone divan, which he overlaid with blankets, and lay down beside her.

Dreamy with satiation, she loved the feel of his strong hard body next to her naked skin.

She loved the thick probing of his tongue into her mouth in the darkness while she slept. She answered his kisses languidly, wetly, letting him seduce her with the succulent caresses of his tongue.

His kisses aroused her, slowly and expertly, swirls of sensation centered in her mouth, deeper and deeper; taking her tongue, sucking it avidly, licking her lips, whispering his ravenous need for her.

Her body curled against him languorously.

"I want you now," he whispered.

"Take me now," she breathed, her body pliant and ready for him.

He mounted her, slick and sliding easily into her welcoming fold. He took her gently, firmly, rocking his hips against her, warming her body from the cold.

He took her with kisses, with sweet caresses, and gentle words.

He took her with feeling, as though his body knew their erotic games not only pleasured them but bonded them in a way he could not yet admit.

He took her softly, reverently, so deliciously she felt she was floating on a cloud. And then the feelings thickened and clotted and melted into a creamy thick squeeze of sensation that erupted into her very vitals.

So soft . . .

Her kisses muted; he pushed himself one more time, soft, thick, driving into a spume of a release that pulled out his very soul.

And then he slept.

Chapter 18

He was gone in the morning, and she knew a frightening moment of unreasoning panic.

She was alone in a windowless room that reeked of the scent of sex in an abandoned dig thousands of miles from her home, and just maybe she was being pursued by a madman. How Culhane could have left her alone, she could not understand.

There was barely any light in the room either—it filtered in through the door to the courtyard, but that was shaded by a column of arches.

She groped around on the floor to find what remained of her dress and, by feel, determined that it was salvageable if she could find something to tie around her waist . . . a stocking perhaps or that cursed veil.

The stockings were ruined, so she braided them together and belted the dress and put on her boots, then rummaged for the necklace and the veil to cover her head. Thus armed, she went out into the courtyard.

Culhane was there, waiting for her, his cool gray gaze flickering over her makeshift dress without expression, the heat of their coupling once again utterly dissipated in the light of day.

"We need to stay here for another several days."

She hesitated a moment. "All right."

"I have to go back into the village for supplies and water for the horses. I want to go now and be back before noon."

"I can't stay here alone."

"You have to. No one could find us here."

She sniffed. "Anything is possible—you have said so your-self."

"I'll be gone no more than two hours. It has to be, otherwise we would have to leave before sundown. I'm leaving you the gun—"

"I won't touch the weapon of an assassin."

"Nevertheless . . ."

She made no move toward it, and he set it on the ledge of the fountain.

"*Alexandra. . . !*"

She looked at him with stormy eyes. "I don't want you to go."

"You'd rather return in the morning."

"I—no . . . I don't know. I'd rather go with you."

"Back to the *caravanserai.*"

"Yes! No . . ."

"I will be back in two hours, Alexandra, and the sooner I go . . ."

She took a deep shuddery breath. "All right."

He gave her a hard swift kiss and ducked into the *serdab* and out of her sight.

She had the eerie feeling she was tumbling back in time. The silence was unearthly. Her heart pounded like a thunderstorm. Fear washed away her common sense like a drenching rain.

She ran after him, through the *serdab,* and out onto the plateau of rocks—just in time to hear the clatter of hooves as he made his way up into the hills.

She was truly alone now, and she had never felt anything like this emptiness—not even when her father died.

She cautiously made her way through the *serdab* and into the courtyard, where she felt safer and she could see everything.

Hesitantly, she picked up the gun.

She hated the weapon; it just fit into the palm of her hand, and the weight and heft of it were perfect for her.

She knew so little about guns: he ought to have taught her.

He had taught her other things.

How far she had come since one month ago. And now the story was almost at an end.

Her father might be a hero, who had tried to stop a disaster with subtle clues and the knowledge that the minions of Dzmura marched everywhere.

How clever he had been then to bypass them through Khuramafar, and to plant false clues in the face of his enemies.

She had hardly known her father at all.

And now she did not know herself.

The silence was deafening. She sat curled up just inside the column by the princess' chamber door.

She wished she could sleep. If she could, the time would pass quickly and he would be back before she knew it.

Nor could she lose herself in the reverie of what had passed between them the night before. In the daylight, it became just another dream, delicious in its intensity, and fraught with consequences she did not wish to think about.

And she could not bring herself to think about Allegra. It was easier to think about enemies and clues than to try to imagine what Dzmura might have done with her.

The whole thing was unimaginable, and as she sat in the steepening silence and the sun rose farther and farther into the sky, she thought she might be the only person alive in the whole world.

The silence was getting to her.

She got to her feet and went back into the princess' chamber, but she didn't see that there was anything she could effectually do in there.

Out in the courtyard, the sun was blazing. The silence expanded. Her feeling of abandonment intensified.

And then she heard a whickering sound—a horse. A horse! Culhane was back—and just in time. She had thought she was going mad!

She ducked into the *serdab* and raced out onto the plateau.

For a moment, the sun blinded her eyes.

And then she saw him.

"*You!*"

And that was the last thing she knew.

* * *

He felt the exact moment when he disconnected with her, and he had never known such a moment of impotence, had never raced anywhere so fast in his life.

Futile . . . He had known it even as he was pounding back to the Bazzi Palace.

. . . *gone* . . .

The word settled in his mind like a ten-pound weight.

Dzmura was everywhere, his methods of infiltration beyond rationality.

He raced like the wind toward the palace, tumbled off of his horse and dashed through the *serdab* into the courtyard.

The gun lay ominously on the ground.

There was nothing else.

Her tunic lay on the floor in the corner of the princess' chamber; the blankets on which they had lain were undisturbed.

He retraced his steps, and just as he was coming through the *serdab* he heard the soft whickering of his horse.

. . . as she had heard—

He felt it clearly: she had thought he had arrived.

She came willingly, and as she stepped onto the plateau she would not have known it was not he until it was too late.

Her horse was still tethered to a stand of trees near an outcropping behind the plateau.

He walked slowly back to the courtyard, bringing with him the saddlebags loaded with provisions.

He had brought her milk to slake her thirst.

He picked up the gun, pocketed it, unpacked the saddlebags and drank the milk himself.

And then he sat down to wait.

They had thrown a blanket over her and they had tied her up, had thrown her like a sack of flour across a saddle, and now they were racing across a hellish landscape that bounced and jounced her until she thought all her bones had jarred loose.

It only intensified her terror. Dzmura had spread his web once again, and this time he had intentionally caught her . . .

. . . Dear God, she couldn't move; she lay in muffled blackness, as helpless as she had ever been in her life . . . a moment away from death if the horseman let her slip . . .

Her screams had been lost in the wind.

Her panic bound her tighter than any bonds.

She wanted to live, and they were racing toward the prophet of death.

Hours. They had been travelling for hours. She thought she had fainted. She thought she felt her captor's hands all over her helpless body, but she could not retaliate and her convulsive protests raged into the silence.

She was so thirsty she thought she would die.

She heard no conversation at all among the conspirators. They were acting in concert. She heard the simultaneous clop of hooves as her rider suddenly pulled in the reins and the pace slackened and then slowed further and still further until they were at a canter.

Dear God, she wanted some respite from the bone-wracking journey and the horrible violation of her captive body.

She didn't dare move.

The horses began climbing: she felt the push of gravity and the slant of the horse's back.

Now the pace was slow, a hesitant *clip-clip* over sharp stone. Up and up and then a final levelling out.

Clip-clip—slowly now. Maybe they were almost there. Almost. Almost there.

The horses stopped.

A bell. Jabbering voices. Her rider dismounted, his weight depressing the saddle so that her body shifted.

The hands were at her again, and she squirmed frantically away.

She felt other hands grasping her, pawing at her, pushing at her to move her forward, roughly squeezing her buttocks.

She was like a mummy, tied and wrapped in coarse sacking, at the mercy of her captors. They lifted her, carrying her like a coffin, one at her feet and two at her shoulders.

The only sounds she heard were the shuffling of their feet and the chittering sound of people following them, speaking a tongue she did not understand.

It was like dying, floating along like a cloud and hoping she wouldn't fall off.

... She could die ...

... *Culhane ...!*

More shuffling, more voices and then one above the rest, forceful, resolute—authority:

"*Hakkam. Hakkam. Salaam, Hakkam!*"

Everything stopped. Her captors slanted her body to the floor to a standing position.

The voices muted into silence and the silence blanketed everything, everyone.

And the waiting.

Did she not know the power of waiting?

Waiting dredged into a depth of feeling, but this time it was pure unalloyed fear.

Her heart started pounding. She felt a hand on her, sliding down her back and cupping her buttocks.

A gong sounded somewhere in the distance; those around her murmured, "*Salaam, Hakkam, salaam,*" and she heard the shuffle of bodies dropping to the floor.

Then a reverent hush.

And then *his* voice: "You have done well, *khouans,* very very well. The end is near. We will conduct a *medha* in your honor for the work you have done today. And now ... now it is time to unveil the captive so she may take her place among my chosen."

Rough hands pulled at her ropes, seeking in any way possible to degrade her still more by their touch.

And then they lifted the blanket, and one by one, she memorized their faces: Colonel Rosedale, Freddie Alderson, Barclay Gore, traitors all, and agents of the man before whom she stood.

"My dear," Dzmura said condescendingly, "welcome to Bakharha Palace. And now, of course, you will please remove your clothes."

He prowled the Bazzi Palace, feeling her anguish, suppressing his own.

The impressions were intermittent, gritty with determination and futile protests. And then the aching wail of his name ...

Dzmura had her; he was as sure of that as he was of his life. And Dzmura would use her; it would be yet another reason for him to calmly and without compunction take the bastard's life.

And still he waited, with all the ingrained patience he could muster when that little pulse in the back of his mind thrummed her name, breathed her scent, remembered their thousand and one nights, swore that she would belong to no other man.

He had meant it; he hadn't known he meant it.

He waited.

Dzmura blocked him, willfully and triumphantly, after the last mournful call. And he knew, as he had always known, he would never find Dzmura without the key to the bracelets.

And he waited. Had he not taught her about waiting? But she could not know of the waiting that dredged the depths of a man's fear and anguish, the will to action that was stultified by the need for knowledge that did not come easily or obviously.

He waited, sitting in the sanctuary of the chamber where they had become the first man and woman on earth, he waited.

The fire he had built out of coals he had brought banked low in the *tandur,* throwing little heat as the night poured over the valley.

The sense of her permeated the chamber.

He closed his eyes and he could feel her. He had only to think of her to want her.

And they had gotten her, somehow. In spite of precautions, in spite of ruses to throw them off the track, they had gotten her.

Was there no end to Dzmura and his treachery?

Sir Peregrine had known, and somewhere in these ruins he had left the answer. He had come deliberately to Khuramafar, after planting the false cylinders, to leave the answer.

He had left a trail of convoluted clues all wrapped up in his most sensible and down-to-earth daughter, and he fully expected that his protégé would somehow appear on his doorstep to follow through.

He must have expected that Dzmura would claim him.

A clawing hatred knifed through Culhane's heart.

The thing was done, and retribution must be paid. It was the way of desert; he was nothing more than an instrument.

It was a matter of putting himself in the mind of his mentor and finding his way.

He settled back against the stone divan and prepared himself for a long and sleepless night.

She fought them. His followers stood back, astonished by her powerful resistance.

Dzmura was amused. Alexandra had always been the stubborn one, and in her rank insubordination, she was utterly desirable and totally unaware that they were ripping what was left of her dress to shreds.

"I get the cheeky bitch first," Colonel Rosedale panted, his thick hands barely holding onto her writhing body. "The little she-wolf teased the life into me and then balked at the last minute. So wise of you to bring her here to learn the lessons of submission, *Hakkam*. I beg for the privilege of teaching her."

"Oh no," Alderson protested, surrounding her from the front, tearing at her dress and trying to capture her flailing hands. "Let me. Young flesh. Fresh. Pliable. Smooth and unblemished. I'll whip her into shape in no time, *Hakkam*."

"Gentlemen," Dzmura said chidingly, and immediately the two desisted and moved away from her. "Miss deLisle is a woman of the world. Such women are treasures and must be shown the value of the ways of the harem. We do not force. We only show—and contain."

Barclay Gore shoved her forward. "You owe great gratitude to the mercy of the *Hakkam*. He doesn't intercede for everyone."

"Only for you," she spat, wheeling on him.

He immediately grabbed her shoulder, wrenched her back against his thick body and grabbed her breasts. "*Hakkam*, should not such disobedience be punished? It would be my pleasure to serve you in the capacity of disciplinarian."

Dzmura raised his hands. "My gratitude to you all, but I intend to take a personal interest in Miss deLisle's education. A very personal interest. Therefore, it will be my pleasure to guide, correct and chastise her as the need arises. But Alexandra is an intelligent woman. She will see very soon there is no need for punishment when she surrenders herself to her female instincts and her senses."

Alexandra stared at him mutinously. "How kind of you to save me from the gross debauchery of these libertine traitors. Surely you can't believe I am so biddable?"

"I could leave it all to their discretion, my dear, and then, perhaps, we would see."

She bit her lip, knowing he was fully capable of unleashing these animals on her. But what would amuse him most, to see her debased or to see her compliant?

"Where is my sister?"

"Ah, the beautiful and luscious Alya. Her harem name, Alexandra, just as we will bestow one upon you. Alya awaits my pleasure, gentlemen, and yours. Esmat will escort you."

He waited and watched as one of his company stood aside and motioned to her abductors. One by one they followed him through a brass door, and it closed ominously behind them.

"Excellent. Excellent men, don't you think, Alexandra? Would you ever have conceived of Sir Barclay Gore as one of my initiates? I have lured him by the promise of things to come and by the heaven he has found at Bakharha Palace. And so it will be with you once you understand what is expected of you. I will send you now with Biju who will be responsible for your obedience. Biju speaks some English, and she will make everything known to you. And then—perhaps—if you are obedient, I will let you see . . . Alya."

She hated him; she had hated him before, but she positively despised him now. And she would beat him. Somehow she would beat him and would repay him in kind for what he had done to her and for his insidious subjugation of her sister.

She picked up what was left of her clothing and the beautiful necklace she had worn around her neck and followed the woman Biju through the brass door.

She entered a wonderland; it was the only word for it. Behind the stone walls of the plateau were tiles and arches, mirrors and fretwork, nooks and fountains, vaulted cove-molded ceilings and dazzling mosaics—greens, blues, fawn and brown, umber and purple against a background of ivory and white. These were set off by glorious carpets and several excellent pieces of imported European furniture.

Biju, who was dressed in a pair of thin black silk trousers gathered at the ankle and waist, an embroidered black vest which barely covered her breasts, and a *yashmak* which concealed her hair and the lower half of her face, said not a word as they passed through room after splendid room, all empty, all glorious in color and conception.

Finally they stopped at still another door, this one arched and surrounded by a molding above which there was a marble frieze with words inscribed on it.

"This is the house of women," Biju said, and she threw open the door.

Here too was splendor: large clustered fretwork-covered windows and languid divans draped in silks, and carpets beneath; a table with a tray still on it, a drift of transparent gauze trailing over the edge of a chair. The air was redolent with the scent of attar of roses.

She had the impression of a covert presence, as if the women were watching her, and she wondered if Allegra was among them. Allegra, *not* Alya.

She wondered where Biju was taking her, as they passed through two rooms which were heated much more intensely than those through which she had come and then into a vaulted arched tunnel at the end of which was a vast pool surrounded by marble.

She could see the steam rising from the water, and the sunlight filtering in from the skylights above gave it an unearthly air. All around there were built-in marble benches, stone jugs were placed at intervals along the ledge and the ever-present rugs were scattered on the floor.

The bath was empty, but still there was that sense of a hidden presence, watching and watching, to see perhaps what she would do.

Biju indicated a bench and she moved to it and sat down.

"Bathe you will now please," she said, holding out her hands.

"I? No," Alexandra shook her head. *"No."*

"Yes, you will bathe. *Hakkam* commands it."

"*Hakkam* does not command me."

"In the house of women, we obey."

It is so simple for her, Alexandra thought, and she found that perfectly logical.

"Water is warm, feels good. Will make you ready for what is to come. Clothes, please."

"*No!*"

"As you wish." She clapped her hands, once, twice and once again, and then she spoke: "Najib. She will not obey *Hakkam's* command."

Alexandra jerked her head around. Standing behind her was the biggest man she had ever seen; he looked ten feet tall, he might have been six; and he was broad and muscular with huge flexing hands and an impassive expression that said volumes about his willingness to aid Biju in her quest for obedience.

She swallowed hard and took a deep breath. "I will bathe."

Biju nodded because of course she had expected capitulation. "You will give clothes to Najib."

Alexandra froze at the thought of disrobing in front of this massive black man, even if half of her body was already exposed, but there was no arguing with Biju—not over this at any rate.

She stood up reluctantly and untied her stocking sash and shrugged out of what remained of her dress, handing it to Najib, then her boots.

All that remained was the necklace tied loosely around her neck with the ends hanging.

Biju motioned to it.

Alexandra balked. "It was a gift to me. I will keep it."

"No gifts, only gifts from *Hakkam*."

God, she hated her nakedness in this place of women, and she hated arguing with this obdurate zealot.

"*Hakkam* will give me no gifts. I will keep it."

She stared at Biju, at her unfathomable black eyes and elongated brows, the only thing visible over the mask of the *yashmak*, and Biju bowed first, but only to keep peace as *Hakkam* had adjured her.

"*Hakkam* will decide. The necklace."

Alexandra handed over the necklace, which Biju folded into her hand and tucked into the pocket of her trousers. She then waved Najib away.

"The bath, *mem-sahib.*"

There was nothing left to her incipient rebellion. She stepped down into the water and was instantly enveloped by the scent of perfume and oil.

"Jada!" Biju called and snapped her fingers.

Instantly a dusky young woman appeared, naked except for the turban wound around her head.

"Your slave, *mem-sahib,* who serves both you and Alya. Jada will wash you and see to everything until I return."

Alexandra took a tentative step out of the bath as Jada marched right in. "But—"

"I will wash," Jada said, grasping her shoulder firmly with one hand and lifting a jug off the ledge with the other. "I . . ." This last sentence was spoken as if she expected Alexandra to produce others to fight over the favor.

Again, she was left with no way to protest. It was easier to let Jada carry on.

From behind the columns and the latticework doors, she heard murmuring.

The women were watching, curious, envious perhaps, of *Hakkam's* new toy.

They drifted out slowly, cautiously, from the arched tunnel into the bath. Eyeing her suspiciously, they slipped into the water and circled around her as Jada scrubbed her tender skin.

They murmured behind their hands as they scrutinized her; she heard laughter and a buzzing sound, whispers as she examined them boldly.

They were hardly any different than she. They were all sizes and shapes, dark and light, fair and plain. And there were so many of them, wandering in and out of the room, and the bath, sitting on the stone benches, whispering confidences to each other as they strolled around the ledges, or just disappearing as suddenly as they had come through another of the vaulted tunnels which led in a different direction.

She didn't know what to make of it. Three dozen women, naked and unself-consciously bathing and gossipping as if this were some ritual and nothing out of the ordinary.

She hated it.

"Come," Jada said, holding out her hands.

She grasped them and Jada pulled her from the bath and onto the ledge.

The whispering grew more intense.

"There," Jada said, pointing to the second tunnel, and she led her past the languidly gossiping women, through the tunnel and into a room steaming with warmth where she toweled her off and then pushed her to lie down on a covered bench, then proceeded to massage every inch of her body and rub oils and scent into her hair, her hands and her feet.

Alexandra resisted, tensing her muscles against the touch of Jada so that she would not relax into it as she so dearly wanted to do.

But her body was not proof against such delightful handling after all she had been through. It rebelled; her aching limbs melted under the brisk and stimulating massage, and in the end she almost fell asleep under Jada's ministrations.

But there was more: Jada roused her and led her into another room which was furnished with overstuffed divans and sumptuous rugs and hangings on the wall. In the center was a fountain gently splashing, and to one side a musician played a lilting song on a rippling harp.

Slaves meandered among the women, offering coffee, fruit and sweetmeats; several of the women were smoking pipes; others were exchanging secrets; still others napped.

Jada sat her down on one of the opulent little sofas, twisted up her hair and pinned it and then enfolded her in a warm blanket, laid her down and covered her with still another blanket.

"You sleep. Biju come," she said, patting Alexandra's shoulder.

And Alexandra could sleep. The air was heavy with a mixture of scents: the coffee, the perfume, the sweet dreamy opiate. She was aware of the heat of her body as she sank into oblivion.

She was succumbing too easily; she wasn't even fighting, she

thought dreamily. Culhane had taught her well. Submission, subjugation, all at the man's will.

It wasn't an erotic game anymore. It was something infinitely
more real—and more insidious.

But she would think of that later—that and the mystery of
Allegra . . . Allegra who was now Alya . . .

. . . She slept.

Chapter 19

Who was she? Who *was* she?

Wrapped in splendor, deep in dreams, she was the houri who could enslave a suzerain; her power was absolute, her surrender her scepter. And for her he would provide this eden of luxury in which she would tend her nakedness all for him to ready herself to submit solely at his demand. How little to pay to subjugate a king.

And she could immerse herself in this world of sensuality forever.

. . . Forever . . .

. . . She craved it. She wanted it. Even in her dreams, her body yielded to it. She would be his, silk against stone, forever . . .

In his mind's eye, Culhane walked the path of Sir Peregrine, from the moment he received the telegram through his feelings of desperation at having to give up his quest and return to England.

What would he have known? He would have known Dzmura was watching.

He would have known that his protégé would eventually follow him home.

He would have felt utterly defeated, would have been frantic to find a way to communicate with *him*.

He would have immediately thought to use that medium which linked them. Then . . . how?

It had to be portable, something which Dzmura would apprehend—not immediately. And it could not be all in one piece because that would negate the function of it.

He would need to think of distracting Dzmura just in case Dzmura did discover what he was about.

He would have to have started the thing as he travelled from Alekkah to Tirhan in order to have the counterfeit cylinders ready.

Which meant he must have found the votive receptacles in Alekkah and sacrificed them to the greater need.

Perhaps he had planned even sooner to leave some communication for him, and the receptacles had been decided upon long before the death of his wife.

Two similar vessels on which he had begun to inscribe the message—and then the telegram came . . .

He must make arrangements to leave immediately. He knows not where Culhane has gone or when he might expect him.

He has no choice: he must take the votives with him. He knows that the first place Culhane would come before starting for Alekkah would be the Legation House.

He wants to leave a message for him.

. . . *Do not trust* . . .

The impression was strong, immediate and clear: . . . *Do not trust* . . .

He reached for his pouch and pulled out the rubbing he had made of the cylinders and the bracelets.

Even by the light of the fire—the candlelight in the bedroom of the Legation House—he saw the markings did not match.

But he had not looked for a message.

He removed the rubbing of the cylinders and studied it.

. . . *Gore* . . .

He didn't see it: the name flew up at him from the fire, from the instinct in his belly . . . and then it grew out of the markings on the tissue.

. . . *Gore* . . .

Bloody damn . . .

Something had to have happened at the Legation House. He had changed his mind about the missing pieces; he had meant to leave them there, simply and in plain sight, clues that only Culhane could interpret but which would look, along with the several other valuable artifacts, just like pieces he wished to leave in safekeeping with Lady Gore—as *she* had told them.

. . . *Gore* . . .

Goddamn . . .

And so he had left them, and instead of proceeding to Tabriz, he had gone south to Khuramafar, and somewhere in the Bazzi Palace, knowing his protégé would immediately head there first if he had construed the clues properly, Sir Peregrine deLisle had left the rest of the message of the bracelets.

So many ifs . . . He had counted on so much: that Ryder would come, that his *knowing* would sense the things he must do. He had counted on his questioning Alexandra, on his being allowed into the secret room, on his finding the duplicate set of bracelets and his understanding exactly what they were.

And he had relied on his keeping his promise regarding the reckoning with Dzmura.

"Mem-sahib."

The voice was flat, commanding, and Alexandra opened her eyes dreamily.

It was Biju, standing directly over her, and calmly waiting for her to come fully awake.

"It is time."

Alexandra struggled to a sitting position. "Time for what?"

"We must go." She pulled away the cover and motioned for Alexandra to rise.

"I need a robe."

"No robe, *mem-sahib*. You understand. Nothing is hidden. We will go."

"I will not go without a robe."

Biju regarded her dispassionately. "This is the way. Nothing is hidden. Everything is displayed for the pleasure of *Hakkam* who delights in the beauty of all his women."

"I am not his woman, and I wish for a robe."

"Najib will carry you."

She felt the first stirring of panic. *"No!"*

Biju shrugged. "You must do as is the custom. You belong to

Hakkam, and his command must be obeyed. Nothing is hidden, everything is displayed for the pleasure of he who by his will and wish deigns to pleasure us. You will come with me please."

They were all naked, every last one of them, except Biju, with her small rippling body, who walked ahead of Alexandra with conscious grace as if she were hoping *Hakkam* was watching and that she pleased him.

Again, Alexandra had no choice but to follow, and again, she had the distinct impression that the women were looking at her and judging her; she stiffened her spine and tossed her head as they left the rest room and padded through elaborate hallways strewn with carpets and fragrant with the scent of the flowers in vases set in niches high above them in the walls.

Somewhere in this labyrinth, she would find her sister.

Biju stopped before an archway that led into a room which was as sumptuous as all of those through which they had passed, except here there was an alcove in which was a raised stone bench, obviously a bed.

"This will be your place. You will learn everything very soon. *Hakkam* will send your sister to you, and she will explain the rest."

She bowed then, and withdrew, walking slowly backwards, her head bowed, until she was out of sight.

Alexandra ran to the doorway, and immediately Najib appeared, tall as a mountain, threatening as a storm.

She backed away until she stumbled over the covers and rugs that were heaped on the bed, and she fell backwards onto its hard surface and just lay there, propped up on her elbows, frantic with fear and humiliated by her nudity.

The sun filtered into the princess' chamber, and slowly he awakened from a sleep fraught with nightmares. There was something he had to remember, something that had seemed so obvious in his dreams.

He built the fire again, and poured out some water into a tin and set it on the coals.

. . . circle . . .

As always, the impression came out of nowhere. He studied the tin for a moment, dredging up the sense of his dreams, all of which were senseless, except for this one pertinent thing.

The fire pit was circular, the tin sitting on the coals. The water was steaming, a moment away from the boil.

What had been the dream? Alexandra in the arms of Dzmura, submitting to his will, Allegra in the corner wielding a knife; the two vying for the attention of Dzmura, clashing, fighting, stealing from each other the paint and jewelry to beautify themselves to attract Dzmura. Alexandra, with bracelets, a gift from Dzmura, flaunting them in front of her sister; beautiful gold, inlaid with jewels, crisscrossing in a matching pattern, to be worn together to dazzle Dzmura's eye; Allegra, furtive and wily, stealing one—only one—knowing even that would bring down Dzmura's wrath. Hiding the bracelet so that no one would ever find it, and watching with malicious glee as Dzmura meted out the punishment: the taking of Allegra before her sister's very eyes, making an example of Allegra's abject submission to his will . . .

. . . *circle* . . .

He had expected such dreams, rife with components of the thoughts which occupied his life.

But still—*circle*—and a nightmare of subjugation and repression, complete with bracelets—

—*matching* bracelets . . .

. . . bracelets were circular . . .

. . . the cylinders were circular . . .

. . . something circular—because—because—

. . . because otherwise he would not be able to match the bracelets to the message . . .

. . . *circle* . . .

What in the whole of the Bazzi Palace was circular?

. . . the fire pit . . . the fountain . . . the columns—

He jumped to his feet and made for the courtyard.

She had wrapped herself in the thinnest of the blankets and sat brooding on the bed.

Time had passed: she marked it by the way the light streamed in through the latticework shutters that covered the windows.

She had even tried opening them, but they were fixed in place to discourage the recalcitrant slave who thought to open the window and jump.

After a long long while, she heard voices beyond the columns of the recess of the entrance to her room, and then a woman walked in slowly and warily.

She was naked as well, her skin rosy and rich, her glossy dark hair streaming down her back and caught around her forehead by an ornamental gold circlet from which golden discs were appended. Attached to this was a silver embroidered cloth which covered her mouth so that all Alexandra could see were bright green eyes rimmed with kohl and brows which had been darkened and elongated so that they met over the bridge of her nose.

On her wrists she wore diamond bracelets, and around one ankle was a thick gold cuff.

But when she spoke, the voice was Allegra's.

"Alixe? Alixe? Oh, Alixe . . ." She ran lightly to the bed and gathered Alexandra up in her arms. "I'm so glad you're here. Oh, Alixe—look at you . . ."

Alexandra couldn't say a word. She was utterly bewitched by her sister's appearance and by the obvious: Allegra was not a bit unhappy.

"Ah! Tebo told me you would come, and here you are. Let me look at you."

She pushed away the concealing covers and nodded her head knowingly. "You have been to the baths already. Aren't they wonderful? How perfect of Tebo to understand you would want to refresh yourself before we saw each other! He thinks of everything. Now, my darling, we must talk. I have sent for some food and Tebo says I may stay with you as long as I like today. The reason is, of course, that I am his attendant, and he cannot do anything without me. Isn't that like a man? But he chose *me* from all the women, even though he could have another half-dozen at his beck and call . . . It is just as he promised me when we left England—"

She broke off as Jada entered bearing a tray.

"Ah . . . food. You must be so hungry and thirsty by now, darling Alixe, and I have so much to tell you."

She motioned for Jada to set the tray on the bed between them. "Oh look, good strong tea—Russian, you know—and cheese and jam and some halvah and a special treat: nougat, lovely with tea. Help yourself, please—oh! I am *so* happy to see you!"

Alexandra poured some tea just to stem this ingenuous tide of enthusiasm.

"What," she said ominously, "have you done to your hair?"

"My hair?" Allegra touched it, smoothing it back, preening, Alexandra thought. "Isn't it so much better in this color? This is the standard of beauty, Alixe; of course I had to dye it. I wanted to please Tebo and to be everything he wanted me to be."

Alexandra bent her lips to her cup and sipped slowly to calm her rising anger and fear; there was no use arguing with this idolatry of Dzmura. She had to keep her temper, she had to *listen* because only in that way would she learn from her infatuated sister everything she wanted to know.

But she felt like strangling Allegra. What kind of golden lures had Dzmura used to enslave her? She couldn't begin to imagine; she couldn't bear to think about it. But she saw immediately that Allegra did not mean to spare her any detail.

"Alixe . . . oh, I've been dying to have someone of intelligence to converse with—besides Tebo, of course—I mean, he can't concern himself with the mundane matters of his women, so who can I talk to? Biju? She is so jealous, she could kill me. He hasn't looked at her in months, even before he brought me to Bakharha. I think there is one other woman who speaks some English. The slaves don't really count. You can't tell them secrets and expect them to be honored when your enemies are willing to exchange jewels for information.

"Oh! I am ecstatic that you are here. How generous of him to remember and to keep his promise! My compassionate master, taking pity on me and giving me the jewel of my heart—my very own sister. Ah—!"

Alexandra clamped down on her temper. Dzmura—generous! It defied all norms of convention how he had bewitched her sister. She swallowed her angry words, bit back her censure, clenched her hands so tightly around the fragile cup she thought she would break it.

"And how," she managed to get out at last, her voice shaky with rage, "how did this all come about?"

Allegra looked at her as if she were stupid. "Why, it was always meant to be. Tebo told me, and then it was. All the time I was growing up, when I would visit him at Renwick House, he would talk to me of this splendorous heavenly palace where I would have all the wealth and luxury I could command. You must have known: he has always told me how much he has wanted me, how long he has waited for me. You know he took photographs of me so that he could carry me with him wherever he went.

"Oh, they were dear little secret photographs to stir his imagination and keep him hungry for the day when he could possess my charms. It was quite something, really, to see him grovelling to me, begging me to give him a treasure of remembrance. I did so love posing for him. Every year he would take new pictures and talk over and over about our life together at Bakharha.

"And now I am here, and it is more wonderful than I ever could have imagined. He gives me everything, and he expects nothing but my complete love and devotion to his needs.

"And here is what I have learned: woman was born for this, to reap the rewards of submitting utterly to her lord. No man on earth could provide me with jewels and pleasure except my king of masters.

"Do I look unhappy, Alixe? I do not. The pleasure is unimaginable, and Tebo cruelly only gave me the teeniest taste in all those years. He reminds me of it sometimes, just to make me obey. But I do what I want to; the trick is, he doesn't know it."

"All those years . . ." Alexandra said faintly.

"Oh yes. He loved my innocence. He told me often that a woman must be molded from a tender age to become the perfect thrall. He couldn't have me all the time, of course, but he was so expert in the way he made me hungry for more and more of what he would give me when I was ready, I couldn't wait. It was all I thought about between his visits to England, how this time, and then this time, he would initiate me into the ultimate pleasures for which he was preparing me.

"But he wanted it perfect—he wanted me in his pleasure

palace where at last I could be free of all constraints. When I came here—oh, when I came here Alixe, imagine my joy when I understood that I need never conceal anything from my master again!

"I tore off my clothes, and his slaves prepared me on his strict instructions. They dyed my hair, and made up my face to his exacting demand of beauty; he sent me treasures to gird my arms and feet. He sent me silks and satins; he piled my bed with soft soft pillows on which I would recline and wait for him and only for him.

"And then he brought his camera, Alixe, that first time; of course, he did it in secret, because photographs are strictly forbidden, except by the master's whim, because he had so loved to photograph me all those years before.

"And he arranged me on the pillows just so: he must have my naked womanly image to carry with him everywhere. And then he came to me, and—how can I tell? The kiss of a man in your most secret place recorded for a lifetime for him to remember: it thrilled my soul.

"And he was so wise: he did not take me—not that night or the next. He let me think of the pleasure, and remember the thrill of his kiss until I was ravenous with desire.

"Then he sent for me, and this is how you will know: he sends a little ring to the woman he favors. It looks like an earring, but it is to be placed on your right nipple as a reminder of the excitement you feel for him.

"That night you go to him, and everyone will know. And if you continue to pleasure him, you will keep the ring which is cunningly devised to keep his woman in a state of arousal. It is all you will think about when you wear it.

"But of course, he will not send for you soon. There is too much yet to be done. Your hair, for one thing. It must be dyed, and all traces must be removed from your body. Look, see? Nothing is hidden. Everything is revealed. All for his pleasure. It is the dominating rule here and I love it. It is everything Tebo said it would be: an immersion of the senses into pleasure and torment and rewards beyond your wildest dreams.

"And now you will share it with me, just as I will share Tebo with you. No one else, mind you, and all those bitches wish they could have him. But their dreams are futile. Tebo is mine—and for whomever I wish to share him with."

"And does he share you?" Alexandra whispered.

"Of course. Just today, he was desirous of rewarding the good men who brought you to me. What better way for me to show my gratitude? They envy him terribly; they wish I could be their slave. But I could only give them a half-hour of pleasure; I don't particularly like their ways; but Tebo was insistent, he wanted it; I think he photographed it actually; he said he would and that he would show it to me someday."

Alexandra closed her eyes. The scene was unimaginable—or too imaginable: her horribly impressionable sister being commanded to satisfy the traitor pigs who spoke only in terms of punishment and pain.

Allegra saw her distress. "Oh, it wasn't that bad, Alixe. There were the three of them at once—what harm could they do? One wanted to tie me up, the other wanted to watch and the third wanted to do it; so it was done. Little enough, if it rewarded them and pleasured Tebo and brought you here to me."

Men are all the same, Alexandra thought wrathfully. In any case, she would not give Dzmura that power over her.

"I must have something to cover me," she said.

"But you will—when you are allowed out of the palace. You have no need of that here."

"I need a robe. You cannot expect me to dive feet first into this life when I am not prepared for it; Dzmura did not see fit to give me a lifelong course in becoming his slave. I need a robe . . . until"—she tempered her growing anger—"until I can get used to things around here."

"Oh yes, of course. I forget; Tebo should make allowances—he will, for me. Tell me, do you like the food? Isn't it beautiful here? Couldn't you just stay forever? Oh, Alixe, if I find something for you to wear, will you come strolling with me? I will show you the palace."

Alexandra nodded.

"Oh, darling girl. Stay here, stay right here—I'll be right back . . ."

* * *

... circle ...
... circle ...

At the very base of the two most recessed columns in the *serdab,* hidden away in the shadows of the marble room, he found the writing.

It had taken him all of the morning and most of the afternoon, crawling around on his hands and knees by candlelight, and he found it in the place he had least expected yet the place that made the most sense.

No one ever looked downwards when traversing a room. Nor had he when he had examined the columns in the porticos outside the excavated rooms.

But here, in the dim cool silence of the underground room, he found it as he was tracing the circular motif which ended at the base of a column.

Sir Peregrine had not made it easy: he had not etched the message into the stone—he had painted it there in tiny brisk strokes all around the base, circular, so that when Ryder traced it onto a piece of tissue paper, by the light of three candles, it would fit between the rubbings of the two bracelets and reveal the message at last.

Sir Peregrine had counted on the thoroughness of his methods, as well as his rituals. In all likelihood, he had made the same rubbings, and then fit the brush strokes to that. Probably then he had buried the bracelets for several days in the sands of the desert as he'd made his way from Khuramafar to Baghdad.

He had been so close himself: the distance between Baghdad and Khamaquil was almost negligible, yet Sir Peregrine had made a definitive choice: he had gone home to Hidcote and his family and left Bakharha Palace to Culhane.

"Tebo sends you this with his felicitations," Allegra said, coming into the room with a drift of white gauze in her hands. "It is the greatest allowance he can make for you, Alixe, and you must be grateful; he has extended that condescension to no one else."

Alexandra took the tunic from her hands and held it up in

front of her. "It is as good as wearing nothing," she protested, running her hand over the silky material.

"But that is the point, sister dear. You may hide nothing from the *Hakkam,* and so Tebo has given you the best situation: you feel dressed, yet you are perfectly naked for him to see."

Alexandra draped the tunic over her head. White gauze, as light as a feather came over her body like a halo. Nothing was left to the imagination except the notion of breaching a barrier.

She bit her lip. "It will do."

"Of course it will, but you will feel sorely out of place as we walk around the palace."

She felt sorely out of temper instead. There were too many naked bodies and too much time to refine the beautifying of them. And there was hardly much more they could do than bathe several times a day, arrange their hair, eat, relax, gossip, play games, tell fortunes and sleep.

Not a soul wore any clothes except the eunuchs who served Dzmura. The women were not permitted to dress within the women's house, except to adorn their hair or their bodies with ornaments.

To a woman, they had long dark hair and all their feminine hair had been removed.

She could not bear to look, and she could not keep her eyes away.

None of them wore the ring of possession. All of them seemed suspended in a state of languid waiting, and they all sent malicious looks Allegra's way as they passed by.

"Ignore them," Allegra said. "Who among them has known Tebo longer than I? Who has a greater claim? Who has been tutored only by him to serve his needs? And who willingly submitted herself to his dictates? I am the queen of his desire—and they will obey me.

"Now—darling Alixe, you can see—so much room, so much beauty, all sustained by the intensity of Tebo's desires and our willingness to submit to them. It is in our nature, but where we come from, it is ever suborned to propriety. We never know the depths of passion of which we are capable.

"Here, though, in all this sensuous luxury, we can explore the carnality of natures which have been repressed for so long. Tebo will show you. You have only to be willing to give yourself over to him and he will take you to a realm of pleasure where no woman has gone before.

"When you are ready, of course. But don't you feel silly wearing that old tunic now?"

"Everyone is whispering about me."

"You have too much hair—anybody can see that; really, it's thought to be sinful. It's so much cleaner the other way, and there is no barrier to Tebo's senses when he makes his sensual demands on you. I still revel in the day he crawled to kiss my naked mound; he abased himself to me, Alixe, and it was then I understood my power, the more so because it was meaningful enough for him to want to preserve it.

"He told me"—she lowered her voice to a whisper—"he told me he looks at that picture every hour of every day, and that sometimes he keeps it out where he can see it all the time. It makes him yearn for me. It makes him hunger for me. It makes him ache with desire for me. Sometimes he calls for me twice and three times a day because his need is so great. He has such a capacity for sensuality, and he tells me I am the only woman who can please him.

"I am the favorite—I am his queen. Look, I wear the ring of possession which was delivered to me once again this afternoon."

Alexandra had not missed it. Allegra's nipples were taut with excitement and the symbol of her status was evident to everyone.

"I think of him constantly; I would do anything for him. I have done everything I can think of. I cannot give him enough in my gratitude for his keeping his promises to me. I strut my way down the corridors as I go to his bed so those stupid bitches can see what I wear and envy me. I want them all to imagine what it feels like to submit to the *Hakkam* and to know that I am the one he has chosen for pleasure. He has had no one else but me.

"Ah—here we are, Alixe, back at your room. Now you have only to relax until your slave returns with dinner. But I will leave you now: I must prepare myself for a night of pleasure, and I will return in the morning to tell you how it goes. Oh!" She hugged Alexandra. "It is so good to have someone to share all this with. I would burst from the joy of it otherwise!"

She flew out of the room in a flurry of excitement, and Alexandra sank onto her bed.

Her head was spinning: the thing was hopeless. Allegra was drunk on power and lust, and between the two there was nothing else for her.

And that had been the doing of Dzmura; Dzmura had educated her and trained her, had led her along like a dog until she could want nothing but the allurements he held out to her: a life in a luxurious prison in exchange for total submissiveness.

Oh, truly her sister had made the bargain of a lifetime, her uncherished freedom for the life of a slave.

There was nothing to do in this godawful place but eat and sleep, and she was sure the hour was not even advanced in the evening when she felt herself being shaken awake by a tearful Allegra.

"Get up—get up! Damn you, *get up.* He wants you. He sent me to get you. Damn you, damn you, damn you. He made me take off the ring, and he sent me with it to give to you. Alexandra— *do you hear me?*"

She shook off her sister's hand as she rolled over and sat up.

The scene was unearthly: Allegra stood over her, tears streaming from her eyes, Jada behind her holding a lamp and Biju waiting by the door to attend her.

"You bitch, how did you manage so quickly to seduce him? He sent me to get you—do you hear me? He sent *me,* his queen, to get my *replacement.* He made me remove the ring of possession, and he told me to give it to you. How cruel, how ungodly cruel of him to do this to me."

"Take it back to him then," Alexandra said matter-of-factly. "I don't want it. I don't want him."

"But you don't understand. Of course you want him. You have no choice. Nobody has a choice. You must go to him, *now;* in his name, I command you."

"This is nonsense—" Alexandra began.

"She is so stupid," Allegra moaned to no one in particular. "You are the chosen, Alixe. Get up, and I will put on the ring. Then you *must go* to him. No one refuses the *Hakkam*. You must offer yourself to him, naked and with his gift, the ring, encircling your nipple, and you must submit to his desires. And that is the way of it whatever I may want. My duty is to submit to his wishes and give you the gift of his favor."

Alexandra was appalled. "I won't go. You go back to him and tell me I am grateful, but no thank you."

"Stupid, stupid . . . He will kill me if you do not obey his command. Now get *up*, Alixe, and let me dress you in the ring."

"Are you crazy? *Dress* me?"

"It is the *Hakkam's* wish that I dress you in the ring of favor. Biju will witness and report to *Hakkam* that I obeyed him implicitly, so that he may find favor in me again. Sit *up*, Alexandra. You *will* go to my master tonight, naked and wearing the ring."

She looked into her sister's eyes, and she saw that Allegra was dead serious. Dzmura was playing some cruel and deadly game and she was a mere pawn.

But Allegra did not know that; she was sure he would kill her if she did not obey his command to the letter.

She got up on her knees in front of her sister. Surely she could handle this despot better than Allegra. The little ring couldn't hurt her, else why would Allegra be so proud and excited to wear it.

"Do what you must," she said resignedly, cupping her breast so that her nipple would peak.

She watched curiously as Biju edged in closer and Allegra bit her lip and wiped away her streaming tears before she produced the ring.

It was tiny, of gold strands wound around a stiff little piece of wire, with smooth silky flat gold wires at either end that were slightly concave to fit around the contour of the nipple. It took only the slightest pressure to set it in place, and the little flat wires held, caressed and encircled the tip of her breast. No one could mistake what it was.

"Your breast was made for the ring," Allegra said stiffly. "The

Hakkam will be pleased, and Biju will testify that I submitted myself to his will. Now I must take you to him, and he has required that Biju arouse the others to watch my humiliation.

"But it is *Hakkam's* will, and I surrender myself to him in all ways. Biju returns; all is ready. The women are waiting. It is time to go . . . to him."

Chapter 20

The women did not know, and they whispered and tittered behind their hands as Allegra walked down the corridor with Alexandra.

And then they saw the mark of favor, the coveted ring, and they quieted instantly as Allegra's face flushed with disgrace.

In a moment they were past the women's apartments and into the long hall leading to the wing of the palace Dzmura occupied.

"Address him as *Hakkam,*" Allegra whispered. "Suborn yourself in all things, and you will reap the rewards. Here is the door. Najib will announce you."

She turned away then, and Alexandra felt a frisson of fear. She had not the strength to deal with Dzmura when she was naked and he was not. She was not now playing erotic games that would culminate in an evening of supreme pleasure.

This was truly a scenario of master and slave, and he could exercise his power over her. Najib could kill her in an instant if commanded to do so, and that might be simply because Dzmura did not like something she said.

She had not for one moment appreciated the impregnability he enjoyed in this place. This was his world, of his making; here he was king and lord—God for that matter—and he was cruel and capricious.

Najib motioned to her, and she swallowed hard as she followed him into the golden chamber.

It was high in a tower with windows on three sides and she could see the moon and the stars and the lights of habitations below.

His bed was in a pit, three steps below the rest of the room, and was spread with satin covers and piled high with pillows. All around the ledge surrounding the bed were lamps, lamps and photographs, photographs of Allegra in all stages of growing up, and the final one, of her gratifying his guests, was perched on a writing surface against the far wall.

Dressed in loose baggy trousers and a turban, he lay sprawled on the bed, watching her.

"Beautiful Alize—that is your harem name, dear Alexandra—come. Let me look and be sure you wear my mark of favor. Oh yes, it is just as Biju reported: your breasts are splendid, made for my ring. And your hair—I love your hair. We will not depilate your hair—it is so deliciously bushy; it begs for one to explore its delicious secrets.

"Sit, Alize, and do not look as if you would kill me. On the bed, my dear, where I may gaze my fill upon you. On the pillows, over there . . ." His voice got tighter and tighter as she moved reluctantly to do his bidding. "And do not be shy about spreading your legs, my dear."

He shook his head exasperatedly. "That is *not* the way. I want to see *everything,* so you will recline on your left side, please, with your breast towards me and your legs straddling those pillows."

She shook her head mutinously as she curled her body stubbornly away from him.

"No? My dear, Najib will be perfectly happy to help you if you are having trouble . . . Ah! *That* is much better. Look at how you please me already, Alize. You are a wanton, waiting for arousal, and my ring of favor is but the first step in your ultimate surrender.

"Does it not make you more aware of your desire? Does it not excite you to feel it squeezing your flesh ever so gently? Did you think of me when Alya dressed you in it?"

She gazed at him steadily, watching him arouse himself to a fever pitch while she said nothing. What was the power of a slave, after all? She was a vessel, waiting to be filled. He filled her with words and they were like dross, sloughing off her.

He came closer to her, his protuberant silk-shrouded erection but inches away.

"Did you, Alize? Did you think of the power I have over you? You are the only one with such a lush body. I command you never to remove the ring. It arouses me just to look at it. I have never been so aroused by the sight of a woman; you please me, Alize, and that is good. Your body pleases me, hair and all.

"You will wear the ring from now on always. I will know if you disobey my command, and you will be punished. I will think of you wearing it in your daily pursuits, and everyone will know you are favored. Does it please you, Alize?

"But you are a woman; you understand some of the pleasures of the flesh. I truly tire of the artlessness of your sister even as I have molded her to my desire. She knows not how to excite me, and thus I resort to artificial means. I abased myself to her to remind myself to never seek out a child again. But then I found that the picture excited me—see for yourself, Alize, the *Hakkam* on his knees to a female's sex.

"Notice her ring—not nearly as arousing as you. Between the two of you, I will not want for variety. I have been waiting for this moment, Alize, for a long time."

She felt her body close up like a shell at his words; this was as unlike her games with Culhane as anything could be. She hated Dzmura.

"See how I have waited, Alize—look at how my manhood wants you, how it revels in your nakedness, how it loves the sight of my ring caressing you, how it yearns to feel your feminine hair surrounding it . . . surrender to it, Alize; let it enslave you with its power even as you enslave it with your wanton desire to submit to it. Alize . . . Alize—surrender to me and the world will be yours forever—"

"*No—no—no!*"

Allegra threw herself in the door and onto the bed before Najib could stop her, shrieking at the top of her lungs. "I can't bear it, I can't—*Hakkam* forgive me, I cannot see another woman in my place.

"I will *not* submit to your will in this. I can't bear your caressing her with the same words you used with me—I won't have it, I *won't*, I *won't*. You are *mine, mine*—you swore, you promised; I let you touch me and feel me all those years ago because of your promises of never-ending pleasure. *Hakkam*—master—take me, take *me* . . . "

Dzmura pushed her away, and she fell sobbing onto the side of the bed.

"You will be punished for this insubordination, Alya, I promise you. Now stop your futile sobbing and take heed. Your sister wears my ring from now on, and as a mark of my desire for her, I give her the second one. You . . . you dress her—*now* or I will banish you forever."

He thrust the ring into her hands, and screaming and sobbing, she took it and crawled over to Alexandra and gently squeezed it around her left nipple.

"Now get out of my sight."

"*Hakkam*, forgive me, forgive me; I am desperate for the love of you and the loss of your mark of favor."

"And you have lost it doubly, stupid bitch. Get out of my sight until I refine your punishment for this outrage."

The room was hot and tight with emotion as Allegra crawled away sobbing hysterically.

"She is a child," Dzmura muttered, "a selfish child, thinking she could have the *Hakkam* for herself. Now she bears the worst of her punishment—I have chosen you as my queen, and everyone will witness her degradation. Perhaps that is enough. Perhaps.

"But enough of her, let me look at you. Yes, you were made for this—the most erotic ornament a woman can wear."

She shuddered in horror. He was an amoral monster, and it was obvious that her sister's hysteria had aroused him still more. She did not know what she would do if he came an inch closer to her.

"Arch your body towards me, Alize, so that the light catches the rings. You see, that way a man's eyes are directed to the most erotic part of your body, and he knows instantly that that part has been subjugated by your *Hakkam* and that you willingly dress to please him.

"I wonder . . . I wonder—I need to see . . . " He reached behind him and then moved up closer to her. "You are subject to my whim in all matters, Alize, is that not so? Excellent, you understand this. You will wear two more marks of my favor, and I will dress you. This will be for me: you will wear two sets of rings when you are with me as the mark of your submission to my will.

"And now Alize, you are ready for me. You cannot escape this destiny—you are mine . . ."

She closed her eyes against the most unbearable moment; she felt him coming closer and closer—she could hear his panting breath, the beating of her heart.

His hand touched her leg as he placed himself to begin his brutish conquest of her . . .

And she reacted, instantly, with no thought but to save herself from his obscene possession of her: her leg thrashed outward, catching him at the peak of his desire, and he fell over, growling in animal pain.

In an instant, Najib jumped on her, hauling her up to her knees and roughly pulling her arms behind her.

"You bitch, you stupid bitch! *Get her out of here!* You will pay for this, Alize, *you will pay . . . !!!*"

Najib dragged her away, out of the sunken bed and up the steps, as if she were no more than a sack of potatoes, stopping by the door as Dzmura regained some of his composure and signaled to him.

"We will try again, whore, but Alize you had best make up your mind that obedience is the best route to a place in my heart. Do you understand me? Because I will have you, one way or the other—*next time.*"

He waved his hand negligently, and Najib unceremoniously pulled her away.

The rings were erotic, but once the arousal had dissipated they were downright irritating. She removed them, all of them, then buried them under a pillow and donned the gauze tunic and sat on her bed to think.

She had to get out of this place. It was not possible to count on Culhane; she must save herself and her besotted sister somehow. And she knew deep within her heart that the only way to escape was to pretend to submit to Dzmura.

He favored her already, for whatever obsessive reason, so if she could just act compliant and do what he wanted, she would be able to move freely around the palace and find some escape route.

Simple as that. . . . She was mortified to think how much time it might take, with Dzmura growing more and more crazed and perhaps, in an instant, reducing her status to slave of the baths.

Who knew what he might do next?

In a moment, she found out: Biju appeared at the door. "*Hakkam* awaits you, *mem-sahib.*"

Oh God—and she had removed the rings.

She dug for them frantically, found them, and saw Biju's impassive gaze on her. "*Hakkam* awaits. You must come."

She came, tossing the tunic over her head as she followed, and attaching one ring to each nipple as they strode down the corridor to his palace wing.

The door was open—she had only to walk in; no one would announce her this time.

She stepped across the threshold and saw the implacable Najib placed where he could enforce his master's commands.

"Close the doors, Alize," Dzmura commanded from his place in the bed, and it was as if they were beginning over again, as if he were giving her a second chance to become the slave he wanted her to be.

There was no escape this time, she thought, casting a covert glance at Najib and then slowly grasping the doorknobs and backing against the doors to close them.

"Come forward, Alize, and kneel to your master."

He was lying naked on the bed, and she hesitantly stepped to the edge of the pit and sketched a curtsy.

"Najib, remove that excrescence the slave is wearing to conceal her body from me."

And this was how it was going to be: Najib would obey his every command if she would not. The eunuch took the filmy material of her tunic into his huge hand and ripped it off her body.

The rings glistened in the low sensual light.

"There were two sets, Alize. *Two,*" he reminded her as his manhood lazily began rising to power.

Now . . . now she must lie. "You removed the second. You said they were our secret."

"A secret? What kind of secret, Alize? If you are lying to me . . ."

"You said I would wear them only when I was with you, *Hakkam*. I could not disobey you. You wished to have the pleasure of dressing me, and I could not disobey you in this."

She held her breath, her heart beating wildly. She couldn't imagine what he had in mind for her now, but she would bear it—whatever it was, she would take it. He was massive now, anticipating the ritual of dressing her again.

"None of my women can wear two sets of rings. And so, in spite of your rebellion, you still have special favor in my eyes, Alize. Come here, and I will dress you."

She could not stand feeling his hands on her body, but she clamped down her revulsion as once again he brought out two rings and appended one to each of her quivering breasts.

"Don't move now, Alize. Every man respects the symbol of the rings and will envy me the slave who can wear two. You cannot refuse me this time, Alize. This time I will punish you.

"Now fix yourself against those pillows just as you did before . . ."

She swallowed her dread as he turned his pulsating manhood away from her for a moment, and then turned back, fastening something around his waist, above his throbbing member.

It looked like . . . she couldn't believe it—it was long and thick and rubbery, the very embodiment of him, permanently aroused and ready to possess her in an instant as he could not.

She began to laugh. She could not believe he was serious, but she saw, as Najib came down onto the bed and forced her onto her back, that he was and that her derisive laughter had diminished his erection so that what was the impostor now looked impossibly real.

Dzmura loomed over her, the essence of evil.

"You will comply, lovely Alize, because Najib has only to reach over and pull up your legs to immobilize you completely and put you at my mercy."

Immediately, her body stiffened and she began thrashing her legs.

He slapped her, and she was so stunned, she stopped in midcourse. "You bastard . . . !"

"Who are you to deny *me*, your *Hakkam* who has gifted you with his favor? All you are allowed to do, stupid woman, is lie down and wait for me to spend my seed whenever I choose."

"Your seed is as dry as your bone," she spat out, and he slapped her again.

"Keep your mouth shut, bitch. You are here for one reason and one reason only"—he reached out and took her chin roughly in his hand—"to abase yourself to my needs, my whims, my desire—my demands . . ."

He thrust her face away from his as if he could not bear to look at her.

"Bah! I cannot. The bitch has unmanned me. Najib—"

"All is in readiness, *Hakkam*."

He clapped his hands, and the doors opened to reveal Biju waiting outside, her hand restraining a slender young woman.

"Bring her here."

Biju thrust the girl into the room and slammed the doors behind her.

"Get down here, girl."

The girl came, looking like a frightened deer.

"Lie down."

The girl obeyed him, and looked up at him with suddenly adoring eyes as she understood what he wanted.

"The girl shall be annointed," Dzmura said, straddling her body and parting her legs. "And you, stupid bitch, you shall be her voice."

Alexandra struggled against the iron hands of Najib. "I *won't*."

"How she defies me; she knows nothing of the power of Dzmura. Najib . . ."

Najib was subtle. He knew just where to pinch and pull while he held her immobilized so that she was soon ready to scream, to beg him to stop.

"Yes, I thought you might see it my way," Dzmura said with satisfaction. "Now. . ." He mounted the girl and inserted his surrogate manhood into the vessel of her willing body. "Yes . . . see how it works . . . see how I grow more powerful with each thrust. Now, Alize, pretend . . . pretend it is you, and let everyone hear your moans and groans of satisfaction . . ."

"I—" she began, but Najib applied his insidious pressure before a defiant refusal took shape in her mouth.

"Obey *Hakkam*," Najib said, and she whispered, "Stop, stop, I will—"

"*Now!*"

And she did; she moaned, and she begged, and she cried out for more and more; she praised his prowess, his manliness, the size and the shape of him as he plunged the shape of something into the poor pliant body of his worshipful young slave.

"Scream with pleasure," Najib commanded her, applying that same subtle hurtful pressure.

And she could not get away from it. She cried out in her frustration, and it sounded like the joy of her culmination. She exclaimed at the wonder of it, the unbelievable power of him, until the girl fainted and he had to remove himself from her.

"It is well," Dzmura said, unstrapping his apparatus and secreting it behind him someplace within the confines of the bed. "You have done well, Alize. Even I would not have believed that your pleasure was not real."

He turned to the eunuch. "Get rid of the slave."

"Master . . ."

Najib released her abruptly and she fell backwards onto the bed.

Dzmura held up his hand. "Never fear, Najib; she will not betray me. I will now make her understand that I brought her here solely to lure the elusive Culhane to my kingdom. I have no compunction about killing her if she does not cooperate. After all, it is the fate even of those who do cooperate. The girl, Najib!"

Najib arose and took the limp body of the girl and waded off the bed and onto the floor. "It is done, *Hakkam*."

Alexandra curled herself into a defensive ball. "You would kill her?"

"I would kill you, Alize, so my secrets would die with you. But there is still more to come. Betray me, and Najib will see that you suffer. Cooperate . . ."

He clapped his hands, and Alexandra finished bitterly, "And I will die a quick death."

"Stupid woman!" Dzmura slapped her yet again as the doors opened to admit Biju.

"Summon our guests," Dzmura commanded and Biju withdrew.

Alexandra levered herself upward in protest, and he pushed her back hard and began arranging her body into a more languorous and revealing position on the pillows.

She pulled her legs together rebelliously as she heard the voices beyond the door, and then it opened.

"Ah, gentlemen," Dzmura said heartily, "come, come. Let me show you how I have tamed the slave. Look how she rests in satiety after a night of forbidden lust. She withholds nothing from her master, nothing.

"She pleases your master. He has never had such a wanton slave who could wear two sets of rings. I have taken her for my own, and none of you will touch her. But I will allow you to look your fill.

"This, gentlemen, is the perfect slave, obedient, wanton, naked to her master's gaze, willing to submit to whatever form of gratification he desires.

"It is too bad you could not take her when you had the chance, Rosedale . . ."

"I told you she was a teasing little bitch. Look at her, so smug and insolent down there, knowing I can't get to her now. But times change, my haughty darling. You will not wear the *Hakkam's* mark of favor forever. Tell her to stand up and let us see them."

"Stand up, Alize. Let Colonel Rosedale envy how I possess you."

She rose, knowing full well that Dzmura would pull her to her feet if she did not obey, and she hoped that Rosedale would explode in his pants at the thought of what he had been cheated out of.

She hated him. She hated them.

She would make Dzmura pay someday. She would kill him if she had to.

"God, look at those nipples; did you ever see—how do you suck them, *Hakkam?*"

"I prefer to own them," Dzmura said coolly. "She wears the rings only for me. I have only to think of her moving among my women wearing them and I am instantly aroused to a frenzy. Even now, watching your lust for her, I am consumed with desire. I want to take her right before your eyes because the thought of it excites me."

"Let us take her instead," Rosedale suggested lasciviously. "We know what to do with those succulent breasts, and it ain't putting rings on them."

"Najib," Dzmura shouted, not liking that comment at all. "Choose a woman for the gentlemen, one who can satisfy their desires. Take them away . . . Ungrateful bastards . . . Infidels unable to appreciate the *Hakkam's* mark of favor. Boorish barbarians. And you"—he rounded on Alexandra—"have gained another night of life."

Allegra crawled in to see her the following morning.

"He has made you his own; word has gotten around that you wear his symbol of favor. Rumor says you can even wear two. I am mortified and humiliated that he would do this to me."

"I hate him," Alexandra said vehemently. "And why are you crawling on the floor?"

"It is part of my punishment to abase myself so that I will not climb so high in my pride again."

"This is nonsense," Alexandra snapped. "You have given him the power over you—now you must take it back."

"Oh no, no. I want only to be his queen once again. I want my nipple ring, and if I am good enough, he will take me back as his queen among women."

"He is a phony and a fraud."

"You shared his bed, what more could you want? He spent his passion on you; you wear his symbols. He has made you his queen, and you are still ungrateful. I could kill you for taking with no compunction what I honor and revere. He spent a lifetime teaching me to want him, and he turns away from me now and degrades me in the process."

"That is the reason a man declares himself a king: he is a little man who cannot rule without debasing his subjects. He is a very little man who has no power with women at all, and so he must pretend with whatever willing accomplice he can find."

"Oh God, never say so—*pretend*—when he is the most wonderful lover in the universe?"

"He has tutored you well," Alexandra said dryly. "I don't suppose you have ever thought of getting out of here."

"That is heresy," Allegra whispered. "Never let those words pass your lips."

"Who would stop me?"

"Najib for one. And Biju is everywhere, a spy for him, hoping against hope that he will take her into the fabled realms of pleasure that only I have reached."

"This is such nonsense. The man cannot sustain himself, and he pleasures only one."

"You lie, Alexandra; the word goes around that you moaned and begged for pleasure."

Dear lord, these women had nothing better to do than listen at doors and peepholes to see what the master was doing.

And not see what the master was using. Or on whom.

"How long must you demean yourself until the bastard is satisfied?"

"Today. And of course I spent the night with his guests, so I heard all about *you*. I wasn't going to tell you, but I can't believe how you will lie, even to your own sister, about the pleasure you found in his arms when there were three live witnesses to the aftermath. Oh, and they just loved how you showed off his rings. It made them crazy. But I proved I could drive them crazy too."

Alexandra realized that she was getting nowhere with Allegra. He had made her a slave and a prostitute, and still she defended him.

"I trust they reached some realms of pleasure," she said tartly.

"They will never be the same after last night," Allegra said, preening. "And I pray that they brag to *Hakkam* the way he bragged to them. Then, perhaps, he will seek me out again from curiosity."

So sensuality was all, and possession. Allegra could not care less about anything beyond these walls.

She couldn't bear the thought of sacrificing her sister, but

Allegra had been programmed to become the very thing she was; Alexandra did not know how to combat that.

"I don't hate you, you know," Allegra said, as she got down on her hands and knees again. "It's just that you always spoiled everything. Here I had everything I ever wanted. And what happens? You come along, and you spoil everything all over again. I hope you find a way to escape, Alixe, because then you'll be gone and everything can go back to the way it was. So I won't tell on you, all right? Just be wary of Biju. Don't let her catch you, because if *Hakkam* finds out, he will kill you. I want you gone, but that way just wouldn't be right."

Chapter 21

The very next hour her life shifted into the focus of what it would be like if she were to stay at Bakharha forever.

Jada brought her breakfast and then took her to the baths. There, she was the object of derision and curiosity, the more so because Dzmura had made it plain he was changing the rules for her.

She wore the rings—she had to, for Biju was everywhere—and the women wanted to see them and examine her hair. They wanted to touch her skin, to compare their bodies with hers. They couldn't understand why the *Hakkam* wished her so different *there*.

Afterwards, Jada massaged her, and folded her in for her nap. When she woke, there was eating and drinking, along with some discussion, interpreted reluctantly by Biju, of the rumors flying around the palace about Alya and what she knew of that. And then there was another nap. Perhaps songs or games or stories followed. There was the oblivion of the hookah for those who were trapped, and the everlasting presence of the eunuchs who monitored everything.

It was closed in and stultifying, it was Dzmura's own little world, run according to both his specifications and the ancient rituals.

The women must wait. But waiting enhanced nothing once he had made his choice. The women were there for diversion, to amuse themselves, the favorites and Dzmura. He walked among them, the women said, secretly observing, hoping to find his secret desire.

He was a *voyeur,* enjoying his power over these women, none of whom—especially her sister—had the will or the instinct to fight back.

They had been taught passivity forever. How could they resist him?

And he sapped their wills, gave them luxury and opiates and a woman's kind of hope. Who would not find satiety in surrendering everything else? The rewards were so great that the negatives seemed few. Until it was too late. Until they realized they were trapped in oblivion to eternity.

There *had* to be a way out. And she had to find it, now that she knew he was waiting for Culhane as eagerly as she. Her life hung merely on his whim.

She wondered when he would summon her next.

He called for her again that night, and she reluctantly followed Biju to his opened doors.

Once again, she entered and closed them; once again he awaited her naked in the opulent luxury of his bed, but this time Najib did not keep watch over him.

And there was someone waiting to attend her: Allegra, seated at the edge.

"*Hakkam,*" she began heatedly and he stopped her.

"You have no say in the matter, Alize. Come to me for the dressing."

She stepped reluctantly onto the bed, holding Allegra's eyes. Allegra hated her. Allegra wanted her gone. Allegra might kill her if he didn't first.

"In this private act of dressing you, I made you my slave. But tonight, I will punish you once again. You will not wear the mark of my favor. Tonight Alya will be your surrogate, and you will see what it means to be chosen by the *Hakkam.* Alya!"

Allegra looked at her triumphantly and kneeled down on the bed.

He needed no surrogate tonight to possess her. His was the way of the ancients of Rome, and she felt disgusted by his fervor and the eagerness of her sister to yield to it.

But she knew no different: this was the way he had trained

her; this was how he had visited himself on her, on the slender weightless body of a young girl—boyish at best, culminating in curves later, when her tastes had been formed and the way had been set. No wonder she had been his favorite: who would surrender everything to this?

And behind her feminine body, he could hide the secret of his. For that her sister would abase herself; for that she would be queen.

But he was not done yet; he had spent himself on her sister in that pagan way, and now he wanted her. He reached out, and pulled her legs, and she toppled onto the bed.

"Now moan for me, Alize. Make them hear how you want what I give you—louder, Alize," he commanded in a guttural hiss as he straddled her legs.

She knew he would kill her now; one false move, one hysterical note . . . He did not need to possess her to take her pleasure: she gave it to him in long languorous moans that were loud enough for all to hear and to assume that the *Hakkam* had brought his chosen to the very peak of ecstasy.

Allegra watching her—furious, envious, murderous—as she moaned and begged and cried out in simulated pleasure, timing it, hoping it wasn't too soon or too late.

"More . . ." Dzmura hissed, "more."

Damn, she thought frantically, what could she tell this despot about an act in which she had not participated?

"The certain way you move your hips *Hakkam*. Every Western man alive would pay to know your secret . . ."

"You excite me," he murmured, looking down at his burgeoning manhood. "You are more arousing than Alya just with your words; you give me hope."

"I am privileged to be the voice for the *Hakkam*," she said sarcastically.

"And I am privileged to show you once more the delights you have forsworn. Alya!"

His eyes glittered as Allegra crawled towards him.

"I could kill my little slave as easily as I would kill you," he said musingly, as Allegra positioned herself to receive him.

And then he mounted her, his evil dark eyes reading Alexandra's horror and her acknowledgement that he held the upper hand and that she must, and she would, in the end, obey.

There was no time now to think of consequences: it was imperative she escape this madhouse, with or without her sister and under the watchful eye of Biju and Najib.

They followed her even now, maintaining a careful distance behind her as she tried to plot some plan of action.

But there was absolutely nothing between Dzmura's apartment and the seraglio. The rooms were a puzzle, boxes within boxes, and misleading to the untutored eye.

She slipped into her bedroom and curled up in one of the satin covers and waited for Biju to check on her presence.

Biju was her first obstacle; Allegra her last.

Out on the ramparts above the palace Culhane silently crept through deep darkness. It was night, and the silence was preternatural, weighty with the timelessness of the ages. He thought it was curious how similar this seemed to the palace at Bazzi.

The silence was close, the danger ever imminent.

He stopped, he knelt down and then he listened. Not a whisper stirred the air.

It was hours away from dawn, and there was nothing he could do until daylight.

He mustered his patience and prepared to wait.

Allegra crept into her room early in the morning as she lay tossing and turning on her bed.

"What do you want?" she demanded in a fierce whisper, pulling her blanket closer against her body to ward off the revulsion she felt. "Wasn't tonight enough? Haven't I heard enough? Is your watchdog out there—the one that runs protection for you?"

"I will help you," Allegra mouthed. "I want you to go away—*now*, today."

"How can I trust you?"

"I want him more than I want you. He will kill you eventually to keep his secret when you tire of the subterfuge. The only way it will work is if you go."

"How?"

"I don't know yet. I will find out and meet you later, at the baths. Trust me."

But she didn't know whether she should—or could. Her own sister. She had travelled thousands of miles to have it all come to this: a jealous hair-pulling over who would take the prize.

She was so disgusted and so consumed with guilt that somehow they had both given Dzmura this power, she wanted to scream.

But the more practical thing to do was to have breakfast and make ready to go to the baths; she was bored already. Being a harem slave was absolutely no fun.

Jada accompanied her as usual, and women drifted in, in twos and threes, chittering and chattering and either slipping into the perfumed oil-rich water or gathering around benches to exchange gossip.

Two dozen women, bored and alone, at the beck and call of a man who didn't want them. At what cost to maintain appearances?

This morning she took a careful look around her, and noted for the first time that there were other exits from the room besides the two vaulted tunnels.

One of the doors had to conceal a closet for the towels and blankets that were continually refreshed in the outer fountain room.

But the other two, in opposite walls of the baths, just beyond the tunnels . . .

Jada appeared with her clogs and a towel and wrapped her up into it and began leading her away to the fountain room.

"Jada?"

"*Mem?*"

"The doors—what is behind the doors?"

Jada shook her head. "Come . . ."

She felt a signal frustration that only Biju spoke any English at all; Biju was not the one to ask, but spies were everywhere. She had no sooner lain down on her couch all wrapped and ready for a nap when Biju appeared.

"Jada says you have questions."

Oh, Biju was sharp. But so was she.

"I was curious as to what was behind the doors in the baths room."

"Why so? It is nothing, merely storage closets for linens and towels and the perfumes and oils we employ."

"Thank you, Biju," she said caustically, turning over and showing Biju her back. She hated the woman, just hated her. Biju would be watching her now. How stupid she had been to question Jada. Even with her good nature, the young woman would report it to Biju.

Nevertheless, she had to take a chance. Sometime during the naptime, she would sneak into the baths and open those doors.

He eased himself downwards from the ledge onto the plateau. The entrance was here, his instinct told him so.

He moved his hands slowly and patiently over the rock formations, seeking with all of his power, the secret entrance.

Dzmura had been so smart: a fortress in a stone mountain to be blown to kingdom come. He had laid the charges himself all around the perimeter of the mountain, taking no chances.

Dzmura's acolytes would be safely below, and unknowingly headed towards oblivion.

A little bit more now, and a little bit more—his *knowing* would not fail him, not with Alexandra's life at stake.

He moved his hands slowly, as softly as a lover's in the sunlight.

She didn't know how she contained herself and waited out the time. Some of the women were sleeping; others engaged in drowsy conversation or lapped the last drops of sherbert from icy little bowls.

Slaves were everywhere, watching over their mistresses, but Jada was nowhere to be seen, as Alexandra cautiously raised her head and looked around.

No one paid any attention to her, and she wondered if this was some kind of trap that Biju had devised.

Still, the risk was worth the punishment. She swung her legs over the divan and wrapped herself in the towel and headed back through the tunnel to the baths.

Slowly the rock formation moved, a soft scraping noise that was jarring in the silence.

Beyond it rose two thick wooden doors, impregnable, with thick locks and undoubtedly bars across the other side.

He set the dynamite at edge of the wood where the doors met, and lit the fuse.

The explosion was forceful, shattering rock and punching an opening in the door big enough for him to climb through. He couldn't be sure no one had heard; he ducked into the cavern as he heard a babble of voices and the sound of running feet, but there was only one place to hide.

A phalanx of guards rushed into the anteroom just as he leaned against the rock and it quietly turned and shunted him into another room.

There were several women seated on the ledges by the fountain, idly flicking their fingers through the water and conversing earnestly.

Alexandra passed by them on cat-silent feet and edged towards the farthest door, her heart pounding, her senses pitched almost to hysteria.

The knob was gilded and incised with symbols. She reached for it boldly, turned it forcefully and was shocked when it opened in her hand.

She darted into the space without thinking and pulled the door closed behind her only to find she was standing in the dark with no way of knowing where this space led.

She took a tentative step and another, holding out her arms and bracing for a fall into oblivion.

Her foot encountered a step and she went down and down and down . . . She thought she would die in the dark all alone . . . down and down again . . . She could not see . . .

And down—the staircase was steep and the stone was cold and her towel was slipping. She tied it around her waist and kept going, down and down . . .

And then she saw a glimmer, just a finger of light permeating the darkness. It grew brighter and brighter as she went farther and farther down.

And then she could see it—an underground room, so similar to the one at Bazzi, it might have been designed by the same architect: marble floors, slender columns supporting the ceiling, circular motifs, a beginning going somewhere . . .

She raced back up the stairs, and listened intently at the door before she opened it a crack.

Oh God—it was way past the time when they would have left the fountain room and gone on to some other occupation.

The wonder was that Biju was not standing by the door, waiting for her, a knife in hand.

She slipped out the door and raced into the fountain room. Everyone was gone.

She ran through the puzzle rooms without thought as to where she was going. She only needed to be somewhere that was not near the door in the baths.

"*Mem!*"

Jada's voice, reproachful. "I look."

"I'm sorry."

Jada shook her head. "Come." She took Alexandra's arm and pulled her.

But it was too late. Biju stepped from behind a column, her expression engorged in wrath.

"And so, precious Alize, where have you been?"

He listened closely by the wall, but he knew already that the guard had no idea this secret room existed.

It was black as a tomb within, and he lit a match the moment he was sure it was safe.

The room was no bigger than the vestibule at Hidcote, and at the far end of it there was a staircase.

Slowly he eased his way down, counting the steps, and marking his way.

She was confined to her room for insubordination, and she felt faintly grateful that the punishment was not more severe.

Biju brought her her meals, guarded her door so that Allegra could not come to see her and brought her Dzmura's summons.

"*Hakkam* sends for you tonight. He wishes you to dress for him in the garments I will bring you."

"I obey his commands," Alexandra said meekly.

Biju's expression said she thought not. But it was not she who had to endure Dzmura's attentions.

The costume consisted of a pair of thin silk trousers, girdled at the waist by a thin jeweled belt, and a matching *yashmak* which was stiffened at the forehead and whose veil fell over her shoulders and down her back.

Over Alexandra's mouth, Biju appended a long oblong of silk which hung right between her breasts. Her feet were bare and her arms, but Biju gave her a bracelet to wear on each wrist.

"You will keep your arms down by your sides, precious Alize, and of course the reasoning for that is to divert *Hakkam's* eyes to the enticing slit in the trousers that he may imagine the delights which lay beyond. *Hakkam* wishes the excitement of the seduction tonight, precious Alize. I hope you can play your part well."

Alexandra viewed herself in the mirror Biju had provided. She was all mystery and light, her face and hair veiled, her breasts adorned with the rings, the rest of her shrouded in feminine eroticism.

She looked up sharply at Biju as she comprehended the gist of her comment. What did Biju know? Or was the comment designed to trap her?

"*Hakkam* is satisfied," she murmured. "Does he not call me back night after night?"

"Then we will please him again tonight," Biju said, "and I will be watching." With that ominous comment, she gestured for Alexandra to follow her out of the room.

The women watched covertly from their rooms. *Hakkam* was besotted they said. They whispered about the potency of her unshorn femininity. They cast spells on her body as she passed. They raged with jealousy over her beautiful breasts.

The doors to his apartment were open as usual.

Najib hovered nearby.

She stepped into the room and closed the doors.

Dzmura lay sprawled on the bed, a male slave at his side; sated, sedated and utterly oblivious to her presence.

She backed against the doors, nauseated by the scene, feeling trapped. It was a moment suspended in time: she did not move, he did not stir.

She had to get out of there, even if a battalion of servants waited in the hallway to grab her and force her back.

She opened the door slowly, just a crack, and looked cautiously out into the hallway to her left. It was dimly lit, empty as far as she could see.

Which was meaningless. If Najib was hovering, she had no chance at all of avoiding Dzmura this night.

She shrugged her veil over her shoulders to cover her breasts, and then pushed the door open just wide enough so that she could slip out.

Hushed . . . the hallway was silent, respectful of the master's wants. She saw not a soul, but surely Najib awaited his commands someplace . . .

She ran, scurrying across the cool tile floors in her black costume like an ambitious little nun fleeing the infidel, righteousness on her side.

Back into the seraglio . . . where? Where?

To the baths, where no one would be watching, no one would think to look, and to the mysterious steps leading underground . . .

It seemed to take forever as she scrambled from one arch to the next, flattening herself against walls, terrorized and terrified that Najib would find her.

Through the tunnel she sprinted, hanging onto her veil, holding onto hope.

The baths were like a cavern, the spigot of pouring water the mouth of a jaguar, monstrous in the dim light of one torchère.

She was a shadow here, parsed out by the flickering light as she moved to the far door and grasped the knob.

Her hand froze. What if she was walking from one nightmare into another?

The cavernous room was eerily silent. She was just a long shadow against the wall.

But Biju would not be fooled.

And then she heard a step, the echo of it reverberating through the room like a cannon.

She wrenched open the door and slid into the darkness.

Guards were everywhere, but nowhere did Culhane feel the mind of Dzmura working.

It made avoiding them that much easier, and simplified the matter of finding him.

He slipped through the extravagant halls of the palace in the shadows of the night.

The guards were innumerable, stationed at every corner, but were oblivious, stupefied with boredom. Some even slept.

He moved slowly and steadily through the palace, his senses unfailing: ... *here—there—this door ... that hall ...*

Every step of the way, he thought of all the steps it had taken to get to this point ... *in the barren potato field there was always the hope of spring ...*

But buried in the field was the root of man's monstrosity to man, festering, growing underground, seething with maggots and the religion of nullification. Man fed on it, grasping for power, hiding from the sun.

The source of nourishment and the cult of death.

Culhane would bury Dzmura in the desert dust from which he had grown.

Steep and dark as midnight. She followed the steps shakily one by one, her arms outstretched wall to wall, holding her up, balancing her terror.

In the baths of the harem, who would have expected a staircase in a closet? she thought hysterically. And how could anyone have predicted she would choose the right door?

She could be walking into the jaws of death; the only saving grace was she was not naked. How thankful she felt for small favors as she edged her way slowly and fearfully down the narrow staircase.

Her hands were frozen; the walls were rough, striated stone carved out of a mountainside. The steps were wooden, built into the space, and her feet were cold and bare, and she was scared witless that a splinter of wood would stop her altogether.

Down and down she went, her courage sapped by facing the unknown in darkness.

. . . she could always go back . . .

But she might face the punishment of the *Hakkam* for abandoning his bed; she would lose the status of favorite, and he might well kill her. The choice between two darknesses—two evils.

It pushed her determination to keep on going until she became aware of that slim dart of light directly below her.

She hadn't imagined it. She hadn't; in the overwhelming blankness of the dark, she had begun to question whether the underground room had been real.

And then the light expanded, inch by warming inch until she was almost at the bottom of the stairs.

Empty space: it was the first thought that hit her. It was as empty as the *serdab* at Bazzi, and as full of portent. This place would not lead to a princess' chamber.

She slipped into the room and against the far wall, as distant from the light as possible, and she followed it.

It was a wide corridor, running on endlessly underground. There were rows of columns in threes supporting it. Every few yards, there was a niche in which an oil lamp burned to provide minimal light.

Far up ahead, finally, she could see a curved arch, and she hesitantly edged her way towards it.

In the flickering light of the oil lamps, she peered out into what looked like a garden, with tall hedged bushes and the fragrant scent of flowers.

She could not go any farther without some light. She ran back into the room and took one of the lamps and then slowly and cautiously proceeded into the garden.

It was so dark. The lamplight flickered eerily in a light wafting breeze. She kept walking and walking, shielding the flame, and she felt as if she were toppling headlong into one of her nightmares.

The hedge wound into a maze. Fear pounced on her. She began to run, hysteria following her like a bat out of a cave.

She heard a voice behind her—the dwarf, the dwarf—and there were no trees to hide behind . . .

She was dreaming—she had to be dreaming . . .

She ran, holding the lamp above her head so she could see the trees—but there were no trees: the hedge turned into the impregnable stone wall and curved and angled into impossible places. Dead ahead she could see there was nowhere else to run.

"Alexandra—Alexandra . . ."

The voice pursued her; terrorized, she raced for the edge of the plateau where there was nowhere to hide.

And she stopped, stricken by the scene below.

Torchères burned everywhere, and an army of men marched in the night, their voices, in cadence, rising to the moon.

"Alexandra!"

She heard her mother, she heard her father—and she whirled, dropping the lamp, expecting the panther to pounce and devour her.

She teetered on the edge of madness, hearing the screams—the whoosh of flames climbing up the wooden barricades at the sides of the plateau.

A pair of hands wrenched her away from the edge.

She screamed and she screamed: Khurt's hands were holding her; her nightmare had come true.

Chapter 22

He did not try to calm her hysteria; he needed only to get her away from the ledge and the chaos below as the flames spread and bells began clanging.

He pulled her, shaking and screaming, back the way she had come, through the gardens and into the underground room, stopping only to appropriate a lamp so they could see the way up the steps.

By then she was silent, frozen with terror and a sense of unreality; she moved like a puppet, proceeding in whichever direction he pushed her.

"Hurry!" He propelled her up the stairs, then raced ahead of her, pulling her by her limp hand.

She sensed his urgency, but only her body responded; her mind felt lifeless—Khurt was dead; she must be dead too.

But the rough edges of the wooden steps felt real enough against her bare feet, and the compelling note in his calm voice, that seemed real: her body responded, racing up the steps to keep up with him, her gaze on the circle of light he held in his hand.

Her heart was pounding frantically when they reached the little landing.

They could still hear bells clanging and the distant frenzied shouts behind them.

Khurt doused the flame and slowly opened the door.

The clanging bells, the chaos, the confusion gave him the cover he needed; no one noticed when he grabbed a guard, rendered him senseless and appropriated his uniform.

And then he moved among them, undetected. Like a panther, he sprinted down hallways and up shallow steps and no one questioned why he was heading in the opposite direction.

He sought the tower, the pinnacle of the palace, the height of Dzmura's dreams.

He stalked his enemy like a cat, deliberately, purposefully, heeding his instincts, measuring his chances, his spaces, his luck.

Dzmura was waiting—he sensed it now.

Hastening down a long empty corridor, embellished with Dzmura's dreams, he came to the massive double doors which guarded Dzmura's apartment.

The reckoning was here. Dzmura expected him.

He pushed open the doors and entered.

Now the disorder had invaded the harem. The noise from beyond the fountain room was tumultuous.

"You must return to your room," Khurt whispered, as they made their way carefully through the puzzle rooms. "I must seek both your sister and *caid* Culhane. It is imperative you stay in your room, for it is there I will come for you."

"But the fire—you—"

"Explanations later, *mem-sahib;* my duty to *caid* takes precedence. Let no one deter you. The fire will spread, and we will use it to our advantage. Go now."

She went, her mind a jumble of bewilderment, but she had to keep her wits and move carefully through the confusion of guards and eunuchs running every which way.

She flitted like a long shadow through the rooms, skirting the panic and edging her way against the walls.

She was not dreaming: the thing had happened; an army had been marching; Khurt was alive.

. . . And where was Allegra . . . ?

Her room, just past the arched entryway. She prayed Allegra had taken refuge there . . .

"Precious Alize."

Biju's cool unemotional voice belied the bitter enmity in her boring, black gaze.

Her heart dropped. Biju—of course. Who else wished her fall from grace more than Biju.

"*Hakkam* was disappointed, precious Alize. He wonders if you did not only lie to him when you allowed him to dress you in the symbols of his precious favor but whether you are responsible somehow for this catastrophe. *Hakkam* you see is very distrustful of women. Even those he has trained from childhood. Especially those he has given his confidence and who betray him.

"He waited for you, precious Alize. He yearned to see you in the dress of his beloved. Instead he waked to disaster, and his precious Alize was nowhere to be found.

"As if you had the power to snap your fingers and resist his will.

"Stupid Alize—but he knows that now. He will take another as his chosen, more willing than you."

"And who would that be, Biju—you? You jealous tyrant. You have the body of a child. If the *Hakkam* wants you, he must tell me himself."

Biju spat at her. "The *Hakkam* has used my body for his pleasure, and he will discover its gratification again. He commands that you remove the mark of his favor."

She was becoming insensate with anger, and Alexandra wondered how wise it was to bait her. Still, Biju was a puny thing that stood in the way of her ultimate escape.

She had to get rid of her, but she couldn't think straight. It was so much easier to clash with her over the mundane concerns of women, which were paramount to her.

She tossed her veil over her shoulders to expose her breasts.

"Let us compare our bodies, Biju. Let us see between ourselves which of us *Hakkam* must prefer."

Now she knew she had the right of it. Biju's face contorted in rage and she leaped at her, her hands clawing, raking at Alexandra's veil and at the most feminine part of her.

Alexandra hadn't expected that; Biju caught her off guard, and she went down heavily onto the bed.

"Stupid infidel," Biju panted, "bitch-woman, sister of a camel wallowing in its dung . . ." Her hands were everywhere, reaching, tearing; her fury driven by her epithets which descended into guttural slang, incomprehensible but needing no translation.

Alexandra pushed, shoved, rolled; her body taking the awful pummeling of Biju's fists, her ears filled with the woman's curses.

"You rutting goat; you daughter of a swineherd; your disgraceful infidel's body is a mockery of womanhood—arrggh!" She swiped at the headdress and pulled it from Alexandra's head, then grabbed a handful of hair. "And your English hair, the indecent body hair *Hakkam* permitted you . . . you are a disgrace to his harem; your body is bloated and unseemly—you fat, ugly, horsefaced English woman . . . ahhh!"

She grunted as Alexandra grabbed for her, wrenching away her veil to reveal something wrapped around her hair, something with golden and blue links—the necklace she had taken at the baths.

Biju pulled her hair still tighter as she reached for it. "The trinket is mine, stupid Alize. *Hakkam* decreed it."

"Yes," Alexandra grunted, reaching futilely for it, "and it is the only token you will ever get from him. But it is *not* his mark of favor."

Biju screamed and relinquished her grip to gain purchase to attack Alexandra.

Alexandra rolled frantically out of her way just as Biju slammed herself down on the bed; and before she could right herself, Alexandra climbed onto her and straddled her.

"Puny Biju," she taunted, wondering how smart it was to enrage her more. She grabbed a handful of her hair, and ripped the broken necklace from her oiled tresses as Biju bucked and screamed curses at her.

"I will kill you—kill you—you English women ruin everything, everything—sheep fodder, camel dung, horse manure, whore—" She heaved upwards and Alexandra toppled back onto the floor.

And then Biju was on her, her hands around her throat. She thrust her body upwards frantically before she could get purchase and shove Biju back against the bed, holding the broken necklace tight against her throat.

"Puny woman," she muttered. "You are an embarrassment. Who is stupid now, Biju? Who has the power? Envious Biju, to think I care about the symbols bestowed by a man who resorts to fakery to please his women. Should a manly man wish to possess me, I would wear his tokens proudly. But I am more woman than Dzmura is man—and you, you puny dog, you are welcome to his flaccid manhood which revels in reversing the natural order. But you knew that already, you heathen whore, and I did not."

Biju shrieked. "*Hakkam's* will is above all things; maggots in his harem make no judgements. Insects in his harem bow to his will and kiss his feet that they may serve him." She struggled against the inexorable press of the chain. "You are lower than ants; dirtier than mosquitoes; who are you to judge *Hakkam*? You fester with jealousy because *Hakkam* has rejected you. Poor fool, poor stupid fool who could have had the world at her feet if only she had obeyed *Hakkam*. He would have given you to the boy and then taken you himself. But you rejected his pleasure, and someone else fulfilled his fantasy. You are finished . . . A-li-ze—"

She tightened the chain to stem the tide of Biju's words, to cut off the images of what must have happened after she had slipped away.

"So he admired your beauty did he? I wish I could have heard those lies," she growled. "But your body is much like that of boy, isn't it, Biju? And that is why he keeps you by his side and uses my sister so badly. He trained you both to do his will, and now neither of you can withstand his power. But can you withstand mine? Can you? *Can you?*" she raged, pressing harder and harder into Biju's throat.

Then Biju stopped struggling; her body went limp and Alexandra released her hold in an agony of fear.

Now she was a murderer too.

From the tower windows overlooking his domain, Dzmura watched the fire spread, and as he sensed a presence outside his door, he turned.

"Come in, Culhane."

Culhane entered, to be greeted by a panoramic view of the fire, Dzmura's lean hawkish body outlined in profile against it.

"You have done your work well, Culhane. I did not expect this."

"You expect everything," Culhane said.

"As do you, most prescient Culhane. We are a pair."

"It is the eternal conflict," Culhane said, "which you can never win. You are the darkness and I am the light."

"I have not yet lost," Dzmura said. "I am a *sherif Kartir;* my followers will live forever, underground, preparing for the next coming, accepting their fate in this generation. You cannot vanquish the idea or the ideal. The Zoran lives, most learned Culhane—but I think you know that already."

"Evil will always flourish; the world needs no Zoran to define the way."

"And evil will thrive where there are men who grasp for power. I have been one of them. I have seen the defeat of the forces at Khartoum; I have built an army of acolytes as zealous in the cause of Kartir as they were for Islam. I have constructed my palace, and I will reign here. All over the world I have placed my followers, and not even you, most zealous Culhane, can ferret them all out."

"But when the point of power diminishes, when the energy which feeds the fire is extinguished—what then, Dzmura, what then?"

"But who says the fire is extinguished, most deductive Culhane? Who says the point of power has diminished? I have built this fire well, most philosophical Culhane; soon, very soon, it will feed itself and my *khouans* all over the world will rise up in its light.

"And I, most patient Culhane, will be the phoenix rising from its ashes . . ."

He spread his arms and he fell back against the window glass with a jarring crash, disappearing through the window into the smoke and the flames below.

And then there was no time for anything except finding Khurt and Alexandra and then burying this place.

He raced down the corridors, his senses guiding him unerringly towards the seraglio.

God, there was no time, none. The flames were spreading as if oil were feeding them; too soon they would ignite the dynamite and blow Bakharha Palace and the town of Khamaquil to kingdom come.

He paused for a moment in one of the large, empty interlocking rooms. Allegra was that way—Alexandra this. He felt brutally unconcerned about Allegra's well-being and sprinted towards her room exasperatedly, passing empty bedroom after empty bedroom.

Allegra's room was abandoned as well.

With a curse, he dashed back in the opposite direction towards Alexandra's room.

He found her there, hysterically shaking the limp body of one of Dzmura's slaves.

"Oh my God, Culhane—I killed her, I killed her . . ."

He wrenched her away, and knelt down to feel for a pulse, all the while drinking in the improbable vision of her in her trousers and veil, her breasts bared and her nipples adorned with the most erotic little rings.

He didn't want to know about it; he felt the heat rising in his body even as he tore his slatey gray gaze away from her.

"You nearly choked her to death, yes, but she's still breathing. It doesn't matter. This place is going to blow any minute. We have to get out of here—no explanations—*now!*"

She swooped up Biju's veil and her headdress as he grabbed her hand and pulled her into the corridor.

The place was ominously empty, the silence catastrophic with the fury of the flames and the chaos below.

They could feel the heat as she hurriedly pulled the veil over her nakedness and tied it with the silken length from Biju's headdress.

"Ready?"

She nodded; they linked hands and they ran.

Explosions boomed in the distance as they swerved into a vaulted reception room.

"I entered here," Alexandra whispered, "but I couldn't tell you where the door was."

"Shhh . . . I'll find it."

"Oh God—what about Allegra?"

"Khurt has her, I'm sure of it," he said confidently though he wasn't sure of it. He had no sense of Allegra whatsoever.

"She was crazy, stupefyingly loyal to that . . . that—"

"He jumped out the window," Culhane said, patiently going over the lines in the tile of the least likely wall.

"Oh God," she moaned, wrapping the thin material of the veil more tightly around her. "He had an army—"

"I know . . . shhhh."

"And the others—"

"I know . . ."

"*How* do you know? I went through agony with this madman—and you know everything?"

"Shhh. Look at how clever this is. The common slave would never think there was a door embedded in these tiles. Just like your father with his safes. Perfectly obvious when you look for the key."

The doors swung open, the exterior side the ornate brass that she remembered—three days ago, was it?

They stepped out into the anteroom, and it was the place where he had blown in the door and gone into a secret room.

The hole was still there, and the door was bolted from the inside.

She jumped as another explosion went off.

"Get out, quickly. We have got to get off this plateau."

She crawled through the opening, and he swung out after her. She thought she would be breathing the air of freedom; instead it was the stench of death.

"Get me out of here," she moaned as another explosion sounded.

He swung her into his arms and complied.

He had brought horses, some food, and the answers to her questions, but first he went back and set off the interlocking explosions that would engulf Bakharha.

"Allege—"

"I promise, she is safe."

"All she wanted was *him.*"

Khamaquil was burning in the distance, the conflagration feeding off the flames that spread from the marching grounds beyond the garden.

The thing was done, the promise fulfilled.

"Where will we go now?" she asked sadly.

"To Baghdad—and home."

She couldn't conceive of it; she had no idea what "home" meant.

But Baghdad meant a bath, a bed and clothes, and she found that utterly foreign as well.

It was strange how used one could get to being naked all the time, she thought mordantly, sifting through the packages Culhane had brought back to the hotel in which they stayed.

Here were the undergarments and the stays. A blouse and a suit, a pair of sturdy boots. A cork helmet. Everything to withstand the brutal sun and brutal man.

Her luxurious immersion of the senses was over; she gave herself up to the bath water which was hot, unperfumed and curiously bland: there was no one to scrub her, no one to command.

And she didn't feel like a nap afterwards either.

Home . . .

When Allegra arrived, they were going home.

She didn't know if she wanted to go home.

She didn't know how she would live without this erotic heat within her. She wanted to stay naked for the rest of her life.

He could not expunge his vision of her in the harem, with her breasts naked and the symbol of the ruler's favor adorning her nipples. Two . . . He knew what that meant, and he seethed with violence that things had progressed beyond her control. Two— when he wanted her and he owned her and she was his by her own volition.

Two . . . Dzmura would have dressed her with his own hands

and sent her among his women to validate his claiming of her body.

Two . . . the symbol of favor, to be worn only by his command.

Two . . . She would remember it always; he could never erase the thought and feeling of it from her mind.

Or his own.

Two . . . She would be forever and always the odalisque of favor in the harem of Bakharha . . .

And when he opened the door, he found her naked and waiting on the bed, beside her a little silver tray on which she had placed one of the rings, and one only.

"It seems my odalisque loved her taste of the harem," he murmured as he entered the room.

"Your odalisque loved the taste of you," she whispered, her blood thrumming with excitement.

But he couldn't let it go; he felt like a bulldog about to gnaw on a meaty bone. "Tell me the lessons of the harem, odalisque. Tell me what you loved."

"I loved being your harem of one, Culhane. That is what I loved."

"But the *Hakkam* presented you with his mark of favor. Surely you earned it, odalisque. How could you not?"

"He wished to degrade my sister, so he chose me in her place. He gave me a harem name, and I did not love that. He dressed me in the symbols of his favor, and I did not love that. He had not the manliness to take a woman, and I did not love that. That is what I learned in the harem."

"Still, you wore his rings."

"I would wear yours," she said boldly. "I would answer to the harem name that you would give me. I would beg for your favor; I would do anything if you would dress me in the token of your chosen odalisque. I would wear it always and you would know, when I am dressed, that I am yours, whenever you want me. That is what I learned in the harem."

"You went to him at night, when he sent for you. Deny that."

"I went to him; you can guess why. He humiliated Allegra before me and made her dress me in the symbol of his favor. He talked and he talked, and he could not arouse himself to do anything. What he really wanted was to show off his power by conferring the token of it on the powerless."

"And you talk and talk with tales of a thousand and one nights, odalisque. You have learned well. You have learned to want me; you have learned the secrets of the harem; you have learned to be bold and to ask for what you want."

"I want only what you want."

"And what is that, odalisque?"

"I want to surrender to you; I want a symbol of your favor."

"Such an obedient naked odalisque; you want everything now, don't you?"

"I want you," she whispered.

"Get up."

She rose gracefully and watched as he picked up her blouse and handed it to her.

"Put it on."

Her eyes pleaded with him, but he was adamant. She began to button it up, but he stopped her and pushed it aside to reach for her breast.

In his hand, he held a ring, a different one but of the same fine tensile flexibility, with the two concave heads. This ring was of fine gold and was carved with symbols.

He pushed aside her blouse and thumbed her right nipple until it peaked into a long hard point and then he dressed her in his ring, squeezing it gently until it hugged her firmly and she swooned with pleasure.

He finished buttoning her blouse and made her stand back so he could look at her.

He could see it, just pushing against the fine lawn of the blouse.

"Get dressed."

Her chest swelled with disappointment, but she did as he commanded and he watched so she made sure that she made an erotic tease of it—pulling on her stockings, her skirt, checking the thrust of her nipples against the fine material of her blouse.

She was awash with desire for him, thrilled he had claimed her. Murderously angry that he wished to walk with her on the hot sultry streets of the city instead of surrendering to his need for her.

And when they returned, he undressed her, all of her except her blouse. Her eyes glittered with emerald insolence. She felt the awesome power of the odalisque.

"Unbutton your blouse."

She began at the collar and worked her way downwards slowly, savoring the slatey gray look in his eyes as he stopped her and pushed aside the thin material to expose her breasts.

"Let me look at you," he commanded, and she turned in profile, arching herself forward so he could see that her nipples were stiff with arousal.

"Seductive odalisque," he muttered convulsively; he had thought he could resist her. "Made to wear my ring. Made to wear two, three—a hundred." He moved behind her and grasped her hair. "I claim you again, odalisque. You will wear my rings on both breasts as you so ardently desire."

He had the second one in his hand, and he slipped it on, gently squeezing to close it, then he bent his head to suck the luscious point.

She arched her nipple into his mouth, feeling all of it: the wet heat of his sucking, her streaming body reaching for the pleasure point he drew and drew against the succulent thickness of his tongue.

She almost gave in to him, almost, but she didn't want any substitute for him, the whole, full, forceful maleness of him.

"I want you," she whispered. "All of you."

"Odalisques make no demands."

"This odalisque demands you."

His slatey eyes turned dark with passion. She was the embodiment of passion, there was no one like her, and now he was not the only one who knew.

"Lie down."

She crawled onto the bed, still half-clothed in the blouse, her breasts thrust forward so he could see the rings.

"Turn around so I can see you."

She knew how to do that; the bed was piled with the ubiquitous pillows and she arched herself against them.

"You have claimed me, Culhane. Now take me."

"Odalisques express no desires."

"I desire you," she whispered.

"The odalisque has learned her lessons so well."

"You have taught me, Culhane. I want you, and no one else can claim me. Only you. Claim me, Culhane; I want you."

But he didn't know—he did not know: three days in the harem at Dzmura's mercy, and she had not removed his rings even in her flight.

They looked as though they belonged there, as though she had worn them from the beginning of time.

She was the essence of Eve, the consummate temptress, and she had honed her natural abilities in the opulent sensate world of the harem.

Now she waited for him, wanted him, and he could not clear his mind of the notion that she had waited for and wanted someone else as well.

After he had claimed her and made her his own.

But what had he expected when she had been at the mercy of Dzmura? She was too willing to live, too willing to love. And she had been, for that incremental amount of time, a slave of the harem, with all that implied.

Desire and danger blocked his senses. He wanted her and he rejected her at the same time.

His feelings were not his own.

It was enough that he had reclaimed her. But after that, he did not know.

She felt the heat dissipate between them and bore the onus of rejection. It was too much for him, the man of the world, that she had been claimed by Dzmura's hands. He, who knew better than she, the hierarchy and the demands of the harem would put the blame and burden on her, as if she had had choices and could have denied her captor. It was infuriating, a purely and unforgivable male response. Forget that she had suffered; that they had abducted her, that she had been at the mercy of unmanly lust. She was to blame because he could not accept that she had been initiated into the harem.

She wanted to remove his rings and throw them at him, wanted to stamp her foot and scream. She wished she had the strength to overpower him. She would have straddled him and taken all of his power and siphoned it off to be her own.

She flounced off the bed and shrugged on her blouse, buttoning it tightly over her breasts. He would see who had the power, she thought vengefully; he would see who would blame who for what. And she would make certain that he knew she wore his rings not for his pleasure, but for her own—and then let him imagine what he would.

This odalisque would wield the most sublime power of all.

Chapter 23

It was war between them, and nothing else mattered.

"You have claimed me, and you will not take me," she murmured at one point. "A situation that may well never end."

"Bitch," he hissed at her. "We have finished with our bargain; you got what you wanted. You found your sister. We are done with my promise to your father. There is nothing more to be said. A woman learns her potency only in one place: my instincts are right about that."

"Yet I still wear your rings."

"You may remove them then, because I will not. And you may keep them, because I won't take them back. I relented in the heat of the moment, but it won't happen again. The important thing now is your sister, and then to make arrangements to get you home."

She wanted that less than anything; if he had asked her, she would have stayed with him in the desert and lived with him in the princess' chamber where he would make love with her forever.

But Dzmura stood between them—and all that she knew and he did not.

There were not enough words in an ocean to combat that. It was not enough that only she wanted it; it was too much that he could not believe it.

Slowly she opened the blouse and removed the rings. "I meant to wear them always," she whispered, setting them on the nearby table. "The other was meaningless to me."

* * *

They could see the smoke from Khamaquil late into the afternoon from the window of the hotel.

"She is alive," Culhane said. "They are coming."

"How do you know?"

"I know."

"I *hate* your smug certainty," she raged at him.

"And I hate it that you have no faith."

"I had more faith than you, Culhane. You were terribly willing to let it go."

"Let it go anyway," he said grittily. "Your main concern is for Allegra."

And she would never let him see that it wasn't. It was as he said: the thing was done, and she had stupidly removed the rings; that was the end of it.

She was an odalisque no more.

They had escaped through the palace, stopping only to ascertain that Dzmura was not in his apartments and to take a robe with which to cover Allegra's nakedness.

She couldn't bear to look at Allegra in the normalcy of a hotel room.

"Where is he? What did you do with him?" Allegra kept asking her and finally Culhane told her the truth.

She immediately broke into a fit of wailing, and beat her chest until she wore herself out and fell asleep on the bed.

Khurt volunteered to arrange for dinner, and an hour later, a servant delivered a tray full of dishes of lamb and pilau and eggplant and vegetable pastries, water and wine and tea, and cakes and a compote of fruit.

They were hungry; they ate ravenously without waking Allegra.

"You did not see her," Alexandra said. "She was completely obsessed with being with him. He had trained her for this, behind closed doors at Hidcote, behind everyone's back. He had taken pictures of her, had wooed her with promises of his great love and of how he would make her his queen. She has known nothing else all her life . . ."

She broke off, wondering whose fault that was—hers, her

mother's, her father's? Who could have prevented Allegra's fall into Dzmura's hands?

"Fate," Culhane said.

"She knows nothing else," Alexandra said again, "nor does she want to. He has trained her to be his slave in all ways, and to accommodate his preferences. When you know that, you can see how suited a child is for his purposes: all arms and legs and no body. Feminine but not . . . pliable, eager to please. It makes me sick . . . and then for him to demean her by choosing me—and do you know why? To enhance his status among his women and his illustrious visitors. Gore . . . Rosedale . . . Alderson—the kindly gentlemen of the Legation who abducted me."

"And who may have perished in the conflagration," Culhane said. "It is burning still, and we have no time for a body count."

"I need to know how Khurt is still alive."

"The victim was one of our enemies, of course. Khurt and I had decided that we had to try to infiltrate Dzmura's stronghold and it would be best if Khurt were declared dead so that he could operate freely. Neither of us knew he would ultimately come to Bakharha; we were looking for information, a way to get at Dzmura before he got to us. Fate once again. Fate which moves in strange ways. A man is lost in a fire; another comes to replace him. Dzmura vets no one; he asks only for loyalty to his cause. Khurt was among the soldiers training under cover of darkness. Fate, he saw you just as he was sneaking up to the palace on a nightly foray to gather information."

"And fate that it was *my* father who must devote his life to chasing after Dzmura. Fate," Alexandra said bitterly. "And Dzmura was a murderer without compunction. He murdered my sister too."

They left Baghdad the following morning. By then, Alexandra had convinced Allegra to bathe and wash away all vestiges of the harem, then don western clothing for the journey to Istanbul.

Allegra hated it. She had spent two months in the harem, free of all constraints. She hated her clothes. She hated Alexandra. She abhorred the ever-patient Khurt, and she would not speak to Culhane, the agent of her beloved's death.

The trip went slowly—too slowly. There was too much time for Allegra to brood on the waste of Dzmura's death.

"Perhaps he did not die," she said craftily. "You know how devious he always was. Perhaps he ended your quest the way he knew you wished it to end. The fire had barely started then. I think he's alive, Alixe. I think he's alive, and I think he will be waiting for me when I return to England."

It was a most unsettling theory, but Allegra fairly reeked with certainty.

"You need to," Alexandra said. "You could not bear it otherwise. How could he have survived a leap from that height into a frantic crowd escaping a fire which was billowing up the very walls?"

"Dzmura has magic," Allegra said. "But you've always known that."

Dzmura did have black magic, she thought, perturbed by the possibility.

Culhane said nothing. Allegra got sick on the ferry to Varna, but they travelled with the certainty that no one was after them, that all the secrets had been solved except the one in Culhane's heart.

Allegra hated the little rickety train that would take them to Bucharest.

"This is not how Dzmura travels. He always promised to take me in style. I am his queen, you know."

Alexandra said, "She is going mad."

They spent the night in Bucharest to take the train through to Vienna the following morning.

"This is quite adequate," Allegra said, surveying the compartment she would share with Alexandra, while Khurt and Culhane would occupy the one next door. "Quite adequate indeed. And if you pulled all the shades, Alixe, we could pretend we are back in the palace and get rid of all these awful clothes."

Khurt brought their meals; they could not take Allegra into the dining car. Allegra grew frenzied with joy that they were going to meet Dzmura, and the more she talked about it, the more silent and withdrawn Culhane became.

In Vienna, Alexandra finally asked him, "Why does her talk so disturb you?"

He looked at her, and his gray eyes were distant, focused somewhere beyond her as if she did not exist. "Because he spoke of the fire that fed itself and of his rising like a phoenix from the ashes. Anything is possible, Alexandra, not the least of which is *that*."

His words chilled her. "You saw him."

"I saw him jump. I did not stay around to see if someone caught him."

Anything is possible.

By the time they stopped at Munich, it was Khurt who was spending most of his time with Allegra.

"He understands, Alixe, and you don't. I don't want to go back to that awful Hidcote. What will I do at Hidcote? Who will be my master there?"

How could it be that she could just dive so completely into the sensate world of Dzmura and be so willing to submit to all of its strictures?

She hated Dzmura for what he had done to Allegra, and she hated herself for succumbing to some of the seductive components of it. The closer they got to Paris, the tighter she must draw in her nature, until it was so constricted her natural desire would die away altogether.

She had left it all in a hotel in Baghdad anyway; and two months past she had had no conception of the passion of which she was capable.

How could she go back?

Nevertheless, the train rocketed towards Paris with alarming speed, and she found herself counting the hours: how many more till she was home?

Khurt said, "You must not blame *mem* Allegra; the man was a demon who used her cruelly and now she knows only one thing. Permit me the privilege of taking care of her, *mem* Alexandra. I know the ways, and I can slowly ease her back into the life she once knew."

She wasn't sure she wanted that either. They changed at Paris for the Bournemouth boat-train. England was too close, too close and all the passion was so far away.

* * *

They reached Lavering two days later, and it was like entering another world. She had never been there, ever.

Mrs. Podge answered their summons and almost fainted in shock. "Oh, miss—miss—we was so worried for you . . . What happened to you? When my boy returned—oh, and all the bills come due and me not knowing how to pay them—miss, I'm so glad you're home."

"The gentlemen will be staying the night," Alexandra said, unmoved by this display and rather taken aback by how huge Hidcote seemed to her now and how run-down. Surely she had been aware of that?

"It's just as awful as it ever was," Allegra said snittily. "I never liked it here. I always liked Renwick House better. If only Tebo had stayed at Renwick . . ."

"Well, he didn't," Alexandra said sharply. "He had bigger fish to fry, including our father, so just stop talking about him and go to bed."

"You're jealous because in the end he wanted me and not you."

Her heart sank. How could Culhane hear that loud declaration and not add it to the list of her deceits? An eyewitness account that Dzmura had indeed pursued her charms, but had backed down in the end and taken her sister . . .

It was so cold in the house, and drafty and creaky, but Allegra would walk its halls no more.

Mrs. Podge brought them tea, then went up to ready their rooms.

They sat in the dimly lit parlor beside a roaring fire, exhausted to the point of almost falling asleep there.

The size of the house weighed on her; it was too heavy for her slender shoulders, she thought. And she would have to provide for Allegra. And herself.

The two eccentric Misses deLisle—she could hear it now; the neighbors would talk about them forever. *Did you hear? They went to Persia, and they picked up some heathen notions. That younger deLisle girl—they say she runs around the house naked. They have a foreign-born servant, a man, who lives with them. And her father died mysteriously, his reputation in shreds . . .*

She rubbed her hands over her face. That was exactly how it would be, and she was resigned to it.

Wearily, she went to bed.

Damn and blast!

She heard the faint shuffling footsteps and jumped up and out of bed.

This was not supposed to have happened: this was over, Dzmura was dead and they were home.

She flung open her bedroom door and ran smack into Culhane who immediately put his hand over her mouth.

"Shhh—she's walking."

"Oh God, what does that mean? He's alive? He's *here?*" she whispered frantically, clutching him tightly.

"*Caid* . . ." Khurt, on cat-feet, slipped down the hallway.

"Oh my God," Alexandra moaned.

"Shhh . . ."

They moved forward in the dark, the three of them, and made their way slowly down the stairs.

They heard the click of the door to Sir Peregrine's study as Allegra entered.

"I can't believe this," Alexandra muttered. "This is over; he is *dead.*"

Anything is possible . . . his words came to her mind: he had put them there.

"Why don't you know?" she demanded in a furious whisper.

"It doesn't work that way."

They reached the bottom of the steps, and they eased their way down the hall to the study.

There was an ominous silence beyond the door.

"She's not there," Culhane said.

"Damn you—how do you know?"

"I know." He opened the door slowly and there was nothing, except a rush of air from the French windows by her father's desk.

"Oh my God," Alexandra shrieked, "she's gone to *him.*"

Culhane grabbed her and forcefully held her back.

"There's something more to this; it isn't him. I swear it—it isn't him."

"Oh yes, you know—you know everything," she said bitterly.

"Shhh . . . listen . . . This is what he said: he asked what made me think the fire would be extinguished and the point of power would be diminished with his death."

"Gobbledygook," Alexandra snapped.

"Someone is in that house with Allegra," Culhane said.

"I won't even ask how you know," Alexandra said waspishly. "I just want to go and get her."

"Not yet—not yet . . . The point of power—think, Alexandra— the point of power. His people were everywhere. Of course he would have a plan for someone to take over in the event of his death."

"Oh no, oh no," Alexandra moaned. "No no no no. No one, no one—*who?*"

"I don't know."

"How refreshing."

"I don't know . . . but she is with him: he has the power. Bloody damn, he planned for every contingency except your father's single-mindedness. And those damned bracelets."

. . . The bracelets . . . she had almost forgotten about the bracelets. How many people had been after the bracelets, starting with her own sister and the head of the Museum?

"Oh my God, oh my God," she whispered, her heart accelerating like a drum.

"Tell me—quickly." But he knew; the impression leaped from her stunned consciousness to his in a heartbeat.

"Oh my God—Sir Arthur. He took an amazing amount of father's stuff and paid us enough money for it so that we could invest in funds and live thriftily. But then later, after father died, he wanted the bracelets. I thought it was a little strange, but I had decided not to give them up—and he never asked again."

"He didn't have to: Allegra was searching for them by then. What far-reaching arms the director of the British Imperial Museum has . . . how diabolical . . . how clever . . . how perfect . . ."

He listened for a moment. "It is time." He moved, taking

Alexandra's hand, and he led them out of the French door and across the desiccated garden which was lit by a three-quarter moon.

"I'm freezing."

"Shhh . . ."

They skirted the edge of Hidcote and then made their way down the short pathway between the two houses, the route Allegra had traversed for most of her life.

The house was dark, but somewhere within Sir Arthur Hadenham was taking on the mantle of Dzmura's power.

Culhane felt it; he was sure of it. And Allegra was with Hadenham, was his devoted disciple.

They cut through the garden where Dzmura had posed her, skirted the side door and edged around to the front entrance.

"I should have brought a light," Culhane muttered.

The front door was open and Alexandra, unheeding of Culhane's detaining hand, dashed inside.

She wondered how reckless this was and stopped dead in the vestibule. Now there were lights everywhere—in the parlor where Dzmura had entertained them, in the library, in the hallway . . .

She felt Culhane's presence behind her.

"He is waiting. In the library."

She didn't ask how he knew.

She drew herself up and slowly, cautiously, opened the door.

"My dear." And there he was before her, sitting benignly at Dzmura's desk with Allegra by his side. "Come in. Tebo would have been delighted. A regular family affair. The same old people all the time, including the elusive Culhane who ventured through the deserts of Persia. Haven't changed a bit, have you, old boy? Clever of the old man to use you to try to get me. It never ceases to amaze me. I always thought Tebo was a little naive about that aspect of it. His loss is irreparable to me. But as you so aptly deduced, I am ready to go on. Have been for years.

"I'm sure I don't need to explain the rest to you, Culhane. It's pretty black and white. Of course Tebo never did believe it when Alexandra denied having found the bracelets after her father's death. A waste of my time sending me there. A waste of my time altogether. But I took good care of you, Alexandra, did I not? I was fond of old Sir Peregrine in my way.

"What I'm really sorry about is that you and Culhane had to poke your noses into Tebo's business; I really wish you had left well enough alone. Allegra would have been perfectly happy with him. He had planned it for so long.

"Well, in any event I will take care of her, just as he would have wished, and she will be my consort when I rebuild and restore the legacy of Bakharha Palace. That will be no more than a snap of one's fingers compared to the lasting impact of the Zoran.

"Yes, dear boy, I have it here; it has always been here, but Tebo just blocked it out of existence.

"So you know everything now, except the final disposition, and that will come in a moment.

"Alya dear . . ."

Oh God Alexandra wheeled to face the doorway.

Allegra stood there with a gun.

"Culhane first, I think," Sir Arthur said conversationally, gathering up some papers and hardly paying attention to her at all.

A shot rang out: Alexandra screamed as Allegra slumped to the floor.

Sir Arthur looked up.

"Ah Khurt . . . I wondered when you would appear. How convenient, Culhane, and nicely done. Khurt is a valuable man to have on one's side. He did yeoman service for Tebo on the train to Istanbul. What? You look shocked. My dear man, you never saw the half of what supposedly went—"

"Oh my God, Allegra—*Allegra!*—Culhane, she's *dead.*"

"And now, Khurt, there is no choice," Sir Arthur said imperturbably. "You must end your mission honorably. Tell Culhane . . . he still looks as if he can't believe it."

But anything was possible, Alexandra thought as she hysterically, on the floor where she was hunched, rocked Allegra's limp body. And now Khurt—dear God—now Khurt . . .

"I am the servant of the *sherif* Kartir, *caid,*" Khurt said calmly, swinging his gun around. "It was the only way. I was the watcher. I was the one who instigated the threats. How else could I have gotten into Bakharha? How else could I have fooled you except to pretend loyalty to you? All the time I was watching, looking for ways to make the threats look real. And now it is my honor and my duty to kill you in the service of the new *Hak*—"

Another shot: Khurt looked utterly dismayed as his body crumpled at Sir Arthur's feet.

Alexandra looked at the smoking pistol in her hand, the one with which Allegra would have killed her at Sir Arthur's command.

It was so easy—too easy to dispatch one's enemies. How easy it must have been to murder in the name of fanaticism, and Khurt had done all that and more as they pursued Dzmura across Europe.

Now Sir Arthur would step into his shoes and take his place, and there would be another "Khurt" to do his bidding . . .

No!

"And now Sir Arthur . . ." She climbed tremulously to her feet.

"You cannot kill me, my dear. Khurt was expendable, and of course I'm so sorry about your sister—"

"*So* sorry," Alexandra mimicked, waving the gun, her steady sense of Culhane soothing her anguish. She had to be calm; she needed every ounce of her strength, guile and determination because she was going to kill this man, and she was going to kill him because she could not kill Dzmura and because she wanted to kill him in Dzmura's house.

It was so simple really. They had, between them, destroyed her life. It was just and right, Biblical really.

"Alexandra, my dear. You've known me for years. Do give me the gun."

"Stay away, Sir Arthur; I will shoot."

"You're hysterical," Sir Arthur said coaxingly. "Culhane, convince her to let go of the gun and we'll talk about this like reasonable people."

She almost wavered; she had known him all her life. But there wasn't time to throw the gun to Culhane. She must do it or die in the attempt.

"He wears the mantle of Dzmura," Culhane said coolly, pronouncing sentence on Hadenham. "He carries the message of the *sherif Kartir*. He is the new *Hakkam*. He will seduce away another sister and make her his slave."

"Culhane—what nonsense—I'm a married—"

She closed her eyes and squeezed the trigger.

Bam!

Bam! The second shot rang out, a requiem for her sister.

Bam! And a third, a judgement for all the lies.

"He's dead," Culhane said, taking the gun. "And now we will consign his soul to hell."

They burned Renwick House.

The flames etched the morning sky long before any fire apparatus could be called from the village. By the time help came, the house and its contents were a smoldering ruin.

Alexandra and Culhane watched from her neighboring garden. "She is with him now," Alexandra whispered. "They shared the same fate."

"It is fitting."

"And it is the end?"

"For now."

It was an anticlimax. She had witnessed the death of her sister, and she had killed a man. Her father had been avenged, but she could not count the lives it had cost—including her own.

She wondered how she would now endure, while the archaeologic world mourned the loss of Sir Arthur Hadenham and wondered how it would survive.

She did not go to the memorial service.

The newspaper account said he had gone to Lavering to dispose of the estate of the highly respected antiquities dealer, Tebo Dzmura, who had perished in an accident only weeks before and who had kept a home in England for many years.

Lies.

Found with him, said the paper were his trusted servant, Khurt, and the daughter of his eminent colleague, Sir Peregrine deLisle, who had been a neighbor of Mr. Dzmura, and who was thought to have been acting as his assistant in the matter of the disposition.

Lies.

She mourned, but she didn't know how to cry.

They arranged for a service at the church to honor Allegra, and they interred her body beside those of her parents.

It was over; the thing was over.

She was back home where she belonged, and Culhane had fulfilled every promise.

Her father would be proud.

Rest in peace, Father . . .

It was over.

She could not believe the thing was over.

Culhane went back to London.

It was as if there had been nothing between them—nothing.

She paced the halls of Hidcote restlessly; what was there for her here?

Memories and sadness, futility and silence.

There one less mouth to feed, ten shillings more in her pocket every month. Where would she go from here?

Her body cried out for the sultry heat of Khuramafar.

In that moment, she had been sublimely happy, alone with him at the Bazzi Palace with nothing between them but the silken breath of their desire.

If she had that, it would make up for everything.

He had only to snap his fingers, and she would come.

The waiting was intense and fraught with that peaking pleasure of anticipation: she understood now what it meant.

It meant that she remembered every moment between them, every word that had been said. It meant that her clamoring body re-created their every coupling, and that heightened her yearning. It meant she hungered for his kisses and counted the minutes until he would claim her forever.

She hated her clothing. She wanted to be dressed in his rings and naked in his bed. She wanted to watch him grow thick and rigid with desire for her, and she wanted to surrender to the primitive male essence of him.

She waited.

The odalisque makes no demands.

She wanted to be his harem of one forever, naked and willing and waiting, her body awash in anticipation of the moment he would come.

The note came in the next morning's mail: *Make yourself ready for me.*

She was ready, so ready.

She awaited the day, shuddering with excitement, her need for him burning to fever pitch.

At six o'clock that evening, a coach drew up before the house, and Mrs. Podge answered the door.

"A coach has come for you, Miss Alexandra," she announced.

Alexandra ran out into the courtyard, and the driver met her.

"Get in, mum. No questions."

No questions. She climbed into the carriage and closed the door.

"Odalisque . . ."

Oh God—his voice.

The coach lurched forward, and she fell into his arms.

"Naked for me, odalisque," he murmured, capturing her lips.

"Yes," she breathed.

"Willing for me . . ."

"Oh yes . . ."

"Take off your clothing."

"Here?"

"Wherever I desire," he commanded, crushing her lips.

But she had planned for this, craved this—this wanton demand that she instantly strip naked for him. She slipped out of her skirt in an instant, kicked off her shoes, unbuttoned her blouse as she returned his thick hungry kisses and offered herself to him.

As his hands touched her flesh she caught her breath: *oh yes . . .*

She felt his finger playing with her nipples, and she gasped: *oh yes . . .*

She felt him ripping away the barriers, *oh yes,* and then slowly easing her onto his ramrod heat, *oh yes.*

He never broke the kiss as he grasped her hips and pushed her down tightly, down against his stiff male root.

She wanted to stay that way forever. She rode him just like that, kissing him wildly, wantonly, never moving, just feeling the thick rigid maleness of him contained within her.

And his hands were all over her, feeling her soft womanly flesh, fondling her hard, pointed nipples, caressing the sweet erotic curve of her buttocks.

"I claim you as my odalisque, and I dress you in the symbol of my possession."

She felt his fingers squeezing the cool flat of the rings against her breasts.

"Now you are mine forever. When a man claims his odalisque thus, she can never leave him."

And he pictured her, in the dark, as he drove himself into her, her body arching with pleasure, the glint of his rings adorning her—symbols of his naked possession of her—and his body stiffened and then plunged into a driving endless release.

He stayed enfolded in her.

"Where are we going?" she murmured after a long long time.

"We are almost there."

"Shall I get dressed?"

"I will have the pleasure of dressing you."

"I love it when you dress me," she whispered. "I loved your dressing me tonight."

He caressed her breasts as he buttoned her blouse, and then he cupped his hands over them so he could feel the rings.

"I want every man to envy me," he murmured, sliding his hands into her blouse and feeling her breasts.

"Every woman is jealous of me," she whispered, offering her mouth for his kiss.

The carriage jolted to a halt, and he reluctantly removed his hands.

"Where are we? Where are we going?"

He opened the door and she saw then: they had come to Victoria Station.

"The Museum has offered me the Directorship," he said quietly. "And I have said yes. But I said yes on the condition that I could work in the field—and on the condition that you would be mine."

"I am yours," she whispered. "You have claimed me."

"We are going to Khuramafar. I need to take you there."

He climbed down from the carriage to help her out. She stood, tall and proud, at the entrance of the station, waiting for his lead.

"The train leaves in minutes. Will you come?"

She smiled seductively. "I have no luggage."

"You will need none."

He held the door as she walked into the station, and they joined the crowd of bustling passengers; but he was aware of her only, and the evidence of his possession.

She knew it. The claim of the rings was overpowering and unconditional, an erotic secret known only to him. She thrilled to the feel of them and to his unswerving awareness of her as they made their way through the crowd. She walked taller and prouder now, her breasts thrust arrogantly high to heighten his engorged hunger for them.

And she surrendered to the power of them, to the potency of him.

Molten with excitement, she mounted the steps to the vestibule of their car.

This was so familiar and known. She entered the compartment without looking back, and began to strip off her clothes.

He closed the door behind him and watched her make herself ready for him, the rings of his possession glinting as she moved.

He felt the urgent thrust of his still-unslaked desire. She belonged to him, *she* was his joy.

And he was her slave—forever.

"I will buy you silks and satins," he murmured, forebearing to touch her, heightening the anticipation by prolonging his explosive desire for her.

She walked towards him slowly, insolently, cupping her breasts with their golden adornments, tempting him, enticing him, the embodiment of Eve.

"You need not bother, Culhane of my heart," she whispered, her voice sultry with invitation. Her body shuddering with excitement as she offered herself to him. "I am wearing everything I will ever need."